Praise for Susan Fleet's Frank Renzi crime thrillers

ABSOLUTION

Best Mystery-Suspense-Thriller — 2009 Premier Book Awards

"Relentless tempo . . . sharp writing." — Kirkus Discoveries

"Creole-flavored suspense." — Attleboro Sun Chronicle

DIVA

"Absolutely fascinating ... a very suspenseful book!" — Feathered Quill Book Reviews

"Fleet subtitles Diva a novel of psychological suspense. That's an understatement." — Jan Herman, Arts Journal

NATALIE'S REVENGE

Best Mystery-Thriller — 2014 Feathered Quill Book Awards

"Fast paced, well written and extremely challenging to put down." — Rebecca's Reads

"The coolest detective in literature at the moment [is] Frank Renzi." — Feathered Quill Book Reviews

JACKPOT

"Thrilling and gripping. The writing is tight and builds to a tense climax." — Readers' Favorite

"A page-turning thriller. Frank Renzi hunts a disturbed serial killer." —Tom Bryson, author of *Sarcophagus*

"A tremendously great series." — Feathered Quill Book Reviews

NATALIE'S ART

"Compelling characterization and a surprising conclusion. That's fine art, indeed." — Midwest Book Reviews

"Non-stop twists begin on page one. A fast-paced, action-packed read!" — Feathered Quill Book Reviews

MISSING

"Opens with a bang, fast-paced and hard-hitting. An emotional roller-coaster ride far above the usual whodunit." — Midwest Book Reviews

[The] action never stops, and the suspense is palpable." — Feathered Quill Book Reviews

Praise for Susan Fleet's non-fiction

WOMEN WHO DARED: MAUD POWELL and EDNA WHITE

"Fleet is an expert on American female musicians who deserve wider recognition in the history of jazz and classical music." — Matt Morrell, 'Jazz at WGBH,' Boston, MA

"Fleet's heroines were successful, artistic performers, attracting and enriching broad audiences." — Howard Mandel, music critic, *Billboard*

DARK DEEDS, Vol. 1: Serial killers, stalkers and domestic homicides
DARK DEEDS, Vol. 2: Serial killers, stalkers and domestic homicides

"Well researched and well written. The inner world of these killers is vividly and psychologically portrayed." — Arthur Smukler, MD, psychiatrist

NATALIE'S DILEMMA

A FRANK RENZI NOVEL

"Tomorrow's not guaranteed."
– Jazz drummer and band leader Art Blakey

Dedicated to the police officers
who put their lives on the line every day to protect us.

SUSAN FLEET

Music and Mayhem Press

Natalie's Dilemma is a work of fiction. All names, characters and events are either products of the author's imagination or used fictitiously. Any resemblance to actual persons living or dead is entirely coincidental.

Published by Music and Mayhem Press

ISBN-10 0-9847235-9-5
ISBN-13 978-0-9847235-9-1

Cover photographs used with permission:
from Fotalia, Chinesische Mafia Gangsterbraut, © Haramis Kalfar
from Shutterstock, Sad little girl with toy, © altanaka

Author photo by Pete Wolbrette

Printed in the United States of America

CHAPTER 1

FRIDAY December 10, 2010   5:35 AM – New Orleans

Riding shotgun in an unmarked Chevy, Homicide Detective Frank Renzi held his SIG-Sauer in his lap, hoping he wouldn't have to use it. The tension in the car was palpable, no lights and sirens, but they were moving at a good clip. Four NOPD detectives on a dangerous mission.

He glanced at Kenyon Miller, his longtime partner and friend, whose eyes were fixed on the road. Sweat beaded the veteran detective's dark--skinned face and muscles bunched in his jaw. They all knew King Rock wouldn't go down without a fight. Frank knew for a fact that he'd killed two 'bangers to gain control of the B-n-L gang, but he couldn't prove it. Nobody would talk, fearing King Rock would kill them.

"I just sent Angelique a text," Kelly O'Neil said. "Told her we'd be there soon."

Seated in back with David Lee, another District-8 homicide detective, Kelly worked Domestic Violence. An hour ago, Angelique had sent her a frantic text, saying King Rock was in her apartment, threatening her. "Beating the crap out of her," Frank said, lying in bed beside Kelly.

They didn't flaunt it, but everyone in Homicide knew they were lovers. "We better get over there," he said. So he'd rounded up his best detectives, Kenyon and David, to help with the take-down.

He rubbed his bleary eyes, wishing he'd stopped for coffee, but there was no time. Stress and a rush of adrenaline would keep him alert.

As jazzman Art Blakey once said, Tomorrow's not guaranteed. For gangbangers or cops.

Last week he had attended a memorial service for Hank Flynn, his boss when he worked for Boston PD and a cherished friend. Four months ago they'd met for dinner in Boston. Now Hank was dead. A stark reminder of how fragile life could be.

Kenyon slowed as they approached the Iberville public housing project, a two-block assortment of three-story, red-brick buildings. An hour from now Basin Street would be jammed with traffic. Now, in the gray light of dawn, theirs was the only car.

Plastic trash bags, discarded fast-food containers and empty drug vials littered the sidewalk. No lights in the windows facing the street, but that didn't mean no one was watching. Christmas lights around one door blinked, a forlorn reminder of the approaching holiday.

As Kenyon pulled to the curb, two figures in dark hoodies sprang out of the bushes beside a fence and ran off.

"Damn," Frank said. "The lookouts just made us."

"Twelve years old, already armed and dangerous," Kenyon muttered.

"Deadly," Frank said. "So is King Rock, so stay alert."

Bulked out in Kevlar vests, they gathered on the sidewalk beside the unmarked car, Kenyon, a rugged six-foot-six, Frank a lanky six-one. David was built like a runner, a wiry five-nine. Kelly, a curvy five-seven, worked out at the gym, took no shit from anyone, including him.

"Watch out," she said sternly. "She's got a three-year-old."

Frank shuddered. His worst nightmare. A child hit by a stray bullet. He'd seen it happen.

"Lead the way," he said. Kelly had been to Angelique's apartment many times, trying to convince her to leave her abusive boyfriend, King Rock, the father of her three-year-old son and leader of the B-n-L gang currently dispensing drugs in and around Iberville.

Alert for any sudden movement, they silently entered the project, weapons drawn, Frank and Kelly in front, followed by Kenyon and David. Faded Day-Glo gang tags on the cement walkway reminded Frank of his run-in with another gang leader. AK-47 had murdered a fourteen-year-old girl who'd lived in Iberville with her mother.

Focused on King Rock, Kelly had her game-face on, jaw clenched, eyes purposeful. She had no use for men who battered women. She turned left and marched down the walkway past red-brick buildings with darkened windows decorated with decals of snowflakes and Santa Claus.

Three doors down, she led them into a building. The lobby stank of urine, stale cigarette smoke and the odor of fried bacon. Metal mailboxes lined the wall on the right. Ahead of them to the left, a staircase was littered with cigarette butts.

Kelly checked her cellphone. "Damn. She just texted me. He, then nothing."

The bastard knows we're here, Frank thought. To David and Kenyon he said, "Cover the back in case he tries to run down the fire escape."

Kenyon frowned, his dark eyes troubled. "Okay. But you two best be careful."

"We will," Frank said grimly. "You be careful, too."

David and Kenyon hustled out the door. Gripping their weapons, he and Kelly quietly mounted the stairs. The building was quiet. Too quiet.

As they crept down the second-floor hallway, a door opened a crack, then closed. Frank sometimes thought public housing residents had a special antenna that told them when the cops were there.

At the end of the hall Kelly stopped and pointed to the door on the left. Frank put his ear to the door. Hearing nothing, he quickly stepped to the side. These days, gun-wielding bangers had ammo that would slice through a wooden door like butter.

He gave the door three hard raps. No response. He glanced at Kelly.

Clearly worried, she frowned and called in a loud voice, "Angelique, are you okay?"

A high-pitched scream came from inside the apartment.

The hairs on the back of his neck prickled.

"He's hurting her!" Kelly said. "We have to go in."

"No!" screamed a shrill high-pitched voice. "Don't!"

Then, a gunshot.

"Fuck," Frank muttered. He drew back his leg and kicked the wood beside the doorknob. The wood splintered but the latch held.

Another gunshot.

He kicked the door again, harder. The wood splintered and the latch gave way. He burst inside and dropped to a crouch. Arms extended, he gripped his SIG in both hands, inhaling the smell of gun powder.

Alert for any movement, he scanned the room. No shooter. A dilapidated couch. A maple coffee table. Colorful plastic toys scattered over an oval rug. The apartment was deathly silent.

Kelly crept up beside him, pointed her chin at a half-open door to their left.

"Mama!!" a child's voice wailed.

Then came the sound of breaking glass.

His heart zoomed into overdrive. Kelly flattened her back against the wall beside the door, gripping her Glock, eyes squinty, her lips set in a grim line. Frank crept past her to the open door, SIG raised, and charged into the room. No shooter, just a brutal scene, blood spatter on the wall beside the bed, the air thick with the odor of death.

Clad in her underwear, Angelique lay face up on floor, her eyes vacant and staring, her mouth twisted open in a silent scream. Blood puddled on the hardwood floor beneath her head.

Worst of all, a pajama-clad little boy stood beside the body, staring at his mother, his eyes wide with fear, mouth agape, chest heaving.

Kelly scooped him up and pressed his head against her chest, shielding his eyes from the carnage.

Frank ran to window. Broken glass in the lower sash left a gaping hole. He stuck his head out.

No one on the fire escape. No sign of King Rock.

"Stop, police!" called a deep voice. Kenyon Miller.

More shots, a series of them. Pop-pop-pop.

His heart lurched. "Kelly! Call for backup and stay with the kid. I'm going after King Rock."

He climbed out the window onto the fire escape and raced down the metal stairs, sickened by what he saw. Twenty feet from the bottom step, David knelt beside Kenyon, who lay on the ground, sprawled on his back, motionless. David had removed his sweatshirt and was pressing it against Kenyon's thigh.

"He's bleeding bad," David said. "The fucker shot him."

For an instant Frank was too stunned to move, staring at Kenyon, his best friend. Then he got on his radio handset. "Code 3! Officer down! Send an ambulance to the Iberville project, ASAP." To David, he said, "I'll stay with Kenyon. You get King Rock. Go!"

David took off running.

Frank knelt beside Kenyon and gripped his hand. "Hang in there, man. Help is on the way."

But would it get here in time? Feeling helpless, he glanced at Kenyon's thigh, nauseated by the blood,

A petite black woman shoved him aside. "I'm a nurse," she said. "He needs a tourniquet on that leg. Give me your belt!"

Grateful for the help, he took off his belt. The woman grabbed it, slid it under Kenyon's thigh and pulled it tight.

"What's your name?" he said.

"Ella," she said, her eyes wary. "Ella Hughes. But I didn't see anything, only heard the shot."

Kenyon, his face ashen, squeezed his hand. "Two ..."

"Two shooters?" Frank said.

But Kenyon's eyes closed and his body went slack.

Frank got on his cellphone and called Kenyon's wife.

———

Venice, Italy – 12:45 PM

"Can we decorate the tree today, Mamma?"

Sophia Ruffino smiled at her daughter, dancing around the living room in her favorite red dress and white leggings, her dark eyes wide with excitement. Curly ringlets of dark hair framed her angelic face. Bianca was only five and Christmas was still new and exciting: the towering fir tree, the gaudily wrapped presents, Santa Claus.

"Not today, my sweet," Sophia said. "Papà has to work late. Maybe tomorrow."

Bianca ran to the sideboard opposite the tree and picked up one of the ornaments, a white angel with gold glitter. "I like this one best." She twirled over to the tree in front of the window that overlooked the Grand Canal. "Can we put this one on the top? Can we, Mamma? Just this one?"

"Papà will have to do that one. He's taller than I am." In fact she was taller than most Italian woman, five-foot-nine like Sophia Loren and full-figured. Even more so these days. Her breasts were tender and swollen. She ran a hand over her stomach. Not showing yet, but soon she would. She was three months pregnant, eating for two now.

"What shall we have for lunch? Stuffed ravioli? Some lentil soup?"

"Soup," Bianca said decisively. "And lots of Goldfish crackers."

With an indulgent smile, Sophia said, "Come help me fix it then."

Her stiletto heels clicked on the ceramic tile floor as they walked to the kitchen. Built for a wealthy shipping magnate, their magnificent palazzo had cost the earth, but her husband loved it. "We've got plenty of money," Dominic had said. "Why not spend it?" Dominic had inherited the family business, a jewelry firm that imported uncut diamonds. Dominic cut them to order and created elegantly designed, and very expensive, jewelry.

She took out a sauce pan and set it on the stove. The appliances were state of the art, not that she gave a fig about cooking. The maid did the food shopping and cooking. But she could heat up some soup.

The doorbell rang. Sophia frowned. She wasn't expecting anyone. Fatima had gone to the market to buy fresh ingredients for dinner, but she had a key.

"Who's at the door, Mamma?"

She tousled her daughter's curly dark hair. "I don't know, but it's not Santa. He won't be here until Christmas Eve."

She walked down a carpeted hall to the front door. The rear of the house overlooked the canal, but the front faced the street. She put her eye to the peephole. A well-dressed couple stood on the sidewalk. Dressed in a chic suit and high heels, the woman appeared to be her early twenties, her blonde hair perfectly coiffed. The man looked older, in his thirties, wearing a designer suit, a Gucci perhaps, charcoal with thin gray pinstripes.

Sophia opened the door. The woman smiled, displaying even white teeth. Her makeup was nicely applied, subtle eye-shadow and mascara to match her royal blue suit. "Good day, Madame Ruffino. We're from the Montessori School. It would be perfect for your daughter. May we come in and tell you about it?"

Reluctant to allow strangers into her home, she hesitated. But they looked respectable, well-dressed, not scruffy like the homeless people.

"I have a present for Bianca." The woman held up a small stuffed toy, a puppy with tan spots and large button eyes.

"Oh, Mamma, isn't she cute?" said Bianca. "Now I get a present before Christmas!"

Unwilling to appear rude, Sophia opened the door and let them into the foyer. The woman gave the stuffed toy to Bianca.

"Thank you!" Bianca said. "Mamma, feel her fur! It's so soft!"

"How kind of you," Sophia said. "Come and sit down in the living room."

Clutching her new toy, Bianca ran down the hall. Sophia followed, saying as she entered the living room, "I'm sorry but I didn't get your names."

"Ricci," the man said. "Mr. and Mrs. Ricci."

A handsome man, but his eyes darted around the room, taking in the Christmas tree and the ornaments on the sideboard. The woman smiled at her and said, "What a gorgeous home you have, Mrs. Ruffino. I love the tile floor."

"Thank you." But the compliment made her uneasy. Now that they were inside, they didn't seem eager to tell her about the Montessori school. She gestured at the sofa. "Please sit down and tell me about the school."

But the man strode to the sideboard. "Is this the only phone?"

Why was he asking about the phone? Now her stomach felt queasy.

Gazing up at him, Bianca said, "Do you like the ornaments? I like the angel the best."

The man ignored her, his dark eyes fixed on Sophia. "Is this the only phone?"

The queasy feeling in her stomach grew worse. Something wasn't right. "Why do you ask about our telephones?"

The man reached inside his jacket and took out a gun. "Who else is in the house?"

Sophia gasped. "Bianca, come here to Mamma right now."

But the woman took Bianca's hand and said, "Stay here while your mother makes a phone call."

Her heart pounded her chest. Phone call? Why would she make a phone call?

The man grasped her arm in his hand. The hand without the gun. "If anyone one else is in the house, you need to tell me right now."

Paralyzed with fear, she couldn't speak. Should she tell him the maid was upstairs? But then he might search the house. When he didn't find the maid, he would be angry. "No one else is here."

"Good. Call your husband."

A feeling of dread swept over her. These people weren't here to talk about school. They were criminals. The man had a gun.

He leaned closer, so close she could smell his spicy aftershave.

"Call your husband," he whispered, "or the girl is dead. I will dial the number. When your husband answers, I will hand the phone to you. This is what you will say."

———

1:10 PM

Fatima Amato trudged down a narrow side street, weighed down by the groceries in the shopping bags she held in each hand. She turned onto the main street and breathed a sigh of relief. The Ruffino residence was only one block away.

A big black car was parked in front of the house. Someone must be visiting Sophia.

The front door opened. Holding Sophia's hand, a man in a well-tailored suit escorted her to the big black car, opened the back door and helped her inside. Then a blonde woman came out the door holding Bianca's hand and put her in back with Sophia.

Fatima's heart thumped her chest. Something didn't seem right. She backed around the corner and set the grocery bags on the sidewalk.

Moments later the black car zoomed past her. The blonde woman was driving. The man sat in back with Sophia and Bianca. Before the car disappeared, she glimpsed Bianca's tiny face in the back window.

A chill skittered down her spine. Recently there had been some kidnappings in Venice, wealthy people held for ransom by gangsters. Lord knows the Ruffino family was wealthy.

Fatima made the sign of the cross. Should she call the polizia?

Sophia hadn't told her she planned to go anywhere, but maybe some friends had stopped by unexpectedly and invited her out for lunch.

If she called the polizia and made a fuss, the Ruffinos might dismiss her. With a heavy sigh, she picked up the grocery bags and set out for the house.

She was probably worrying over nothing.

CHAPTER 2

"Bottom line," Morgan Vobitch snapped, "the maggots got away."

Frank bit back a sharp retort. Vobitch supervised the D-8 homicide detectives and was furious that one of his men had been shot. Frank was too, but his primary emotion was overwhelming relief. Kenyon was alive, in stable condition now that he was out of surgery.

"David did the right thing," Frank said, "stayed with Kenyon until I got there."

"Of course he did. It just galls me that we didn't catch them. We're gonna get those motherfuckers." Vobitch didn't raise his voice, but it seemed loud in the hushed corridor outside Kenyon's hospital room.

Frank glanced at the nurse's station down the hall, hoping they didn't hear the F-bomb. No point telling Vobitch to cool it. He looked haggard, his face unshaven, his silvery-gray hair disheveled, his temper frayed to the breaking point. It had been a long and stressful four hours.

"David saw them take off in a dark SUV, but he was too far away to get the plate number. We'll check RMV, see if we find an SUV registered to King Rock."

"No ID on the other shooter?" Vobitch said.

"Not yet. David and I talked to Angelique's neighbors—"

"But nobody's talking, right? Nobody saw nuthin. Our only witness is a traumatized kid."

"Beyond traumatized. When we went in the room he was standing there, staring at his mother's bloody corpse. Once the crime scene was secured, Kelly took him to Social Services."

"Good luck with that. Get caught up in the red-tape, could be a nightmare."

"Exactly. Kelly said it took three hours to get him squared away. She called Angelique's mother, hoping she'd take him, got no answer. When we talked she was on her way to the mother's house to do the notification." No need to mention that Kelly was also traumatized, devastated that her client had been murdered.

"We got two different caliber casings," Vobitch said, "but no guns. Christ, they could be anywhere. Drop 'em down a storm drain, we'll never find 'em. We need to ID the second shooter."

"David and I drove past the B-n-L pharmacy, corner of Basin and Louisiana, figuring we'd talk to King Rock's bangers, but they made us and scattered. Then we went to his mother's house. She said he wasn't there, she hadn't seen him in weeks."

Vobitch curled his lip in disgust. "His own mother wants nothing to do with him. These scumbag drug-dealers would shoot their own mother if she got in their way. Hell, King Rock shot the mother of his own child."

Frank scratched the jagged scar on his chin, stark white against the dark stubble. He hadn't shaved or showered since yesterday morning. Not even the antiseptic hospital smell could override the stink of sweat emanating from his shirt. "Maybe they both shot her."

"Wouldn't surprise me." Vobitch gazed at him, his pale-gray eyes full of outrage. "But King Rock shot Kenyon, damn near killed him. David saw him do it. "

"Good thing the nurse came out and helped. I stopped by her apartment before I came here. Nobody answered the door, but she might be working."

"Or hiding. Doesn't want to talk to us."

"What did you tell the media?" After the EMTs loaded Kenyon into the ambulance, he'd called Vobitch, who arrived ten minutes later. By then Iberville was swarming with cops, and the media was out in full force, camera crews, reporters and photographers.

"Nothing. One unidentified female, murdered, one NOPD officer shot, transported to the hospital, no suspects." Vobitch flashed his evil smile. "But we know damn well King Rock did it. If the fucking surveillance cameras in Iberville were working, we'd nail his motherfucking ass."

The door to Kenyon's room opened and Tanya stepped into the hall. Every time Frank had seen her—at Kenyon's house or NOPD parties—Tanya looked like a fashion model, impeccably dressed, not a hair out of place. Now her face was drawn, her shoulder-length dark hair uncombed, wearing a worn pair of jeans and a sweatshirt, probably the first thing she grabbed when he'd called her with the news every cop's wife dreaded. Your husband's been shot.

He went over and hugged her, felt her chest heave as she stifled a sob. "He's gonna be okay, Tanya. Do some PT, he'll be as good as new."

"You saved him, Frank."

"No, I didn't. The nurse did. She put a tourniquet on his leg." Even now he got queasy, remembering Kenyon's bloody thigh.

Tanya nodded but her eyes remained somber. "If they hadn't gotten him here fast—"

"Don't even think about it. This time tomorrow he'll be flirting with all the nurses."

That got him a tiny smile. Outgoing and full of pizzazz, Tanya worked for a public relations firm. She was smart, attractive and a great mom, dealing with two teenagers, a full-time job and a husband who often worked overtime.

Vobitch joined them, his steel-gray eyes somber, and took Tanya's hands in his. "You need anything, no matter what it is, call me and I will make it happen." Built like a Sherman tank and twice as tough, Vobitch could be foul-mouthed and obnoxious, but under the gruff exterior he had a heart of gold.

Tanya's eyes welled up. "Thank you."

"We take care of our own," Vobitch growled, visibly fighting to control his emotions.

As Tanya walked down the hall toward the elevators, Frank's cell-phone rang, shrill in the quiet hallway.

He answered before it could ring again.

"I got a lead!" David said. "Went back to the B-n-L corner, grabbed one of the bangers. Jeez, a nine-year-old kid selling drugs. At first he wouldn't talk, but when I threatened to bring him to the station, he told me Rocket Man was driving King Rock today."

"Great!" Frank said. "The name doesn't ring a bell, but the Gang Unit might know him."

"I'm on it," David said, and ended the call.

Frank told Vobitch the news, ended by saying, "A nine-year-old kid delivering drugs."

"That's why they use him. No jail time for juvys." Vobitch massaged his bloodshot eyes. "I'm going home for a quick shower and shave, pretty up for my next press briefing. Keep me informed. You get anything on King Rock, I want to hear about it ASAP."

"Will do," Frank said, and headed for the elevators, already planning his strategy, eager to find Rocket Man. King Rock's wheel man. Another gangbanger, who might also be a killer.

———

Venice, Italy 5:40 PM

In the courtyard behind the Peggy Guggenheim Museum, Natalie leaned over the balustrade, gazing at the Grand Canal. The setting sun cast golden light over buildings on the opposite bank, sending dazzling reflections over the water. It was almost as gorgeous as the special exhibit she'd come here to see, paintings by French Impressionists: Claude Monet, Edgar Degas and Édouard Manet. The Manet Olympia was her favorite, on loan from the Orsay Museum in Paris.

It brought back memories of Willem, her first love. She'd met him at the Orsay, years ago. Before she began killing people. Before she escaped from Frank Renzi.

The thought made her shiver. Renzi, the relentless detective who never gave up, was still looking for her. Of this she was certain. But she felt relatively safe in Venice. Ling Lam was the name on her passport, but she called herself Laura, enjoying life in this beautiful city.

Reluctantly, she turned away from the Grand Canal. She was alone in the courtyard. Most of the visitors had left. At six o'clock, the museum would close. On her way to the entry door she paused beside the Marini sculpture, Angel of the Citadel, a naked man astride a horse, legs dangling, arms flung wide, his face turned up to the sky. The most startling element was his large erect phallus.

According to the guide-book, when Peggy Guggenheim had Marini cast the sculpture in bronze in 1950, she asked him to make the phallus removable, to hide it from guests arriving at her home via the Grand Canal who might be offended. Some museum goers took selfies beside the statue, pointing at the erect phallus, and posted them on Facebook.

She would never do that, of course. She couldn't afford to have anyone see her here.

A sudden noise startled her. *Rat-a-tat-tat.* She knew that sound. Some might assume it was firecrackers but she knew better. The rat-a-tat-tat came from an automatic weapon.

She held her breath. Heard more rapid-fire shots.

Terrified, she looked around. Nowhere to hide in the courtyard. If she went inside the gunmen might see her, but out here she was a sitting duck. She ran to the entry door, ducked inside and froze.

More gunshots and faint voices coming her way down the corridor, shouting "Stop!"

Was this an art heist? Her heart pounded in remembered fear. She'd stolen a few paintings herself, but never in the daytime, never shooting at guards who were chasing her.

She dug her nails into her palms. The footsteps were louder now, closer. A large bushy shrub stood ten feet to the right of the entry door. She darted behind it and squatted, hiding behind the thick greenery.

Seconds later she heard footsteps.

Through a small gap in the greenery, she saw a black-clad man with a knapsack in one hand. A balaclava covered his face. In his right hand he held an automatic rifle. His finger was on the trigger.

Her stomach clenched in a knot. If he saw her, she was dead. Motionless, she held her breath.

He ran out the exit door, shouting over his shoulder in Italian, "Hurry! The boat is here."

Another man raced into view, followed by the slender form of a woman, also dressed in black, their faces hidden by balaclavas. The second man held an automatic rifle. The woman held the hand of a little girl in a red dress, dragging her toward the exit door.

"Get in the boat!" the second man yelled. He turned and fired down the corridor.

Yes, get in the boat, she silently implored. Then she might be able to escape before the guards arrived. She studied the girl, five years old perhaps, wearing a red dress and white leggings, her face frozen in fear, her large dark eyes full of terror.

As though sensing her scrutiny, the girl turned and spotted her. But then the woman dragged the girl out the exit door.

Distant footsteps pounded down the corridor, museum guards pursuing the gunmen. Soon the police would arrive, and certain disaster. She couldn't let them find her. The polizia would ask too many questions and the carabiniere officers would check her passport.

She left her hiding place, ran out the exit door and saw the black-clad men jump into a cigarette boat. The woman scooped up the girl and jumped in after them. The whine of high-powered engines reached her ears as the boat sped away on the Grand Canal.

She raced past the Marini sculpture to the boat dock.

The footsteps were closer now, the voices louder. "Polizia! Stop or we'll shoot!"

Her heart slammed her chest. Already the police were here.

She kicked off her leather sandals and threw them in the canal. With trembling hands, she took out her identification papers, put them in the plastic bag with the museum guide-book and sealed it. She studied the water three feet below her, filthy and stinking of discarded refuse. Disgusting, but it was her only hope of escape.

She took a deep breath and jumped into the canal.

The frigid water shocked her. Ten seconds later she surfaced, brushed long black hair away from her face, took a big breath and dived under the water. Hugging the side of the canal, she swam to the left as far as she could. Lungs bursting, she surfaced, took another breath and dove again. She stayed underwater as long as she could, rose to the surface, took another breath and dived again.

The next time she surfaced a twenty-foot yacht was five yards away, moored to a wooden dock outside a large palazzo. She dog-paddled to the yacht, turned and looked at the museum.

Now it was bathed in light. Uniformed officers swarmed the rear courtyard near the canal, and spotlights stabbed the darkening sky. No police boats yet, but soon there would be, powerful vessels with guns mounted on their decks.

She clambered up a ladder to the wooden deck, shivering in the night air, her clothes drenched with filthy canal water. Buffeted by a brisk wind that chilled her to the bone, she checked the seal on the plastic bag to make sure her documents were dry. They were.

Her heart jolted. Distant sirens heading this way. Soon police would swarm the neighborhood.

Clenching her teeth against the chill, she scuttled along the dock toward the street, hoping no one in the palazzo would see her.

Her apartment was only a mile away. If she avoided streetlamps and stayed in the shadows, maybe she could get home without someone stopping her. She'd be safe there, for tonight anyway.

CHAPTER 3

FRIDAY – 7:00 PM – Venice

Generale di Brigatta Cesare Valenti squatted beside the body on the sidewalk, consumed by righteous anger and profound sadness. Rivulets of congealed blood extended from the woman's head into the gutter in front of Ruffino & Son Jewelers. He had met her once at a benefit for disabled children with his wife. His second wife. Elana was twenty years younger than his first wife who, like him, was fifty-three. As his former mother-in-law never failed to remind him.

That night at the benefit, Sophia Ruffino had been the most beautiful woman in the room, bellissima in an elegant satin gown, her dark hair impeccably coiffed, her face radiant, her eyes joyful.

Now her face was a death mask, eyes vacant, lips drawn back in a grimace, a single bullet hole in her forehead.

An hour after the shooting, the odor of gun powder still lingered in the air, and whistles tweeted at the end of the block, polizia officers directing drivers onto side streets away from the carnage. Police vehicles lined the street behind the dark SUV parked outside the jewelry store. Dominic Ruffino had been taken to the hospital, comatose, his skull fractured, unaware that his wife was dead and his five-year-old daughter was missing.

The chief of the Venice carabiniere questura rose to his feet. *Merda!* All this misery because of a fucked-up robbery. The clerk in a nearby shop had described what happened. A young polizia officer approached the SUV and engaged the female driver in conversation, probably because the SUV was parked with two wheels on the sidewalk. Then a shot rang out from inside the SUV, striking the polizia officer, who fell to the ground, mortally wounded.

Then everything happened fast. Dressed in black, his face hidden by a balaclava, a man with an Uzi slung over his shoulder burst out the door of Ruffino & Son Jewelers, a canvas bag in one hand, a pistol in the other. A second man, similarly dressed, climbed out of the SUV, dragging Sophia behind him. When she struggled with him, the first man shot her in the head. By then, people had emerged from other shops along the street. The first man fired at them with his Uzi, striking several, who fell to the ground as others fled.

The driver of the SUV, her face hidden by a balaclava, took Bianca Ruffino out of the car and shielded the girl with her body, an apparent attempt to protect her from the two gunmen. They knew it was foolhardy to flee in a car. The streets here were narrow and winding, and polizia could easily set up roadblocks. They had a different getaway plan.

Valenti studied the sprawling white building across the street. The Guggenheim Museum had drawn more visitors than usual today due to a special exhibit of Impressionist art. Fortunately, most had departed before the shooting began. The main entrance where visitors entered to buy tickets was in the middle of the building. On the right-hand corner, a second door opened into the gift shop. Now yellow crime-scene tape blocked both entrances.

According to witnesses, the first man sprinted to the gift shop and sprayed the store with gunfire, killing a clerk and a museum guard. The second man followed, dragging the woman and girl into the shop. As people cowered behind displays, the robbers ran to the rear of the museum, firing at the unarmed museum guards who tried to stop them.

In the choppy waters of the Grand Canal, gondoliers took evasive action to avoid a speeding cigarette boat, which stopped at the dock behind the museum. Several gondoliers saw two men, a woman and a little girl get into the boat, which immediately sped away. By the time a carabiniere speed boat and three polizia officers on jet skis arrived, the cigarette boat was long gone.

Valenti looked up at the darkening sky. Soon it would be pitch dark. With a heavy sigh, he walked toward the museum. His officers were in a conference room with the witnesses: museum guards and visitors, gondoliers, shopkeepers and passersby who had witnessed the massacre.

His cellphone rang, an annoying chirp designed to get his attention. He checked the ID. Not someone he wanted to talk to, but there would be serious repercussions if he didn't.

In English, he said, "John, you heard what happened?"

"Yes," said a familiar deep voice. "I need to talk to the people in the museum. My target was there. Please detain all visitors."

Valenti grimaced. John Conti was a *cafoni di prima classe*. A first class asshole. When it came to police matters these self-important Europol agents considered the carabiniere ignorant locals.

"We have done that already. Who is this target? Describe him."

"Her. A Vietnamese woman. Tall and slender with Asian eyes and long black hair."

"How do you know she was in the museum?"

"I know. And I want her detained."

"It is chaos here. Many wounded and four dead, including a polizia officer. Only twenty-four, with a wife and two young children."

"My condolences. Any police officer who dies is a brother to us all."

But not as important as a Europol agent, Valenti thought.

"You think this was a Mafia stickup?" Conti asked.

He didn't answer immediately, thinking *stronzo mafiosi maledetto.* Vicious gangsters, like the Antonetti brothers. *Per il mafioso la morte e un modo di fare.* For the mafioso, death is a means to an end.

But why share his suspicions with this insufferable boor?

"A witness said an armored van arrived an hour before the shooting. Dominic is known to receive shipments of uncut diamonds from time to time. Unfortunately, no one can give us a list of the store inventory. Sophia Ruffino is dead and Dominic is in the hospital, comatose with a severely fractured skull. The robbers took their five-year-old daughter."

"Maybe the robbers used the wife and the girl to make him let them into the shop."

Valenti clenched his teeth. These Europol agents were all alike. No concern for the victims. They wanted to ride in on a white horse like John Wayne and nab the bad guys. No, not a horse. They preferred sleek Ferraris, like James Bond with his fancy toys and sexy women.

"I will check to see if we have your target and call you back." Valenti closed his cellphone without waiting for a reply.

———

7:45 PM

Drawn by the whistling teakettle, Natalie entered the kitchen, shivering inside a thick terrycloth robe. For twenty minutes she'd stood in the shower under the steamy water, but she still felt cold, chilled to the bone by her frantic mile-long run to her apartment in sopping wet clothes. Maybe some green tea would calm her frazzled nerves.

Ordinarily the kitchen felt cozy and cheerful, but not tonight.

She shut off the gas under the kettle and poured hot water into a mug, her mind seething with questions. How could this happen now? She had a job she loved, working with kids, a nice apartment in a good neighborhood. Her Italian was, if not fluent, more than passable.

Sipping the steamy tea, she wandered into the living room and shut the Venetian blinds on the window that overlooked the street. A flowered-print sofa faced a TV set, a stereo system and a wire rack with her jazz CDs. A comfortable apartment, but she was no longer safe here.

The telephone rang, startling her. She checked the Caller-ID. Giancarlo. Normally, she would be pleased, but nothing was normal tonight. Should she answer or let it go to voice mail? But then he would expect her to call him back. Reluctantly, she picked up and answered.

"Hi, Laura, how was your day? Did you do anything interesting?"

Interesting? How about her worst nightmare? Hiding from men with guns, jumping into the canal to escape security guards and polizia. But her escape was only temporary. She didn't know what the masked gunmen had done, but shooting inside a famous art museum would draw serious attention. Security cameras in the museum had recorded her face. The cops would study the tapes and see her. They could easily identify her. She'd used her credit card to buy the ticket.

But Giancarlo wasn't a cop. And he was waiting for her to answer.

"Nice to hear from you," she said. Recalling his dark sexy eyes and her contentment after they made love three days ago, she didn't have to fake her enthusiasm.

"I got off work early tonight. Would you like to go out for a drink?"

Impossible. She was exhausted. Her nerves were shot. "Not tonight. I have a migraine. The kids were very rambunctious today."

"I'm sorry to hear that. Shall I come over and give you a massage?"

No, no, no! A frisson of fear prickled her neck. "Tempting, but I need to lie down in a dark room and get rid of this headache."

A brief silence, then, "Okay, I guess. Sorry you aren't feeling well. Call me tomorrow, okay?"

"I will," she said, and clicked off. But she wouldn't be calling Giancarlo tomorrow. In fact she might never see him again. She had to leave Venice as soon as possible.

A week after she arrived, they'd met by accident in a small cafe near her apartment. She smiled, remembering his abject apologies when he'd jostled her arm and spilled her coffee. He asked a waiter to bring her another latte, mopped up the spilled coffee with some napkins and sat down. "You are American?" he said, in English.

Taken aback, she said, "Why do you ask?"

"You're reading an American newspaper."

She usually read the local papers to expand her Italian vocabulary, but she'd bought a *USA Today* because it was the twelfth of September, one day after the ninth anniversary of 9-11.

Avoiding a direct answer, she said, "I have friends there."

Well, she used to have friends there, until Oliver betrayed her. Now she had only enemies. Oliver's CIA friend was still looking for her, and so was Frank Renzi. She said nothing about this to Giancarlo, of course. It had been a long time since she had enjoyed the company of an attractive, charming man. When she complimented his fluent English, he said he had a degree in languages from the University of London and had done graduate work at Georgetown University in Washington.

"I travel a lot for business, often to New York City. Have you been there?"

That sent her into deception mode, a skill she had acquired, of necessity, as a child. Answer no questions. Reveal nothing of yourself. Flatter your inquisitor and learn more about him.

"No, but I hear it's a great city. You must be good at your job. What sort of work do you do?"

"I work for an international real estate firm." Not looking at her, rushing his words. A sure sign of deception. She didn't believe him.

Perhaps sensing this, he flashed a smile, took out a business card and gave it to her, a fancy one with embossed letters. Worldwide Properties.

But anyone could create a fake business card. She'd done it herself several times.

"Let's have a drink sometime," he said. "Call me and we'll go hear some jazz."

A week later she had called him. They went to a jazz club to hear an East German jazz band and had a wonderful time.

But the good times were over. Tonight she had witnessed a crime at the Guggenheim Museum, which had security cameras.

Picturing men in black balaclavas wielding automatic rifles, and a little girl looking at her with terrified eyes, she went in the bedroom, took a suitcase out of the closet and began packing. Where would she go?

Not Paris. Not London. No hiding in those cities.

Now it was eight o'clock, six hours earlier in Boston. The Mountain Man was probably in his office. She took out her iPhone and punched in a number. Pak Lam was the only person she trusted. He would help her figure out what to do.

CHAPTER 4

Standing beside David Lee, Frank looked through a one-way-glass window. Slumped in a chair inside the District-8 interview room, Jawon Taylor stared at the tabletop, maybe hoping it held the solution to his predicament. A scrawny five-seven, he'd earned his street name—Rocket Man—due to his ability to outrun most anybody, cops included.

Yesterday he had eluded David. Not today. A Gang Unit detective had caught a tip. Rocket Man was staying in an abandoned cottage a few blocks from the B-n-L drug corner.

At 5:00 AM they went in hard and fast, screaming, "Police. Don't move or you're dead!" Rocket Man yelling, "Don't shoot, don't shoot!"

The place was a pig-sty reeking of pot and rancid garbage. Empty 40-ounce bottles of malt liquor littered the floor beside two mattresses. Tattered blankets nailed over the windows protected the room from the sun, and the eyes of unwanted visitors. No electricity and no furniture, just two trash bags full of clothes pushed against one wall to sit on.

Hidden under one bag, they found a loaded Tec-9 with a home-made silencer and a Smith & Wesson .38 Special, both serial numbers filed off. Not the guns that killed Angelique, but they had bagged and tagged them and taken Jawon Taylor to the station to book him.

But Frank wanted to squeeze him for information first.

"Sad case," David said. "According to the file at juvenile hall, his father left right after he was born and his mother's a crackhead, been sitting in prison for the past four years."

"Tough. You can be the good cop. I'm gonna make the little shit wish he never met King Rock. Put a fresh tape in the video machine but don't roll the tape."

David frowned. "Why not? Department protocol—"

"Fuck protocol." He didn't give a damn about protocol, nor would any other cop in the city. When a scumbag shot a cop, sometimes rules had to be broken. "If we catch heat, I'll take responsibility. He's an accessory to murder. Let's see what he says before we roll tape. He plays nice, we tell him we might cut a deal. Get the DA to go easy on him."

"And if that doesn't work?"

Frank smiled grimly. "You go get him a bottled water. I'll handle the rest." He went around the corner and entered the interview room.

Rocket Man looked up, gazing at him with a sullen expression. Frank sat across the table from him. David took the chair beside his.

He put King Rock's mugshot on the table. The bastard had a cocky look on his face, staring at the camera, light-skinned and good-looking, unlike Rocket Man who had dark skin and a face only a mother could love: a low forehead, a big nose, acne scars on his cheeks.

"Where's your scumbag leader?" Frank said, tapping the photograph.

"How should I know? He don't tell me where he goes when I ain't with him."

"Don't dick me around. No sleep for two days, I'm in no mood for your bullshit. We got you for illegal possession of firearms. You better start talking."

"Ain't giving up nuthin to no cops."

"Why? Because King Rock will kill you if you do?"

The kid stared at him, fingering the scraggly hairs along his jaw.

"Where's he hiding?"

"Just tol' you I don't know where he at!"

"We know you were in Angelique's apartment yesterday. That makes you an accessory to murder." But they couldn't prove it. Yet.

"Can't put that on me. Wasn't nowheres near the place."

"Bullshit. Where were you yesterday morning at 5:30 AM?"

"Sleeping." Taylor raised his chin, gazing at him, belligerent now. "With my girlfriend."

"What's her name?"

"Daisy." Something flickered in his eyes. "Daisy Buchanan."

Frank shot out of his chair and got in his face, so close he could smell the stink of his filthy T-shirt. A lot of 'bangers dropped out of school barely able to read, got their information from TV shows and movies.

"Listen up, asshole. Don't give me a name from some movie you saw on TV. Daisy Buchanan? In your dreams."

David tapped his pen on the table to get Frank's attention. "Maybe he'd like a bottle of water."

"Maybe he should give us some information first," Frank snapped. He went back and sat in his chair and locked eyes with Taylor. "Where'd you dump the guns?"

"What guns?"

Fury stabbed his gut, already churning with acid from all the coffee he'd consumed in the past twenty-four hours, running on adrenaline for most of those hours, running on fumes now.

"The guns King Rock used to murder Angelique. Sooner or later we'll find them. We already got you for illegal possession of firearms. You're an accessory to murder. Tell us where King Rock is, maybe the DA will cut you a deal. Reduced time for telling us where he's hiding."

"Reduced time?" Taylor said. "How 'bout no time. How 'bout dead."

"How about King Rock murdered his son's mother and you watched him do it."

Taylor straightened in his chair. "Fuck this, man. I want a lawyer."

He was certain Taylor was hiding something, his body language screaming deception, but the kid had just spoken the magic words. *I want a lawyer.*

"Detective Lee. Go get him a bottled water out of the vending machine." Better that David didn't see what was about to happen.

David left the room, and Taylor leaned back in his chair, smirking at him. He went around the table, grabbed the punk by the throat and squeezed. "Tell me where King Rock is hiding," he said quietly.

Taylor clawed at his fingers, a futile attempt to pry them from his throat, eyes bulging, his forehead damp with sweat.

Frank squeezed harder. "Tell me where he is and I'll let go."

Taylor's mouth opened, emitting a croaking sound.

He let go and flexed his fingers. "Tell me."

Massaging his throat, Taylor said, "Might be at his cousin's in Mississippi."

"Where in Mississippi?"

"Bay St. Louis."

"What's his cousin's name?"

"Ace be his street name."

Frank slapped the side of his head. "His real name, asshole."

"Tariq Barrett."

Not much but it was something.

"We know you were with King Rock at Angelique's apartment. We found casings from two different guns in her bedroom. Maybe he made you shoot her, too, so he'd have something on you."

Taylor clamped his lips together and looked away. Frank got the feeling he'd struck a nerve.

"We got a hundred cops combing the city looking for the murder weapons." A gross exaggeration, but nothing in department protocol said he couldn't lie to a suspect. "When we find them, we'll use DNA to nail both of you." Another empty threat. DNA was no magic bullet. Depending on when and where the guns were found, any DNA on them could be degraded by moisture, extreme heat and a dozen other factors.

"You got no right to put your hands on me, no cameras running, no witnesses."

Fury rose up inside him again. He pictured Kelly, close to tears, devastated that Angelique had told her King Rock was in her apartment and wound up dead. "What about Angelique's rights? What about her three-year-old son? Detective Lee saw you and King Rock drive away after he killed her. Tell me where you dumped the guns."

"Ain't telling you nuthin. Told you I wanted a lawyer."

"Listen, right now I'm the best friend you got. It doesn't matter if you talk to us or not. I can put the word out that you did."

Taylor stared at him, naked fear visible in his eyes. "Yo, man, you wanna get me killed?"

He didn't want him dead, he wanted information, but he wasn't going to get any more out of the punk.

"When Detective Lee brings your water, we'll roll the tape and you will tell us the whereabouts of King Rock. You even mention the word lawyer and I will fuck you up so bad you'll never stick your slimy dick in a girl again. You'll be lucky you can walk, you hear me?"

Taylor stared at the tabletop and nodded.

"Say it out loud. You understand me?"

"I understand."

The door opened and David entered the room with a bottled water. He looked at Frank, his eyes sending a message: *What's going on?*

"Hold on while I start the tape." Frank took the bottled water and left the room, hit Record on the video camera, went back inside and set the bottled water on the table in front of Taylor.

"Here's your water, Mr. Taylor. Homicide Detectives Frank Renzi and David Lee commencing an interview with Jawon Taylor at—" He checked the clock on the wall. "6:45 AM, December eleven, 2010. Mr. Taylor, we have reason to believe that Rufus Barrett, also known as King

Rock, murdered Angelique Vaughn in her Iberville apartment yesterday. We saw you leave the scene with him. Tell us where he is."

Taylor unscrewed the cap on the bottle, drank some water and glowered at Frank. "Can't swear to it, but he might be at his cousin's in Bay St. Louis, Mississippi."

"What's his cousin's name?"

"Tariq Barrett. Street name Ace."

"Did you drive Rufus Barrett to Mississippi yesterday?"

"No."

"But you often drive Mr. Barrett around, correct?"

"Sometimes. But not yesterday." Taylor smirked. "Not that I recall."

The punk spouting lines from reality TV shows now, gangsters denying their crimes. "Maybe when we charge you with being an accessory to murder, your memory will improve. If King Rock isn't in Bay St. Louis, we'll be having another conversation."

He checked the time and announced he was ending the interview at 6:55 AM. "Detective Lee, can you shut off the camera? I'll take Mr. Taylor and get him booked on the firearms charges."

He waited until David left the room, gave him two minutes to shut off the camera, and said in a quiet voice, "I meant what I said, Jawon. If we find King Rock at his cousin's house, you're home free. If not, we might put the word out on the street that you gave up your boss."

"Get me killed you do that," Taylor muttered.

True. No snitchin ruled the street. If King Rock thought Rocket Man ratted him out, he was a dead man. Not that Frank intended to make good on his threat. Which reminded him of another threat, CIA Agent Clint Hammer, vowing to capture Natalie Brixton.

If Hammer found her, he'd pull a CIA snuff job, and no one would be the wiser, including Frank.

———

4:10 pm – Venice

Natalie pretended to take a sip of wine and set her glass on the bar. Giancarlo had ordered an expensive Valpolicella, tart with a hint of sweetness. But she needed to stay alert, needed to deflect any more invitations from him.

He ate another piece of fried calamari and licked his lips.

"Fantastico! So crisp and tender. You should try some."

"Not for me," she said with a smile. "All the more for you." Her stomach was too jumpy. Playacting for Giancarlo. Pretending everything was normal. She shouldn't have answered his call this afternoon. When he invited her out for dinner, she said she had work to do, but had agreed to meet him at a wine bar near her apartment that hip young couples frequented, drinking cocktails and sharing appetizers before moving on to a restaurant for dinner.

Giancarlo lighted a Benson & Hedges, the British cigarettes he preferred. He was a heavy smoker, and she hated it. She could smell the smoke on his clothes, and if he didn't use mouthwash, his mouth tasted vile when he kissed her.

"What did you do today?" he asked, smiling mischievously, seducing her with his dark sexy eyes. "Anything exciting? Or were you lying in your sickbed, fighting off your migraine?"

"I slept late and spent the rest of the day cleaning the apartment and doing laundry." So she could pack the rest of her clothes, close her bank account on Monday and leave town.

"I'm so happy to see you." He leaned closer and kissed her cheek. "You don't usually brush me off like you did last night."

Her antenna went up. A provocative statement. Should she ignore it? Act annoyed? No. She couldn't afford to arouse his suspicions now.

She caressed his hand. "Don't be silly, Giancarlo. I didn't brush you off. I wasn't feeling well."

"No time for dinner tonight," he grumbled. "What is this work you have to do?"

"Homework for my child development course," she lied. "For my job. To help me understand the children better."

He drank some wine, puffed his cigarette and set it in the ashtray. "A terrible thing, that shooting at the Guggenheim. It's all over the TV."

As if she didn't know. After watching the morning news, she'd gone out and bought Il Gazzetino and La Nuova Venizia. Both newspapers had run photos on the front page: carabiniere officers with rifles, crime scene tape across the doors of the museum. The articles told of a young family decimated, the mother shot dead, her husband comatose in the hospital, their five-year-old daughter kidnapped. Not to mention a dead museum guard and innocent bystanders wounded.

She didn't want to talk about it, but that might seem odd. Everyone else was talking about it. Why wouldn't she?

At last she said, "These gangsters are ruthless."

Giancarlo made his eyes go wide. "You have experience with gangsters?" he said, teasing her.

Or so he thought. He had no idea what her life had been like, dancing as a stripper in New York, working as a high-paid escort in Paris and London. If she told him, he'd be shocked out of his mind.

Not that she would ever tell him.

If only she could. She had no family, no girlfriends to confide in.

"From what I hear," he said, "the body count would have been worse if it had happened earlier. Most of the visitors had left the museum. There's a special exhibit there. Have you seen it?"

Her stomach clenched in a hard knot. Why was he asking all these questions? She raised her wineglass and pretended to take a sip.

"Not yet. I haven't had time."

"A colleague of mine saw it last week. He said it's fabulous, famous paintings by French Impressionists. The museum is closed tomorrow, but it reopens on Monday. Let's go see it. I'll get off work early."

Her palms grew sweaty. Another invitation, one she couldn't possibly accept. With her most seductive smile, she said, "I'd love to, Giancarlo, but not on Monday. I have to work late."

He snubbed his cigarette out in the ashtray and gazed at her, his mouth set in a line. "Are you trying to dump me, Laura?"

Shocked, she stared at him. She had expected annoyance, even anger. Not this. Feigning dismay, she said, "Giancarlo! How can you say that?"

She was about to say more but caught herself. Protest too much and he won't believe you.

He gazed at her, his dark eyes smoldering with anger. "Last night I ask you out for a drink and you plead headache. Today I invite you out for dinner, but you say you have work to do. Now I invite you to see a fantastic art exhibit on Monday, and you're too busy. Three strikes and you're out. Isn't that what you Americans say?"

"Nonsense, Giancarlo. You've been watching too many movies. You're so sweet to invite me. Let's go on Tuesday. All my work will be done, and I can enjoy my time with you at the museum." Gazing into his eyes, she caressed his cheek. "And at my apartment afterwards."

His expression softened. "I like the sound of that, Laura. What time shall I pick you up?"

CHAPTER 5

SATURDAY 5:25 PM – Venice

Cursing under his breath, Cesare Valenti leaned over the porch railing at the rear of the cottage, smoking a cigarette. *Merda!* They were paying the woman a small fortune, but she would only allow them use her home if they promised not to smoke inside. In the front room, two of his carabiniere officers were monitoring the house across the road with surveillance equipment. The 'Netti brothers were hiding there, Orazio and Tomasso, Tomasso's wife and Bianca Ruffino, a defenseless five-year-old girl whose mother was dead and whose comatose father might die at any moment.

Valenti spewed cigarette smoke into the chill air. His most ruthless interrogator had persuaded a low-level member of the Antonetti gang to reveal the location of their hideout. He didn't ask how his officer had obtained this information. He didn't want to know about such unpleasantness, which undoubtedly involved pain and suffering, screams and quantities of blood.

His thoughts turned to the Ruffino maid. Another aggravation. When he told Fatima Amato what happened to her employers, she became hysterical, ten minutes of unrelenting shrieks. Then she screamed, "It's all my fault!" And told him what she had seen when she returned to the Ruffino home from la groceria. But did she call the polizia? No!

She went inside, put away the groceries and waited for Sofia to return. But her description of the couple who spirited Sophia and Bianca away in a dark SUV had been helpful. A dark-haired man in a fine-looking suit, Gucci, Fatima believed. A woman with long blonde hair in a fancy blue outfit, who painted her face like a trollop, Fatima had sneered.

Cesare drew deeply on his cigarette. For years he had been trying to put the 'Netti brothers in jail. The younger one, Tomasso, was married to a twenty-two-year-old woman with long blonde hair. Catarina dressed like a fashion model in expensive outfits and wore heavy makeup.

Footsteps sounded behind him. "Sir, come quickly. They are talking about the girl!"

He tossed his cigarette on the ground and hurried to the parlor. Two of his officers sat in front of the electronic equipment: video cameras and tape-recorders hooked up to loudspeakers. Powerful microphones were aimed at the windows of the house across the street.

One of his men turned up the volume on the speakers. Two voices, a man and a woman, arguing.

"I can't take care of the girl by myself, Tommy. I need help!"

"We should have killed her. She's a stone in our shoe."

"Mother of God, you're so cold. You'll go to hell."

"We can't take her to New York with us."

"Why not? She doesn't speak English. She's so terrified, she won't open her mouth."

"Plane fares are expensive. Leave her here."

"No! Your brother will have his men kill her!"

"Calm down, Catarina. Don't be foolish."

"What about your niece? She speaks English. She would love to go to New York City!"

"Absolutely not! Find someone who doesn't know us. A nanny who speaks English."

"Where do I find someone like that around here?"

"Catarina, you give me the mother of all headaches."

Through the speakers, Cesare heard a door slam. Then silence.

"Good work," he said to his men. "But this talk of killing the girl worries me."

He massaged his forehead. If the 'Netti brothers killed the girl and the press found out he knew where they were and didn't arrest them immediately, his reputation would be ruined. But in his mind, the safety of Bianca Ruffino was paramount.

A voice called from the kitchen. "Cesare, are you here?"

Merda! Another aggravation. "Just a moment," he called.

When he entered the kitchen John Conti was waiting for him. To prevent the 'Netti gang from detecting their surveillance, anyone coming to the cottage parked on the next street over and walked through the woods behind the cottage.

"Have you obtained any information?" Conti asked.

Stone-faced, Cesare regarded the Europol agent, dressed in a tailored suit that probably cost the earth, his hair styled in what passed for fashion these days, curly locks falling over his forehead, thick dark hair falling to his collar in back.

"We believe they intend to fly to New York City," Cesare said. "To fence the jewelry perhaps."

"To deliver stolen diamonds to their boss is more likely. According to our information, the *capo di tutti capi* lives in America."

Seething with fury, Cesare said nothing. Earlier, the Vice Comandante Generale dell-Arma had informed him that Europol Agent John Conti was now in charge of the case. And how could Cesare Valenti argue with a man with three stars on his uniform? His had only one.

But the fact that this insufferable man could exert power over him filled him with rage. Conti cared nothing for the girl. He had bigger fish to fry. The Mafia and their criminal activities had bedeviled northern Italy for many years. Conti and his Europol boss wanted to crush them. To be sure, there were rumors, faint whispers here and there, that the man who ruled the Antonetti Family lived in America. But not his name or where he lived. Still, Cesare knew for a fact that Orazio, the older brother, flew to the United States from time to time.

"I am worried about the girl," he said. "Tomasso spoke of killing her, but his wife wouldn't have it. At least someone in that house has a shred of humanity. Catarina wants to take Bianca with them to New York, but she wants to hire a nanny to take care of her."

Conti looked at him sharply. "A nanny? Interesting. Perhaps we can get them to hire my target. Then Natalie can feed us information."

"Natalie is this Vietnamese woman you spoke of?"

"Yes. She would make an excellent nanny. Her job involves working with children. She speaks fluent English and French, and decent Italian, and she lived in America for a time."

Outraged, he said, "You want to let these murderers fly to America? Not if I have a say in it. The only reason I did not arrest them already is because they have Bianca. Her safety is my priority."

Conti looked at him, his dark eyes as cold and hard as granite. "You want to arrest the 'Netti brothers. We want their boss, this American capo di tutti capi. If we arrest him, we will destroy this Mafia gang, not just in Venice, in America as well."

Cesare clenched his jaw to keep from screaming. This self-important ass didn't care about obtaining justice for Sophia and Dominic Ruffino, or the safety of their young daughter. "How will you persuade this woman to do this?"

"Don't worry. I have plenty of crimes to hold over her, several murders in fact."

"She's a killer?" Disquieted, Cesare fingered his mustache. Conti wanted a *killer* to take care of Bianca? "How can we trust her?"

Conti smiled, but his eyes were cold. "I will be her minder every step of the way. She will do what she is told. Or else." He checked his watch. "I must return to my hotel and prepare my plan. Call me immediately when you learn the date and time they depart for New York City."

Cesare watched him leave the cottage and jog into the woods. The Europol agent believed he had everything under control. But Cesare Valenti had a few cards up his sleeve.

He returned to the parlor and spoke to his officers. "I will sleep here tonight. This talk of killing the child disturbs me. I have assembled an elite team of military officers armed with stun grenades and assault rifles. They await my orders in an armored vehicle one kilometer from here. If you hear any more talk of killing Bianca, tell me immediately, even if I am asleep. I will have them mount an assault on the house and rescue the girl."

"Yes, sir. Any talk of harming the girl, you will know instantly."

"Hold these details close to your chest," he said sternly. "No need to tell the Europol agent."

His officer smiled faintly. "Of course, Generale. That is understood."

He returned to the porch, pulling out a cigarette with one hand, his cellphone with the other. Elana was expecting him for dinner. She would not be pleased to learn that he was sleeping here tonight, but he would make it up to her, take her to Paris for a weekend after this nasty business was finished.

Europol Agent John Conti could sleep in comfort at a fancy hotel. Generale di Brigata Cesare Valenti would remain on duty and protect Bianca Ruffino. If Orazio Antonetti harmed a hair on her head, Cesare Valenti would personally arrange for this ruthless mafioso to go to an early grave.

———

11:30 PM   New Orleans

Kelly took a slice of apple pie out of the microwave and said, "Want ice cream on it?"

"No, but I'll take a beer," Frank said, admiring her curvy figure. She had on a blue T-shirt and a pair of cut-off jeans now, but her Glock was on the table. Wearing casual clothes, but keeping her weapon handy.

His SIG was inches away from his right hand.

Working the mean streets of New Orleans, he seldom left home without it. Two cops, armed and dangerous. A gun was an intimate thing, like a lover almost. Either it fit or it didn't. Most of the time he and Kelly were a good fit. But she had a temper. He didn't want her out hunting for King Rock, also armed and twice as dangerous.

She brought the pie and two Heinekens to the table and sat down opposite him. "Great combination," she said. "Apple pie and beer."

"And my pistol-packing girlfriend," he said, nodding at the Glock.

"Damn right. If I see King Rock, I'll shoot him, ask questions later."

He swigged some beer and forked up a bite of apple pie. He knew she wasn't joking. No storm clouds yet on her olive-skinned face, framed by a fringe of short dark hair. But her eyes told the story, sea-green and seductive when she wanted them to be. Hard as agates now.

"Great pie," he said. "Juicy and lots of cinnamon."

"I got it at Whole Foods. Expensive, but worth it."

"Why not? You've been working your ass off." The physical strain on her was bad enough—no sleep, getting Jacques settled—but the emotional toll was worse. A client had called her and wound up dead.

Kelly shrugged. "You are, too. Did you eat anything?"

"Coffee and crap mostly. David and I had takeout sandwiches a while ago." He set the plate aside and drank some beer. "How's Jacques?"

"So traumatized he won't talk. Three years old and he sees his father shoot his mother."

"You tried to get her to leave him, but she wouldn't."

"She was afraid of him! Afraid of what he'd do if she ditched him."

He took her hands in his and looked into her eyes, glazed with tears now. "It wasn't your fault, Kelly. You did the best you could."

She set her jaw and pulled her hands away. "Not this time."

"What did her mother say when you told her?"

"She didn't shed a tear. Looks me in the eye and says—quote—'I haven't seen Angelique since she took up with the no-good thug that got her pregnant.' When I asked if she'd be willing to take Jacques, she said she's never seen the kid and wants nothing to do with him."

"Man, that's cold. Her own grandson?"

"Right," Kelly said, her eyes blazing fury. "But she gave me her mother's name and phone number. Angelique's grandmother. She was at work

31

when I called. She broke down and cried when I told her about Angelique. She loves Jacques, and she's worried about him. I'm going to see her tomorrow."

Frank yawned and glanced at the clock. Almost midnight. He needed sleep, but he wanted to tell her about Rocket Man. "David and I interviewed the other shooter."

Kelly perked up a bit, clearly pleased. "Great! Who is he?"

"Jawon 'Rocket Man' Taylor, age 19, no outstanding warrants, one conviction as a juvenile, got busted for purse-snatching. At first he wouldn't talk, but I leaned on him. He said King Rock might be hiding out with his cousin in Bay St. Louis, Mississippi."

"King Rock, bullshit! He's no king, he's a maggot that crawled out from under a rock."

Frank grinned. "Now you sound like Vobitch."

Kelly drained the last of her beer. "Morgan's a good guy, always treated me right when I worked for him. I think I'll ask him to let me transfer back into Homicide. So I can find the no-good prick that murdered Angelique."

Stunned, he said nothing. Vobitch knew they were involved and was willing to look the other way as long as Kelly worked in a different unit. She was a great detective, but both of them working Homicide would cause problems. "He might not go for it," Frank said. "You're too emotionally involved."

The moment the words left his mouth, he knew it was a mistake.

Anger flared in her eyes. "I'm too emotionally involved? What about you, Frank? What about Natalie Brixton? You're obsessed with her."

He bit his tongue and said nothing. Rafe Hawkins, his best friend when he worked for Boston PD, thought he was obsessed with her, too.

Last week when he was in Boston, Rafe had asked if he was still hunting for Natalie, which elicited his usual response. "Yes, and I'm going to find her."

"Where d'you think she is?"

"I have no idea. Could be in Europe, could be in Mexico or South America for all I know."

"You think that CIA agent, Clint Hammer, is still looking for her?"

Hammer was just as obsessed with Natalie as Frank was. "I don't know, but he's got more resources than I do, and if he finds her he'll kill her." Rafe had told him to forget Natalie and get on with his life.

Like hell. He still checked the Interpol website once a week looking for any trace of her.

"Admit it," Kelly said. "You're still hunting her. You told me Hank's widow thanked you for helping him go out in a blaze of glory. You solved the Gardner heist, captured Natalie and returned the stolen art."

He said nothing, recalling the memorial service, a moving tribute sprinkled with laughter and more than a few tears. Diagnosed with advanced bile cancer, Hank had taken early retirement and moved to California with his wife to be closer their two daughters and grand-kids. Frank was glad they'd had a few months together.

But that didn't change the facts. He might have helped crack the Gardner case, but Natalie Brixton had escaped.

He checked the time. 1:15 AM. Already Sunday, Day Three on Homicide #98, Angelique dead on the floor in a pool of blood, her distraught son wailing for his mother, who'd been shot by his father. By the end of the year the homicide count would be over a hundred.

"Okay, Frank, truce," Kelly said. "It's late and we have to work tomorrow. You want to sleep here?"

"Not tonight. I need to grab a few winks before I go back to the office." If he could get to sleep, his mind going 100 mph, reviewing what he'd already done and what still needed to be done.

Kelly rose from her chair and kissed him. "Thanks for letting me vent, Frank. Not that it changes anything, but it helps to know that you understand how I feel."

He caressed her cheek. "I understand completely. We'll get him sooner or later, Kelly."

And sooner or later he was going to get Natalie Brixton.

CHAPTER 6

SUNDAY December 12 1:30 PM – Venice

Mired in a melancholy mood, Natalie wrote her landlord a check for the balance of the lease and put it in the envelope on her kitchen table with the note. *So sorry to terminate the lease, but I must go to America. My mother is ill.* She included no forwarding address. Other than utility bills she received no mail here. Her check would cover any recent charges.

Last night she had talked to Pak Lam, leader of a Chinese tong in Boston, known to associates as the Mountain Man. She leaned back in the chair, picturing her adopted father, his glossy black hair, warm dark eyes, and the terrible scar on his face. The disfigurement he had suffered when he took revenge upon the men who had murdered his wife and six-year-old twins.

In August he had given her the passports he had obtained for his son and daughter, born two months before her own birth. Now her photos were on the passports. In the Ling Lam photo, the one she was using now, she had long black hair. In Liang's passport photo her hair was short. Disguised as a young man, she had used it to escape her pursuers and fly to Europe. Tomorrow she would use it to escape from Venice.

Take a train to Geneva, Switzerland, Pak Lam had told her, and board another train to Lyon, France. His contact would meet her at the station. Chinese tongs knew no borders. Pak Lam had contacts all over the world. As soon as her bank opened tomorrow she would close her account and take a taxi to the train station.

Giancarlo wanted to take her to the Guggenheim tomorrow, but she'd managed to stall him off until Tuesday. When he came to get her and she didn't answer the door, what would he think? Would he miss her?

She'd grown rather fond of him, not the intense love she'd felt for Willem, but he was a pleasant companion and a considerate lover. Unlike some men she'd known, he had treated her well.

Two weeks ago he had taken her to La Perla, an expensive restaurant on the island of Murano, where the world-famous Venetian glass was made. After a sumptuous meal—zuppa di pesce, ravioli stuffed with chicken, and grilled sea bass accompanied by glasses of fine wine—they walked hand in hand to the vaporetto stop. But Giancarlo said, "No water bus tonight. I'll hire a gondola."

"No," she protested. "It's too expensive." But he had insisted.

Their gondolier, an older man dressed in the traditional white shirt with horizontal navy stripes and dark baggy trousers, said, "I give the two lovebirds a romantic ride back to Venice and sing for you, no extra charge." His price: almost 200 dollars, by her calculation.

They stepped into the gondola and settled onto the padded seat. Giancarlo put his arm around her, holding her close as the gondola cruised under the moonlight and the twinkling stars. After they passed the St. Mark station and entered the Grand Canal, the gondolier began to sing "Nessun Dorma," from Puccini's opera Turandot.

"A beautiful love song," Giancarlo murmured, hugging her closer. "A fitting aria for a beautiful woman who has charmed me completely." Then he launched into a lusty version of O Sole Mio. The gondolier frowned at him, and they fell out laughing. Captivated by the moonlight and Giancarlo's amorous overtures, she had invited him into her bed for the first time. She could still remember her shuddering climax and his murmured endearments as they lay in bed afterwards.

But she couldn't think about that now. She had to forget Giancarlo's endearments, his charming smile and his sexy dark eyes. Forget Venice, too. She was no longer safe here.

She went in her bedroom, towed her suitcase to the living room and parked it beside the sofa. Her travel outfit was in the bedroom, a short black wig, well-worn jeans and the MIT sweatshirt she wore when masquerading as Liang Lam. Another chapter of her life was about to begin. C'est la vie. After tomorrow she would be speaking French again.

She returned to the kitchen and heated some minestrone soup for lunch. But she had no appetite. For many years she had made her way through life alone. No family. No close friends. Always running. Always hiding. Trusting no one. Tomorrow she would leave Venice forever. She should be relieved. Instead she felt only a deep sadness.

She didn't want to live in another new city, hiding her identity, lying to people, keeping her distance, confiding in no one.

Venice held so many happy memories. The elderly Italian men in the cafe where she got coffee each morning, smiling at her and saying good morning. Her daily run along the canals, the glorious sunlight sparkling on the still waters, her camaraderie with the women at the shelter.

Most of all she would miss the children in her ESL class, gazing up at her with adoring eyes. For the first time in her life she felt like she was doing something positive and good. Teaching little kids in a shelter for battered women how to speak English in case their mothers had to flee to a safer city, or another country perhaps, where English was spoken.

How could she leave them?

The doorbell cut into her joyous memories, sending her heart racing.

Polizia! They had seen her on the security tapes at the Guggenheim Museum and wanted to question her. But if she didn't answer the door, they would assume she wasn't home and come back another time.

She ran to the living room and shut off her stereo, cutting off the Chet Baker CD she'd put on to dispel her mournful mood. She heard footsteps on the stairs.

Rigid with fear, she stared at the door.

A soft tap sounded on it. "Laura? It's Giancarlo."

At first she felt relieved that it wasn't the polizia. But why was he here? He never came here without calling first. She didn't want to talk to him, but there was no way to avoid it.

She took a deep breath to calm herself and looked around the room.

Damn! Her suitcase stood beside the sofa, and her Beretta was hidden inside. "Just a minute," she called.

She carried the suitcase into her bedroom, ran to the far side of the bed and laid the suitcase flat on the floor out of sight. Giancarlo would-n't be coming into her bedroom today.

She returned to the living room, took a moment to slow her breathing, unlocked the door and opened it.

Giancarlo stood there, not smiling, his dark eyes serious. "Sorry to stop by without calling, but I've got some questions for you."

Alarm bells clanged in her mind. "About what?" she said, making no move to invite him inside.

"About what you told me last night." He pushed open the door, stepped into the room and shut the door, gazing at her, his lips set in a grim line. He seemed angry. But no more angry than she was.

An eerie calm settled over her. If someone challenges you, attack.

"Is this so important you had to interrupt my lunch and barge into my apartment uninvited?"

His expression hardened. "You've been lying to me, Laura. Or should I call you Natalie?"

Her stomach clenched in a spasm of fear.

How did he know her real name?

"What are you talking about?" she said.

He smiled, not his usual charming smile, a triumphant smile.

"Ever since we met you've been lying to me, Natalie. Pretending to be an innocent teacher of English. Ling Lam on your passport, calling yourself Laura."

Stunned, she saw her world crumble like an iceberg shedding chunks of ice into the frigid sea, just as it had in Boston four years ago. Oliver, her lover, saying his CIA-agent friend had investigated her, saying he knew who she really was. Forcing her to kill him.

Now it appeared that Giancarlo also knew who she was.

Her heart turned to stone.

Like Oliver, Giancarlo had deceived her, pretending to be her friend, lying even as he made love to her. Questioning her, like Oliver.

How did he know about her fake passport? Not that it mattered. She had to get out of here, now, not tomorrow. The Beretta was in her suitcase, fully loaded. She didn't want to shoot him, but if he tried to stop her, she would. As these thoughts whirled through her mind, she maintained a neutral expression, revealing nothing.

Which seemed to make him angrier. "My Europol colleagues and I have been tracking you for months. Natalie Brixton, traveling under false names on fake passports. Probably because of the warrants for your arrest in America. One murder in Boston, three more in New Orleans. Another for stealing two priceless paintings from the Gardner Museum in Boston."

Bile rose in her throat. He knew everything. He worked for Europol. If they sent her back to America, she would spend the rest of her life in jail. No way was she going to let that happen.

Anger exploded inside her like a mushroom cloud, worse than when a wealthy businessman had held a gun on her in a New Orleans motel, intent on raping her. But she had defeated him, and she would defeat Giancarlo, too. Every man she'd ever known was susceptible to flattery.

She would lull him into a false sense of security, disable him with one of her Taekwondo moves and escape.

"You never cared for me at all," she said tonelessly. "It was all an act."

Emotion flickered in his eyes. Embarrassment? Regret?

Then his eyes grew cold. "You are a very attractive woman, Natalie. You use this to make men do what you want. You've had plenty of practice, right? Working as a prostitute in Paris and London?"

Fighting the fury that raged inside her, she said nothing.

This evil man had slept with her, knowing all along he was going to arrest her. He didn't deserve to live.

"You lied when you told me you hadn't seen the exhibit at the Guggenheim. You were there on Friday when the shootings happened."

Her worst fears, confirmed. He'd spotted her on the security tapes.

Damned if she'd admit it. How could she have allowed this vile man to seduce her? But she could play a role, too, submissive woman, distraught that he didn't love her.

Using the acting skills she'd studied in high school, she conjured a few tears, brushed them away as they spilled down her cheeks. "You lied to me, Giancarlo. Even when we were making love, you felt nothing for me. It was just business, to make me think you cared about me."

He clenched his jaw, gazing at her. He opened his mouth as if to reply, closed it, and gestured at her sofa. "Sit down. We need to talk."

"Don't order me around. I'm not your property." She turned and stalked into the kitchen. Standing beside the table, she spooned up a mouthful of minestrone soup and forced herself to swallow, planning her moves as he entered the kitchen.

He studied the table, then the counter, searching for something incriminating no doubt. He wouldn't find anything. Her passports were in her purse in the bedroom, but she'd make sure he never saw them. He turned away from the stove and approached her.

Now that she was cornered, a distraught woman scorned by her lover, he seemed happy. *Strike when he least expects it.*

Her body tensed. Coiled like a cobra.

Without warning, she whirled in a spin move and kicked his head.

But at the last instant he pulled back, so it was only a glancing blow. He fell to the floor with a heavy grunt, massaging his head. But sprawled beside the table, he lay between her and the doorway to the living room. She had to get the Beretta before he recovered.

She took two steps back, gathered herself and leaped over him.

Quick as a snake, his hand shot out and he grabbed her right ankle.

She lost her balance and fell to her hands and knees beside the table. Bracing her hands on the floor, she jerked her leg, kicking at him.

But his fierce grip imprisoned her ankle. Damn him to hell!

She grabbed the bowl of soup and threw it in his face.

"Aaah!" He let go of her ankle, grimacing as he wiped broth and bits of noodles from his eyes.

She sprang to her feet and raced through the living room, breathing hard, her heart pounding.

Seconds later she heard footsteps behind her.

Frantic, she raced into the bedroom, circled the bed and opened the suitcase. She pawed through her clothes, flinging them aside, desperate to get her hands on the Beretta.

He charged into the room. "*Strega!* You're all packed and ready to go, aren't you?"

Like a dog digging up a bone, she flung T-shirts and trousers on the floor until she saw the Beretta, inches from her grasp.

His fist hit the side of her head. Pain shot up her cheek into her eye socket. Before she could recover, he yanked her to her feet.

She slapped his face. "*Basta! Vafangulo!*" Bastard! Go fuck yourself!

He laughed. "Such naughty words from the prim English teacher!"

She clawed his cheek with her nails, drawing blood.

He hit her again and shoved her down on the bed, pinning her against the headboard. Through clenched teeth, she said, "What, you're going to rape me now?"

"I have no interest in having sex with you," he said coldly. "Now we will sit down and I will tell you what will happen if you do not cooperate."

Gripping her arms, he dragged her into the kitchen. Avoiding the puddle of soup on the floor, he sat her down at the table. "Do you promise not to run? Or must I tie you to the chair?"

She spat in his face. "I promise nothing."

He slapped her again, bringing tears of pain to her eyes.

"Suit yourself, bitch."

He took plastic flex-ties out of his pocket and cuffed her to the chair, first one wrist, then the other. Gripping her jaw in his hand, he said, "You have two choices, Natalie. Cooperate or go back to America to face those murder charges."

She closed her eyes, picturing Frank Renzi, the relentless homicide detective.

"Look at me!"

She opened her eyes and glared at him. "You're disgusting."

He smiled, the pseudo-charming smile she knew so well.

"No, I am Europol Agent John Conti, working with Generale Cesare Valenti, head of the Venice carabiniere. We want to catch the men who murdered Sophia Ruffino and put her husband in the hospital. We hope to rescue their five-year-old daughter, Bianca."

The girl she'd seen in the museum with the terror-stricken eyes.

"Soon they will fly to New York City. The wife of one of the robbers wants to hire a nanny to care for the girl. We want you to be their nanny."

Natalie said nothing. If that's all they wanted, maybe she would cooperate. For a time she had lived in New York City. After she got there, she would find a way to escape.

"What do I get in return?"

"The murder charges in Boston and New Orleans will be dropped. You will plead guilty to the theft of two paintings from the Gardner Museum and be put on probation. No jail time."

"He will never agree to this."

Conti frowned. "Who?"

"Frank Renzi. He will never agree to it."

"How do you know?"

"He hates me. I shot him once and he has never forgotten it."

Her tormentor smiled. "Perhaps I can persuade him."

She said nothing, thinking, *When hell freezes over.*

CHAPTER 7

Frank finished checking his messages, left his desk and stared out the Homicide office window. It was a gloomy day, dark and dreary to match his mood. Seventy-two hours after Angelique's murder they didn't have squat. Nothing useful from the tipline, no chatter on the street, no tips from any CIs. David was at Iberville digging for leads, hoping to catch people before they went to work.

Yesterday he and David had wasted three hours driving to Bay St. Louis. Rumor had it that King Rock, supplier of good times in New Orleans, had branched out to the Gulf coast, using his cousin to supply gamblers with their drug of choice: crack, heroin, coke or Oxy pills. His cousin, Tariq Barrett, street name Ace, lived near two gambling casinos.

Feigning innocence, Ace said he had no clue why they had any interest in him. Frank told him to cut the shit and tell them where King Rock was. Ace claimed he hadn't seen him for weeks. They searched the apartment, found nothing to indicate King Rock had been there, and drove back to New Orleans.

Because Rocket Man had fed him a load of crap.

Contemplating the day ahead, he sipped his take-out coffee. Last night he'd slept almost four hours, not nearly enough to prepare him for today's problems. Vobitch was at Headquarters. Thanks to the incessant media drumbeat, the NOPD top brass were up in arms because a young woman had been murdered in a public housing project. When Vobitch got back, Frank had to deliver his daily report. No murder weapons, no SUV registered to King Rock, no clue as to his whereabouts.

The only good news: last night he'd gone to see Kenyon, who looked a lot better than the last time he'd seen him. Last night he was sitting in a chair beside his hospital bed, his bandaged leg elevated on the footrest. Tanya was thrilled. Kenyon was going home on Monday. Kenyon was too, but he had put on a show, pissed and moaned, saying he'd have Tanya on his back, making him do his PT exercises.

His phone rang. Hoping David had a lead on King Rock, he grabbed it and said, "Renzi."

"Detective Renzi, this is Agent John Conti calling from Venice, Italy. I understand you were involved in the investigation of an art theft at the Gardner Museum four months ago."

41

That got his attention. Agent John Conti, calling from Italy. Maybe he worked for Interpol. His English was fluent, though it had a certain rhythmic pattern that Frank recognized. His Sicilian grandparents had spoken with a similar cadence.

"Peripherally involved. The Boston FBI office was in charge. Why do you ask?"

"I am working on a recent case in Venice that involved the Peggy Guggenheim Museum."

The hackles rose on the back of his neck. *Natalie.*

"How many paintings did they steal?"

"You misunderstand. No art was stolen. Two Mafia thugs robbed a nearby jewelry store. They killed a police officer, shot several bystanders and ran across the street to the museum. They killed an unarmed guard and escaped by boat via the Grand Canal."

"So why are you calling me?"

"In 2008, you assisted in the investigation of the murder of a former CIA agent, correct?"

"Yes. Oliver James. Are you CIA?" If Conti reported to Clint Hammer, it meant Hammer was hot on Natalie's trail.

"No. I work for Europol, but we have an interest in the case. Can you put me in touch with the Boston detective in charge of the Oliver James murder and the Gardner heist?"

"Lieutenant Colonel Harrison Flynn was in charge, but he passed away recently."

"How unfortunate. My condolences. We know Natalie Brixton was involved in the Gardner heist and the Oliver James murder. I understand you are looking for her."

Damned right he was looking for her. A black cloud of fury rose up inside him, but he forced himself to speak calmly. Why tip his hand to a guy he didn't know?

"She was the prime suspect in the James murder and we know she was involved in the Gardner heist. Do you know where she is?"

"Yes. I took her into custody yesterday."

He felt like he'd been hit with a sledgehammer.

Natalie was in custody?

"Civilians were killed," Conti said, "which means I must work with the carabiniere. Unfortunately, the man in charge can be difficult at times. Generalissimo Cesare Valenti."

Conti's words barely registered. Natalie was in custody in Venice! His heart pounded his chest. He wanted to go get her. Now.

He realized Conti was waiting for him to speak. "Generalissimo? Like Mussolini?"

Conti chuckled. "Not Mussolini. But the carabiniere are military police. They love these fancy titles. We believe Natalie Brixton can help us capture these Mafia gangsters."

"She's wanted for three murders in New Orleans." *And another in Boston, not to mention illegal flight to avoid arrest.*

"So I understand, Detective Renzi. But we hope to obtain your cooperation so that we can use Natalie as our—" Conti paused, groping for a word. "Our undercover agent, so to speak."

He didn't answer immediately. Conti had arrested Natalie, but with Natalie, nothing was certain. She had escaped from police custody before. "How did you find her?"

"I contrived to meet her two months ago and began a relationship with her."

"What kind of relationship?"

Silence on the other end, a telling pause. Did Conti seduce Natalie or did she seduce Conti? She knew how to bamboozle people. Last September she had convinced the Boston cop who was driving her to jail to stop his cruiser, disabled him with a Taekwondo move and escaped in the cruiser. He'd been looking for her ever since.

"An intimate relationship," Conti said. "So I could, how do you say, keep tabs on her. I had reason to believe she was planning to leave Venice, which is why I arrested her yesterday."

"Where is she now?"

"In a hotel in Venice, guarded around the clock by carabiniere officers."

"A hotel? Why didn't you lock her up in jail?" *And throw away the key.*

"A small concession on our part. These robbers are members of a ruthless Mafia gang. They killed the wife of the jewelry store owner and kidnapped their five-year-old daughter. We want Natalie to help us rescue her."

Use Natalie to help them? Was Conti out of his mind? Natalie was the one who used people. "Where's the girl's father?"

"He is in hospital, comatose. The doctors fear he may not recover. But our main concern is the girl. And capturing the robbers, of course."

Amused by the double-speak, Frank smiled. Conti was trying to imply that catching the robbers was an afterthought. Bullshit. Conti and his Europol colleagues wanted to capture the Mafia thugs.

"They stole a large quantity of uncut diamonds. Untraceable, as you probably know. We believe they will fly to New York City soon."

"How do you know this?"

"Valenti's officers are in a cottage across the street from their safe house, monitoring it with sensitive electronic equipment. We heard them talking. The robber's wife wants to hire a nanny to care for the girl. We want Natalie to be the nanny."

Frank conjured an image of Natalie in a hotel room, guarded by cara-biniere officers, her mind working overtime, plotting how to escape. "She agreed to this?"

"We want to sweeten the deal to convince her. Tell her we will make these murder warrants in New Orleans go away. She pleads guilty to the art theft, gets probation and all is forgiven."

All is forgiven? Not in his mind. "No fucking way!"

"She returned three valuable paintings that were stolen from the Gardner, did she not?"

"She murdered four men in cold blood."

"Detective Renzi, this may be the only way to assure the safety of Bianca Ruffino, an innocent five-year-old girl. We heard the robbers threaten to kill her."

Frank weighed his options. Conti might be bullshitting him, but he could sling bullshit, too. Once Natalie landed in New York, she'd be in U.S. jurisdiction. If he agreed to the deal, he could save himself a trip to Venice, serve the murder warrants after she landed in New York.

"How do you keep tabs on Natalie if she's with the robbers?"

"I will fly on the same plane with them to New York City."

"A city Natalie knows well. She lived there for a while."

A short silence. "Really? I did not know that."

You don't know a lot of things. Conti had no idea who he was dealing with, or how ruthless she was. Natalie had waited twenty years to avenge her mother's murder, had murdered four men in the process.

"She told me she shot you," Conti said. "She said you would not agree to this deal."

He smiled tightly. That sounded like Natalie. A step ahead of every-one, cops included.

"I don't have the authority to make the murder warrants go away."

"Detective Renzi, when these gangsters fly to New York, we want Natalie to be with them. Please. Help us convince her."

"I'll talk to some people but no guarantees. If she flies to New York, I want to know when the flight lands so I can be there."

"I can arrange that. Thank you for your cooperation," Conti said, and ended the call.

Frank studied his notes. *Natalie in custody, Venice, Italy. May fly to NYC soon.* Maybe Conti would tell him what flight she was on and maybe he wouldn't. But if she tried to pass through customs, NOPD and Boston PD would know it immediately. Her name and passport were on a watch-list at every international airport in the country.

―――――

Venice 2:15 PM

Natalie studied the man across the table from her, Generale di Brigata Cesare Valenti, head of the Venice carabiniere, stiffly erect in his black uniform, with the red epaulets on the shoulders, a red stripe down the legs of the trouser. A distinguished-looking man, he appeared to be in his fifties, his dark hair graying at the temples, his thin mustache neatly trimmed.

He reminded her of the Frenchman in Paris who had tutored her in art history, so she could converse intelligently with the wealthy men who paid to have sex with her.

But Valenti was no art teacher, he was a military policeman, saying in heavily accented English, his dark eyes boring into her, "These men are not characters in some Hollywood film like *The Godfather.* Like his father before him, Orazio has tortured and killed many people. Strangers fear him because he seldom speaks. They think he is retarded. Nonsense. He is highly intelligent. Tomasso, the younger brother, is better looking but ..." Valenti frowned. "Equally ruthless. For them, killing is a means to an end, to get what they want. And they wanted to steal the shipment of uncut diamonds that arrived at Ruffino and Son Jewelers on Friday."

"Orazio killed the owner's wife," Natalie said. Valenti had already told her this.

"And put her husband in the hospital. The doctors tell me he may not recover." Valenti pinched the bridge of his prominent Roman nose and gazed into her eyes. "If you cross these men, they will kill you."

Chilling words, but she had dealt with ruthless men before. Last summer in Boston two men had tried to kill her. They hadn't, but she had no illusions that her luck would hold if she agreed to this deal.

The 'Netti brothers might kill her no matter what she did.

She fingered her cheek, then her eye socket. They still ached where Giancarlo, the deceitful prick, had punched her. Now purple bruises decorated her face. "What about Tomasso's wife?"

"A well-born woman—her father sits on the city council—but her wealthy parents gave her whatever she wanted. She was not Tomasso's first lover, far from it, but he is handsome and charming. He uses her to help him rob and steal. He only married her so she couldn't testify against him." Valenti grimaced. "Another case two years ago, and poof, Tomasso goes free. Catarina is a beautiful young woman." His lip curled in disgust. "Married to a gangster, but she prances around like a fashion model, wearing fancy clothes, painting her face with makeup."

Natalie sipped from a glass of water. Maybe she could use this to get close to Catarina. She knew all about fashion and fancy clothes and makeup. Another thing they'd taught her in Paris when she'd worked as a high-paid escort.

"What about Bianca?"

Memories of the girl's terror-stricken eyes still haunted her.

"I know nothing about her. But she witnessed the shooting of her mother. Perhaps you can get her to talk. John Conti tells me you work with children here."

Hearing his name fueled her fury. The deceitful prick had charmed her into trusting him, then punched her and took her into custody. The hate she felt for him was like nothing she had ever experienced.

If she had her Beretta, she would shoot him without remorse. She had violated her rule. Trust no one. She would never trust anyone again.

Conti and Valenti were using her, just as Tomasso, the Mafia brother, had used his wife to stay out of jail.

The door of her hotel room opened and Conti sauntered across the room to the table. With grim satisfaction, she studied the abrasions on his cheek. Four jagged scratches, two-inches long, only now beginning to scab over. She should have scratched his eyes out.

"Hello Cesare. Hello Natalie."

Valenti returned his greeting. She didn't.

Conti sat down beside her. "Do you like the room we chose for you?"

No, she hated it. High above the street on the sixth floor, the only window, which opened onto a fire escape, was barred. No window in the bathroom. Two armed carabiniere officers stood outside the door around the clock. The bed was comfortable enough, not that she'd slept much, tossing and turning, by turns angry and fearful, wondering what would become of her.

"You're a liar," she said, shooting him a venomous look.

He smiled, the faux-charming smile he'd used to seduce her.

To make sure Valenti understood, she said, "*Un caffone repugnante. Un culo di merda.*" A disgusting boor. A shitty asshole.

He reeled back as though she'd slapped him.

She saw Valenti's lips quirk in a smile, quickly suppressed. Perhaps Valenti wasn't fond of Conti either.

Recovering quickly, Conti smiled. "It's better than a jail cell."

"Do you fuck all the women you seduce with your lies or just the ones who are good in bed?"

His smile disappeared. Slowly and deliberately, he reached inside his jacket, took out a pack of Benson & Hedges and shook out a cigarette.

"Put that away," she snapped. "Don't stink up my room with your dis-gusting cigarettes!"

He grabbed her forearm and squeezed. "Watch your mouth. I will be your only protector in New York City. Don't piss me off or I might not be there if you need me." He released her arm. "Your favorite detective will be there, too. Frank Renzi."

A spasm of fear jolted her. Renzi would be there? How much worse could this get? Trying to get information from two ruthless brothers for a deceitful Europol agent was bad enough. How would she escape if Renzi was there? He might arrest her as soon as she got off the plane.

"You need an attitude adjustment," Conti said. "You play nice, we play nice. If you don't, you pay. We need to buy you some clothes. It's cold in New York this time of year."

"I have my own clothes."

"Not anymore. We took your belongings and put them in an evidence locker."

To hide her despair she turned and stared out the window. Any hope of retrieving her iPhone, her lifeline to Pak Lam, was gone. Worse, if they had the iPhone, they might call him. Not that Pak Lam would talk to them. They used a coded greeting, but still.

Conti rose from his chair. "Come with me, Laura, otherwise known as Ling Lam, the name on your fake passport. Let's go shopping."

"Momento," Valenti said. "Wait outside, John. I need a private word with Natalie."

Conti frowned and a flush rose on his cheeks. Then he shrugged and left the room.

After the door closed, Valenti said, "You are having second thoughts about this?"

"Not about the deal. But what about my employer at the shelter? What will you tell her?"

"What do you want me to tell her?"

"Tell her my mother is ill and I must go to America to care for her." A lie. Her mother had been dead for years, murdered by a rich bastard who treated women like dirt. Ever since then her life had been a disaster, one problem after another.

She thought about the children she'd tutored, picturing their young faces and adoring eyes. "Ask her to tell the kids that I love them. I will miss them very much." She looked at Valenti, who gazed at her, his dark eyes somber. "I loved working with them. I thought I could start a new life in your beautiful city, but now you force me to return to a life of deception."

"The past has a way of catching up with us." But Valenti said this in a kindly way, as if he were dispensing fatherly advice. "I believe you intended to end your life of crime, Natalie. If you help us capture the 'Netti brothers, you can live out the rest of your life in freedom."

Live her life in freedom? That's what she thought when she had escaped from Boston. And Frank Renzi. But when she landed in New York City, Renzi would be waiting for her.

Valenti gazed into her eyes. "Natalie, I am worried about Bianca. She needs someone to protect her. These Mafia brothers are ruthless. Please, look out for her. As a favor to me."

"Of course," she said, automatically.

But that wasn't her main priority.

She had to find a way to escape from John Conti and Frank Renzi.

CHAPTER 8

12:35 PM – Venice

Bianca hunched over the kitchen table, perched on the phone book Catwoman had put on her chair. That wasn't her real name. She didn't even look like a cat. She had long blonde hair and blue eyes, but the men called her Catarina. She was the woman who gave her the cute little stuffed puppy. But that was a trick to make Mamma let her in the house.

Later they put her in a big black car with Mamma and drove to Papà's store. She didn't want to think about what happened then. Afterwards, Catwoman had to buy her new clothes. When Owl came out of the store and shot Mamma, she'd wet her pants.

She called him Owl because his eyes scared her, like when the owl in the zoo glared at her, only worse. She didn't know his real name.

Catwoman called the other man Tommy. She was pretty sure they were married, because they wore wedding rings. But Tommy talked nasty to Catwoman. Papà never talked to Mamma like that, using bad words. She didn't know what they meant, but she knew they were bad because Catwoman told Tommy not to say things like that in front of her.

Yesterday Owl told Catwoman that people were looking for her. That made her happy, but then he told Catwoman cut her hair so he could take her picture. Now she looked like a boy. She didn't want to look like a boy! She hated wearing boy's clothes, jeans and itchy long-sleeved shirts with buttons down the front. She liked pretty dresses and leggings.

But Catwoman had thrown her red dress and white leggings and shiny black shoes in the trash. She had to wear sneakers, like a boy.

Tears filled her eyes, but she didn't cry. If she did, Owl would get mad. He was bigger than Tommy and scarier, always glaring at her.

He had mean eyes. And a gun.

Did he shoot Papà, too?

If Papà was dead, who would come find her and take her home?

She looked at the sandwich Catwoman had given her, pulled off the top piece of bread and picked out a slice of cheese. She wasn't going to eat the salami. She hated salami and it had mustard on it. She hated mustard, too. Mamma never made her eat sandwiches for lunch. She fixed her a bowl of soup or ravioli stuffed with cheese.

Catwoman brought a glass of milk to the table and set it beside her plate, hovering over her. She smelled nice, some kind of perfume. She was pretty, not as pretty as Mamma, but she wore makeup like Mamma. Blue eye-shadow to match her blue eyes. Mamma's eyes were brown.

She loved Mamma more than anyone in the world, except for Papà. But now Mamma was dead. Whenever she thought about this, it made her cry. But she couldn't cry now. Owl came into the kitchen, frowning like always. Her heart pounded. She could hardly breathe. It felt like Owl had sucked all the air out of the room. She refused to look at him.

"Eat your sandwich, kid."

That's what he called her. Kid. She ate a bite of cheese and stared at the table. He came over and grabbed her jaw and tipped up her face to make her look at him. Terrified, she stared at his eyes. Big and dark, almost black. Hateful eyes.

"You don't eat your food, you might not get anymore."

"Don't say that," Catwoman said. "You'll scare her."

"Shut up, Catarina, or I'll scare you, too."

He let go of her jaw and took out his gun. Was he going to shoot her?

Her stomach heaved and her throat closed up. She spit the cheese onto the plate.

"Stop scaring her!" Catwoman said. "We need her to get on the plane."

"No we don't. Me and Tommy can go to New York without you."

"Tommy won't go without me. When I tell him—"

"Shut up." He aimed the gun at Catwoman's head. "You might be able to pussy-whip Tommy, but he doesn't run this family. I do."

Then he stomped out of the room with his gun. But she still felt sick.

If Owl killed Catwoman, who would protect her?

Catwoman stroked her cheek. "Don't pay any attention to him, Bianca. He just likes to scare people. We're going to New York soon."

She didn't want to go to New York. She wanted to go home.

"Where's New York?"

"Across the ocean in America. We'll fly there in an airplane." Catwoman made her blue eyes go wide to show how excited she was. "You'll love New York City. There are lots of stores where you can buy beautiful clothes. And for the holidays they decorate a big Christmas tree with colored lights in the middle of a skating rink."

Bianca thought about the Christmas tree at home, waiting for Papà to put her favorite ornament on the top.

What would happen to the white angel now?

"Will Papà be there?"

Catwoman frowned. "Want some ice cream? Chocolate? Vanilla?"

Her eyes filled with tears. She didn't want ice cream.

She wanted to go home and be with Papà.

———

10:25 AM – New Orleans

The moment Frank entered the office, Vobitch fixed his steel-gray eyes on him like twin laser beams. "You get anything in Bay St. Louis?"

"No. It was a wild goose chase. Looks like King Rock is using his cousin to deal drugs. Tariq Barrett, street name Ace, lives near the casinos, supplies the high-rollers."

"These fucking maggots make more money than I do," Vobitch growled.

"We searched the place. No weapons, no evidence that King Rock had been there. We could have busted Ace for the baggie of pot we found, but I figured it wasn't worth it. What happened at Headquarters? Did they give you grief?"

"They want results." Vobitch raked his fingers through his silvery-gray hair. "Like I can wave a magic wand and find the fucker that killed the woman. When I asked for more troops to hunt for the prick, not to mention the murder weapons which are probably in some fucking sewer, they politely told me to go to hell. So. You got any good news for me?"

"No. Nothing on the tipline. No vehicle registered to King Rock."

Stone-faced, Vobitch tapped his pen on a yellow legal pad. "Kelly called me yesterday. She wants to get back into Homicide. Figured I'd tell you as a courtesy since you two are such good *friends*." Doing the quote thing with his fingers. Vobitch knew he and Kelly were lovers, but he was okay with it, as long as Kelly was working in Domestic Violence.

"What did you tell her?" he said cautiously.

"Told her I'd think about it."

"So? What do you think?"

Vobitch gave him a sly look. "You go first."

"Well, she's a great detective. I don't need to tell you that."

"And?"

51

"She wants to work the Angelique Vaughn murder, right?"

Vobitch smiled tightly. "She made that crystal clear. Angelique was one of her clients."

"She's too emotionally involved to work the case." True enough, but his main concern was personal. If Kelly transferred back into Homicide it would cause problems. NOPD frowned on relationships between officers working in the same unit, and Vobitch knew it.

"She feels guilty," he said, "Angelica gave her a tip and got murdered because of it."

"Bullshit! Her asshole boyfriend murdered her and shot Kenyon." Vobitch leaned forward, resting his thick forearms on the desk. "But I could use another detective. With Kenyon out of commission, we're shorthanded."

"Maybe we can let her keep an eye on the B-n-L crash pad. See if King Rock shows up."

"Are you crazy? She sees him, she'll shoot first, ask questions later!"

That sounded about right to Frank.

"I think she should stay where she is," Vobitch said, "but maybe we can figure a way to keep her in the loop. Make her feel like she's helping us with the case. Unofficially."

Relieved, he said, "Good idea. Maybe tie it in with Jacques."

"Right. I almost forgot about the boy. How's he doing?"

"Not good. Kelly talks to the social worker every day. He's in foster care, so traumatized he literally won't speak. Not a word."

"Because he saw his scumbag father shoot his mother. We need to find this motherfucker."

"And we will. As soon as possible. Make everyone happy for Christmas."

"Make the NOPD bigwigs happy, for damn sure. Speaking of which, Juliana and I are having an open house the Sunday after Christmas, provided some nutcase doesn't massacre ten people that day. An end-of-the-year thank-you to all my diligent detectives."

The parties Vobitch and his wife threw were legendary. Music by a Tulane University brass quintet, an open bar and a mouth-watering smorgasbord prepared by Juliana. Vobitch could be a hard-nosed SOB at work, but he liked to kick back and relax at home.

And when Juliana was around, he was a pussycat. No F-bombs.

"Make sure you bring Kelly." Vobitch said. "If you two split up before then, I'll invite her myself."

"Last time I checked, we're not planning on splitting up."

"When was that?" Vobitch said, deadpan. "Last night in bed?"

Jiving him. Frank let it go. Now that Vobitch was in a better mood, he could tell him about Natalie. "I got a call from Italy this morning. A Europol agent arrested Natalie Brixton yesterday."

"Jesus! Are you serious?"

"Yes, but here's the deal. He's working a major case and he wants Natalie to infiltrate a Mafia gang and act as his undercover agent. Conti says they're planning to fly to New York City."

"Undercover agent, my ass. Fuck that. I want to put her in jail."

"Hold on, it's complicated." He summarized the robbery, the murders and the kidnapping. "One brother is married. His wife wants to hire a nanny to take care of the girl. Conti thinks he can get them to hire Natalie, but he's not sure she'll cooperate, so he offered her a deal. If she infiltrates the gang and reports back to him, he said we'd forget the homicide warrants."

"Like hell we will!"

"That's what I thought at first, but look at it this way. When Natalie lands in New York, she's in our jurisdiction, not his. Cheaper than sending me to Venice."

"I'm not sending you anywhere. We've got a high-profile murder to solve."

"Morgan, we've been hunting for Natalie since September. Four months. Conti calls me with the details of the flight, I fly to New York, arrest her, bring her back here."

"No fucking way! Get your priorities straight, Frank. Find the scumbag that shot Kenyon. Newsflash. He ain't in New York."

In the tense silence, his cellphone chimed. When he answered, a voice said, "Frank, this is Sergeant Mitchell at the lockup. Got some bad news for you. One of the guards found Jawon Taylor dead in his cell this morning."

His heart slammed his chest. "Jesus! What happened?"

"Someone strangled him with a shoelace. We're not sure when, last night after bed check or early this morning, but we don't know who. We're investigating."

"Thanks for letting me know," Frank said.

When he ended the call, Vobitch was looking at him, eyebrows raised. "What?"

"Rocket Man's dead. Somebody offed him in his cell last night or early this morning."

"Christ! There goes our witness."

"Man, I feel guilty. When he wouldn't give us anything, I threatened to put out the word that he talked, but I never intended to do it."

"People think jail is a safe place to be. Wrong. Getting one inmate to off another one is easy. Hell, a carton of cigarettes would do it."

"True, but I still feel guilty."

"Don't," Vobitch snapped. "These maggots have no respect for human life. The moke fell in with evil companions. His choice. King Rock had him killed so he wouldn't talk. You can take that to the bank."

Frank rose from his chair. "I better go tell David."

When he entered the Homicide office, David swiveled his chair to face him, his short black hair neatly combed, still wearing his sports jacket, but his tie was draped on an open desk drawer.

"How'd it go with Vobitch? Any F-bombs?"

Eight months ago David had joined the District-8 homicide squad and helped him solve a brutal murder-kidnapping. His girlfriend was a grad student at MIT in Cambridge. David claimed she was smarter than he was, but Frank doubted it. It hadn't taken David eight months to get a handle on Vobitch and his volatile temper.

"A few. The top brass roasted him over the coals about Angelique's murder, so he was already in a bad mood. When I said we've got no clue where King Rock is, it didn't improve his disposition. And it gets worse. Rocket Man is dead."

David stared at him. "Dead? What happened?"

Frank told him about the call from the lockup. "Vobitch figures King Rock had him killed. I feel guilty. I should have told them to put him in isolation."

"Hindsight is twenty-twenty. Not your fault, Frank. But damn! He was our only witness."

"Except for Jacques. You get anything at Iberville?"

"No. Nobody's talking, and when they hear about Rocket Man it will get worse. I found out one thing though. The nurse, Ella Hughes? Her neighbor said she went to visit her daughter in Jackson, Mississippi. Maybe she saw more than she let on."

"Maybe." But talking to Ella Hughes was no longer his main priority. The murder warrants for Natalie were at Headquarters. "I've got to run an errand. Be back in an hour."

Vobitch was fixated on King Rock. He was focused on Natalie. When she landed in New York City, he was going to arrest her. All he had to do was convince Vobitch to let him go there.

CHAPTER 9

TUESDAY December 14 – 1:05 PM – Venice

She pushed the carriage along the sidewalk, slowly and carefully so as not to wake the baby. Her hands were sweaty, her mind focused on all the things that could go wrong. The baby would wake up and start crying. She would stroll past the Antonetti house and no one would see her. The carriage would tip over and the baby's mother would shoot her.

Conti was waiting around the corner with the baby's mother, a polizia officer. *If anything happens to my daughter, you will come to an unpleasant end.* A typical Italian mother, sharp claws and teeth. But this mother had a gun.

She and the baby were bait, a ploy to induce the 'Netti brothers to hire her. Conti figured Catarina would see her, come running out and ask her to be Bianca's nanny. *Tell her you work with children, demonstrate your Italian and your fluent English.* Easy for him to say. She was the one who had to convince Catarina. And the brothers. Vicious killers.

If no one came out when she passed their house, she had to push the carriage around the corner and report to Conti. Then she'd have to do it again. What if the baby woke up when she was talking to Catarina? She had no idea what to do with an infant. If she picked her up, the baby would know she wasn't her mother and cry harder.

Sweat dampened the armpits of her black silk pantsuit, gold buttons on the jacket, red-and-gold dragons embroidered on the pant legs. Conti didn't want her to buy it, but she had convinced him, saying Catarina was a fashion maven and the chic outfit would impress her.

In a minute she would pass the Antonetti house, a one-story cottage with a two-car garage. The garage doors were shut, and Venetian blinds covered the windows on either side of the front door.

As instructed, she didn't look at the house across the street. Valenti and his carabiniere officers were inside, monitoring the Antonetti house.

She kept walking, just an innocent nanny taking baby for a stroll.

As she passed the front door she walked slower, mentally imploring Catarina to see her. But nothing happened. When she reached the far corner of the house, she stopped, bent over the carriage and pretended to adjust the baby's blanket. Still nothing.

At least the baby was asleep, her tiny fist pressed against her lips.

Filled with despair, she straightened and kept walking. Now she would have to tell the insufferable John Conti that his plan had failed and reassure Tiger-Mom that her baby was fine.

Behind her a voice called in Italian, "Excuse me, Senora!"

Scarcely daring to hope, she turned. A woman with long blond hair in an elegant blue dress was hurrying across the lawn.

She want to shout for joy. Catarina!

She had a pretty face, smooth creamy skin the color of a vanilla shake and large blue eyes, accented by mascara and eye-shadow.

Smiling at her, Natalie said in Italian, "Good afternoon, Senora. Beautiful day, isn't it? Warm enough to take the little one for a walk."

"A fine day," Catarina said. "I like your pantsuit. Very stylish."

"Thank you. The woman who pays me to babysit—" Switching to English, she said, "She told me not to dress like a slob. Sorry, my Italian vocabulary is not all that it should be."

"Slob. A new word for my English vocabulary," Catarina said in heavily accented English. "You speak Italian quite well."

"Thank you. I'm a student at the university, but we're on break until January. I use the time to make extra money. The books are expensive."

Studying her almond-shaped eyes, Catarina said, "You are American?"

"Chinese-American. My father is Chinese. But I have lived in Italy for several months. Such a beautiful country, and the food!" She spread her hands in a helpless gesture.

Catarina laughed and nodded. "All this pasta is tempting. We have to stay slim for our men. What do you study at the university?"

"Psychology. I volunteer at a halfway house teaching children how to speak English."

"Wonderful! I am Catarina. And you are?"

"Laura. Happy to meet you."

"You cannot imagine how happy I am to meet you. I need a nanny to take care of my cousin's girl. She is only five, and her mother died recently. I do my best to console her, but I have many things to do." She gestured at the cottage. "My husband and I will fly to New York City soon. Would you consider traveling with us? We would pay you well."

A faint cry came from the carriage. Her heart pounded. *Please don't wake up now! Not when I'm about to close the deal!*

"How long would we be in there?"

"Not long. A week perhaps. We will be back before Christmas."

More cries from the carriage. Louder and insistent.

"I need to take the baby home for her bottle. Her mother will be home at three. Would it be all right if I came back then to discuss this with you?" *Please say yes!*

More cries from the carriage.

Her heart pounded her chest like a wild thing.

"That would be fine, Laura. I'll be waiting for you. Ciao."

"Ciao." She turned and pushed the carriage down the sidewalk.

More cries, angry and shrill. She walked faster.

———

8:15 AM – Washington, D.C.

"I'm going to get you, bitch."

Clint Hammer stared with undisguised hatred at the photograph on his desk. Finally, after two interminable years, his assistant had located the woman who'd murdered his friend, Oliver James, the best CIA operative he'd ever worked with. Years ago he had partnered with Oliver in Nicaragua, a top-secret project that was still classified.

Recalling their extracurricular activities, also classified, he allowed himself a tight smile. Oliver, a handsome six-footer with a gift for gab, easily snared the prettiest local girls. Clint happily settled for his castoffs. He was five-six and not nearly as handsome due to his acne-scarred cheeks. When their top-secret assignment and amorous adventures ended, Oliver had left the CIA and started his own business, a highly successful one, buying and selling art antiquities.

Until he met Natalie Brixton.

A beautiful woman, half-Vietnamese and more devious than Mata Hari. Two years ago in Boston she had seduced Oliver, who fell in love with her. How was he to know she was a serial killer? After murdering Oliver in cold blood, she'd gone to New Orleans and killed three more men. The NOPD cops were useless. Just thinking about Frank Renzi and his Jew-bastard boss, Morgan Vobitch, made him want to vomit. First they had her, then they lost her.

He sank into the high-backed chair behind the government-issue metal desk facing the door and surveyed his ten-foot-square office. Two floors below street level, the room was like a bunker. No windows, linoleum on the floor, bare walls painted institutional green.

A three-in-one laser printer-copier-fax machine stood beside his desk. No file cabinets. He never left paper trails.

His thoughts returned to the Brixton bitch. It frightened him, how badly he wanted her. He'd come to think of this as his own little covert operation, but he had to be careful. If he deviated from his usual routine, others would notice. One way to put yourself in serious jeopardy was getting caught with a file that was none of your business. So for the past two years he had performed his duties as though he had nothing else on his mind. Like hell.

A sharp rap sounded on his door.

Clint aligned the photo of the Brixton bitch in the center of the desk. Placed his pen beside the photo. Checked to make sure his desk drawers were closed. "Come in, Jason."

His assistant entered the office and approached the desk. Jason was five-two, four inches shorter than Clint. His liquid brown eyes were hidden behind thick glasses, but he was the best computer hacker the agency had, able to crack the most deviously encrypted files.

"Where is she?" Clint snapped.

"Well, sir, I've got good news and bad news."

He ground his teeth, sending shooting pains down his jaw. "Don't fuck with me, Jason. Where is she?"

"I can't tell you where she is now. I can only tell you where she was two months ago."

"Damn it to hell! You said you found her!"

"I did, sir. I spent all my free hours working with the face-recognition program. We've got the most advanced face-recognition software in town."

Jason had explained it to him in excruciating detail. The software reduced human faces to 600 tiny measurements: the distance between the pupils of the eyes, the width of the nose at seven points, more measurements for lips, even more for the ears, every crease, curve and earlobe like a fingerprint. A database held three million faces from all over the world, convicted criminals, spies, immigrants, legal and illegal, tens of thousands of protesters chanting slogans. Jason almost got a hard-on, explaining this to him.

"I know that. Tell me what you found!"

"The first week in October she was in a train station in Venice, Italy. But I can't guarantee she's still there. Venice might have been a stopover."

"So? Keep using the software and find her." Given the CIA's interest in criminals world-wide, they had cameras in key airports and train stations across the globe.

"Yes, sir, but—"

"But what!!" His acne-scarred cheeks grew hot, reddening in a flush.

"I'm checking every major airport and train station in Europe, but if she rented a car, she might be holed up in a small city. Where we don't have cameras."

Jason gazed at him, his eyes magnified by the thick lenses. "And then there's the bad news."

He ground his teeth, sending another painful jolt down his jaw. He didn't want to hear about bad news. He wanted results! "What?"

"Someone else accessed the facial recognition file."

"Who?"

"I don't know."

"Find out!! Call me immediately if you spot the Brixton bitch!"

Jason bolted out of the office like a cat with a Rottweiler on its tail.

He took a deep breath to calm himself, set his laptop on the desk and opened it. Natalie Brixton had been in Venice two months ago. Jason thought she might have gone somewhere else, but he didn't believe it.

He'd go there and find the bitch. But he needed a reason to get his boss fly him to Venice. Budgets were tight these days.

He did a computer search: *Organized Crime + Venice, Italy*. The Mafia still ruled in Italy.

He got a zillion hits. Perfect. His boss had a hard-on for these Mafia motherfuckers.

Two days from now he'd be in Venice, hunting for the bitch who'd murdered Oliver. If she wasn't there, he'd track her down. He knew how to make people talk.

What was she doing now, he wondered. Six hours ahead in Venice, almost three in the afternoon. Maybe she was sitting in an outdoor cafe, eating gelato, enjoying a nice sunny day.

She'd better enjoy it. Her days were numbered.

CHAPTER 10

3:00 PM – Venice

Steeling herself, Natalie rang the doorbell and faked a smile. Her face muscles felt stiff and her stomach was churning like a blender. Catarina seemed eager to hire her, but the 'Netti brothers might not be.

If you cross these men, they will kill you. Valenti's warning.

This was a high-stakes gamble, one she couldn't afford to lose. If she didn't convince them to hire her, Conti would ship her back to the States to face four murder charges, and Frank Renzi.

Catarina opened the door and beamed her a big smile. "Hello, Laura, please come in."

"Thank you," she murmured, and followed her into a small, sparsely furnished living room. The window blinds were closed but two table lamps gave the room a cheery glow. A man rose from a three-cushion sofa facing a television set. Catarina beckoned him closer.

"Laura, this is my husband, Tomasso. Tommy, say hello to Laura."

He was three inches taller than she was, five-ten and darkly handsome in the classic Italian mold, dressed in well-tailored slacks and a white shirt open at the throat. Visible in the V were several gold chains and a thick mat of dark hair. Like many Europeans he wore his wedding band on his right hand. Like many gangsters, he wore a gaudy ring on his left pinky finger.

She smiled and said in Italian, "Hello, sir, I'm happy to meet you."

"My pleasure," he said with a suave smile, exposing even white teeth. An attractive man, and like many such men, he knew it, studying her reaction to him. He took her hands in his, and his dark eyes roved over her body, evaluating her, a sexual appraisal she knew well. Tits, average. Ass, skinny. Face, exotic. For some reason men seemed to think Asian women were hot in bed. She hoped this wouldn't be a problem.

"My brother-in-law is in the kitchen," Catarina said, gesturing at a doorway. Tomasso released her hands, returned to the couch and turned on the television. Other than sexual interest, he seemed indifferent to her. The older brother would make the decision. A chilling thought. According to Cesare Valenti, Orazio had killed many people.

The kitchen was unremarkable: a gas stove, a refrigerator, a porcelain sink. In the center of the room, chairs surrounded a square table with a white Formica top. Dressed in a dark suit, Orazio leaned against the counter beside the sink, his arms folded across his chest. He was bigger than Tomasso, six feet tall with a powerful physique that signaled brute strength. Mirrored sunglasses covered his eyes. It made him look like some futuristic warrior in a sci-fi movie.

"This is Laura, the woman I told you about," Catarina said in English. "Laura, this is—"

"Sit down," Orazio said in English, indicating the chair facing him.

Annoyed, she did as he said. He had deliberately put her in the subordinate position, the usual tactic of men who wanted to intimidate people. She had encountered many such men, one in Boston, another in London. They were dead now, but Orazio Antonetti was very much alive, and very much in control.

He removed his mirrored sunglasses, but his expression remained inscrutable. He wasn't as handsome as Tomasso, but his body language and demeanor radiated power.

"You are American?" he said, studying her eyes.

She forced a smile. "Yes. My father is Chinese-American. My mother's ancestors are English."

"Where did you live in America?"

"In Needham, Massachusetts, a small city west of Boston."

"I have been to Boston. The Italian neighborhood has excellent food. It is near the waterfront. You have been there?" His English was fluent, with only a trace of an accent.

"Yes. The North End has many fine restaurants." It also had coffee shops and restaurants where the Boston Mafia congregated.

"Show me your passport." When she hesitated, he said, "Did Catarina not tell you we fly to New York soon? You will need a passport."

Reluctantly, she took her Ling Lam passport out of her purse and gave it to him. What if he kept it? Conti had confiscated her Liang Lam passport, Ling's twin brother. She glanced at Catarina who leaned against the doorjamb, docile and submissive like a good Italian wife.

Orazio flipped through her passport. "You have only one entry stamp, the one when you landed in Rome in September. Why is this?"

Her heart pounded. If she claimed to be a world-traveling student, her cover story, her passport would have several stamps.

Years of lies and deception saved her. "That is my new passport. The other one expired. It has many entry stamps."

Speaking rapidly in Italian, Catarina said, "Why do you question her? She has experience with young children. She speaks English and Italian. What more do we need to know?"

Orazio replied in Italian, "Where is the child?"

"Taking a nap in the bedroom."

"Wake her up and stay there until I call you."

After Catarina left the room, Orazio said in English, "You understand what we said?" His eyes bored into her, predatory eyes, relentless and implacable.

Her mouth felt dry as toast. She wanted a drink of water, but if she asked for one, he might take it as a sign of weakness. "You asked where the child was and told Catarina to wake her."

"Close enough," he said.

"What is her name?" she asked.

His eyes turned black with fury. "The child is five years old. That is all you need to know. Catarina tells me you are a student at the university. What is it that you study?"

"After high school I got a degree in psychology." She knew enough about this to discuss it in general terms. "My major at the university is child growth and development."

"Who pays for this?" His lips curled in a sneer. "Your passport says you were born in 1978. Thirty-two years old and you don't have a job?"

Now he was browbeating her. Damned if she'd put up with it. If someone attacks you, strike back. "You don't even offer a woman a glass of water when she enters your home?"

His eyes widened in surprise. Then, a faint smile. "A woman with spirit. I like that."

He opened a cupboard, took out a glass and ran water in the sink. He filled the glass and set it on the table, looming over her. She smelled smoke on his suit jacket, cigar smoke.

"What have you been doing for the last ten years? Four years of college, then what?"

She drank some water and put the glass on the table. This was an exercise of wills. He was trying to intimidate her. But her momentary defiance had intrigued him.

"I have held many jobs in America and a few in Europe. I would show you my resume, but my laptop was stolen recently."

"Have you ever lived in New York City?"

"No." Conti had warned her about this. *If he asks, deny it.*

"Catarina," he called in Italian. "Bring the child in the kitchen."

Her heart caught in her throat and her palms grew sweaty. Would Bianca remember her? Her fate hung in the balance. If the girl let on that she'd seen her in the museum, she was done for.

Footsteps sounded in the hall, the click-clack of Catarina's high heels. Holding Bianca's hand, she entered the kitchen. The girl's appearance shocked her. Someone had cut her curly dark hair. Now it was cropped short, and she was dressed like a boy in jeans and a blue-plaid shirt.

But her eyes were the same, large and dark and wide with fear.

To her dismay, she saw recognition in those eyes.

"This is Laura," Catarina said in Italian. "The lady who will help me take care of you."

Smiling at Bianca, she said in Italian, "Hello, I like your blue-plaid shirt. It's very pretty."

The girl's eyes filled with tears. "Mamma!" she wailed. "I want Mamma and Papà."

"Catarina," Orazio said, "take the child in the living room."

Like a soldier following orders, Catarina hustled Bianca out of the kitchen. Fearing Bianca's reaction would kill the deal, she said, "I'm sure things will be fine once the child gets to know me."

"This does not concern me. Be here Thursday afternoon at two. Do not be late. Bring only one suitcase." Orazio smiled. "We discuss your salary on the plane. I am sure you will be pleased."

Relieved that he had decided to hire her, she didn't argue.

———

Bianca sat on the couch beside Catwoman, anxiously fiddling with the buttons on her shirt. When they came in the room, Catwoman grabbed the clicker and said to Tommy, "Let's watch something for *children*, not half-naked women!" Tommy frowned and stomped out of the room. Catwoman changed the channel to a cartoon, but lowered the volume, like she was trying to hear what was happening in the kitchen.

Owl was talking to the woman who was going to take care of her. The woman she'd seen at the museum. That scared her. Today the woman had on a pretty green-and-gold pantsuit, but she was positive it was the same woman. Her name was Laura. She had long black hair and a pretty face and Asian eyes.

She would never forget those eyes. Staring at her while Owl was shooting his gun. Trying to kill more people.

How many people had Owl killed, she wondered. Maybe he would kill her, too, like he killed Mamma. She knew he wanted to, glaring at her with his mean, hateful eyes.

In the kitchen Catwoman acted like Laura was her friend. What if Laura was friends with Owl, too? But if Catwoman and Tommy and Owl were Laura's friends, why didn't she get in the boat and come with them? Thinking about it made her head hurt.

She glanced at the cartoon. A dog was chasing a cat, but the cat ran up the tree and yelled at him. The dog got mad because he couldn't climb the tree. He barked at the cat and ran away. Mamma never let her watch cartoons. She said they were stupid and made her watch Sesame Street instead. So she could learn her letters. And a little bit of English.

"That was a funny cartoon, wasn't it?" Catwoman said.

"Very funny," she said. Catwoman didn't scare her as much as Owl, but Catwoman didn't like it when she cried. Or didn't agree with her. Or wouldn't eat her sandwich.

Now Laura was going to take care of her. The woman who might be friends with Owl. Thinking about it made her tummy hurt. She picked at the buttons on her shirt. Should she ask Laura why she was hiding behind the bushes at the museum? Maybe not. Laura might get mad.

Catwoman said they were going to New York where there were lots of stores. Catwoman loved shopping. It was all she ever talked about.

Which meant she would spend a lot of time alone with Laura.

But she didn't have to talk to her.

If she didn't say anything, Laura couldn't get mad at her.

She missed talking to Mamma. Every day when they ate lunch, they would talk about Sesame Street or the stories Mamma read to her before she went to sleep at night.

But not any more.

Tears flooded her eyes and rolled down her cheeks.

She would never talk to Mamma again.

CHAPTER 11

3:15 PM – Venice

Oratzio settled into the soft leather upholstery of his black Mercedes SUV. It had dark-tinted windows, an armor-reinforced exterior, and the powerful engine ensured that it could outrun any pursuing vehicle, his enemies or the polizia.

From the front seat, his driver asked, "Where to, Boss?"

"Soon I must take a trip. You know where to go." Thanks to the hysterical news reports about the jewelry store heist and the owner's family, they had to get out of Venice as soon as possible.

Julio was his most trusted soldier. A hail storm could be raging outside, but if anyone asked about the weather, Julio would say, "I don't know. Don't ask me." One could never be too careful. As Father said, secrets and silence go hand in glove.

He took a Cuban cigar out of his pocket, removed the wrapper and held the cigar to his nose. His earliest memory was the aroma of Father's cigar and the distinctive man-smell when Father cradled him against his chest, giving him his undivided attention. He adored everything about his father: his leonine head, his thick black hair, his craggy features, his wide powerful shoulders. He especially loved the way Father puffed his cigar when he was thinking.

Now Giovanni Antonetti was dead, brought down by a massive heart attack two years ago. Octavio, a grown man of thirty, had wept at his funeral. Father had been the center of his world.

Now he had only memories. Even now they remained vivid.

Born with one leg shorter than the other, when he began to walk, he often fell. One day he fell on the hardwood floor and began to cry. His mother rushed to console him, but Father shouted, "No! Let him get up by himself."

He loved his mother. A magnificent cook, she pampered him with delicious treats. But he loved Father more. He would do anything to win Father's love and respect. He became hyper-vigilant, studying the floor and the ground outside to make sure he didn't trip and fall. Soon Father praised him for being so sure-footed. And overcoming his disability. Not saying this in so many words, but Orazio knew what he meant.

Immersed in memories, he held a Zippo to his cigar, puffing just so to get it started.

When he was four, Mother went away and returned with a baby. Soon Father was hugging Tomasso to his chest. If Orazio tugged his trouser leg, Father spoke sharply and told him to stop. When Tommy began to walk, he never fell. Soon he could run as fast as Orazio. Handsome and athletic, Tommy used his persuasive charm on everyone in the family.

Orazio saw the gleam of admiration in Father's eyes when he looked at his younger son, but Orazio was certain this would change when he went to school. He already knew how to read and Father had taught him how to add large sums in his head. St. Anthony's was the best Catholic school in Venice. He excelled in class, but on the playground other boys taunted him, calling him Razzi the Cripple. Humiliating.

When he told Father, expecting to be consoled, Father grew angry. "Don't be a pussy! Stand up for yourself. Show them who's boss."

He tried, making fists with his hands to threaten them. But one day a fourth grader bloodied his nose, knocked him down and kicked him in the ribs. That night at Mother's urging, Father examined his nose and bruised ribs, and declared, "You must learn how to fight, Orazio."

Father took him to the gym where he worked out with his friends and told the owner to teach him to fight. The Ringmaster, an older man with white hair and brawny arms, made him jump rope until his legs were so tired he could hardly stand. The Ringmaster gave him a drink of water, then wound heavy tape around his hands and showed him how to hit the punching bag. At school, he went to the library, not the playground.

After school he worked out at the gym. The Ringmaster had him spar with another boy in the ring, shouting, *Circle and jab, Orazio, circle and jab.* He tried, but his limp hindered him.

This made him so angry he broke the boy's nose.

The Ringmaster took him aside and gave him a heavy roll of coins. "The most important factor in a fight is surprise. Go to the playground tomorrow. If a bully hits you, wrap your fist around the coins and punch him in the nose." The next day, he did. When his fist hit the bully's nose, it gave a satisfying crunch and blood spurted. The boy screamed in pain. The other boys stared at his bloody nose, then at Orazio.

Using an expression he had overheard at the gym, he yelled, "*Vafangulo! Un colo di merda!*" Go fuck yourself you shitty ass!

When he told The Ringmaster, he said, "Good, but some other

fucker, bigger and stronger, may take his place. You learned the first rule. Surprise. Now you must master other weapons."

The Ringmaster took him to a room he hadn't seen before. Inside glass cases were knives and daggers, curved scimitars and foot-long swords. The Ringmaster taught him how to feint and parry before he went in for the kill. Then he told him the second rule. "Kill only when absolutely necessary. Killing brings too much attention. Wound these bullies and hurt them, but do not kill them."

The next time he went to the playground with a knife hidden in his sleeve. Sure enough, a bigger boy confronted him. Orazio whipped out the knife and sliced his arm, drawing blood. Enraged, the boy put his head down and charged. Octavio ripped his cheek with the blade. The bully backed away, clutching his cheek, his eyes fearful. A moment of triumph he never forgot. After that, none of the boys bothered him.

But he still felt like a cripple.

He massaged his right leg. Sixteen years after the operation his leg still pained him at times, especially in damp weather or when he was forced to sit for long periods of time.

Julio slowed and stopped at the corner of a narrow street.

"I won't be long," Orazio said. "Park here and stay alert."

He got out and studied the narrow street. Stylishly dressed women and men in business suits approached him. Seeing no threat, he set off down the sidewalk. He always made his travel arrangements in person. Phones could be tapped, but Luigi, another trusted soldier, owned a travel agency. Luigi also created false documents and passports for him.

No need to worry. Luigi's lips were sealed. Comforting when his travel needs were urgent, as they were now. He had to get Tommy and Catarina out of Venice until the heat died down.

He puffed his cigar. Catarina was getting on his nerves, always complaining and so manipulative. Tommy let her lead him around by his dick. Stupid! Orazio did no such thing. In Italy, men ruled the family. He used women to satisfy his needs and discarded them.

As he strode down the sidewalk, his thoughts turned to the girl. He had intended to kill her, but upon reflection he had changed his mind. Why not take her with them? When they landed in New York City, they would look like a happy Italian family coming to America for a vacation, the perfect cover to get the spoils of their heist through customs undetected. Now that he'd hired the nanny, he could finalize the trip.

Something about the woman grated on his nerves. Still, she might be useful. She could stay with the girl in one room. Catarina could sleep with Tommy in another and fuck him senseless. Then Tommy would be more compliant, less apt to question Orazio's orders.

He tossed the cigar in the gutter and entered the travel agency. He would have Luigi book five tickets to New York and five more to their final destination. Tommy and Catarina thought they were staying in New York City. They were in for a surprise.

———

12:30 PM — New Orleans

"One day," Frank said. "That's all I meed."

"No fucking way!" Vobitch said. "Do you know how much heat I'm taking? Headlines in the fucking local rag every day? The Assistant Super called me at home last night, said the reporters are hounding him. A young mother shot in a public housing project and NOPD can't find the killer. And I got nothing to tell him because we can't find the fucking scumbag. How's it gonna look if I put in a travel voucher for you to fly to New York?"

Frank squirmed in his chair. He didn't like the headlines either, but he was going to New York City come hell or high water. A half hour ago—6:00 PM Venice time—Conti had called him. The 'Netti gang would land at JFK on Friday morning at 11:30 AM.

Natalie would be with them, and he was going to arrest her.

"I'll put it on my own credit card."

Vobitch crossed his arms, leaned back in his chair and gave him his patented frosty stare.

"If I arrest Natalie and bring her here, we can close three murder cases and up our clearance rate. The Superintendent should like that."

"You got an answer for everything, Frank, I'll give you that."

His heart sped up. He was almost there, could sense Vobitch weakening, already picturing himself on the early bird flight to JFK. Three hours non-stop, he'd be there in plenty of time.

Vobitch heaved a sigh. "Okay, book the flight, but keep it quiet. And if Natalie pulls a fast one and escapes—"

"She won't. Conti will be on the same flight. He'll meet me outside of Customs. They collect their bags and go through Customs, we follow them and I grab her. I didn't tell Conti about that part of the plan."

"Screw him. We don't owe him anything."

"He figures they'll stay at a hotel. I figure they'll put Natalie and the girl in a separate room. That's why they hired a nanny. I go to their room and grab her."

"What about the girl? She's five years old, you said."

"The woman will take care of her." But a nagging voice in his mind said, *Would the wife of a Mafia goon really protect the girl?*

"Okay, Frank. Get out of here so I can dream up some bullshit statement for the media, keep them off our backs." Vobitch glowered at him. "But remember. One day. No more."

Energized, he left the office, planning what he needed to do.

When he got to the Homicide office, Detective Orville Wilkes was coming out the door. Vobitch had pulled him out of the D-5 homicide office to fill in for Kenyon. Like Kenyon, Wilkes was African-American, an older man with years of experience working homicides.

"Good to see you, Orville. You look beat. What's up?"

"Good to see you too, Frank. Caught a fresh one, four o'clock this morning, a drive-by in Tremé." Orville ran a hand over his salt-and-pepper hair and pulled a face. "Enough of these bangers kill each other, maybe the law-abiding folks can stop dodging bullets."

"Thanks for helping out. David and I have our hands full, looking for King Rock."

"No problem. How's Kenyon?"

"Much better. The doctor let him go home yesterday. Tanya's riding herd on him."

Orville laughed. "Nothing new there. See you around, Frank. Gotta go squeeze some witnesses."

"Good luck," he said and entered the office. David was at his desk, working on his computer. "What's up, David? You get anything?"

David swiveled his chair and shook his head. "Not a peep. People are too scared to talk."

"With good reason, probably. A detective friend of mine in Boston works in the BPD Gang Unit, keeps tabs on a drug dealer who went up there after Hurricane Katrina. The kid left New Orleans but didn't stop dealing." Frank shrugged. "New city, new customers. The kid told him King Rock was the baddest motherfucker in town."

"Maybe he's hiding up there," David said. "Maybe we're wasting our time looking for him in New Orleans. Or anywhere else in Louisiana."

"We'll get him. He can't hide forever. I'm flying to New York City on Friday."

David frowned. "Why?"

Seeing the dismay on David's face, he said, "Just for one day. A woman is flying into JFK. We've got three outstanding murder warrants on her. I arrest her, bring her back here, we clear three cases."

"Fine, but that won't help me find King Rock."

"Kelly can help you, go talk to some people in Iberville. You know, give it the woman's touch. She's good at that."

"I know she's good, but she works Domestic Violence."

"True, but she's working this case on the QT. Does her stint with her clients, works after hours on Angelique's murder. She wants King Rock even more than we do."

David's face brightened a bit. "Okay. I'll email her my reports."

"Great! I'll call and tell her." Frank zipped out the door, hustled out to his car and called Kelly.

She answered on the second ring. "Detective O'Neil." Her usual greeting when other people were around. She knew it was him.

"How's my favorite detective today?"

"Just got out of a meeting. You?"

"I'm in my car. How about some hot phone sex?"

Kelly laughed. "I might enjoy it, but certain other people wouldn't."

"Vobitch told me to keep you in the loop on the murder. David struck out when he talked to Angelique's neighbors. I told him it needed a woman's touch. Can you go to Iberville and talk to some people?"

"Hell yes! I'll do it tonight after I get off work."

"I've got more news, but it's complicated. Can we have dinner at your house tomorrow night?" Kelly still lived in the house she'd shared with her husband, Terry O'Neil. Terry had been an NOPD cop, too, until he died in a senseless car accident.

"Sounds good to me. Bring some take-out. I'm working till six."

"I will. See you then," he said, and ended the call.

For the first time since Angelique's murder, Kelly sounded happy.

Which made him happy.

But when he told her he was going to New York on Friday to arrest Natalie, he had no illusions about what her reaction would be.

Happy? Fat chance.

His fiery Italian lover might blow up like Vesuvius.

CHAPTER 12

WEDNESDAY, December 15 — 2:15 PM — Venice

Venting his fury, Orazio attacked the punching bag, a vicious right, then a left. Had the diamond heist gone as planned, he would be flying to America alone. No Tommy, no Catarina, no girl and no nanny.

But his original plan had failed. Tommy was supposed to hold Dominic's wife and the girl hostage at home, have Sofia call Dominic and tell him to bring the uncut diamonds home. He'd told Tommy to explain what would happen if he didn't. His wife and daughter would die. But Dominic hung up on him.

So he had to revise the plan. *Merda!*

His fists slammed the leather bag, a left jab, a right hook.

When Catarina parked in front of Ruffino Jewelers and beeped the horn, Dominic saw Tommy holding a gun to Sofia's head, unlocked the door and let Orazio into the store. He told Dominic to hand over the diamonds or Sophia would die. Dominic readily complied, pleading with him. "Please, don't hurt my family." He put the diamonds in his duffel bag and slammed the Uzi against Dominic's head, rendering him unconscious. Using Dominic's keys, he unlocked the glass display case and began stuffing jewelry into the duffel. But then he heard a shot.

When he ran outside, a polizia officer lay dead on the sidewalk. Already a crowd was gathering. When Sophia tried to escape he shot her. The rest was chaos. More gunfire. More bodies. The only part of his revised plan that went as planned was their escape in the cigarette boat. Now, thanks to the outcry over the dead polizia and the Ruffino family, they had to leave Venice immediately.

Sweat dripped from his nose as he slammed his fists into the bag. Dante's Gym smelled the same as it had when he'd come here as a boy, a robust man-smell, the odor of worn leather and sweat. After the Ringmaster died, his oldest son had taken over the gym.

This was as it should be. In Italian families, fathers passed their wisdom and experience to the oldest son. And their businesses.

He turned away from the punching bag and mopped his face with a towel, honest sweat from pushing his muscles to the limit. He glanced at the men on the other side of the gym, grunting as they lifted weights. Some were bare-chested. Orazio wore a T-shirt. He didn't want them to see the scars on his torso, inflicted years ago by two shopkeepers who refused to pay tribute to the Antonetti Family. He allowed no one see them, not even the women he paid for sex. The scars were a sign of weakness. He had allowed these men to injure him.

They would never speak of this, of course. He had killed them.

He tossed the towel on a chair and attacked the punching bag, thinking about the woman he'd hired to mind the girl. She claimed to be Chinese-American. He didn't believe it. She looked like Maggie Q, the half-Vietnamese actress who starred in the TV series he liked to watch. *Nikita*. Ling Lam was the name on her passport, but she called herself Laura. When he asked why it had only one entry stamp, he'd seen the momentary rigidity of her body as she groped for an answer. The passport was new. Her old one had many stamps. Or so she said.

But she had *coglioni*. Balls of steel. Rebuking him for not offering her a glass of water. He respected her for that. Still, her story seemed too convenient, tailor-made to win the job. She was studying psychology at the university. He knew a thing or two about psychology. Observing people to see if they were lying, employing certain unpleasant tactics to make them speak truthfully.

Laura was thirty-two and unmarried, with no children, he assumed. What American woman in her thirties was still in college and unemployed? He had been working since he was a boy. For years he had envied Tomasso's agility, his handsome face, his ability to charm people. Envied Father's love for his youngest son most of all.

That changed in 1992. On his twelfth birthday, Father had taken him into the library where he met with his friends, a room Orazio had never been allowed to enter. He would never forget that glorious day. Father had him sit in a leather recliner opposite a large mahogany desk. The only light came from elegant wall sconces. Enthralled, he stared at the books on the floor-to-ceiling shelves. He wanted to read them all.

Father cut off all thoughts of books, saying in a stern voice, "You must never reveal what I am about to tell you. Not to your brother. Not to your mother. Not to anyone."

Eager to please the man he loved more than anyone in the world, he said, "Not a word, Father."

"The time has come for you to know your family heritage. We are La Cosa Nostra. Some call us The Black Hand, others call us the Mafia."

His heart thumped his chest. At the gym, he'd heard Father's friends talk about this when they thought he wasn't listening.

"I am *capo di tutti capi* of the Antonetti Family in Venice." His father smiled at him, a proud smile as though he'd done something special. "Someday you will take my place."

Thrilling words. He knew what this meant. Someday he would be as powerful as Father, the man he loved and respected above all others!

"We live by a strict code of silence. *Omerta*. Break the code, you die."

"I will never break the code, Father. Never! I swear it!"

"I believe you. That is why I reveal to you that I answer to only one man, a man whose ancestors left Italy long ago and became the first of our kind in America."

He gazed at his father, rapt. "Is that why you told me to learn English?"

"Your ability to speak English will be an asset, but the reason I have chosen you to inherit my place in the family is your loyalty. The most important trait a soldier can have."

Father went to a sideboard and picked up a glass decanter filled with amber liquid. He poured a small amount into cut-crystal glasses and handed him one. "Today, we seal our promises with brandy. Later, after you prove yourself, we seal it with blood. Drink your brandy and listen carefully while I tell you about the *capo di tutti capi* in America."

Orazio stepped back from the punching bag, sat on a chair and mopped his face. Recalling this day brought him great joy, but now the family responsibilities rested on his shoulders. His alone.

His thoughts returned to the nanny. The girl seemed to be afraid of her, had refused to talk to her. Good. If the girl wouldn't talk to her, she wouldn't tell her what happened to her mother. But Father had warned him about Asians. They were smart, but treacherous.

Over the years he had read many books in Father's library. One told of an FBI agent who infiltrated the Bonanno Family in New York during the '70s. Joseph Pistone was his real name, but he called himself Donnie Brasco. He spun an elaborate story—completely fabricated—but a Bonanno hitman fell for it. Hollywood had made a movie about it. Johnny Depp played the FBI agent. Al Pacino played the hitman.

An entertaining film but also instructive. He would keep a close eye on this woman with the Asian eyes and the balls of steel.

After he completed his business in America, he would have no further use for the girl. Or the nanny.

———

7:30 PM — New Orleans

Frank rinsed the dishes, loaded them in the dishwasher, stored the leftovers in a container and put it in the refrigerator. He usually had dinner at Kelly's house on Fridays, relaxing over a glass of wine after their work week.

But this Friday he would be in New York to arrest Natalie.

He hadn't told Kelly yet. One of her clients had called just as they finished dinner, sobbing hysterically. Kelly was on the phone in the living room, trying to get her to leave her boyfriend, who'd just beaten her bloody. Frank couldn't understand how men could beat up women they supposedly loved, in many cases the mothers of their children. Or kill them, like King Rock.

Kelly walked into the kitchen and said, "Thanks for cleaning up, Frank. Sorry for the interruption."

"No problem. How'd it go?"

"She said she'd think about it. The usual bullshit. He'll give her a fancy present and she'll stay, until the next time he hits her."

"Has she got kids?"

"No, but she's pregnant. That's one of the most dangerous times for women in violent relationships. I get tired of trying to get them to leave these assholes."

"You do the best you can. Bottom line, it's her decision." Just as it had been Angelique's choice not to ditch King Rock. A fatal decision.

"I need some ice water to cool down. Want some?"

"Sure." He sat at the table and watched her add ice cubes to two glasses and fill them from a container of filtered water. She looked just as sexy as she had when he'd met her four years ago. Five years younger than him and not a speck of gray in her short dark hair. Smart, slender and fit, and never boring. She could be volatile and obstinate as hell, but he'd take sexy over boring any day.

She brought the glasses to the table, sank onto her chair and chugged some water. Knowing Angelique's boy weighed on her mind, he said, "Tell me about Jacques." By mutual agreement, they stuck to benign topics while they ate.

Predictably, she looked even less happy than she had after the phone call from her client. "I talked to Angelica's grandmother." Kelly shook her head. "She's only forty-two, a year younger than me! I can't imagine being a mother, never mind a grandmother."

Nor could he. Kelly had no interest in having children, or pets for that matter, had complained when her now-deceased husband adopted stray dogs. Back then she'd been working hard to win her NOPD detective shield. When she had time, which wasn't often, she fashioned earrings, bracelets and tie-clips out of metal. He hadn't seen any new ones lately.

"She loves Jacques," Kelly said, "but she's not going to quit her job. She's a mid-level executive, making good money. Which means Jacques will be in day care all week. Not what he needs."

He thought about five-year-old Bianca, her mother dead, her father comatose. "Maybe she could find a nanny to stay with him. An older woman experienced with young children."

Kelly twirled a lock of curly dark hair around her finger, gazing at him. Normally he loved her sea-green eyes, but now they were hard as granite. "I'm packing my Glock all the time these days. If I spot King Rock, I'll arrest the motherfucker and bring him in!"

He believed it. When Kelly made up her mind to do something, there was no dissuading her. But trying to arrest King Rock could get her killed. *The baddest motherfucker in town.* He'd seen the damage a bullet could inflict, and plenty of cops died in shootouts with criminals.

During his twenty-plus years as a cop, he'd been shot at several times, a life-changing experience, each one etched in his mind. He could still remember thinking: *You're dead, Renzi.* Could still remember the euphoric rush when the shot missed. The sudden appreciation of being alive, hyper-aware of the sights and sounds and smells around him.

Three times he'd been hit, most recently by Natalie two years ago, a gunshot wound to the leg. It put him in the hospital and sidelined him for two months while he did rehab to get back in shape.

Earlier that year, Kelly had taken a bullet too. She had been lucky to survive, a nerve-wracking close call. He reached over and caressed her cheek. "I know you want this guy, but promise me one thing. Call for backup before you make your move."

Kelly frowned at him, her sea-green eyes sending a clear message: *I'm gonna get the fucker.* "You think I'm too emotionally involved, right?"

He sipped some ice water. She wanted him to deny it, but he wasn't going to lie to her. She was over-the-top involved. But who was he to judge? He was obsessed with Natalie. In two days, he would see her.

"I'm flying to New York on Friday. Guess who's landing at JFK?"

Kelly cocked an eyebrow and grinned at him. "That sexy blonde on *House of Cards,* Robin Wright? I know you're wild about her."

He burst out laughing. "You know how to hurt a guy. Come on, Kelly. You know you're my one and only."

"So who's flying into JFK on Friday?"

"Natalie Brixton."

Her mouth dropped open. "Are you serious? I thought you were joking. You're really going to New York City on Friday?"

"Yes. She flies into JFK on Friday morning."

Thunder clouds gathered on Kelly's face. "What about King Rock?"

"I'll only be there one day, fly back Friday night, Saturday morning at the latest."

He summarized what John Conti had told him about the heist, the murders and the kidnapping. "He got Natalie to infiltrate the Mafia gang, play nanny to Bianca and feed him information so he can find the kingpin, who lives somewhere in the United States, allegedly."

"Wow," Kelly said. "That sounds like a made-for-TV movie."

"Conti doesn't know that I plan to arrest Natalie."

"Be careful, Frank. She shot you once. She could do it again."

"Not this time. She won't have a gun. She'd never get it through security and Customs."

"If she's with a Mafia gang, what's to say they won't have weapons?"

"She's the nanny. They're not going to give her a gun."

Kelly said nothing, but he could see her mind working.

"You want to capture King Rock. I want to arrest Natalie." Again, his thoughts turned to Bianca. What would become of her after he arrested Natalie? He didn't share his concerns with Kelly. She would be outraged.

"Frank, I'm serious. Natalie already shot you once."

He didn't want to think about Natalie. Didn't want to think about King Rock or the two little kids—one five, the other three—whose mothers had been murdered. He wanted to take his lover to bed.

He rose from his chair, pulled Kelly to her feet and kissed her, a long lingering kiss.

"You got too many clothes on. Can I sleep here tonight?"

She wrapped her arms around him and pulled him close.

"Sounds good to me, Frank. It's been a while."

CHAPTER 13

THURSDAY December 16 – 3:35 PM – Rome

When their car pulled to a stop behind Orazio's SUV at Leonardo Da Vinci Airport, Natalie got out right away. She was desperate to call Pak Lam. This might be her only chance.

Orazio dashed her hopes.

Wearing a dark business suit and mirrored sunglasses, he called to Tommy and Catarina, "Hurry up or we miss our flight!"

A highway construction project had delayed them. Seated in front with the driver, Tommy cursed at the drivers who tried to cut in front of them. Catarina told him to stop swearing. Dressed in navy-blue pants and a long-sleeved boy's shirt, Bianca sat between her and Catarina. The girl still wouldn't talk to her, unlike Catarina, who went on and on about shopping at Saks Fifth Avenue.

How could she think? Conti had confiscated her iPhone, laptop and credit card, had given her a cellphone that only sent and received texts and said if she texted anyone else he would know it.

She had to find another way to contact Pak Lam.

Orazio's driver took their suitcases out of the SUV and put them on the sidewalk. Tommy grabbed Bianca's pint-sized suitcase, but Bianca said, "No! Mine!" When Tommy didn't give it to her, she stamped her foot. "I want my suitcase!"

"Catarina," Orazio said sharply, "get her into the terminal. Laura will take her suitcase. We'll take the rest." Barking orders like a general.

She slung the strap of her leather purse over her shoulder, collected Bianca's suitcase and followed Catarina. The terminal was jammed with travelers. Catarina, walking as fast as she could in her spike heels, hurried Bianca along. When Tommy and Orazio caught up to them, Orazio gave them their boarding passes and said, "We check the bags at the gate. Follow me to Security, and remember. No names."

She knew they were traveling on false passports, but Conti had told her they would have no problem passing through Security. His boss had spoken to the security chief.

When they got to the checkpoint, Orazio seemed nervous, a sheen of sweat dampening his forehead. Recalling her anxiety in similar situations, Natalie suppressed a smile. The agent checked Orazio's ID, comparing the photo on his passport to his face. At last, he waved Orazio through and repeated the procedure with Tomasso, Catarina, and Bianca.

Bianca seemed mystified, gazing at the crowd of passengers and the security equipment. What name had they given her, Natalie wondered. A boy's name, probably.

The agent checked her Ling Lam passport and waved her toward the security machines. Orazio and Tomasso had already put their luggage on the conveyor belt. Orazio placed his worn leather briefcase on the belt, lined it up just so, then removed his shoes and his watch. She wondered where the stolen diamonds were, not that she cared. Her mind was focused on one thing: Call Pak Lam, get to New York City and escape.

Tomasso put his shoes in a gray-plastic bin, added Catarina's purse and a plastic bag with Bianca's toys. Natalie put her leather handbag and suitcase on the conveyor belt. After she passed through the metal detector, Orazio waved to her impatiently. "Hurry up! Our flight will board in ten minutes."

Wishing she'd worn running shoes, she lengthened her stride, cursing her luck. If their flight boarded in ten minutes there would be no opportunity to call Pak Lam.

But when they reached their gate, a sign behind the desk said their flight had been delayed. Frowning, Orazio marched up to the gate attendant. Catarina settled Bianca onto a chair in a row of seats against the wall and sat beside her. Tommy took the seat opposite them and took out a newspaper, one from Venice, Natalie realized. She could see the headline on the front page: HUSBAND COMATOSE, GIRL STILL MISSING. No wonder Orazio was in a hurry to leave town.

She took the seat beside Bianca, who was paging through a book with colorful illustrations of two children building a snowman.

"All this rushing," Catarina said, smiling at her, "and now we wait. But this gives me an opportunity to visit the duty-free shop!"

Orazio joined them and said in Italian, "Good news. We will make our connection."

"But the news from Venice isn't," Tommy said, showing him the newspaper.

"Put that away," Orazio said. "Help me bring our luggage to the desk so they can check it."

Catarina rose to her feet. "I'm going to the duty-free shop."

"Okay," Orazio said, "but if you're not here when they start boarding, we leave without you."

"Don't worry," Catarina said, "I will be back in plenty of time."

Natalie glanced at Bianca. She seemed content, paging through her picture book. Now that Catarina was gone, maybe she could find a way to call Pak Lam. He must be frantic. She was supposed to have met his contact in Lyon on Monday. But Conti had foiled her escape. In forty minutes they would board the plane. She couldn't call Pak Lam if Bianca was with her, but she couldn't just get up and leave. Orazio was watching her, his expression stony.

Bianca dropped the book on the floor and began swinging her feet back and forth under her seat, faster and faster. Orazio frowned at her and said, "Stop that."

She leaned down and whispered to Bianca, "Let's go to the restroom." She rose from her seat and said to Orazio, "She needs to use the toilet." He waved a hand, dismissing them.

The nearest restroom was opposite the gate adjacent to theirs. She took Bianca inside, stopped at the first stall and said in Italian, "Do you need me to help you?"

"No! I can do it myself!" Bianca went in the stall and shut the door.

She waited, anxiously checking the time. She heard the toilet flush. Bianca came out of the stall, her shirt hanging over her pants.

"Let me tuck your shirt into your pants."

"No! I hate this shirt."

The girl was impossible. If she let her keep acting like this, the girl would never respect her.

"Stop!" she said. "Let me tuck in your shirt. People will laugh at you!"

Bianca stuck out her lip in a pout, but allowed her to tuck in the shirt.

"Good," she said. "Let's go for a walk."

As they left the restroom she checked their gate. Catarina wasn't back yet. She turned and walked along the concourse. Bianca seemed content to burn off some energy, not talking, but not throwing a tantrum. The girl pulled her to a kiosk that sold candy and snacks and cold drinks, and pointed at the Goldfish crackers.

"You want Goldfish crackers?" she asked. "Which kind?"

Bianca put her tiny forefinger on the glass, pointing at a bag of regular-flavored crackers.

She took out her wallet. Conti had given her twenty dollars, but she might need some of it for the telephone. If she could get rid of Bianca. She asked for the regular Goldfish crackers and gave the clerk the twenty-dollar bill. The clerk gave her the crackers and her change. A ten and three ones. Eight dollars for a bag of crackers! Outrageous.

But the smile on Bianca's face when she opened the bag was almost worth it. "Thank you," she said in English. "I love Goldfish crackers."

"You're welcome. Now we have to go back to our gate. Soon we will board the plane."

And her opportunity to call Pak Lam would be gone.

They walked back to their gate, Bianca happily munching Goldfish crackers. But when they entered the gate area Bianca stopped, anxiously staring at Orazio. *She's afraid of him,* Natalie thought.

Using a hand-held microphone, the female gate attendant announced in a cheery voice with a British accent, "We shall be boarding in five minutes. Please have your boarding passes ready."

She looked over at their seats. No Catarina. Her heart sank. No way could she leave Bianca alone with Orazio. Then, a miracle. Catarina came up behind her and said, "Laura, see what I bought!" Hoisting a plastic bag labeled Gucci, she said, "Beautiful shoes and so cheap. No VAT. And you bought Bianca Goldfish crackers. How nice of you."

But Natalie ignored her, watching a young woman with carrot-red hair approach the restroom. The letters on her sweatshirt said NYU. Maybe she was a student. Every student had a cellphone. "Catarina, could you watch Bianca for a minute? I need to use the restroom." She made a face. "I just got my period."

Catarina made a face, commiserating with her. "Isn't that always the way? You're about to go on a big trip and get The Curse. Go ahead, I'll watch Bianca."

She hurried to the restroom. When she went inside, the red-haired NYU student was nowhere in sight. Assuming the girl was in one of the toilet stalls, she stood beside the sinks, mentally urging her to hurry. A toilet flushed. Moments later a dark-haired woman left one stall and came to the sinks. Natalie leaned close to the mirror and pretended to check her eyes, pulling the lower lid down.

"Contacts?" the woman said in English. "My eyes get so bloodshot on these long flights."

She nodded and forced a smile. As the dark-haired woman left the restroom, boarding announcements floated through the open door. She heard another toilet flush and dug her nails into her palms.

Please, let it be the red-haired student.

The girl in the NYU sweatshirt came out of a stall and approached the sink. "Excuse me," Natalie said, "I lost my cellphone and I have to call my boyfriend. Do you have a cellphone I could use?"

The girl looked at her, aghast. "Lost your cellphone? How awful! I'd be frantic if that happened to me. All my phone contacts are on it."

"Can I borrow yours? I'll pay you for the call."

The girl waved her hand. "Hey, you've got an emergency. Where's your boyfriend?"

"He's supposed to meet me at JFK, but he doesn't know what time my flight lands."

NYU Girl pulled an iPhone out of her backpack. "Here, use mine. It won't cost that much."

"Thank you," she said, and punched in the number. "It won't take long." After a moment, the call went through and the phone rang. *Please be in your office.*

"Hello?" said a familiar voice.

"Hello Mountain Man." Their coded greeting.

"Natalie! I have been so worried about you!"

"I lost my cellphone and my credit cards and my cash," she said, rushing to tell him what she needed. "I land at JFK tomorrow, British Airways Flight 123 at 11:15 AM."

"Understood. I will have someone meet you in the baggage claim and give you what you need. Have a safe journey. Call me when you can."

"Thank you," she said, and ended the call.

"Mountain Man?" the girl said, grinning at her. "He must be a hunk."

Natalie gave her the iPhone. "He is and I adore him. Thank you so much."

"No problem," NYU Girl chirped. "Have a good flight."

She dashed out of the restroom and rushed back to the gate. Only five people remained in the boarding line. No Tommy, no Catarina. But Orazio was waiting for her. Bianca stood beside him, staring at the floor.

"What took you so long?" he demanded.

Her heart pounded. He seemed suspicious. What should she say?

Bianca came over and tugged her hand, gazing at her with fearful eyes. Ignoring Orazio, she said to Bianca in Italian, "Let's board the plane. I'll let you have the window seat so you can look out and see the ocean." Bianca could be impossible at times, but clearly she was terrified of Orazio. If she could get the girl to like her, she might be her best ally.

———

6:15 PM –- Dulles International Airport, Washington, D. C.

Clint Hammer studied the passengers waiting to board the Alitalia flight to Venice. He never stood in lines. After the gate agent sent the others into the boarding tunnel, he'd stroll up to the gate and board in comfort. He had checked his suitcase, and his weapon, in the terminal. As a law-enforcement officer, he was allowed to carry a firearm, unloaded, in his checked luggage. He'd buy some ammo after he got to Venice. He might need it. He was certain the bitch who'd murdered Oliver was there. All he had to do was find her.

Convincing his boss to send him there had been easy. An internet search for violent crime in Venice provided the perfect excuse. Last Friday—a mere six days ago!—a brutal crime had shaken the city. A diamond heist, several murders and a kidnapping. Police believed a local Mafia gang was responsible. When his boss heard this, he had immediately signed the travel voucher.

His cellphone rang. He checked the Caller-ID and answered.

Agitated, Jason said, "Did you board your flight yet?"

"No. I never board until the last minute. Why?"

"Don't get on the plane! An hour ago Natalie Brixton went through Security at Leonardo da Vinci airport in Rome."

"Jesus!"

"I'd have called you sooner, but I pulled some strings and got their security info. She's traveling on a U.S. passport under the name Ling Lam, flying to London Heathrow to board an overnight flight." Jason paused. "You're gonna love this, Boss."

"Stop fucking around, Jason. Tell me!"

"Her flight lands at JFK on Friday morning at eleven-thirty!"

"Fantastic!" He glanced at the boarding line. No more passengers. "Hold on, Jason, I've got to get my luggage off the plane." He darted to the gate, flashed his ID at the agent and said, "I can't take this flight and I need to get my luggage off the plane."

The woman frowned. "I'm not sure we can do that—"

He glared at her, his eyes cold. "This is a law enforcement emergency. Make it happen!"

"Yes, sir. I'll call the baggage chief. What do your bags look like?"

"One suitcase," he snapped. "A hard-case, black."

He clenched his teeth as she spoke into her handset.

After an endless wait, she pointed to the boarding tunnel and said, "The baggage crew will bring it to you, Agent Hammer."

He rushed down the tunnel. Stopped near the portal to the plane and waited anxiously. Saw the baggage dolly approach the ladder beside the door. Yes! His suitcase was on the dolly.

He raised his cellphone and said, "Jason, you still there?"

"Yes. Did you get your luggage?"

"It's coming now. Was she traveling alone?"

"No sir. She's traveling with four other people, two men, a woman and a young child."

Strange. The serial-killer bitch usually acted alone.

"Here's the interesting part," Jason said. "I found out who accessed the data on the software face-recognition program. A Europol agent."

Hammer ground his teeth. How dare they? The CIA trumped Europol every time.

"I pulled some strings, contacted Europol and got their names. You want them?"

"Of course I want them!"

"They all have the same last name, Volpe. John, age 32, Joseph, age 28, Noreen, age 22, and Bruce, age 5. But according to Europol, the passports are fake. Their real names are Orazio Antonetti, Tomasso Antonetti, Catarina Antonetti and Bianca Ruffino."

It hit him like a hand grenade. "Are you sure?"

"Positive."

He could hardly believe it. The serial-killer bitch had hooked up with the Mafiosos who were responsible for the murders and kidnapping in Venice. But he had no time to think about it now.

"Call you later, Jason. I need to book a flight to New York."

"No need to do that, sir. I already booked one for you."

CHAPTER 14

FRIDAY December 17

Frank sipped his bottled water and extended his legs under the seat in front of him. His bag in the overhead bin held everything he needed, the warrants, handcuffs and fresh underwear in case he had to stay overnight. Some of the other passengers were catching a few winks, but he was too wired to sleep. He'd already set his watch to Eastern time, 8:15 AM in New York now.

His non-stop Jet Blue flight would land at JFK at 10:05 AM. Natalie would arrive on a British Airways flight at 11:35. After she cleared Customs, he would be waiting for her. But arresting her might not be as easy as he'd led Vobitch and Kelly to believe. Conti would be a problem, and he was certain Natalie was already planning her escape.

The first time he saw her was on a security video at a ritzy French Quarter hotel, striding along in a slinky dress and spike heels like she knew exactly where she was going and what she'd do when she got there. Kill Arnold Peterson. He and Kenyon had worked the case. Peterson wasn't the man who murdered Natalie's mother, but he told her who did. It wasn't a friendly chat. When she shot him, Peterson had been tied up naked on the bed, one to the head with a silenced Beretta.

At the time he thought it was a cold-blooded hit. Later, he'd changed his mind. Ruthless and single-minded was more like it.

He checked the in-flight map on the seat-back in front of him—two hours and ten minutes until his flight landed at JFK—and returned to the highlight reel of Natalie's life of crime. The man who murdered her mother was dead, so she killed his only son. No video on that one, just one shot to the head. That happened in the summer of 2008. During a late-August hurricane evacuation, he almost caught her outside a B&B in the Garden District, their first face-to-face meeting. After a foot-race, she ambushed him in an ally and shot him in the leg.

She could have finished him off, gazing at him as he lay on the ground. Even now he got chills thinking about it. Natalie staring at him, holding the Beretta in her hand. A few minutes later Kenyon found him and got him into an ambulance. By then, Natalie was gone. Before she got on a plane and disappeared, she'd mailed an audiotape and a note addressed to him personally, telling him who killed her mother in 1988.

85

They put him on medical leave until his leg healed, which left plenty of time to read the diary Natalie had abandoned in the B&B. It started when Natalie was ten, soon after her mother was murdered, a road-map of her life for the next twenty years.

She fell in love with a man when she lived in Paris and another when she returned to the States, a former CIA agent. The man in Paris lived to see another day. Oliver James didn't. Natalie shot him in a Boston hotel.

After she escaped, Frank checked the Interpol website twice a week for any sign of her. In June 2010, he saw a report about an art heist in a museum near London. A witness saw the thief leave and believed it was a woman, because of her sexy walk and distinctive stride.

He was convinced it was Natalie. It was, and it involved a twisted tale of treachery. In cahoots with a vicious thief and an insider guard, Natalie had stolen priceless paintings from the Gardner Museum in Boston. The thief and the guard wound up dead. During another foot-chase at a train station near Boston, he'd caught her. She told him the stolen art was in a car in the parking garage. Eager to retrieve the priceless paintings, he told a Boston police officer to drive her to the station in Boston. But Natalie had conned the cop into stopping the cruiser and escaped. Again!

This time she wouldn't. This time he'd handcuff her and put her on a plane. Fearing he might not be able to arrest her before the last flight left for New Orleans, he hadn't bought the tickets yet. On the plane, he'd have plenty of time to grill her. He had a million questions.

Why did she turn to a life of crime? Why did she kill Oliver James?

And the biggest question of all: Why didn't she kill him in that Garden District alley when she had the chance?

––––––

6:30 AM — British Airways Flight 123

Unable to sleep, Natalie leaned back against the headrest. Beside her in the window seat, Bianca was fast asleep, her tiny fist pressed to her mouth. In the seat ahead of her, Tommy was reading *Playboy*. Beside him, Catarina was mercifully silent. Orazio was across the aisle, one row behind her in an aisle seat. The power position, so he could watch them.

Earlier, Bianca had begun kicking Tommy's seat. To distract her, Natalie took out a box of crayons and a holiday coloring book and found a big Christmas tree. Bianca took out a black crayon and scribbled all over it. A bad sign. Some of the kids at the shelter who'd witnessed violence at home did this. Black pictures to depict their bleak existence.

What had Bianca seen?

She found a page with Santa Claus and gave her a red crayon. But Bianca kept the black crayon, scribbled over Santa and said, "I hate Santa! I hate Christmas. And I hate *you*!"

Tommy turned around and said, "Mind your manners, kid. Don't talk like that."

Natalie whispered to Bianca, "You miss Mamma, don't you." After giving her a strange look, Bianca had curled up and gone to sleep.

Conti had a seat in first class. She'd seen him use the restroom outside the first class cabin. How on earth could she have fallen for him? Was she losing her ability to assess people? It had happened once before. Oliver had charmed her into thinking he cared about her. Later, it became painfully obvious he didn't. Willem was different.

What marvelous times they'd had in Paris, going to art museums, listening to jazz, discussing films over dinner at posh restaurants. She was certain Willem loved her, but when she asked him to leave his wife, he wouldn't. A painful end to her only love affair.

She drank some water. Forget Willem. She had to focus on her escape. Soon they would land in New York and Renzi would be there. She hadn't seen him since he'd captured her at a train station last year and questioned her. Oddly, she'd found herself attracted to his deep melodious voice and dark penetrating eyes. Was this some kind of reverse Stockholm Syndrome, the prey falls for the hunter? At least Renzi was honest. He didn't pretend to like her. He despised her.

If all went well at JFK, she would never see him. Pak Lam had said he would have someone meet her at the baggage claim, and when Pak Lam said he would do something, he made it happen.

She glanced across the aisle. Orazio was staring at her, expressionless. The hackles rose on the back of her neck. She might not be good at choosing lovers, but she knew how to evaluate criminals. Orazio suspected something. She didn't know why, but she'd need to watch him carefully if she was going to escape. Earlier, in the plane's restroom she had checked the cellphone Conti had given her. He had already sent her a text. *"See you when you come through customs. Good luck."*

Good luck. Bullshit. He wasn't worried about her safety. He wanted her to make sure the 'Netti brothers didn't find out she wasn't who she said she was. Wanted her to eavesdrop on their conversations and report back to him. What would he do if Orazio killed her?

A shiver ran down her spine. She had to stop thinking like that.

Pak Lam's contact would give her a cellphone, a credit card and some cash. Then she would find a way to elude Orazio and Bianca and escape. She suspected Bianca understood more English than she let on. One thing was clear. She was terrified of Orazio. At the airport in Rome, perhaps sensing his animosity toward her, Bianca had tugged at her hand to help get her away from Orazio.

After she escaped, Orazio would be furious.

Would Catarina protect Bianca from him?

A cold hard knot formed in her stomach. She couldn't afford to worry about that. She had her own problems to solve.

———

11:45 AM --- JFK International Airport, New York City

Orazio herded his companions onto the escalator that descended to the baggage claim area and massaged his aching leg. *Merda!* If not for the fucked *up* heist, he could have flown first class, plenty of leg room, a fresh cup of espresso and a sweet roll for breakfast. But no. During this interminable seven hour flight he had to sit in the main cabin and keep an eye on Catarina and Tommy, the girl and the nanny.

Below him, Catarina was prattling about the fabulous stores she intended to visit. But she would not be buying clothes in New York. Silent and subdued on the stair below him, Tommy appeared anxious. This would be a new experience for him. Yesterday, Orazio had explained what would happen if the customs officers discovered their swag. Detention, then jail.

He focused on the perils that lay ahead. Collecting the bags did not worry him. Passing through Customs did. As he had instructed, Catarina and Tommy had on their most elegant outfits. He'd made Tommy leave his pinky ring at home, knowing it would attract attention. He had worn a tailored Gucci suit for his entry into the United States. Just a wealthy Italian family eager to begin their vacation in New York. The kid and the nanny reinforced this deception.

But hidden in small fabric bags, the uncut diamonds were inside the briefcase he carried. They had cleared security in Rome without incident, but clearing Customs would be more problematic. Catarina was wearing the diamond earrings and matching necklace he'd stolen. The rest of the stolen jewelry was in her suitcase.

An announcement on the PA system advised passengers on British Airways Flight 123 to collect their luggage at Carousel Two. Catarina and Laura stepped off the escalator and headed in that direction with Bianca. Orazio said in Italian, "Don't worry, Tommy. I packed your suitcase carefully. The cash is inside the secret compartment at the bottom, dusted with talcum powder to throw off the sniffer dogs."

Tommy mopped sweat from his brow. "But what if they search my bag and find it?"

"Stop acting like a petty thief," he snapped. "You are a wealthy man vacationing with your family. You're the charming one. Ask the customs official how to get to the World Trade Center Memorial. They love it when visitors show respect for the Americans who died on 9-11."

Tommy clenched his jaw and said nothing.

His brother hated taking orders, especially from him.

A mob of British Airways passengers stood around Carousel Two, but the metal conveyor belt wasn't moving. He walked over to Laura and said in English, "How is our little traveler?"

The girl shrank away from him, avoiding his eyes.

"She will be fine as soon as she has a good meal and sleeps in a real bed."

Perhaps, but the nanny seemed anxious. "What's wrong, Laura? You look worried."

A flash of dismay crossed her face. Recovering quickly, she said, "One time when I landed in Boston they lost my luggage. The airline put my bags on a plane to California."

This disturbed him, but he did not allow it to show on his face. What if they lost Tommy's suitcase with the cash? "I am sure that will not happen. We will have our bags in no time."

Still, sometimes thieves lurked in the baggage claim area and stole expensive-looking luggage. He edged through the crowd toward the opening where the baggage handlers would dump their luggage onto the conveyor belt. If a thief stole any of their suitcases, the *cafone* would regret it. He'd cut off his balls and stuff them in his mouth.

―――――

Shaken to the core, she watched Orazio push through the crowd. He was watching her like a hawk, had spotted her nervousness. She ran sweaty palms over the front of her denim jacket. It had patch-pockets on the front, ready to receive what Pak Lam's contact gave her.

But she had to get away from Bianca, who was already fussing, asking for more Goldfish crackers. She whispered to Catarina, "I need to use a restroom. You know, to change ..."

Catarina smiled. "No problem, Laura. Bianca can stay with me."

She circled the crowd that surrounded the metal carousel. Her contact knew her flight number, would expect to see her near Carousel Two. She saw an older Japanese couple, and a young Chinese woman with an infant, but no Chinese-Americans. With a metal clank, the conveyor belt began to move. She kept going, inching through the crowd as suitcases, knapsacks and packages tumbled onto the conveyor belt. Her suitcase had a gold ribbon tied to the handle to make it easy to spot.

But if she grabbed it now, Orazio would expect her to join him, and kill her chances to escape. They would go to Customs. Conti and Renzi would be waiting outside.

Someone bumped into her from behind and thrust something into her hand. Her fingers closed around a soft bag. Her heart surged. It felt like a cellphone and a power cord. She slowed but didn't turn around, kept her face blank in case Orazio was watching. She dropped the bag into one pocket of her jacket. "Good luck," said a male voice as he put a wad of cash in her hand. "Call our friend."

A young Asian man with glossy black hair walked past her and kept going. She shoved the cash in the other pocket, wanting to shout with joy. Now she had a cellphone and some cash.

Ducking around British Airways passengers that surrounded Carousel Two, she hurried to the nearest restroom. Several women stood at the sinks, washing their hands or peering into mirrors to tidy their hair. She went in an empty stall, shut the door and opened the drawstring bag. Inside was a power cord and an iPhone.

She turned it on. Fully charged. Perfect. Giddy with excitement, she counted the wad of bills: nine hundred dollars in fifties, wrapped around a Master Card in Ling Lam's name.

She put the cash and credit card in her wallet and stuffed the bag with the iPhone and charger into her leather purse. Forget the suitcase. She had what she needed to escape. She'd buy whatever else she needed later. All she had to do was hide until Orazio and the others collected their luggage. He'd be furious when she didn't claim her suitcase, but he wouldn't waste time hunting for her. He wanted to get his ill-gotten gains through Customs.

But Conti and Renzi would be waiting for them.

If she wasn't with the 'Netti brothers, what would they do? Conti was focused on the 'Netti brothers, but Renzi wasn't.

Renzi, the relentless hunter who never gave up.

No way was she going to let him arrest her. She would hide long enough for Orazio and the others to pass through Customs, then go through Customs by herself. But she couldn't stay here. The restroom was too close to Carousel Two. Orazio might send Catarina in here to look for her. She'd better find another restroom and figure out how to disguise herself.

She saw a woman head for the door, a large black woman, taller and wider than she was. If she stayed close behind her, maybe no one would notice when she came out the door.

She followed the woman outside.

And came face to face with Orazio.

Her heart almost jumped out of her chest.

"What were you doing in there? Talking to someone?"

"No, no," she stammered. "I just … I wanted to wash my face."

"Why do you leave the girl alone for so long?"

"Catarina—"

"I did not hire Catarina to mind her, I hired you."

She said nothing. He was already furious. Why provoke him?

"I have your suitcase. Come with me, we go to Customs now."

CHAPTER 15

12:35 PM – JFK International Airport

Frank stood behind a crowd of people jabbering excitedly in various languages, awaiting the arrival of friends or relatives. Off to his right, livery drivers in dark suits held cardboard signs with names printed on them in Magic Marker, awaiting their passengers.

But he wasn't waiting for friends or passengers.

Any minute now Natalie Brixton, the woman who'd shot him once and escaped from him twice, would come through the exit door, visible through the clear plastic barrier ahead of him.

British Airways Flight 123 had landed on time at 11:35. On his way to Customs he'd stopped for a Dunkin Donuts coffee. No rush. Natalie and her companions would have to collect their bags and pass through Customs. But that was an hour ago and he was getting antsy, eager to see the woman he'd been hunting for months.

He scanned the faces of people coming through the exit door. No Natalie, but then John Conti walked through the door. Towing a large suitcase with a laptop strapped to it, holding a leather briefcase in his other hand, he looked around, scanning the crowd. Frank waved his Yankee baseball cap, their agreed-upon signal.

Conti saw him but his expression didn't change. Six-feet-tall in his well-tailored suit, he looked as handsome in person as he did in the photo Frank had found on the Internet: Italian movie-star handsome. thick dark hair, sexy dark eyes. Women probably fell all over him.

The Europol agent circled the crowd, greeted him with a confident smile, set down his briefcase and extended his hand. "Nice to meet you at last, Frank. They should be out soon."

He shook Conti's hand. "Likewise. Natalie's with them?"

"Yes. She is traveling on a U.S. passport under the name of Ling Lam. These days she calls herself Laura."

Shocked, he thought, *How the hell did Natalie get a new passport?*

"After they clear Customs," Conti said, "they will probably go outside and take a taxi to their hotel. We shall follow them."

Frank parsed his words, delivered in English with a slight accent.

"Good luck with that. There'll be a line for the cabs. New Yorkers despise people who crash lines."

Conti took out his Europol badge. "This will take care of it."

But he was no longer looking at Conti. Natalie walked through the Customs exit door. She looked the same as he remembered, tall and slender, long black hair. But she didn't look happy.

He studied her companions, memorizing faces and attaching names to them. Two men in suits and an attractive woman with long blond hair. He assumed the child clutching her hand was Bianca Ruffino, but she looked like a boy, close-cropped dark hair, dressed in jeans and a boy's shirt. A disguise, he assumed, to thwart anyone who was searching for her. They didn't know Agent John Conti was onto them, or that he had facilitated their passage through Customs.

"We must follow them," Conti said," but not too close. I don't want them to see me."

Conti didn't seem to care if Natalie spotted *him*. And she would if they got too close. Clearly, this operation was all about Conti, not him.

They watched the group leave the Customs area, expecting them to head for the airport exit doors that led to the street. They didn't. They turned and set off down the concourse toward Departures.

"Jesus!" Conti muttered. "Where are they going?"

"Not to the taxi stand, that's for sure. We better hang back so they don't spot us."

Dodging harried travelers and hiding behind others, they followed the 'Netti brothers. Five minutes later they saw Orazio herd the group into a crowded departure gate. The blond woman seemed upset, talking and gesticulating. Frank studied the board behind the desk. JetBlue Airline Flight 2014, bound for New Orleans, boarding in forty minutes.

"Damn!" Conti muttered. "We'll lose them!"

"Like hell we will. Follow me." He turned and trotted back down the concourse to the NYPD cop he'd seen, flashed his badge and said, "Frank Renzi, NOPD. This is Europol Agent John Conti. We're tracking some people who arrived from Italy, figured they'd stay in New York. Turns out they've got tickets to New Orleans."

The ruddy-faced cop grinned at him. "Threw ya a curveball, huh?"

"Yes and we need to get on that plane. Any way you can convince the gate agent to hold the plane while we get tickets?"

Eyeing his Yankee cap, the cop said, "A Yankee fan, huh? No problem. I love throwing my weight around. I'll call my pal at the ticket counter and tell him you're coming. But don't be long."

"We won't," he said, and took off running. Towing his suitcase, Conti struggled to keep up.

When they raced into the ticket area, another NYPD cop waved them to a counter where a female clerk was waiting. Frank thanked him and said to Conti, "Get us two seats in First Class. That way we can board after they do so they won't see us."

Conti grimaced and took out his wallet. "My boss will crucify me."

Frank shrugged. "Some days you win, some days you lose." This was a big win for him. Now he didn't have to pay to fly Natalie to New Orleans. But his car was in the airport parking garage.

He took out his cellphone. He'd ask David Lee to meet the plane and follow their targets.

———

Mired in a pit of despair, Natalie opened the bag of Goldfish crackers she'd bought on the way to their gate and gave it to Bianca. She was trapped in an airport, about to fly to New Orleans. No escape now. Orazio wouldn't let her out of his sight.

Catarina was furious, all set to conquer New York City, decked out in her finery, including a three-strand diamond necklace with matching earrings. She hadn't listed them on the declaration form and the Customs agent had given her a hard time. Waving her hands, Catarina said in fractured English, "They are mine. How can I go on vacation s*enza jewels?* " The agent frowned. Behind her, Natalie said, "Madame is very fashion conscious. She would not dream of visiting your fine city without her best jewelry." Whereupon the agent had flapped his hands and waved Catarina through.

Was the jewelry stolen, she wondered. Not that she cared. But the incident had put her in Catarina's good graces, which might be useful.

Orazio was distributing their boarding passes. When he gave one to Catarina, she said, "Why can't we stay in New York? I went on the Internet and chose the things I wanted to buy."

Orazio looked at her, expressionless, but his eyes smoldered with anger. "Stop all this talk about shopping. We have business to conduct."

"Exactly," Tommy said. "Calm down, Catarina. Be glad we got through Customs."

"No thanks to you," Catarina snapped. "Laura was the one who helped me."

"Be quiet," Orazio hissed, glancing at the other passengers. "You draw attention to yourself."

Catarina lowered her voice and said, "Are we staying at a hotel in the French Quarter?"

"No, a private home with three bedrooms. You and Tommy get one, Laura and Bianca sleep in another. The master bedroom is for me." He paused. "Because I am the leader. Understand?"

Tommy nodded, but he didn't look happy about it.

Natalie glanced at Bianca, wondering if she was listening. They would be sleeping in the same room. How was she going to call Pak Lam?

As a child, she had lived in New Orleans with her mother until she was murdered. To appease the Vietnamese spirit gods, she had returned many years later to take her revenge. But this had set Frank Renzi, the relentless detective, on her trail. Where was he now? Still in New York with Conti? Conti knew nothing about New Orleans, but Renzi did, and he knew how to find people.

The back of her neck prickled. Was he watching her now? She turned and looked. She didn't see him, but that meant nothing. It wouldn't take long for Renzi to find out she was back in New Orleans.

———

Bianca ate another Goldfish cracker. She was sick of eating crackers. Tired of being in airports. There were too many people, talking in languages she didn't understand. Laura seemed upset, her face pinched and anxious, like she didn't want to get on another airplane.

She didn't either. But if she made a fuss, Owl would get mad and yell at her.

Catwoman had said it would be fun to ride in an airplane. It wasn't. She hated it, strapped into a seat with a harness, unable to run around. The only time she got to leave her seat was when she told Laura she had to pee. But then she had to walk past Owl and his scary eyes. She didn't think he would kill her on the airplane in front of all the people. But she knew he was thinking about it.

She ate a Goldfish cracker, then another and another. She was hungry. The food on airplanes was awful. A yukky sandwich with some kind of meat. She didn't eat any of it, just drank her milk. The lady in the uniform said if she didn't like the sandwich she'd get her something different. But when she asked for minestrone soup, the lady said they didn't have any. She didn't bother asking for ravioli.

Catwoman looked pretty in her fancy dress and her sparkly necklace, but she seemed angry. When she said something to Owl, he told her to be quiet. Tommy didn't say a word. If someone yelled at Mamma like that, Papà would have made him apologize.

She put the bag of crackers on the seat beside her. Thinking about Papà made her tummy hurt. She wanted to go home.

But home was far away, across a big ocean.

How would Papà find her? Maybe she'd never go home.

Tears filled her eyes.

Mamma said that Santa would come and leave presents for her on Christmas Eve, and when she woke up the next morning there would be presents under the tree. What if she wasn't there?

Tears ran down her cheeks into her mouth, warm and salty.

She didn't care about the presents.

She wanted to be home with Mamma and Papà.

CHAPTER 16

Clint Hammer collected his suitcase and rode an escalator up to the main concourse. Raucous music greeted him, a trumpet blaring jazz to get tourists in the spirit so they'd spend lots of money. He hated jazz. It was loud and distracting, obnoxious music the jungle bunnies played when they weren't selling drugs.

He bought a *Times-Picayune* at Hudson News, then went to the information counter and picked up a free magazine that told what was happening around town. The gray-haired biddy behind the counter smiled and asked if she could help him with anything. He had a transportation problem, but he doubted she could solve it. That's why he needed the magazine.

All kinds of transportation downstairs near the baggage carousels: shuttles to rental car agencies, shuttle buses to various hotels, and a taxi kiosk manned by uniformed attendants with radio handsets. But that wouldn't solve his problem either.

Natalie Brixton, the serial-killer bitch, was due to arrive at 3:45 PM. But he didn't know where she was staying or how she'd get there. Ergo, he needed to follow her. And her mobster pals.

This morning he had called his boss to tell him he'd canceled his flight to Venice. He didn't tell him the real reason, of course. Follow the Brixton bitch and make her pay for killing Oliver. His boss was pissed about the last-minute cancellation fee, but when Clint said he had Intel that the two Mafia brothers who'd gone on the murderous rampage in Venice were flying to JFK, his boss said, "Even better. No extraditions to worry about. Keep me informed. We have agents monitoring the Mafia families in New York. These thugs are well-known to us."

He hadn't mentioned the diversion to New Orleans. Plenty of time for that. After he landed in New York yesterday, Jason had called with more Intel. A travel agency in Venice had issued the plane tickets for Natalie and her lowlife companions. A grease-ball named Luigi had paid cash for five tickets to JFK and five more to fly them to New Orleans. Jason had booked him a room at an airport hotel and a non-stop flight to New Orleans this morning.

During the flight, he had puzzled over the change in plans. Why come to New Orleans? There were plenty of Mafia hoods in New York.

The only mafioso he knew about in New Orleans was Carlos Marcello, who may or may not have put out a contract on President John F. Kennedy. Carlos was dead now, but when one Mafia boss died, another took his place.

He'd dig up that dirt later, after he solved his immediate problem.

To escape the obnoxious music, he ducked into a dim-lit pub and took a seat at the far end of the bar. He never drank alcohol when he was on duty, so he ordered a Coke, thumbed through the magazine and found a half-page ad for Louisiana Livery with color photos of fancy cars. They operated 24-hours a day, every day of the year, Christmas included, and accepted the usual credit cards or, with proper ID and a 50% deposit, cash.

He got on his Smartphone and called the number.

A male voice said, "Louisiana Livery. How can we help you today?"

"I'm on important government business. I need a car and a driver this afternoon, might need him for twelve hours. I'll be paying cash and I have specific needs."

"No problem, sir. Twelve hours will cost you two hundred dollars. Tell me what you need."

"I want a dark car, preferably black. Nothing flashy, no loud colors. Well-maintained and fast, no clunkers."

"I have a black SUV, a 2009 Lexus RX-350, comfortable, low mileage and plenty of power."

"Okay. Now, about the driver. No darkies." Fuck the PC bullshit. He talked plain. He couldn't use a black driver to tail Mafiosos. They hated blacks. The jungle bunnies had taken over their drug business. "I need a white guy, someone familiar with the area. I tell him to go to Metairie, he doesn't get lost." Show the guy he knew the area.

"I see. Let me check my roster." After a short pause, "Festus is available. He's worked for us five years, an unblemished driving record, no complaints at all."

"How is he at tailing somebody without being obvious about it?"

"Festus could do that." A longer pause. "You won't be carrying a weapon, will you?"

Yes, CIA Agent Clint Hammer would definitely be carrying a weapon, possibly more than one. But this asshole didn't need to know that.

"No," he said, punching buttons on his Smartphone. "I'm emailing my credentials. Tell Festus to meet me at two-thirty outside Departures. I'll be waiting at the top of the ramp, give him a hundred bucks cash up front." Provided the car was okay and he liked the driver. What the hell kind of name was Festus? He sounded like a hillbilly.

"Thank you, sir. And your name is … ah, yes, I just got your email. Everything seems to be in order, Agent Hammer. Thank you for choosing Louisiana Livery."

He drank some Coke. Excellent. One problem solved. Now he could figure out why the gangsters were coming to New Orleans. He used his Smartphone to get on the Internet and found a Wikipedia article: Carlos Marcello, born 1910 in Sicily, died 1993 in New Orleans.

In 1911 Carlos had come here with his parents. His early life involved typical mob shit: petty crime, assault and robbery. He did time for five years, got out and got busted for dealing pot, a more serious crime. Sentenced to a long prison term, he got out in ten months.

Clint smiled. Somebody got paid off. Carlos hooked up with the Genovese Family in New York and soon his muscle-men installed illegal slot machines in several New Orleans establishments. By 1947, Carlos controlled a state-wide illegal gambling operation, making big bucks. Ordered to appear before a U.S. Senate committee investigating organized crime in 1959, Carlos took the Fifth and refused to answer questions. Senator John Kennedy was on the committee. His brother Robert was Chief Counsel. In 1960, using Teamsters Union president Jimmy Hoffa as a conduit, Carlos sank a half-million bucks into the presidential campaign of Richard Nixon. But Nixon lost to JFK, who appointed his brother Robert U.S. Attorney General.

He sucked up the last of his Coke and ordered another. Now he was getting to the good stuff. Everyone knew about the JFK assassination and Marcello's hatred of Bobby Kennedy. In 1961, Bobby had Carlos deported to Guatemala, the country he'd falsely listed as his birthplace. Dropped off in a rural area, Carlos was ambushed by thieves. Badly injured, he returned to New Orleans, Rumors surfaced about his threats against JFK, including the Sicilian curse: "Take the stone from my shoe." A private investigator said Carlos had given him a more colorful version in 1962. "If you cut off a dog's tail, he can still bite you. If you cut off the head, your troubles are over." Carlos hinted that "he might set up some nut to take the fall, like they do in Sicily."

When the bartender delivered his Coke, Clint ordered a plate of sausage with red beans and rice. From long experience, he knew that when an opportunity to eat arose, it was best to take it. No telling when his next meal would be after the serial-killer bitch landed.

He returned to the Wikipedia article. As everyone now knew, Lee Harvey Oswald, a former Marine who'd defected to the Soviet Union, was seen distributing communist fliers in the French Quarter in 1963. Jack Ruby, a known Marcello associate, ran a Dallas strip club. Shortly before the JFK assassination in November 1963, Ruby contacted Carlos Marcello, ostensibly about a union problem he had with his strippers.

Clint clapped a hand over his mouth to keep from laughing aloud. Ruby was getting his orders from Carlos. Kill Oswald.

After the assassination, the FBI investigated Carlos Marcello but concluded he wasn't involved. Marcello wasn't an organized crime figure. He earned his living from real estate investments.

Clint groaned in disbelief. These FBI agents were clueless.

Dubbed "The Godfather" of the New Orleans Mafia, Carlos had held the position for thirty years until the day he died.

There were more conspiracy theories in the article, but the bartender delivered his meal. Clint set his Smartphone aside and devoured it, barely tasting the food. Five minutes later, his plate was clean. He paid the tab with cash and left. Time to meet Festus.

———

3:45 PM

The instant the plane stopped at the gate, Frank got on his cellphone and called David. "We're at the gate. Where y'at?"

"Parked outside of Departures. No hassles with the State cop. He knows why I'm here."

"Thanks, David. I owe you big time." He glanced at the cabin attendant standing by the hatch to the gateway. "We should be off the plane in a minute or so. Our targets checked their bags at the gate in New York so they'll get them as soon as they exit the plane. We'll find someplace to hide and see what they do for transportation. Soon as I know, I'll call you."

He closed his cell and took his bag out of the overhead bin. Conti was already standing in the aisle ahead of him with his suitcase. The attendant opened the hatch and the first-class passengers began filing out of the plane. He and Conti joined them and hustled up the gateway.

As they walked through the gate area Frank said, "Once we reach the concourse, we can hunker down somewhere, wait and see where they go. I doubt they'll stop anywhere inside the airport."

"Your colleague will follow them?" Conti said.

"Yes. My car is parked in the garage."

When they reached the top of the ramp, the usual trad jazz was playing over the speakers. Frank took a right and entered Dookie Chase's Pub, a local restaurant. "We can hang out near the bar where the mobsters won't notice us. But we'll see them when they go by."

Conti parked his suitcase near the wall, looking troubled and anxious.

"I can't figure out why they came to New Orleans. There are several Mafia crime families in New York and some of the best diamond cutters in the world work in New York's diamond district."

Frank stifled a smile. Conti had been wrong and he hated it.

"True," he said, eyeing the passengers hurrying past the pub. "But there are other diamond cutters."

"Here in New Orleans?"

Recalling the jibe from Vobitch, telling him to buy Kelly a diamond ring, he said, "Believe it or not, John, even people in New Orleans get married. I've never needed one, but you never know."

Clearly annoyed, Conti said nothing for a moment. Then, "How long will it take us to get to your car?"

"Relax. David's a great detective. He's in an unmarked and he knows how to do a tail."

Two minutes later the mobsters walked past the pub, towing their luggage, Orazio in the lead, then his brother Tomasso. Natalie, Catarina and Bianca brought up the rear.

"Where are the taxis?" Conti whispered.

"Downstairs."

But the Mafia group didn't take the escalator down to ground transportation. They congregated near a window beside the glass exit doors with their luggage. Then Orazio went outside and lit up a cigar.

Frank called David. "They're waiting near an exit door upstairs in Departures. The head honcho is outside smoking a cigar."

"Roger that," David said. "You think someone's meeting them?"

"I assume so. If they wanted a taxi, they'd go downstairs. Hang tight for now." He ended the call and said to Conti, "Looks like they're waiting for someone. Maybe they've got friends here."

"Look," Conti said, pointing as a big black SUV pulled to the curb beside Orazio. He motioned to the others, waving them outside as a silver Lincoln Town Car pulled up behind the black SUV.

Frank called David and said, "Two vehicles are picking up the targets. They're loading luggage into a black Toyota Sequoia SUV. A spiffy silver Lincoln Town Car is behind it."

"I'm on it," David said.

He ended the call and said, "Soon as they get in the cars, we go to the parking garage."

Five minutes later he opened the trunk of his unmarked Dodge Charger. They slung their bags in the trunk and got in the car.

"If their friends picked them up," Conti said, "maybe they're not staying in a hotel."

Correct, Frank thought and he didn't like it. How the hell was he going to snatch Natalie out of a private residence?

But he'd worry about that later. He backed out of the space, headed for the exit and got on his cell. "What's doing, David?"

"They just got on the I-10 headed east. I'm three cars behind them."

"Excellent. I'm leaving the parking garage now. Keep me posted."

"We got a tip about King Rock yesterday," David said. "Someone spotted him."

"Great! Where?"

"Near the corner where the B-n-L gang sells their product. I was on it right away, but by the time I got there, he was gone. Kelly's out driving around looking for him."

"Fuck. That could be dangerous. Hold on." He pulled up to the cashier's booth and took out his wallet. He paid the cashier, drove out the exit and said, "When did you talk to her?"

"A little after noon. She was on her lunch break, driving around looking for him."

Armed and dangerous, he thought. "Damn. I don't like it."

"Me neither. Gotta go, Frank. They're taking the Clearview exit. Keep in touch."

He closed his cell, zoomed through a yellow light onto the airport exit road and accelerated. His unmarked had emergency lights and sirens, but he didn't want to use them.

"You sounded upset," Conti said. "Is something wrong?"

Yes, he thought. Something was very wrong and if Kelly found King Rock it might get worse. No telling what kind of weapons King Rock was packing.

"Another case we're working," he said. "David has the target vehicles in sight. They just got off the Interstate in Metairie, a suburb of New Orleans. Ten minutes and we'll be there."

His heart zoomed into high gear. He couldn't wait to see where Natalie would be sleeping tonight. If it was a private home, things might be complicated. But not impossible.

Now that he had her in his sights, nothing was impossible.

He'd think of something.

CHAPTER 17

FRIDAY 4:40 PM – Metairie, Louisiana

The house looked haunted. In the fading light, the second floor windows were dark and blank like the eyes of an unlit Jack-o-lantern. On the first floor, slivers of light seeped around drawn Venetian blinds. Standing near the end of the driveway, Natalie glanced at the flowers along the front walk of the lavender ranch house next door. The house where she would be staying had drab chocolate-brown siding, an attached two-car garage, and no flowers, just overgrown shrubs.

Unlike other homes on the street, a six-foot-high plank-wood fence enclosed three sides of the house. Worse, there were security cameras, easy to spot if you knew where to look for them, tucked under the eaves on the front corners. To prevent anyone from escaping? Or to alert the mobsters to approaching enemies?

She felt a sudden chill, the Vietnamese spirit gods sending her a clear message. Evil things happened in this house.

She glanced down the street in both directions. After they landed, she'd seen Conti and Renzi leave their seats in first class and exit the plane. If they'd managed to get on the same flight, maybe they had also managed to follow them. She saw no suspicious-looking vehicles, but that didn't mean they weren't somewhere nearby, watching.

Orazio and the driver of the Lincoln Town Car, an older man with thick white hair, approached the house. The front door opened immediately. Orazio turned and beckoned to them. She was tired and hungry, but she didn't want to go inside. Bianca didn't look happy about it either, fearfully watching Orazio. But they had no choice.

The SUV driver took their luggage into the house. She and Bianca followed. Unlike the grim exterior, the foyer glowed with light from an ornate crystal chandelier. A young dark-haired maid in a short black skirt and white blouse took them into a dining room to the right of the foyer.

Two more chandeliers hung over a long rectangular table laden with food. The delicious aromas made her mouth water. Metal containers held Chicken Marsala, Shrimp Etouffee, and meatballs in red gravy. Beside them was a huge pan of lasagna. On the far side of the table, platters held sandwiches, cold cuts and various cheeses. Bianca tugged her hand and pulled her to a sideboard with cookies and Italian pastries.

The centerpiece was a bouquet of fruit: pineapple chunks, fat red strawberries, slices of cantaloupe and green grapes.

"Strawberries," Bianca said, pointing.

Natalie speared a strawberry with a toothpick and gave it to her. Bianca bit into it and juice dribbled down her chin. In three bites the strawberry was gone. When she gave her a napkin, Bianca wiped her mouth and said in English, "I love strawberries!"

She speared another strawberry and gave it to her. Bianca understood English, not a lot perhaps, but some. How had she learned it? From her mother? From watching television?

"Don't eat too many," she said in Italian. "You'll spoil your appetite for dinner."

Bianca wrinkled her nose and reached for a slice of cantaloupe. Fearing the girl would throw a tantrum, she arranged an assortment of fruit on a small plate and settled her onto a folding chair in the corner of the room. Orazio, Tommy and Catarina were filling dinner plates with hot food. The men seemed pleased. Even Catarina looked happy.

She went to the table, took a plate, spooned Shrimp Etouffee over white rice and added a small slice of lasagna. Everything smelled delicious and she was ravenous. When she returned to sit beside Bianca, the fruit on her plate was gone.

"Want a sandwich?" she said in Italian. Bianca shook her head.

"How about some lasagna? Want to try a bite of mine?"

"No," Bianca said in English. "I want a cookie."

Despite her anxiety, Natalie smiled. The girl definitely had a mind of her own. Fine as long as she didn't make a fuss. If she did, Orazio would scold her. Not what she needed right now.

She wanted to be invisible, wanted Orazio to forget she was even there.

"One cookie," she said. "But no more until you eat some dinner."

Bianca rushed to the sideboard and took a large chocolate chip cookie. Smiling happily, she came back to her chair and took a big bite.

Relieved that Bianca seemed content, Natalie ate her dinner, thinking about her next move. A new iPhone was in her purse, but she and Bianca were staying in the same room. Calling Pak Lam would be a problem.

―――

6:00 PM

Orazio stood at the window of his second floor bedroom and watched Silvano Tucci drive off in his silver Lincoln Town Car. The driver of the SUV sat beside him. Silvano was The Boss's consiglieri and closest confidant. An attorney with a degree in accounting, he invested the family's money in real estate or deposited it in off-shore accounts.

Anthony "Tick-Tock" Rotondo ruled the Rotondo Family in Louisiana and the Antonetti Family in Venice. Few people knew this. Two decades ago, Tick-Tock had retired and kept a low profile. During the ride from the airport, Silvano had set up a meeting. Tomorrow morning Orazio would have a sit-down with Tick-Tock at his mansion.

He lighted a cigar, puffed carefully and blew a cloud of smoke out the window. The Boss had welcomed them with a bountiful meal. A sign of respect. Silvano had lent him his black Toyota Sequoia for the duration of his stay. Another sign of respect.

Now he needed to prepare for the meeting, but a shrill voice distracted him, Catarina berating Tommy for something. How could he think with her screeching? If she didn't shut up, he'd go to their room across the hall and silence her. He rued the day Tommy had married her. A necessity due to legal problems, but still.

Tommy let his dick rule his life. Earlier he'd been flirting with one of the maids. Catarina hadn't noticed, but Orazio had. If Catarina caught him, there'd be hell to pay. Intent on seducing women, Tommy wore flamboyant clothes and flashy jewelry like the Dapper Don. But he didn't have John Gotti's intelligence or the cojones to keep people in line. He expected Orazio to do this.

At least the kid and the nanny were quiet in the room beside his. Catarina was a pain in the ass, but easily controlled. Take her shopping and she was happy. But the girl had eaten no dinner, just fruit and a cookie. Laura wasn't a very good nanny. He'd keep an eye on that one.

He puffed his cigar and studied the Christmas lights on the home across the street. A nice enough house, but it had no security cameras like this one. This was Tick-Tock's hideaway. His mansion was several miles to the north, near Lake Pontchartrain. Orazio had been there many times, first as a youngster with Father, and after Father died, alone.

Tommy wanted to meet The Boss, but he didn't trust Tommy to keep his mouth shut about the stolen jewelry. He didn't want him around when he talked to the diamond cutter, either. The Boss's nephew, Angelo Esposito, owned a jewelry store in the French Quarter.

He'd better find something else to occupy Tommy and Catarina, a visit to the zoo perhaps, or a ride on one of the Mississippi riverboats to see the sights.

But his main concern was tomorrow's meet. It was important to strike the correct pose. Appear confident. Show respect, but do not be obsequious. Years ago before his first meeting with The Boss, Father had said, *Never show weakness. He will respect you more.*

Silvano had given him an untraceable cellphone—a burner, he called it—with 25 hours of calling time. He would use it to call a livery service. Why arrive at an important sitdown in an ordinary SUV? He would hire a limousine and have the driver take him there.

He emitted a soft belch and patted his stomach. The home-cooked Italian food was a welcome relief after the crap they dished out in airplanes, and his bedroom was elegant, Tick-Tock's room when he stayed here. Embossed wallpaper, thick wall-to-wall carpeting, and a bathroom big enough for an elephant. Tick-Tock wasn't as big as an elephant, but he was a very large man.

His gaze fell upon the briefcase on the bed. Inside were the uncut diamonds he would take to the meeting. Tick-Tock would decide how many to take as tribute. Orazio would say nothing about the stolen jewelry. There had been no mention of this in the newspapers. The polizia couldn't ask Dominic. He was comatose in a hospital and his wife was dead. But the kid wasn't.

He'd better figure out a way to get rid of her, too.

———

6:30 PM

Bianca perched on her bed and looked around the room. She liked her own bedroom better. It was bigger and so was her bed. This one was narrow and shoved against the wall. Laura's bed was beside hers with a table between them. Opposite their beds, a television set with a blank screen sat on a low chest of drawers against the wall. Two big chairs in front of a low table faced the TV.

Laura was in the bathroom beside her bed. She could hear the water running. A huge yawn made her eyes water. She hadn't slept much on the plane. When they got off the plane, but Catarina hurried her down a long hall with a million people and they got on another airplane. As it took off down the runway, she watched the signs and buildings whiz by, but then she could only see clouds, and when the plane landed, her ears hurt. Laura said to swallow and her ears would pop. So she'd swallowed three times and then they felt better.

Then they got in a big black car and drove here, another long ride strapped into a seat. Catwoman kept complaining to Tommy. If Owl was in the car, he would have told her to shut up, but he was in another car. On the way they passed a mall with Christmas decorations.

Thinking about Christmas and Mamma made her sad. She wondered where Papà was.

The bathroom door opened. Laura came out wearing a white bathrobe and smiled at her. Speaking Italian with her strange foreign accent, she said, "Time for your bath."

"I don't want to take a bath. I'm hungry."

"There was plenty of food downstairs, but you wouldn't eat any."

"Yucky food!"

Laura sat down beside her on the bed. "I know you feel sad about your mother, but—"

"I hate this place! I hate airplanes! I want my Papà!"

"Shh. Don't make a fuss. If Orazio hears you, he'll come in and make you be quiet."

Her heart thudded against her chest. "Owl?"

"Is that what you call him?"

"Yes. I'm afraid of him." She almost told Laura that Owl shot Mamma, but she didn't.

"He's a very bad man."

"Why are you friends with him then?"

Laura frowned. "Why do you say that? He's not my friend."

She didn't answer. Laura was probably lying.

Should she ask her why she was at the museum that night? No. Laura might get mad, might even tell Owl.

"What would you like to eat?" Laura said.

"Mamma makes me ravioli. And minestrone soup."

"Wait here," Laura whispered. "I'll go downstairs and get you some. But you have to be very quiet. Owl is in the room next door."

That scared her.

"I'll be quiet," she whispered. "I promise."

CHAPTER 18

Clint returned from his recon mission and slipped into the shotgun seat of the Lexus. No overhead light. Festus had seen to that, a precaution even though they were parked a half-block north of the target beyond the next intersection.

He'd revised his opinion of Festus. The guy was no hillbilly. He'd been a private dick for ten years until he got in trouble with the cops and lost his PI license. A middle-aged white guy with a craggy weather-beaten face, who wasn't afraid to break rules. Just what he needed. The mafiosos wouldn't give him a second glance.

"The residence behind the mob house looks deserted," Clint said. "No Christmas lights, dark inside. Maybe they're away for the holidays. No dog, either."

"That's a plus," Festus said. "Dog starts barking, pretty soon the whole neighborhood's awake."

"Exactly. No fence in front, but there's a six-foot fence around the rest of the mob house, security cameras on every corner. Nobody gets near the place without them knowing." Which fucked up his plans. He ground his teeth. "I might need you longer than twelve hours."

Festus regarded him silently, his eyes pale as smoke, one green, the other blue, the weirdest thing he'd ever seen. "Gotta tell my boss if you do. How long you need me for?"

"Hard to say. Your boss doesn't need to know."

"He does if you need the car."

"You got a car of your own, we could use yours."

After a moment, Festus said, "How much you paying?"

"How much you asking?" Let the sucker make the first move.

"Two-fifty a day for me and my car. Plus what you already owe for the twelve hours."

"I can swing that. But how do I watch the house while you return this one?"

"Stroll around the block like before, I drive the Lexus to Louisiana Livery, come back in mine."

"Okay, but after tonight we'll need two cars. Tomorrow I'll pick up a rental."

"That'd be good. People get suspicious, they see the same car all the time."

"Someone needs to watch the house at all times, so we'll work alternate shifts, eight hours on, eight hours off. I'll rent a cheap motel room so we can grab some shut-eye now and then."

Festus frowned. "How long you think we'll be here?"

"I don't know, a couple days, maybe." He took out the photo he'd shown Festus earlier. "This bitch murdered a friend of mine, one shot to the head. If she leaves the house, I want to know immediately." He smiled tightly. "No need for you to know what happens then."

Festus gazed at him for several seconds, then said, "Got it."

———

11:10 PM

Seated at the wheel of his Dodge Charger, Frank rotated his neck and flexed his shoulders to get the kinks out. The front windows were open, but the odor of food lingered in the car. Two hours ago, David had brought them take-out dinners, Chicken Marsala for him, Shrimp Scampi for Conti. The house where Natalie and the mobsters were staying was a half-block ahead.

Earlier when he drifted by it, he'd spotted security cameras under the eaves in front. Fearing the mobsters would spot them if he parked too close, he continued south past the next intersection and parked left wheels to the curb facing north so they could eyeball the mob house.

An hour ago the Christmas tree lights in the house beside him had gone out, then the lights in the rest of the house. The occupants were probably in bed. The Mafia brothers probably were too, jet-lagged after an overnight flight to JFK and another to New Orleans. He doubted they'd leave the house tonight. He'd been up since 5:00 AM. In an hour, he'd go home and hit the sack. Tomorrow would be another long day.

Beside him, Conti shifted in his seat. "Chilly, now that the sun has gone down."

"Balmy compared to Boston where I grew up. You cold? I'll put up the windows."

"No, that's okay."

"Where'd you learn English? You don't have much of an accent."

Conti smiled, clearly pleased. "Thank you. I grew up in Naples, but my parents sent me to a boarding school in London when I was ten."

That must have cost some bucks. No surprise there. Conti had an air about him, the confidence that money and privilege conferred.

"I loved London, took my A-levels and got a degree in Political Science from the University of London." Conti smiled. "Or, as you Yanks call it, Poly-sci. After I got the job with Europol, they sent me to a training facility in Maryland to improve my technical skills and learn American colloquialisms."

Frank nodded, half-listening, preoccupied with tomorrow's chores. Earlier he'd stopped for gas. While Conti used the restroom, he called Vobitch, told him what happened at JFK and waited for the fireworks. His boss didn't disappoint. "Jesus-fucking-Christ, she's in New Orleans? Better grab her quick." When Frank said that might be a problem, Vobitch had said, "Come to my house tomorrow morning, we need to talk." Frank wasn't looking forward to it.

He yawned and massaged his eyes. "What's your take on Natalie?" Stakeouts were boring. Why not stir the pot and get the lowdown on Conti's relationship with her?

"A formidable woman. She tried to kill me."

"Join the club. She tried to kill me, too." He wasn't certain she had, but it sounded good.

"She was angry at me for lying to her."

I'll bet she was. "Women don't like it when you have sex with them and then arrest them."

"Perhaps, but I had no choice." Conti shrugged. "Just part of the job."

Not to Natalie. "Where did she get the Laura Lam passport?"

"I don't know. She refused to tell me. We need someone to help us watch the house."

"Not me. I'm working tomorrow."

Conti stared at him, incredulous. "On a Saturday?"

"Homicide detectives don't get days off. Murders happen every day in New Orleans. Christmas is coming. Lots of crime around holidays, robberies, bank stickups, domestic homicides."

"I understand there is an FBI office here. We can ask them to help."

"No, John. *You* can ask them to help. But watch out. When the head honcho finds out you're watching the mobsters that pulled a big jewel heist in Venice, he'll take over the case."

Conti frowned. "I don't want that."

He stifled a smile. Of course not. Conti wanted to arrest the mobsters and grab the glory. "You could pay some off-duty NOPD cops to help watch the house. I'll give you Tony Caruso's number. Tell him I told you to call. He'll organize it for you." He would also make sure Frank was the first to know if Natalie left the house.

"How much would this cost? I don't have unlimited funds."

"If your boss wants the kingpin who runs the 'Netti brothers, he's gonna have to pay for it."

Conti didn't reply. Frank shifted in his seat and studied the mob house. Tomorrow he'd check the city directory to see who lived there, call the Registry of Deeds first thing when it opened on Monday and find out who owned the property. Not that he planned to share any of this with Conti.

Conti's cellphone rang. Frank wondered who it was. Seven hours ahead in Venice: 6:20 AM. Maybe Conti had contacts in America that he didn't know about.

Conti answered, listened for a while, then said, "I am watching the house where she and the 'Netti brothers are staying. With Detective Renzi in his car." After an extended pause, "I am sorry to hear that, Cesare. Thank you for telling me."

Conti ended the call and said, "The jewelry store owner died an hour ago. According to the autopsy report, his wife was pregnant. Generale Valenti has taken this personally. He knew her." Conti gave him a sly wink. "Valenti is a fine carabiniere officer, but rather softhearted when it comes to women. If you get my meaning."

Frank said nothing. Conti was a fine one to talk. He'd slept with Natalie to entrap her. Now he was hinting that Valenti played around on his wife. Still, the news from Venice saddened him. Now Bianca was an orphan. Soon there might be another. Jacques's mother was dead and Kelly was out looking for his father, King Rock. Which was what he should be doing.

"I need to rent a car," Conti said. "Can you drive me to a rental agency? The closest ones are probably at the airport."

Irritated, he said, "John, we need to get something straight. I'm not your chauffeur. I flew to JFK on my own dime to make sure you brought Natalie to New York like you promised. Call a cab. They'll pick you up here and take you wherever you want to go."

Conti clenched his jaw, glaring at him, then punched numbers into his cellphone. "What is this street and the number on the house beside us?"

After Frank told him, Conti repeated the address into his cellphone and said, "I need a taxi to pick me up. Please hurry, it is urgent." He ended the call and said, "What is the name of this big shopping center we passed with all the Christmas decorations?"

"The Clearview Mall. It's on the corner of Clearview Parkway and Veterans Boulevard."

"Is there a food court?"

"Yes. On the ground level."

"I will text Natalie and tell her to meet us there at 2 PM tomorrow."

"How will she get away from the mobsters?"

Conti smiled thinly. "As you pointed out, Natalie is a very resourceful woman. She will figure it out." That ended that conversation. They sat in silence until the taxi arrived. Conti got out, opened the door to the back seat and retrieved his luggage.

"See you in the Clearview Mall food court at two," Frank said.

Conti slammed the door without answering and got in the taxi.

Frank stared at the mob house. Visible above the six-foot fence, the light in the corner room on the second floor winked out. Was it Natalie's room? He couldn't wait to talk to her, but it wasn't going to happen tonight. He cranked the car and headed home.

———

She stood beside Bianca's bed. The girl's eyes were closed, her breathing deep and even. At last she could call Pak Lam. He was probably frantic, waiting anxiously to hear from her.

No more anxious than she was. After Bianca ate her warmed-over ravioli and took a bath, they had curled up in the easy chairs to watch TV. Surfing past shopping channels, cop dramas and reality shows, she found a show for kids. At nine o'clock, she put Bianca to bed and read her Mother Goose rhymes until Bianca nodded off. But when she shut off the lamp on the dresser, Bianca said, "No. Keep the light on. I'm scared of the dark." So she had turned the light on again.

But surely the girl must be sound asleep now. She tiptoed across the room and shut off the light. Bianca didn't stir. Now the only light was an eerie blue glow from the TV screen. She took her iPhone out of her purse. Finally, after two endless plane flights and agonizing hours of tension, she could call Pak Lam and tell him where she was.

Bam! A sharp rap on the door. Loud and authoritative.

Her heart jolted.

Two more raps, louder, more insistent.

Padding barefoot over the carpet, she crept to the door. No peephole. No chain on the door.

She jammed the iPhone into the pocket of her robe and opened the door. Orazio stood there, still wearing his suit though he'd removed his tie. "How is the girl?"

"Shhh. You'll wake her up."

He strode into the room and looked around.

Just like Mr. Self-Important, Conti forcing his way into her apartment. But Orazio was far more dangerous than Conti. Orazio was a killer.

"Your room is comfortable?" he said in a quiet voice.

"Yes," she whispered.

"Good. My room is right next door. If you have a problem, knock on my door."

When pigs fly.

Gazing at her with dark accusing eyes, he said, "The child ate no dinner. Just sweets."

"She was overtired. Cranky after two long plane flights."

"If she does not eat properly, she will get sick."

"Orazio, I'm very tired. I want to go to sleep now."

Anger flared in his eyes. "Do not use my name. Not ever. Understand?"

The murderous look in his eyes terrified her. "Yes."

"Don't forget it. Forget that you even know my name, understand?"

"I won't use it again, I promise. I'm going to bed now."

"As you wish. Good night." He turned and left the room.

She stood there, frozen with fear, her heart pounding, her stomach churning. What if he'd come in the room while she was talking to Pak Lam? Bile rose in her throat and her stomach heaved. She ran in the bathroom, shut the door and vomited into the toilet, disgorging the food she'd eaten for dinner. Exhausted, she struggled to her feet, went to the sink, ran cold water over a washcloth and pressed it to her face. There was no lock on the bedroom door, no way to keep Orazio out of her bedroom. Or anyone else, for that matter.

The dangers kept multiplying.

She had to out of here as soon as possible.

She opened the bathroom door and looked at Bianca. The girl was sound asleep. She shut the door and pressed the button in the doorknob to lock it. At least the bathroom had a lock. She took the iPhone out of her purse and punched in the number she knew so well.

After one ring, a voice said, "Natalie! I have been so worried about you. Are you okay?"

"For now, but not for long. Your contact met me at JFK. That went fine, but I am in New Orleans."

"New Orleans? Why? I thought you would stay in New York City."

"So did I, but after we passed through Customs, we got on another plane and flew here. These men killed people in Venice. I need to get away from them, and this despicable Europol agent."

And Frank Renzi.

"Do not worry. I will help you, but I must devise a new plan. When it is ready, I will text you. I know your situation is complicated and danger-ous. Call me when you can."

"I will. Thank you so much. What would I do without you?"

A soft chuckle. "Be calm, Natalie. Text me if you are in danger, or call if you must. Sleep well. I will work on the plan. All my love to you."

"And mine to you." Tears filled her eyes as she shut off the iPhone. Pak Lam, her adopted father and dearest friend, would help her.

When she left the bathroom, Bianca was sleeping like a lamb. If only she could do the same. Her mind seethed with problems. Conti wanted her to get information from the 'Netti brothers. Renzi wanted to arrest her. She had no idea what Orazio wanted, but one thing was certain.

He didn't trust her.

When she put the iPhone back in her purse, a red light was blinking on her Conti phone. He had sent her a text. *Meet me tomorrow at the food court in the Clearview Mall. 2PM.*

She knew where the mall was, but how could she get out of the house to meet him? A chill skittered down her spine.

Orazio was watching her like a hawk.

CHAPTER 19

Frank finished his strawberry Danish and drank some coffee. The morning sun gave the dining room a cheery glow, but his boss was giving off vibes darker than a thundercloud.

Vobitch had told him to come here so they could discuss the Natalie situation. Now, seated across the table from him, Vobitch was giving him the silent treatment, a silence fraught with tension, not the usual camaraderie during a sit-down at his house.

Vobitch helped himself to another Danish from the plate on the table. Said nothing.

Irritated, Frank thought, *Screw this.* He hadn't come here for coffee and Danish. "Are you trying to piss me off or has the cat got your tongue?"

A flush mottled Vobitch's cheeks. "I let you go to New York yesterday to serve a warrant on Natalie, but the fucking mobsters pulled a fast one and flew to New Orleans. Now that she's here you got no interest in catching King Rock."

"She shot me!"

"King Rock shot one of my detectives! Kenyon's lucky to be alive, you forget that? Get your priorities straight, Frank."

"Since when is closing three old murder cases not a priority?"

His boss gave him a frosty stare. "Since King Rock murdered the mother of his child and shot one of my detectives!"

Frank knew he was a heartbeat away from blowing up, also knew this would be a bad idea. He was about to get up and leave, when Juliana entered the room. "Good to see you, Frank. Is my esteemed husband giving you a hard time?"

He couldn't help smiling. "Nothing new there, Juliana. Thanks for the coffee and Danish."

A tall woman with ebony skin whom one New York City ballet critic had deemed strikingly beautiful, Juliana studied the plate on the table, pursed her lips and frowned at her husband.

"What?" Vobitch said. "You counting? I'm gonna take you to Vegas, let you count cards for me at the blackjack table."

Juliana circled the table and kissed his cheek. "The day I catch you at a blackjack table, I'm canceling our subscription to the Louisiana Philharmonic."

At first glance the stocky, self-described New York Jew and the statuesque former ballerina seemed like a mismatch, but they shared a passion for fine art, opera and classical music.

"How's Kelly?" Juliana asked.

Blank-faced, Frank looked at Vobitch and said nothing.

"My, my. That look had a certain portent. Pray tell, what is Kelly up to now?"

Gunning for King Rock, Frank thought but didn't say. "She's good. I haven't seen her since Wednesday, but I'll see her tonight."

"Give her my best," Juliana said. "I'll leave you two to talk about whatever it is that warrants a powwow on a Saturday morning. Want me to wrap up the last pastry for you, Frank?"

"No, thanks. I'm good." If he left it for Vobitch, maybe he'd stop being such a dickhead.

After Juliana left the room, Frank said, "The house in Metairie has gotta be mob-owned, there's a six-foot fence around it, security cameras. According to the city directory, Alma Esposito, age sixty-seven, is the sole occupant. Does that name mean anything to you?"

"Yeah. She's Italian. What I wanna know is why did they come here? Plenty of mobsters in New York. I should know. I had to deal with them for twenty years, working for NYPD."

"I don't give a damn why they're here. I want to arrest Natalie."

"Fine. Put together a SWAT team, do an early morning raid when the assholes least expect it, grab poor little Natalie and bring her in. Then maybe you can focus on King Rock."

"That might not work. These 'Netti brothers are killers. If they've got Mafia connections here, they're probably armed. And don't forget Conti. He's watching the house."

"Screw Conti. Him and his Europol pals are no better than the feds. What about the girl?"

"Conti got word from Venice last night that her father died."

Vobitch frowned. "And she's here with the mobsters that shot her mother? They find out she's the last witness, they might kill her. Speaking of witnesses, we better keep an eye on Jacques. King Rock had no trouble offing the kid's mother. What's to say he won't kill his son?"

Frank puffed his cheeks. Man, if Kelly heard that theory, she'd go ballistic. "Maybe we can have Kelly guard him." Then she wouldn't be out gunning for King Rock.

"Maybe, but I can't order it. I'm not her boss. Not only that, it's almost Christmas. You know what happens during the holidays. No shortage of robberies, murders and domestic homicides."

"Carlos Marcello is the name that comes to mind when I think about the Mafia in New Orleans. And he's dead."

"Everybody knows about Carlos and the JFK assassination," Vobitch said. "Hell, I saw the movie. But if New Orleans is like New York, someone else took over after Carlos died."

"Like Alma Esposito?"

"Yeah, pistol-packing Alma." Vobitch frowned. "You know, there's a jewelry store on Royal Street not far from the D-8 station. Esposito Fine Jewelry. Go buy Kelly a diamond and check it out." Vobitch smirked, then sobered. "Frank, I know you're hot to grab Natalie, but King Rock is your priority. The NOPD brass call me every day, got all kinds of citizen's groups leaning on them."

"Don't worry. King Rock is at the top of my list." *Right after I arrest Natalie.* No need to mention he'd see her at the Clearview Mall four hours from now. He couldn't arrest her while Conti was there, but if she managed to meet them at the mall, maybe he could figure a way to get her out of the house to meet him somewhere else. Without Conti.

———

10:00 AM

Orazio strode down the driveway toward the white limousine, trying to contain his fury. Tommy wanted to meet The Boss. He didn't even know his name. Father had never allowed Tommy to meet him. Such meetings required self-confidence, intelligence and skill.

Tommy thought flashy suits impressed people. Nonsense. For the sit-down, Orazio had worn his conservative charcoal-gray suit, one befitting an important businessman.

With an obsequious smile, the livery driver opened the rear door. "Good morning, sir."

"A fine morning indeed," Orazio said, and settled onto the plush leather seat.

The driver, a young white man in a tuxedo, got behind the wheel. "Where to, sir?"

"I must attend an important meeting near the lake." The lake with the strange name that sounded like Punch-A-Train. "But I am in no hurry. Go up West End Boulevard and drive around. I enjoy seeing the elegant homes there." In fact, he intended to purchase one. Silvano would facilitate the sale. For cash, and a few diamonds perhaps.

The driver pulled away from the curb. "Some of those houses are as big as mansions."

"True. In Venice we call them palazzos. I would be happy to tell you about them, but I must focus on my meeting." Enough of this prattle, though it amused him to show off his command of American English. Tommy spoke only basic phrases in a thick accent. With his good looks and charm, Tommy expected everything in life to be easy. Crippled from birth, Orazio had worked hard to master many things, including English.

As a young boy he had watched television programs in English. When he was ten, he discovered *Zorro*. A superb athlete and marksman, Zorro was a master of stealth and cunning. Well-educated and wealthy, he used high-tech gadgets to defeat his enemies. Orazio watched the show alone in his room, without Tommy. *Zorro* was his secret fantasy world. Someday he would be as wealthy and powerful as Zorro. Now he was.

He glanced out the window at the mansions where wealthy white men lived, important men who owned banks or lucrative businesses. Not as lucrative as Don Rotondo's business, but substantial enterprises nevertheless. Some were huge, others smaller, though still impressive. He saw no "for sale" signs outside them. Perhaps millionaires did not allow such tawdry signs on their property. But Silvano would help him find some mansions that were for sale here.

"Would you care for a beverage, sir?" the driver asked. "There are soft drinks and bottled water in the cooler beside you."

Orazio checked his Rolex, rather flashy but a fine timepiece. 10:35. If he arrived early, he would appear over-eager. "Thank you. Keep driving. When it's time to go to my meeting, I will tell you."

He opened a bottled water and drank some as they passed a two-story mansion, almost as fine as his palazzo in Venice. Sunlight glanced off the white-stone exterior. Too bad Father wasn't here. But he would be here in spirit. Father's guidance would govern his behavior at the meeting. The path he intended to travel was dangerous, but he had taken many risks in his life. This would be no different.

He massaged his right leg. Even now if he sat still too long, the muscles stiffened up. As a boy he hated being a cripple. Father had taken him to the best surgeon in Rome, but the doctor said he must wait until he attained his full growth. Finally, when he was sixteen and six feet tall, the surgeon reconstructed his leg.

The arduous rehabilitation process had taken six months.

Then Father gave him the assignment he had long yearned for. Kill a member of a rival gang. He prepared for the hit as diligently as he had prepared to fight his tormentors in school. When the time came, he did not flinch. He looked the man in the eye and pulled the trigger. The next day in Father's library, surrounded by soldiers of the Antonetti Family, he had sworn an oath in blood. Omerta. Silence and loyalty.

To betray The Family would bring certain death.

Not until Tommy was nineteen had Father given him an assignment: Kill a low-level soldier who had betrayed The Family. Tommy needed three shots to do it. He was a wuss, and Father knew it. By then, he had already introduced Orazio to Don Rotondo.

Now it was time for the meet. He gave the driver the address and re-laxed into the leather seat. In the course of his thirty-two years, he had overcome many obstacles. When it came to matters of crucial impor-tance, he felt supremely confident. Tommy said he had ice-water in his veins. Nonsense. Fear was foreign to him, difficult to comprehend. He rarely expressed his emotions, unless something triggered his fury. He had the killer instinct. Tommy did not.

The limousine stopped in front of an imposing four-story mansion surrounded by an eight-foot, wrought-iron fence. Orazio gave the driver a fifty-dollar bill and told him to wait. A man with hard eyes and a scarred face opened the door, took him inside and frisked him. He found nothing. Orazio knew better than to bring weapons to a sit-down. After searching his briefcase, the man took him to the room where the Don received visitors, a twelve-foot-square room with a stone fireplace on the left, two windows with drawn shades on the right.

Ahead of him, two enormous men with hard eyes and bulges under their jackets guarded two men in business suits who occupied chairs in front of a low table. The man he had come to see occupied the largest chair, high-backed like a throne, with red velvet upholstery.

Anthony "Tick-Tock" Rotondo had to weigh at least 350 pounds. Even his fingers were fat, fondling the chihuahua with big brown eyes perched on his lap. Orazio had once seen him on the grounds of his mansion, an enormous fat man walking two dogs no bigger than his fist.

He studied the chihuahua. One twist of the neck and the creature would be dead.

Silvano Tucci occupied the chair beside Don Rotondo, thin and wiry in his pinstriped gray suit. Orazio took a seat opposite Silvano and placed a gift-wrapped package on the table. "A gift from the Antonetti Family, Don Rotondo, an ornament made of Murano glass."

Now seventy-five, Don Rotondo had acquired a fearsome reputation on his way to the top. He had whacked many people. Some hits were merciful, one shot to the head. Others involved ice picks, garrotes and knives. When Anthony Rotondo paid a call, they knew the clock was ticking. Hence the Tick-Tock moniker. Nevertheless, Don Rotondo remained a devout Catholic. He unwrapped the gift, a large multicolored mosaic of The Virgin Mary. A smile suffused his pudgy face. "A most thoughtful gift, Orazio. I will treasure it."

"A fine gift indeed," Silvano said.

"I trust your business goes well, Don Rotondo?" Orazio said, easing into business mode.

"Better with each passing year, even without the drugs. Good riddance to that. Now the blacks peddle drugs on street corners and run around shooting each other to protect their turf." He waved a pudgy hand. "Stupid. This attracts police attention."

Orazio nodded, expressionless. So far no one had mentioned the attention the murders in Venice had attracted, and he did not intend to speak of this.

"The Vietnamese are worse," Silvano said. "They prey on their own people, invade their homes and torture them to find out where they keep their money and jewelry."

Interesting, Orazio thought, storing away this piece of information.

Don Rotondo fixed him with a hard stare. "You have made a big score in Venice?"

"A fine score indeed. I learned that a shipment of uncut diamonds would arrive at a jewelry store and made the owner an offer, but he refused. This I could not tolerate. Now he is in hospital, comatose. His wife is dead." He said nothing about the girl. Why ask for trouble?

Gazing at him, his dark eyes full of greed, the Don said, "You have the diamonds?"

He opened his briefcase and placed the drawstring bags of uncut diamonds on the table. Silvano opened them and carefully spread the contents over the table, diamonds of various shapes and sizes.

The largest was almost as big as a golf ball, impressive, even in the dim light. A hush fell over the room as Silvano counted them, broken only by the Don's labored breathing.

At last Silvano said, "Sixty-eight uncut diamonds."

This brought another smile to Tick-Tock's pudgy face.

Orazio maintained a confident expression and relaxed posture. To conceal the fact that he had also stolen jewelry, he must appear unconcerned, not the least bit guilty. "Take your pick of the diamonds," he said. "Our tribute to you, Don Rotondo."

The Don stopped petting the chihuahua. His hand snaked out and his fat fingers plucked the largest diamond off the table. "What do you think this is worth, Silvano?"

"At least a million. Perhaps more. Your nephew would know more precisely."

Tick-Tock smiled, revealing yellowed teeth. "You did well to smuggle them into the country, Orazio. The feds grow more vigilant every day. I will take the four largest diamonds. You and your family may have the rest. My nephew will cut them for you."

Angelo Esposito, the fagosa. Orazio hated dealing with him, but he had no choice.

Silvano put the other diamonds in the drawstring bags and gave them to Orazio. "Sixty-four uncut diamonds. After Angel works his magic, they will be untraceable. Much better than drugs."

Orazio nodded in agreement. "Thank you, Don Rotondo. And thank you for lending us your home. We especially appreciated the fine meal you provided on our arrival."

Don Rotondo waved a hand. "We take care of family. I will call my nephew and tell him to expect you."

Translation: *I know how many diamonds are in those bags and my nephew will tell me if you bring him more.*

"Thank you," Orazio said. "I will make an appointment to see him on Monday."

CHAPTER 20

SATURDAY – 1:40 PM

"So many cars!" Catarina exclaimed. "The stores in this mall must be bellissimo!"

"You'll love Sears," Natalie said. "It has some fantastic outfits." She had no idea if it did or not, but it was a huge store, which would keep Catarina busy, and away from the food court.

Cursing the line of vehicles in front of her, she gripped the wheel with sweaty hands. Her nerves were shot. Catarina had already given her a hard time about leaving the house. After lunch Orazio said he had to go out, and Tommy insisted on going with him. When Catarina said she wanted to go shopping, Orazio told her to be quiet.

After the men left the house, Natalie had said, "Let's rent a car. Why let Orazio ruin our day?"

With a tense frown, Catarina said, "He can do more than ruin our day, believe me. Besides, I know nothing about how to rent a car."

"I'll rent the car," she'd said. "They'll pick us up. Come on, it will be fun. We'll take Bianca with us." Twenty minutes later, a man picked them up and drove them to the rental office. She used her Ling Lam credit card to rent a four-door Honda Accord, but it had taken forever to complete the paperwork.

She didn't give a damn about shopping, but it was an excuse to get to the mall and meet Conti. Something else she didn't want to do. If they ever found a parking space. Seven days before Christmas, people were hellbent on shopping. And so was Catarina.

The cars ahead of them inched forward.

Behind them in the back seat, Bianca said, "I want ice cream."

"I'll get you some as soon as we find a place to park," Natalie said. Now it was 1:45. If she didn't find a space soon, she'd be late for the meeting. Sweat dampened the armpits of her fancy running suit, the one Catarina so admired. Catarina had on an emerald-green wool dress, better suited to the weather in New York City.

"That car is leaving," Catarina said, pointing at a red Jeep one row over to their left.

"Great! Go stand in the space and wait till I get there."

Catarina got out and rushed to claim the space. Another car tried to pull into it, but Catarina stood her ground. Natalie couldn't help smiling. Catarina could be a pain in the ass, but she was a pit bull if she wanted something. And she wanted to buy some fancy new clothes.

Five minutes later, Natalie helped Bianca out of the car, locked the car and checked the time. 1:55. She'd never make the meeting in time. She took Bianca's hand and hurried toward the mall entrance. Catarina struggled to keep up, hobbled by her spike-heeled shoes. A line of cars halted to let them cross to the mall entrance.

Conscious of the passing minutes, Natalie pushed through the door into the mall. "After I get Bianca some ice cream, I'll buy her some summer clothes, T-shirts and shorts."

"And a new dress," Bianca said.

Catarina trilled a laugh. "That's right, Bianca. We both need a pretty new dress. Shall I come with you and help you pick one out?"

Definitely not. "We don't have much time," she said. "Go have fun shopping at Sears. Target has nice clothes for children. It's the store on the end with the big red-and-white bulls-eye." Pointing to their left, she said, "Sears is the store on that end of the mall." On the mall directory, she touched the star on the first floor map. "We're here. If you get lost, keep walking until you come to the mall directory. We can meet here at these wooden benches."

"Okay, let's meet at four." Catarina pointed at the directory. "Look, there's a movie theater. Maybe we can come and see a film some night."

She forced a smile. If Catarina didn't shut up, she'd be late. Conti would be furious. "Maybe. See you at four. Have fun shopping." *And stay away from the food court.*

Bianca seemed enthralled, gazing at the crowds of people and the stores with their holiday decorations, wreaths and fir trees decorated with gold tinsel and colored ornaments. A short walk took them to the food court. Along the right-hand wall enticing aromas came from take-out stalls. Beside them a vast seating area held dozens of tables. Enjoying their food and beverages, shoppers of all ages sat at them, grandparents, young couples, parents with small children.

Her heart jolted. Frank Renzi was sitting at a table near the back of the seating area. Why was he here? He was just as attractive as she remembered, a pale blue shirt open at the neck contrasting with his tanned face. Almost as though he'd felt her eyes on him, he turned and locked eyes with her.

Then he said something to the man beside him. Conti. She couldn't decide who she feared most, Conti or Renzi.

But to hell with them. Bianca wanted ice cream. Why should she worry about being late? It was Conti's fault, expecting her to find a way to get here. She took Bianca to the Baskin Robbins stall and said in Italian, "What flavor do you want?"

Bianca studied the big tubs in the display case. Finally she pointed at two tubs. One held chocolate ice cream, the other orange sherbet.

"Two scoops?" Natalie said in English.

The young female clerk said, "It's okay. I can put a small scoop of each into a big cup."

"That would be perfect. And a bottle of iced tea for me."

The clerk put their order on a small tray. She paid cash and added several napkins to the tray. Bianca went to the nearest vacant table and climbed onto a chair.

She bent down and said in Italian, "Not here, Bianca. Two of my friends are sitting at another table. Here's the deal. You get to have two flavors of ice cream, but you have to promise not to tell Catarina or Tommy or Orazio I talked to them while you ate your ice cream, okay?"

"Okay. I love ice cream."

She took Bianca to a vacant table beside the one where Conti was sitting. He wanted to talk about the 'Netti brothers, and she didn't want Bianca to overhear them. She settled the girl in her seat and gave her the cup of ice cream. Already, Conti was signaling her to come to their table.

Ignoring him, she said to Bianca, "How is the ice cream? Good?"

Bianca spooned a bite of chocolate into her mouth. "Very good."

She opened her bottle of iced tea and drank some. Conti waved his hand to get her attention. The idiot. Did he expect her to jump when he snapped his fingers? She leaned closer to Bianca and said, "Which flavor do you like the best?"

Bianca smiled and licked orange sherbet off the plastic spoon. "Both. I like both the best."

"Good," she whispered. "I need to go talk to my friends now."

Bianca put down her spoon and looked at her with mournful eyes. "You won't leave me, will you?"

"Of course not. I will be sitting right over there. Just for a minute, I promise."

She rose to her feet, stepped over to the other table and sat on the chair facing Bianca. Before Conti could speak, she said in English, "How did you expect me to get here, walk? I had to rent a car and it took forever. I can't stay long. Catarina is with us. She is shopping now."

Conti studied her for a moment, expressionless, then said, "I told Frank you'd find a way."

Renzi's eyes bored into her. "How did you rent the car?"

She had expected this question. When in doubt, lie. "Catarina has a credit card."

Seemingly satisfied, Renzi said, "How's it going? Do they suspect you?"

"I'm not sure. Orazio trusts no one. Not even his brother, I think."

"Why?" Conti said. "What makes you think so?"

"He went to meet someone this morning. Tommy wanted to go with him and they had a big argument. Orazio left by himself. Tommy was pissed."

"Who was Orazio going to meet?" Conti asked.

"I don't know. He didn't say." She glanced at Bianca, who was intent on eating her ice cream, a bite of chocolate, then a bite of orange sherbet. "Orazio had a limo pick him up at ten o'clock."

"I know," Conti said. "I saw it."

She drank some iced tea. That answered one question. Conti was watching the house. "Where did he go? Did you follow him?"

"He drove around a residential neighborhood with expensive houses. I was afraid he would spot me, so I parked on the main street." Conti shrugged. "And lost him."

"Where is Orazio now?" Renzi asked, gazing at her with his dark, penetrating eyes. Eyes that seemed to probe her inner-most soul. She hoped he couldn't read her mind.

"After lunch he and Tommy went out. I don't know where."

"I received some bad news from Venice last night," Conti said. "The girl's father—"

"Quiet!" she hissed, glancing at Bianca. "My little friend is not deaf and she understands a bit of English. I'm not sure how much, but if something happened to that person, keep your voice down."

Conti shrugged. "Okay. The game is over for that person. Is that cryptic enough for you?"

Her heart sank. How would she tell Bianca? Maybe she wouldn't. That wasn't part of the deal. Now it was more urgent than ever to escape from the 'Netti brothers. Especially Orazio.

"Do you feel safe?" Renzi said, gazing at her.

The question stunned her. How could she possibly feel safe? Playing spy to get information for Conti, hoping Renzi didn't arrest her.

"No," she said curtly. "But what choice do I have?" But she did have a choice. She had a rental car, a credit card, her iPhone and a small amount of cash. Maybe she should leave Bianca and Catarina, get in the car and drive away. But if she did, would Catarina protect Bianca?

She looked over at Bianca, who was spooning melted ice cream out of the cup and dribbling it over the table, pouting. Any minute now she'd throw a tantrum. Natalie left her chair, went to Bianca's table and mopped up the mess with some napkins.

"I want to go buy my dress," Bianca said.

"And soon we will." She looked around saw a kiosk with small plastic toys. "Let's get you a toy to play with."

Bianca hopped off her chair and they went to the kiosk. Natalie said to the clerk, "My little friend needs something to keep her busy."

The clerk, a teenager with braces on her teeth, held out a clear plastic bag with a colorful assortment of tiny rings. "All the kids love these."

"Perfect." She paid cash for the toy, took Bianca back to her table, opened the plastic bag and gave it to her. In Italian, she said, "Let me say goodbye to my friends. So we can go shopping."

"For my dress," Bianca said, sliding a red-plastic ring onto one of her tiny fingers.

She returned to the other table, perched on a chair and said, "I need to go. She's getting antsy. I promised to buy her some new clothes."

"Why is she dressed like a boy?" Renzi said.

Trust the sharp-eyed detective to notice this. "It wasn't my idea, believe me."

"We need more information," Conti said. "I will text you and tell you when to meet us again."

She clenched her teeth to keep from screaming. "I can't keep meeting you. I was lucky to get here today. Already Orazio doesn't trust me. He is a killer. Have you forgotten that?"

"When you agreed to do this, you knew it might be dangerous. Find out who Orazio went to meet this morning in the limousine."

"But she's right," Renzi said. "Undercover work is dangerous. If she turns into a problem, Orazio might decide to eliminate the problem. Then you won't get any information." Turning to her, he said, "We'll figure out a better way to meet and send you a text."

Support from an unexpected quarter, and Conti didn't seem happy about it. Without a word, she left the table.

Renzi hadn't arrested her, but that might not matter.

With Dominic and Sophia dead, Bianca was the only witness.

If Orazio decided to kill Bianca, he wouldn't need a nanny. He'd kill her, too.

———

Frank watched Natalie gather up the plastic toys she'd bought for Bianca. To his surprise, she seemed comfortable with the girl, almost protective of her.

"Why do you care what happens to her?" Conti said angrily. "She has killed four men. You said so yourself."

"Why get angry at her? Focus on your goal. You won't get any information if she's dead. She can't keep sneaking out to meet us. The Mafia thugs will get suspicious. We need to find a better way to meet."

Clearly annoyed, Conti took out a package of cigarettes. "Fine. Got any ideas?"

"Put the cigarettes away. You can't smoke in here."

"Right," Conti said. "You Americans are so worried about my health."

He smiled. "Not me. I'm worried about that security guard leaning against the wall over there. Light up in here, he might arrest you."

Frowning, Conti put the pack of cigarettes in his pocket. "Okay, how do we meet her?"

"The carabiniere general in Venice rented a house to snoop on the 'Netti brothers. Maybe we could do the same thing here."

Conti stared at him. "This is possible?"

"Maybe. I need to find out who lives on that street. Some people go away for the holidays. We get lucky, maybe we can convince one of them to lend us their house."

"Excellent!" Conti exclaimed, all smiles now. "She could walk there with the girl."

Exactly, Frank thought. Then he could arrest Natalie and get Bianca away from the mobsters so she'd be safe.

"How soon can we do this?"

"I've got a directory that lists the names. The tricky part is finding someone to help us. It might cost you to use the house. I don't know how much, but NOPD won't pay for it." He watched Conti, saw the wheels grinding in his mind.

"I will call and ask my superiors about this. I cannot promise, but they are eager to find out who is this Mafia kingpin the 'Netti brothers have come here to see."

Frank rose from his chair. Conti and his boss didn't seem to be in any hurry to arrest the men who'd murdered Bianca's parents. "Okay, call your supervisor. I'll check the directory."

If he found a safe house, he wouldn't be telling Conti about it.

He wanted to arrest Natalie, but that wasn't his only problem. Vobitch would keep hounding him until King Rock was behind bars. And Kelly was cruising the mean streets of New Orleans with a gun, hunting for the bastard.

Tonight he was having dinner at her house. That brought a smile to his face. After dinner, he'd take her to bed and make her forget King Rock. For a little while anyway.

CHAPTER 21

Bianca waited beside the metal clothes rack, getting madder and madder by the minute. Laura was choosing shorts to go with the ugly shirts in the big red basket on the floor. She wasn't going to wear them. A little boy stood on a table beside the rack, dressed in a hideous olive-green shirt and matching shorts. Not a real boy, a plastic model with painted-on red hair and a stupid smile.

Laura had promised to buy her a dress after she talked to her friends, not shirts and shorts for boys. She loved ice cream, but she didn't like sitting by herself while Laura talked to her friends. She couldn't understand what they said. They were speaking English, even Laura.

Maybe they were her boyfriends. She was pretty sure Laura wasn't married. She didn't wear a ring like Catwoman. It seemed like one man was mad at Laura, but not the other one, the one with a tanned face and friendly dark eyes. He looked a little bit like Papà, only not as handsome. Except when he looked over at her and smiled. When Owl smiled at her his eyes stayed as mean and hateful as ever. When Laura's boyfriend smiled at her, his eyes were smiling too.

What if Laura decided to go live with him?

Who would take care of her?

She held out her hands, admiring the rings Laura had bought for her, a different colored one for each finger. She loved them. She liked Laura better than Catwoman. Laura let her stay up late to watch TV and read her stories before she went to sleep.

What if Laura went away and left her, too? Like Mamma.

Tears filled her eyes. Christmas was coming. She couldn't remember how many days from now, but it had to be soon. The store had a lot of Christmas decorations. But she wouldn't be decorating a Christmas tree or getting any presents. Santa probably didn't even come here. It was too hot and there was no snow.

No presents. No Santa. No Mamma and no Papà.

Her throat closed up and tears ran down her cheeks into her mouth. Laura didn't even notice. She was too busy picking out ugly shorts for her to wear. A little girl in a red-velvet dress walked past them, talking to her mother, pointing at the big Christmas tree with blinking white lights at the end of the aisle.

It wasn't fair. That girl had a pretty red dress to wear for Christmas, but she didn't.

She picked up the red basket and dumped the clothes on the floor. "I don't want these! They're ugly and I'm not going to wear them!" The girl in the red dress and her mother stared at her. So did Laura. Then she came over and took the basket away from her.

"I hate you! You said you would buy me a dress!"

"Shhh," Laura said, and knelt down beside her, saying in her strange Italian accent, "Don't make a fuss, Bianca. People are staring at you."

That made her even madder. She stamped her foot. "I don't care! You said I could have a dress. These clothes are for boys! I don't want them. I want a new dress!" Sobbing, she kicked the basket aside, wrapped her arms around Laura's neck and buried her face against her chest. "I want Mamma and Papà."

Laura rubbed her back and whispered, "I'm sorry Bianca. I know you miss Mamma and Papà. I don't blame you for being sad. It's Christmas time and you should be having fun. Tell me what you want most in the whole world for Christmas and I will try to get it for you."

She tipped back her head and looked into Laura's eyes. "I want Mamma. And Papà."

Laura's eyes got sad, like she wanted to cry. But she didn't. She sat on the floor and said, "Sit in my lap, Bianca. I have a secret to tell you."

She crawled onto Laura's lap and said, "About Mamma?"

"No. About my mother. She died when I was young and it made me very sad. I was older than you when it happened, ten years old. But it still hurt and I missed her very much. She used to buy me ice cream and tell me funny stories and take me for walks along the river. And I was angry because would never do that again."

Bianca gazed into her sad eyes and patted her cheek. "Did you cry?"

"Yes. Every night for weeks and weeks."

"And then you stopped?"

"Not really. Even now, thinking about her makes me cry sometimes." Laura heaved a sigh. "But after a while I decided to be the person she would want me to be. Mom always told me I was smart. So I worked hard in school and made some new friends."

"Will I go to school here? And have new friends?"

Laura hugged her. "I'm not sure, but I know you will have many friends wherever you go. You're very smart and you're going to be beautiful like your mother. All the boys will like you." Laura kissed her cheek. "Come on, let's go find you a pretty dress."

Bianca pointed at the pile of clothes on the floor. "Do we have to buy these?"

"No. We'll get you some shorts and shirts in the girls' department."

"I'm glad you told me your secret, Laura."

"I am, too, but we need to hurry. We have to meet Catarina soon."

———

Lurking behind a rack of blue jeans, Clint Hammer eyed the dressing room where the Brixton bitch had taken the kid. Five minutes ago the kid had thrown the mother of all tantrums. When he'd seen Natalie with Renzi, he'd felt like throwing one, too. If Renzi arrested her, his magnificent plan would go in the toilet.

Renzi didn't arrest her, but who the hell was the guy with him? Another greaseball, one of Renzi's NOPD detective pals probably. He hadn't stayed to find out. When Natalie left the food court with the kid, he had tailed them through the mall to Target.

A stout woman with scraggly hair and a thick waist came to the blue jeans rack and gave him a dirty look. He glared at her and pretended to check out the jeans. Jeans for little boys. Christ, he'd never had a kid and he never would. Kids were trouble. Especially the brat with Natalie Brixton. How the hell could he snatch the serial-killer bitch if the kid was with her?

An hour ago when the two Mafia thugs left the mob house, he'd told Festus to follow them. He didn't give a damn where they went, but he needed to know so he could call his boss and deliver his report. His boss wanted him to grab the Mafia hoods and make a big splash in the media, which would be a big feather in his cap. Fuck that.

He wanted to make Natalie pay for killing his friend Oliver. But now she had a rental car. What if she didn't go back to the mob house? What if she skipped town with the blonde and the kid? This didn't seem likely, but it would complicate matters if she did.

This was turning out to be more difficult than he thought. His original plan—grab the bitch, bring her to a secluded spot, yank her chain for a while, then kill her—no longer seemed feasible.

But CIA Agent Clint Hammer wasn't going to let a few complications defeat him, not with his twenty years of experience. He'd think of something.

———

She took Bianca across the aisle to the girls' department. It was 3:20. Maybe she'd put Bianca in the rental car and leave now. But how could she deny Bianca a new dress? She was already pointing at a mannequin at the end of one aisle, modeling a dress with a red-velvet top and a puffy red skirt with white sequin snowflakes on it.

"I want that one," Bianca said. "Isn't it beautiful? I love the sparkly snowflakes."

"Bellissimo! Let's find one in your size so you can try it on." Natalie walked along a rack full of dresses, pulled one out and held it up. "Like this, right?"

"Yes, yes, yes!" Bianca said, dancing around the aisle. "I love it!"

"Come in the dressing room and we'll see if it fits."

The dressing room was small, but it had a full-length mirror and a wooden bench. Bianca sat on the bench and took off her shirt and jeans. Natalie helped her put on the dress and zipped it up. "It seems to fit. Stand in front of the mirror and see how you like it."

Bianca studied herself in the mirror, then gave her a big smile. "This is my favorite dress in the whole world!"

"Then you shall have it," she said. Aware of the passing time, she helped Bianca take off the dress and put on her shirt and jeans. There was no time to get the shorts and shirts. She'd pay for the dress, take Bianca out to the car and leave.

But when they left the dressing room, Catarina was standing there with a big smile on her face.

"I followed the map to this Target store like you said. Did you get a pretty dress, Bianca?."

"Yes!" Bianca exclaimed, holding it up to show Catarina. "A beautiful dress! Laura helped me try it on and it fits perfect."

Abandoning any thoughts of escape, Natalie forced a smile. "Let's hurry and get you some summer clothes. It's getting late."

———

When they got back to the house, she helped Catarina take her shopping bags out of the trunk. On the ride from the mall, Catarina had rhapsodized over her purchases: three pairs of shoes to match her three new dresses, two casual outfits, and two fancy sweaters.

133

Now she seemed subdued. Orazio's SUV was parked in the driveway. But Bianca was happy, clutching the Target bag with her new dress and her new shorts and tops.

When they got to the door, Orazio opened it, expressionless, his body rigid with anger. After they entered the house, he said in a menacing voice, "Where have you been?"

"Shopping," Catarina said, beaming at him. "Stop frowning and get in the spirit. It's almost Christmas." In an off-key voice she sang, "Here comes Santa Claus, here comes Santa Cl—"

"Shut up," Orazio thundered. "Give me the car keys."

Catarina backed away, her expression fearful. "I don't have them. Laura does."

An ice-pick of fear stabbed her gut. Orazio turned his terrifying gaze upon her and held out his hand. Fearing he'd grab her leather purse and find the cellphones, she quickly dug the rental car keys out of her purse.

He took them, but his terrifying eyes remained fixed on hers. "How did you get this car?"

"I called a rental car agency. They came and picked us up."

This further enraged him. "You had them come *here?*" He turned to Catarina and said in Italian, "Idiot! Have you no brains in that pretty blond head of yours?"

She felt a tiny hand slip into hers. Bianca stood beside her, near tears, her chest heaving. She squeezed Bianca's hand and shook her head. *Don't cry now. It will only make Orazio madder.*

Turning back to her, Orazio said, "Give me your credit card."

A bolt of anger overcame her fear. Damned if she'd give him her credit card. "No. I use my own money to buy things for Bianca. Before we came here, you said we would discuss my salary, but we didn't. You give me no money. What am I supposed to do?"

Orazio frowned and stepped closer, looming over her now.

Her palms dampened with sweat and her heart slammed her chest. Every instinct told her not to challenge this man, but she refused to let him browbeat her into submission. "Christmas is next week. I want to buy presents for my parents. I need the credit card to pay for them."

A muscle worked in his jaw and his dark eyes were hard and angry.

Footsteps thumped on the stairs and Tommy entered the dining room. "What is this?" he said, gesturing at the shopping bags.

"Your idiot wife went shopping," Orazio snarled in Italian.

Savvy enough to see that Orazio was furious, Tommy said nothing.

Orazio vented his fury on her. "Do not leave this house without my permission. When we finish our business here, you will get your salary, more than enough to buy Christmas presents." He took out a leather billfold, extracted two fifty-dollar bills and gave them to her. "Use this to pay for whatever the kid needs." His dark eyes bored into her. "If you need to go somewhere, tell me and I will drive you. If you have a headache and need to buy aspirin, tell me and I will take you to a drug-store. Understand?"

In other words, she was his prisoner. "Yes."

"If I am not here, you will wait until I *am* here, understand?"

"Yes," she said. *But you can't make me stay here, if you're not around.*

Orazio said to Tommy, "Help your wife take her packages to your room. Then meet me in the garage." His evil eyes returned to her. "Take the kid upstairs and wash her face. There is chocolate on her chin. From now on someone will guard the door to make sure you do not leave the house without my permission."

Her heart sank like a stone. She had to get away from this evil monster, but how? Not with security cameras outside, no lock on her bedroom door, Orazio in the room beside her, and a guard posted at the front door.

CHAPTER 22

Orazio strode down the hall, his fists clenched, unable to remember the last time he had been so angry. These foolish women would be the death of him. When he entered the kitchen, one of the maids was tending to something on the stove, the woman Tommy had flirted with yesterday. She turned and smiled at him.

"Hello, Mr. Antonetti, can I get you something?"

An attractive woman, big breasts and an ass big enough to grab with both hands. The look in her eyes told him she would be willing to earn a little extra money in the sack. But he had too much on his mind right now. Ask Silvano to have some soldiers guard the house. Make sure Angelo finished his work on the uncut diamonds quickly. Find a suitable property and complete the real estate deal.

"Not right now," he said, in Italian he realized. Sometimes when he was deep in thought, he reverted to his native tongue. "Sorry. I forgot that I am not in Venice. You are most kind to ask if I need anything. I don't, but there will be an extra person to feed at mealtimes. One of Silvano's men will be staying here." *Provided Silvano agreed to this.*

She rolled her shoulders in a sexy shrug. "No problem, sir. I'll see that there's plenty of food."

"Thank you. Excuse me, I must make a phone call." He opened the door to the right of the kitchen counter and stepped into the garage. Standing beside the open door of the laundry room, he took out his cellphone, planning what he would say.

Silvano answered immediately. "Orazio, how are you? You have made arrangements for Angelo to cut the diamonds?"

"Yes. I spoke with him an hour ago." He assumed Silvano already knew this. Angelo, the fagosa, would have called and told him.

"Excellent," Silvano said. "What about the list of homes I gave you?"

"I have not had time to choose one." He paused. "You have been so helpful, I am reluctant to ask for another favor."

"Nonsense. What do you need?"

"Tommy's wife and the nanny rented a car and went shopping. I do not want them driving around unsupervised. Tommy will return the rental car, but I am not always here to make sure they stay in the house. Would it be too much trouble to ask one of your men to stay here?"

"Not at all. I will send one immediately. You need to be free to conduct your business. I will have two more men work with him. Eight hour shifts should do it."

"Thank you, Silvano. I will see that they are well fed."

He closed his cellphone as Tommy stepped into the garage, frowning at him, saying in Italian, "What's the big deal? Catarina went shopping. So what?"

"What if they got into an accident? Did you think about that? What if the police stopped them for some traffic violation? What if the cop saw the kid and recognized her?"

Tommy folded his arms across his chest, glaring at him. "What if someone plants a bomb in the French Quarter and blows up a building? You worry too much, Orazio."

He stepped closer, looming over his brother. "I worry because you are incapable of thinking two moves ahead. You think with your dick and give your wife whatever she wants."

"She got the jewelry into the country, didn't she? The swag The Boss don't know about."

"Be quiet," he snapped. Leaning closer, he whispered, "You don't think that The Boss might have bugs in here?"

Tommy's eyes widened. He looked around the garage, then at the laundry room.

Orazio held out the keys to the rental car. "Have Catarina drive the Honda back to the rental agency. Follow her in the SUV, but *you* make the return. Get a copy of the rental contract. I want to see it. On the way home, talk to this frivolous wife of yours. Make her understand that we are not here for shopping. We have serious business to conduct."

Clearly angry, Tommy snatched the keys and went in the kitchen.

Orazio mopped his brow with a handkerchief. The weather in Venice was pleasant this time of year, unlike New Orleans which was hot and humid. But in a few days he would complete their business. Then he could fly back to Venice, relax in his palazzo and enjoy the holidays. His favorite whore would come to see him on Christmas Eve.

His cellphone rang. He studied the Caller ID. His trusted soldier in Venice. Speaking Italian, he said, "What is it?"

"I have news. According to the newspaper and TV reports, Dominic Ruffino died yesterday."

"You are certain of this?"

"Positive. The wife of one of our soldiers works at the hospital."

"Excellent. Thank you for letting me know."

He ended the call and smiled. Dominic would not be talking to the polizia now, nor would Sophia.

Before he left New Orleans, he would get rid of the kid and the insolent nanny, too. Then no one would talk about anything.

———

7:45 PM

"You did it again," Kelly said, setting aside her dinner plate. "Great swordfish, Frank."

He saluted her with his wineglass and drank some of the Pinot Grigio he'd brought. "Does that mean I'm forgiven for standing you up last night?"

She frowned, pretending to debate the issue. "I guess. But don't let it happen again. I can't believe Natalie Brixton is here in New Orleans. What's this guy Conti like?"

"Hollywood handsome and self-important. He expected me to help him do surveillance on the mob house. But he's after the 'Netti brothers, not Natalie."

Kelly raised an eyebrow. "What's the matter, Frank? Jealous?"

Irritated, he said, "What's that supposed to mean?"

"He slept with her. You didn't."

"So? I'm not interested in sleeping with her. I want to arrest her."

"Why didn't you?"

"In the Clearview Mall food court surrounded by a mob of Christmas shoppers?"

Maybe he shouldn't have told her about seeing Natalie today. Better to focus on the real problem. Kelly's Glock was on the table beside her plate. When he arrived at six, she'd told him he'd have to leave by midnight. She was going hunting for King Rock.

Not if he could help it.

He went to the counter, brought the bottle of Pinot Grigio to the table and added a splash to both of their glasses. "Besides," he said, "the Ruffino girl was with her."

"The five year old?" Kelly said. "And now she's an orphan?"

"Yes, unfortunately. Conti broke the news to Natalie this afternoon." He paused and gulped some wine. "To tell the truth, she surprised me.

She seemed protective of the girl, like she was worried about her. I am, too."

Kelly sipped her wine and stared into space. "A while ago I told you I never intended to have kids. I've never regretted it, but that doesn't mean it doesn't hurt when thugs turn little kids into orphans. Right now Jacques is in foster care. Angelica's grandmother wants custody, but it's complicated, legally. King Rock shot Angelica, but his name is on the birth certificate." She flashed a sardonic smile. "So the killer has to sign off on it. Want to call King Rock and ask him to do it?"

"That sucks. I don't like it any better than you do, but I don't want you out gunning for him by yourself. It's too dangerous."

But she paid no attention, working up a head of steam. "People read about a murder in the paper, think how terrible it was and move on. But it's different when you know the victim. The media raised hell about Angelique for a week and moved on to the next big thing. I saw what it did to her son. Her asshole husband shot her nine days ago, but you don't seem that hot to find him now that Natalie's here."

"Wrong. Natalie's not going anywhere. Conti has people watching the house."

"Yeah? Who?"

"Off-duty NOPD cops. Conti's paying them. Tony Caruso set it up. He's a good friend. He'll tell me if she leaves the house. But King Rock is my top priority." *As long as Natalie didn't try to escape.*

"Why don't we pay some off-duty cops to hunt for King Rock?"

"You know why. Vobitch would do it in a heartbeat, but it's not in the budget. He wants King Rock as bad as you do."

"No he doesn't. Angelique wasn't his client. She trusted me and now she's dead."

The department shrinks advised homicide cops to keep their distance. Don't take it personally. Don't get emotionally involved. He'd never been good at that. He lived the job. And so did Kelly.

"It wasn't your fault, Kelly. Stop guilt-tripping yourself. Her scumbag husband shot her."

Kelly set her jaw, an expression he knew all too well. When she made up her mind to do something, nothing could stop her. But he didn't want to lose her, didn't want her shot by some gangbanger. "Have you been to see Ben Washburn's widow lately?"

Her expression morphed into a stricken, guilty look. Two years ago, Ben Washburn had been her partner. Now he was dead.

"I haven't forgotten the night you and Ben got shot. I sat by your hospital bed for hours after you came out of surgery, afraid you weren't going to make it. I was the one who called your father in Chicago. Not a pleasant experience. I don't want to have to call him again."

She gazed at him, her eyes filming with tears.

He left his chair and pulled her to her feet. "We're both tired, too tired to hunt for a killer. Tomorrow I'm going to see Kenyon. Then I'm going to Iberville to thank the nurse who saved his life. Then I'm going to hunt for King Rock. Believe it or not, I care about Angelica's boy, too."

Kelly wrapped her arms around him and whispered, "I believe you, Frank. Let's go to bed."

A great weight lifted from his shoulders. After all the tension and emotional agita of the past week, he wanted to take her in his arms and make love to her, wanted to feel the warmth of her bare skin against his.

But Kelly had suffered as much as he had, maybe more. She needed comforting, too.

He kissed her deeply, a long lingering kiss, and felt her respond which turned him on even more. He didn't waste time taking off her clothes. He'd do that as soon as he got her in the bedroom.

CHAPTER 23

SUNDAY December 19 – 8:35 AM

Frank parked his car on Basin Street and walked into the Iberville project with a big bouquet of red roses. Twenty yards away, two matronly black women approached him, dressed in their Sunday finery and flowery wide-brimmed hats. He assumed they were going to church.

Other than funerals, he hadn't been to church in years. The son of Sicilian immigrants, Judge Salvatore Renzi still attended Mass every Sunday at a Catholic church in Swampscott, Massachusetts, where Frank had grown up. Six days from now his father would be there on Christmas.

After his mother died, he made an effort to spend the holiday with his father, but he'd had no time to make travel plans or do any shopping. Kelly was flying to Chicago to visit her father and her extended family. Last night in bed when he asked what she wanted for Christmas, she'd said, "King Rock."

"Good morning," said the shorter woman, beaming at him. "Those roses are beautiful!"

Smiling at her, he said, "Not as beautiful as your hats!" Which got him two appreciative smiles.

A minute later he entered the building where Angelique had once lived. The foyer still smelled of urine and stale cigarette smoke. He checked the directory. E. Hughes lived in apartment 101 on the first floor. He went to the door opposite the mailboxes and tapped on it.

After a moment he heard two locks click. A chain rattled and the door opened. Dressed in slacks and a paisley-print blouse, Ella Hughes said, "Hello Detective Renzi. What brings you here on a Sunday morning?"

He held out the bouquet of roses. "I just came from Kenyon Miller's house. Kenyon and his wife asked me to bring you these."

Her thin face lit up in a smile as she took the roses. "How nice. Come in and tell me how he's doing."

Her living room was neat and tidy, but barely large enough to hold a leopard-print sofa and two matching chairs grouped around a low ebony-wood table. "Sit down while I put these beautiful roses in a vase."

He perched on the sofa and studied the magazines on the table: *Ebony, Newsweek,* and *Nursing News.* Opposite him, a television on a TV stand was dark and silent. Golden-rod yellow drapes were open to let in the morning sun, but iron bars protected the window, a testament to the high crime rate in New Orleans' pubic housing projects.

Ella returned with a vase full of red roses and set it on a table by the window. He tried to estimate her age. Mid-fifties, maybe? Nary a wrinkle on her smooth dark skin, but her close-cropped dark hair was flecked with gray.

"Can I get you anything?" she asked. "Coffee? Bottled water?"

"No, thanks." He took an envelope out of the inside pocket of his sports jacket. "Kenyon's wife asked me to give you this."

Ella sat beside him on the sofa, opened the envelope and smiled. "What a beautiful family! And such a thoughtful note." She handed him the card. On the front was a photograph of Kenyon, Tanya and their two kids, taken for their Christmas card probably. Inside, a handwritten note said: *Thank you so much Ms Ella. You saved Kenyon's life. We're so happy to have him home with us. He's getting better every day. We'd like to have you come for dinner sometime soon so we can thank you in person. Love, Tanya.*

'Nice," he said. "I'd take advantage of the offer if I were you. Tanya's a great cook."

"You seem rather fond of them, Kenyon especially."

"I am. Kenyon's a great guy. When I came here in 2001, he showed me the ropes. You know how it is. New job, new people, new rules." He grinned. "Some of which have to be broken."

With a faint smile, Ella said, "Sounds like my profession. Too many rules and regulations."

"I wanted to thank you, too. Seeing Kenyon lying there in all that blood threw me for a loop. If you hadn't come out and helped—"

"The blood scared you."

He fingered the decades-old scar on his chin, a reminder of an injury he'd suffered as a kid. The goriest crime scenes didn't faze him, mangled bodies with terrible injuries, blood spatter everywhere. But seeing his own blood—or the blood of someone he cared about—freaked him out.

"Years ago when I was in nursing school," Ella said, "it wasn't the women who fainted at the sight of blood, it was the men. Not that there were many of them." She raised an eyebrow. "Given your profession, avoiding blood must be difficult, being a homicide detective and all."

He decided not to tell her about the cause of his phobia, if that's what it was. Never complain, never explain. "Some people tell me I'm addicted to risky behavior."

His ex-wife had put it far more bluntly. *You love taking chances, Frank. If there's a dangerous assignment, you're the first one to volunteer.*

"It's risky being a police in this town that's for sure," Ella said. "All these thugs with guns. Angelique was such a sweetheart. I don't know why she got mixed up with King Rock."

"Kelly O'Neil tried to get her away from him. She works in the Domestic Violence unit. But Angelique wouldn't leave."

"With predictable consequences. What happened to Jacques?"

Another topic he'd prefer to avoid. One that wouldn't go away. Last night after they made love, Kelly had told him what the psychologist at social services had said. No matter what she did to get the boy to speak, Jacques said nothing, just stared at her, hugging a stuffed toy.

"He's in foster care. Angelique's grandmother wants to take custody of him, but ..." He puffed his cheeks. "You're not gonna believe this, but King Rock has to sign off on it because he's listed as the father on the birth certificate."

Ella stared at him, clearly outraged. "That's ridiculous. The boy should be with his family! If ever a rule was made to be broken ..."

"I agree. But the folks at social services stick to the rules. A week ago, we nabbed King Rock's driver, took him to the station and grilled him. But he wouldn't tell us where King Rock was."

"And now he's dead. I read about it in the *Times-Picayune*."

"Correct. Now he's dead." And it still bothered him. He should have done more to protect the kid. "I figure King Rock ordered the hit to keep him quiet."

"Sounds about right to me. He's a heartless bastard. I saw him this morning."

Shocked, Frank stared at her. "You did? Where?"

Ella gestured at the window. "Looked out my front window and there he was, sauntering past the building, bold as brass."

"How long ago was this?"

"A half hour, forty-five minutes ago."

He left the sofa and headed for the door. "Thanks for the tip, Ella. I'm going to cruise the neighborhood and see if I spot him."

"Try the B-n-L crash pad," she said. "Word around here is, he's got himself a new girlfriend."

———

9:15 AM

The breakfast choices were bountiful: two kinds of muffins, waffles, bacon and scrambled eggs. Natalie forced down half of a cranberry muffin. Orazio had already left the house. Tomasso was upstairs, sulking, though there'd been no argument today. Bianca had tried a bite of Catarina's waffle. Now both of them were happily devouring waffles drenched with maple syrup.

Which left her free to leave the table. She got up and headed for the kitchen. This morning when she checked her iPhone, she'd found a text from Pak Lam. He had obtained new documents to facilitate her escape and express mailed them to his New Orleans contact. How soon could she meet him? Good question. Leaving of the house would be difficult.

She had texted a short reply: *Complications here. Text you later.* Orazio had made good on his threat. A grim-faced thug had arrived and sat on a padded folding chair beside the foyer to guard the front door. Later, another one had taken his place.

When she entered the kitchen, a young woman with short dark hair stood at the counter making a fresh pot of coffee.

"Hi," she said. "I'm Laura, Bianca's nanny, and I've got a question."

Smiling at her, the woman said, "Nice to meet you. I'm Annmarie. What do you need?"

"I want to wash a few clothes. Is there a laundry room?"

"Yes, in the garage. After I get the coffee going I'll show you."

"You must get here early to make breakfast. Homemade muffins and waffles, scrambled eggs and bacon. Everything is delicious."

"Hey, it's a job, you know? It pays good and I'm done at three." Annmarie poured a carafe of water into the coffeemaker and turned it on. Moving to the right-hand end of the kitchen counter, she opened the door that faced it. "The laundry room is out here."

Natalie followed her into the garage, inhaling the odor of gasoline and grass clippings. Both bays were vacant. The guards parked in the driveway. When she and Bianca came down for breakfast, the hulking guard who had arrived last night was gone, replaced by another one, smaller but no less threatening. If she was going to sneak out of the house to meet Pak Lam's contact, it wouldn't be through the front door.

Annmarie walked past two green trash bins, opened a door and flipped a switch. Fluorescent lights illuminated a small windowless room. Two washers and two dryers lined the back wall. Above them, a shelf held jumbo-sized containers of liquid detergent and smaller jugs of fabric softener. Annmarie put her hand on a top-loading machine. "This is the big washer. We use it for sheets and towels. The other one is smaller. Much better for clothes."

"Perfect," she said. But washing clothes wasn't her main goal. "I don't put all my clothes in the dryer. Is there something I could use to hang a few things in my room?"

Annmarie laughed. "I hear you on that one. Put your best top in the dryer, it comes out fit for a ten-year-old, and bras? Forget it. The elastic is shot in two weeks."

She opened a cabinet and took out a package of white plastic clothes-line. "You can use this. Wait." She turned and took out a package of plastic clothespins. "You'll need these, too."

"Thank you so much. You're a lifesaver." In more ways than one.

"No problem. After I put out the fresh coffee, I'm going to Wal-green's. Need anything?"

She wanted to kiss her. "Could you get me a manicure set with a metal nail file? And a plastic wedge to keep the bathroom door open?"

Or the bedroom door shut, to keep Orazio out.

"No problem," Annmarie said. "You can pay me when I get back."

"What are you doing in here?" demanded a raspy male voice.

Her heart jolted. It wasn't Orazio or Tommy. She knew their voices.

When she turned, the guard stood in the doorway, frowning at her. He was not a large man, but his pale blue eyes were colder than an Arc-tic iceberg.

Annmarie flashed a saucy smile. "Geez, Nicky, give us a break. We're just talking girl talk. I made a fresh pot of coffee. Want some?"

Natalie said nothing, her heart beating her chest so hard she could almost hear it.

Ignoring Annmarie, Nicky glowered at her. "Makes me nervous, you disappear like that. Mr. Antonetti don't want you going nowhere."

"She's not going anywhere," Annmarie said. "I'm showing her how to run the washer."

Nicky silently glared at her for several seconds, then turned and went back in the kitchen.

"What's up with these guys?" Annmarie said. "Gotta keep you on a leash like you're their pet poodle or something?"

Natalie shrugged. "Insecure people will do you in every time."

Annmarie laughed. "You got that right. Speaking of which, did this guy Tomasso ever put a move on you? Whenever I'm around him, he stands too close, you know? Like he wants to jump me."

She hesitated, then said, "That's why I want the metal nail file."

Annmarie's eyes widened. Then she threw back her head and laughed, her eyes full of mischief. "Good idea. Maybe I'll get one for myself."

She laughed too. But it wasn't Tomasso she was worried about.

CHAPTER 24

9:10 AM

Focused like a laser beam, Frank stared through the windshield of his Dodge Charger. For nine days King Rock had eluded him. Now, on this bright sunny morning, he was going to get him. No telling where he'd been hiding, but Ella Hughes had seen him at Iberville an hour ago.

He'd already gone past the intersection of Basin and Lafitte where the B-n-L gang sold drugs. It was warm for December, shirtsleeve weather, but no bangers in baggy pants and hoodies lurked on the corner, no strung-out junkies looking to buy drugs this early on a Sunday.

Now he was three blocks away from the B-n-L dealers, parked left wheels to the curb on a narrow one-way street. The B-n-L crash pad was ahead of him, mid-block on the other side of the road, a first floor apartment in a red-brick row-house where gang members screwed girls they didn't want their steady gal-pals knowing about. The street was deserted, the sidewalk lined with trees, their skeletal branches devoid of leaves. Now and then a chirping sparrow landed on one, then flew off.

Assorted cars lined both sides of the street, most of them unwashed older models, but thirty yards away on the opposite side, headed away from him, was a shiny black Mercedes SUV. Waxed and polished with dark tinted windows and slick hubcaps, it seemed out of place. He didn't know if it was the SUV David had seen speeding away from Iberville after the murder, but he hoped it was.

No lights visible in the crash pad. The shade on the window beside the front door was drawn, like most of the windows along the street, people sleeping in after a night of partying probably. Only one car had passed him since he had arrived, no church-goers in this neighborhood apparently.

He flipped down the visor to deflect the glare of the sun and drank some bottled water. Kelly was probably eating breakfast and reading the newspaper. Waiting for a phone call from him. It had taken all his powers of persuasion to convince her not to come to Iberville with him.

The door of the crash pad opened. His heart sped up, rat-a-tat-tatting inside his chest like a snare drum roll. Who would come out the door? King Rock, he hoped. He had no interest in some low-level banger.

And his wish came true. King Rock appeared. But he had a girl with him, his new girlfriend, Frank assumed. Bad news.

He was certain King Rock was armed and he didn't want to get into a shootout that involved an innocent bystander. Wearing platform shoes, the girl pranced down the cement steps in her white hot-pants and red halter top like she didn't have a care in the world, big smile on her face, grooming her Afro-styled hair. She was curvy but petite, looked about twelve though she was probably fifteen at least. King Rock knew enough not to be banging jail-bait.

The gang leader had on designer jeans with silver studs along the seams and a loose jacket over a white shirt open at the throat. But no shades to complete the rap-star look. Tense and wary with no muscle to protect him, he wanted 20-20 vision, eyeballing both sides of the street.

Frank slid lower in the seat, tugged the brim of his Saints cap lower and kept his eyes on the romantic duo. The girl stopped on the sidewalk, said something and laughed, gazing up at her man.

King Rock didn't crack a smile, all business now, took her hand and led her down the sidewalk to the shiny black SUV with the tinted windows parked just beyond a fire hydrant.

Now that they were only thirty yards away he could see her better, crimson lipstick, thick mascara and sparkly eye-shadow, her fingernails painted a gaudy shade of purple.

King Rock opened the door and the girl climbed into the passenger seat. Frank heard the door slam and breathed a sigh of relief. Get the girl out of the way, he could take down King Rock without having to worry about a hostage situation or stray bullets hitting the girl.

He eased open his door, in a zone of concentration now, adrenaline pumping, heart pounding, aware of the bright blue sky, the chirping of birds, the glare of the sunlight, and most of all, the hands of his target.

He watched King Rock circle the hood of the SUV.

The instant he reached the driver's door, Frank pushed open his door, got out and stood in the V of the open car door. Gripping the SIG in both hands, he drew a bead on the scumbag. "Police!" he yelled. "Stay where you are and put your hands on your head!"

Time seemed to stop, each movement etched in tiny increments like a freeze frame.

King Rock's head jerked up. His hand went inside his jacket. Came out holding a gun. It was huge, dull-black and deadly, looked like a Desert Eagle .50 caliber or a .357 maybe.

Either way, it was a killer. One slug would put anyone down.

King Rock didn't look like half of a romantic duo now. He looked like a stone-cold killer, gripping his weapon, his finger on the trigger.

Bam, bam, bam. Three shots in quick succession, the reports reverberating off the row-houses along the street. Spent brass casings spewed onto the pavement, clinking in the silence.

Frank shut the car door and crouched beside the left front tire.

"Police! Drop the gun!"

Bam. A slug hit the grill of his Dodge Charger with a dull thunk.

He scrambled forward to the rusted-out orange Chevy ahead of him.

"Put the gun down or I'll shoot!"

A barrage of shots came at him. One, two, three. Seven rounds gone, but how many were left? Most Desert Eagles had 9-round magazines, plus a round in the chamber.

He crept between the front bumper of the Chevy and the back bumper of the Jeep 4x4 ahead of it. An eerie silence settled over the street. No shots, no voices, no peeps from the sparrows.

His chest felt tight and his shirt clung to his back, clammy with sweat.

He peeked around the bumper. His heart slammed his chest.

King Rock was twenty feet away, walking toward him, his eyes glittery with rage. Like a marksman at a shooting range, he held the killer gun in both hands, pointed in his direction.

When facing an armed suspect, police are trained to aim for the center of mass and shoot to kill. But he didn't want to kill the bastard. One shot and King Rock's life would be over. That would be too easy. He wanted the bastard to stand trial for his evil deed, killing the mother of his son while the boy was watching.

Frank took careful aim, squeezed the trigger and the SIG kicked in his hands. King Rock spun around, clutching his leg with one hand. But he held onto the gun. "Motherfucker!" *Bam, bam.* Nine rounds gone.

He ran forward to the next car, crouched beside the hood and took a quick peek. King Rock was ten feet away, sprawled on the pavement, propped up on one elbow.

"Give it up, Rufus. Drop the gun!" Damned if he'd use the asshole's street name. Kelly was right. Rufus Barrett was no king. He was a killer without a conscience.

"Fuck you, asshole!"

Bam. Only one shot this time. Was it his last?

Aware of how lucky he was, Frank became aware of sounds, windows opening and distant voices. But no sirens. He'd been in such a hurry to find King Rock he hadn't put on his Kevlar vest. He should have called for backup. Too late now.

He eased around the car, playing Russian Roulette now. Holding the Desert Eagle in his right hand, King Rock aimed it at him, his lips drawn back in a snarl. "Come on, motherfucker. Make my day."

Maybe the gun was empty. And maybe it wasn't.

Frank took careful aim and shot him in the right shoulder. If Kelly had been here, she'd have shot him in the heart. But he wanted to take the bastard alive. Then every gangbanger in town would know what a coward he was, shooting an unarmed woman, the mother of his son.

Screaming obscenities, King Rock dropped the gun.

Ignoring the epithets, he walked closer and kicked the Desert Eagle away. It skittered across the pavement, hit the tire of a blue Honda and stopped. King Rock's thigh was pumping blood through a ragged hole in his fancy jeans. More blood seeped through another hole in his jacket.

A male voice yelled, "What's goin' on out there?"

"Police," Frank shouted. "Stay inside and stay safe."

"Motherfucker!" screamed a voice. "Why did you shoot him? He didn't do nothing to you."

His heart jolted. Jesus, he'd forgotten about the girl! She wasn't in the SUV, she was standing behind it, tears and mascara running down her cheeks. She held a Glock 9mm in her hand, her purple fingernails a stark contrast to the black Glock. One of those fingers was on the trigger.

His heart slammed his chest. Jesus, how could she miss? She was five feet away. Dry-mouthed, he gathered some spit and said, "Put the gun down. I'm not going to hurt you."

"Shoot the motherfucker!" King Rock screamed.

He saw the muzzle flash before he heard the shot. Fortunately, the girl was no sharpshooter. She was holding the Glock in one hand. The kick jerked her arm and the shot went wild.

Cursing his stupidity, he gripped his SIG. He should have worn the vest. Should have called for backup. Off in the distance he heard sirens. A squad car, he hoped. Would they get here in time? He didn't want to kill the girl. But if she shot at him again, he might not be so lucky.

———

9:45 AM

Natalie raised the Venetian blinds on the front window, and sunlight spilled onto the floor, brightening the room. Across the street, a well-dressed couple and two small children were getting into their car.

Unlike her, they were free to come and go as they pleased. She was trapped in a house with two ruthless mobsters and men with hard eyes guarding the door. She had to get out of here, but how?

Turning away from the window, she watched Bianca, kneeling on the floor beside the table in front of the television set, coloring Rudolph's nose. With a red crayon, not a black one. A minute ago she had sung "Rudolph the Red-nosed Reindeer" to her in English. Bianca had smiled and said in English, "I love that song!"

Now, waving her closer, Bianca pointed to Rudolph's nose and said proudly, "Red."

"Yes. A red nose." She smiled and touched her nose.

Bianca laughed and touched her nose too. "Red nose."

She pointed to Rudolph's flanks, took a brown crayon out of the box and said, "Brown."

"No." Bianca took out a blue crayon. "I like this one better."

"Use blue then. Rudolph will look beautiful." She wondered how many English words Bianca understood. Colors were harmless enough, but others might not be. She wanted to talk to Pak Lam and formulate an escape plan, but not in front of Bianca.

She sat on one of the easy chairs, took the iPhone out of her purse and composed a text.

New plan is good, but guard is posted at the door. She hit send.

"What are you doing?" Bianca said in Italian, pointing at the iPhone.

"Sending a note to my friend."

"That man at the store where I ate my ice cream?"

The words chilled her. Bianca was far too observant. To distract her, she said, "Let's go down and see if the wash is done." And find out if the guard who'd yelled at her was still here.

Bianca smiled. "Maybe that nice lady will be there."

She smiled, too. Annmarie was a very nice lady indeed. A half hour ago, Natalie had stuffed their dirty clothes into a pillowcase and took Bianca downstairs to the kitchen. Annmarie gave her the items she'd asked her to buy, Then she had treated Bianca to an orange Popsicle.

"Annmarie," she said. "Maybe she's still in the kitchen."

Bianca rushed to the door and opened it. She put the iPhone in her purse and followed.

When they got downstairs, Nicky, the guard with the icy blue eyes, was sitting on a folding chair, sipping from a mug of coffee. The back of his chair was against the wall beside the foyer, perfectly positioned to allow Nicky to watch the front door and the stairs.

She felt his eyes on her as she and Bianca went down the hall to the kitchen. If she was careful, the clothesline Annmarie had given her might get her out of the house to meet Pak Lam's contact tonight.

But what if it didn't? And that was only the first step. When she left for good, it would be at night. She didn't want to leave Bianca, but if she took the girl with her, they couldn't climb out the second-floor window. The only option would be to go through the front door or the garage.

Just thinking about this made her palms dampen with sweat.

First they would have to tiptoe past Orazio's room to the staircase. But the guard at the foot of the stairs would see them. Could she disable him with one of her TKD moves before he warned Orazio? Nicky was not a large man, but he was armed, like all the guards.

Could she drug his coffee to put him to sleep? Poison his food? Use a gun with a silencer to kill him? But that was wishful thinking.

She had no gun, no drugs, no poison.

And she didn't want to kill anyone.

No more killing. There had to be another way.

―――――

Frank focused on the girl's trembling hand, her finger inside the trigger guard of the Glock 9mm.

In life or death situations his senses became hyper-acute. The sour taste of fear. The damp of his sweaty shirt against his skin. The odor of frying bacon wafting through an open window. Faint sounds from a TV set. Distant sirens approaching but nowhere near close enough.

Ten seconds from now it could all be over.

The girl's eyes, large and dark and filmed with tears, were focused on him, no doubt about that. He studied her right hand.

Her forefinger tightened on the trigger. Situation critical.

"I'm not going to hurt you," he said quietly. "Put the gun on the ground."

"Don't listen to him!" King Rock screamed. "Shoot the fucker!"

Her lips trembled. "You shot my man. Why you do that?"

Why was she defending him? Didn't she know that he'd murdered Angelique, the mother of his son? How could she not? For days it had been the lead story on TV and front page news in the newspapers. But she was just a girl, too young to realize it could also happen to her, caught up in the excitement of having a rich and powerful drug lord pay attention to her. Did she think King Rock would protect her?

He had to talk her down, had to make her understand that King Rock only cared about himself.

"Stop worrying about your man and start worrying about yourself."

Her eyes darted around wildly. "You're gonna shoot me too. I know it! Fucking cops."

Behind him, he heard sirens, louder as they turned onto the street.

The girl heard them too. She turned her head to look. A fraction of an opening but it was all he needed. He leaped at her, grabbed her arm and ripped the Glock out of her hand.

"Noooo," she wailed. "Don't arrest me. I didn't do nothing!"

Waves of relief swept over him. He had the gun. She couldn't shoot him. Behind him, the sirens whooped and stopped. He turned and saw two uniformed officers get out of a squad car, weapons drawn.

Not good. If he didn't watch out, they'd shoot him. "I'm police!" he shouted. "Homicide Detective Frank Renzi! Don't shoot!"

"Let go of the girl! Keep your hands where we can see them."

He spread his hands, holding his SIG by the barrel in one, the Glock in the other. The uniforms, one black, one white, approached him warily.

"King Rock is over there on the ground, wounded," Frank said. "I disarmed him. His weapon is lying in the street beside the Honda. Do me a favor and cuff him."

"Holy shit!" said the white officer. "King Rock? You got him?"

He smiled as they lowered their weapons. "About time, don't you think?"

"Who's the girl?" said the black officer.

He turned and looked at her. Bent over the hood of the SUV with her face in her hands, she was sobbing as though her heart would break.

Better heartbroken than dead.

"King Rock's new girlfriend," he said. "An innocent bystander for the most part. She wanted to stand by her man. I convinced her not to."

CHAPTER 25

SUNDAY 1:45 PM

"Grande," Bianca said, pointing at the riverboat.

"Yes," Natalie said, smiling as Bianca danced around, her face flushed with excitement. "A very big boat."

Years ago her mother had taken her for a ride on the Natchez, but she'd forgotten how big it was, as long as five street cars end-to-end, with three huge decks stacked one above the other. Gleaming white railings topped with red paint lined each deck, and jutting off the stern was a huge red paddle wheel, powered by steam.

Earlier at lunch, when Catarina had complained about having nothing to do. Orazio surprised them. He had booked them on a two-hour riverboat cruise so they could see the sights along the Mississippi River.

Now they were standing in line behind dozens of other passengers waiting to board. Festive and smiling, Catarina had on a short-sleeved lavender dress and high heels. No diamond necklace or earrings today. Tommy was wearing a dark pinstriped suit and a white shirt, but no tie.

Orazio stood off to the side by himself. For the first time since she'd met him, he wasn't wearing a suit. Over black running pants, he wore a black sweatshirt with gold fleur-de-lis on the front. The outfit revealed his muscular arms and barrel chest. To the casual observer, he might be a tourist or a native, but she knew better. He was the vicious killer who'd murdered Bianca's mother. She couldn't wait to get away from him.

The temperature was in the sixties, but thick clouds blocked the sun, and the air felt cool. She had on her long-sleeved running suit, but Bianca had insisted on wearing her pink *Hello Kitty* shirt and her new white pants. When the boat steamed down the river, the wind would make the air feel much cooler.

A breeze brought the aroma of buttered popcorn from souvenir stalls near the ticket office. Perhaps they would have something to keep Bianca warm. Annoyed that she had to ask permission, she went to Orazio and gestured at the kiosks. "I want to buy a long-sleeved shirt for Bianca, and a hat to shade her from the sun."

Gazing at her with granite-hard eyes, he pursed his lips.

After a moment he pulled two twenties out of his pocket and said, "Okay. Buy me a hat, too."

"What size?"

With a faint smile, he said, "Large."

Of course. Your head is as big as your over-sized ego.

She jogged past the line of passengers behind them waiting to board and stopped at a kiosk that sold souvenirs, clothing and hats. She chose a Mickey Mouse sweatshirt for Bianca. At the hat stand, she picked out a Saints ballcap for Orazio, a white broad-brimmed straw hat for Bianca and a larger one for herself. It seemed unlikely that anyone on the Natchez would recognize her, but why take chances? Every police station in New Orleans had a wanted-poster with her photograph.

She took the items to the clerk and said, "Could you add a bottle of sun lotion, please?"

"Sure," the girl said. "That comes to sixty-eight dollars."

She used the twenties Orazio had given her and paid the rest with her own money. She put on her hat and tucked Bianca's hat under her arm. The clerk put Bianca's sweatshirt, the suntan lotion and the Saints cap in a plastic bag, and told her to have a nice day.

She returned to Bianca and gave her the hat.

"Beautiful!" Catarina exclaimed. "Put it on. You look bellissimo!"

Bianca smiled and said in English, "Thank you." To Natalie, she said, "White hat."

"Yes. White hat." Aware that Orazio was watching, she brought the Saints ball cap to him.

He put it on, tugged on the brim and said, "Very good. It goes with my shirt." When she turned to leave, he said, "No change?"

Irritated, she said, "No. I paid for my hat and the suntan lotion with my own money. It came to sixty-eight dollars. Would you like to see the receipt?"

His dark eyes hardened. "No. Laura, why must you always be so ..." He paused, groping for the English word he wanted. "Disagreeable."

Because I want to go away and never see you or your brother or John Conti again.

To placate him, she forced a smile. "Thank you for getting us out of the house. Bianca gets restless when she has to stay indoors."

When she returned to Bianca and Catarina, the calliope let out a raucous blast and honked a lively tune on its massive pipes. Bianca and Catarina held their hands over their ears. "So loud!" Catarina shouted.

Natalie knew why but didn't bother to explain to Catarina. When steamboats began ferrying passengers up and down the Mississippi after the Civil War, some of the boats had gambling parlors. To alert the gamblers that the boat was about to depart, the calliope belted out a tune that could be heard all over the city.

The line straggled forward and they boarded the boat. On the lower deck, wire-mesh chairs lined the rail. Eager to celebrate with a drink, Catarina and Tommy went to the lounge on the second deck. Orazio had disappeared. She was relieved not to be cooped up in the house, but she had the uneasy feeling that Orazio had his own reasons for taking them on the cruise.

She took Bianca's hand and led her to the stern to watch the paddle wheel. As they stood at the rail, the steam engines groaned to life. The enormous red wheel slowly began to turn, and water cascaded off the paddles. Bianca pointed at the water and said, "Canal?"

"No, it's a river. The Mississippi."

Bianca burst out laughing. "Mississippi, Mississippi, Mississippi," she said, jumping up and down in rhythm with the words, her dark eyes full of delight.

Seeing the happiness on her face lifted Natalie's spirits, calming the tense knot in her stomach. Forget Orazio and John Conti. Have fun and enjoy the day. In Italian she said, "When I was a little girl my mother took me for a ride on this boat."

"How old were you? Older than me?"

"A little bit older. I was six."

Bianca's expression grew solemn. "Before your mother died?"

"Yes. We had a great time." Unwilling to dwell on the past, she said, "It's cold with the wind blowing. Let's put on your Mickey Mouse sweatshirt."

She helped her put on the sweatshirt, but as Bianca watched the paddle wheel, Natalie's eyes misted with tears. Every October on the anniversary of her mother's death, she built a Vietnamese shrine in her bedroom: fresh flowers, scented candles and a small bowl of fresh fruit.

Vietnamese families put framed photographs of their ancestors in the shrine. All she had was a worn snapshot of her mother. She placed it in the shrine, lighted sticks of incense and spoke to the spirit gods. For many years she had vowed to avenge her mother's murder. She had, but it brought no comfort, just a bleak empty feeling.

And now the snapshot of her mother was gone. Conti had taken it.

"What's that?" Bianca asked, pointed at a little boy holding a box of popcorn.

"Popcorn," Natalie said. "Let's go inside and get some."

She took Bianca up to the second floor lounge. At the end of the bar a machine spewed popcorn into a large glass container. While Bianca watched this, fascinated, Natalie bought a big tub of popcorn.

"Popcorn," she said, and popped a piece in her mouth.

Bianca did the same. After a moment she smiled and said, "Pupcorn," mispronouncing the word. "I love pupcorn."

"Good," she said. "Let's go outside and eat it while we enjoy the sights."

Maybe Orazio was right. She should stop being angry and enjoy small pleasures while she could. Tomorrow would be a day fraught with peril. Avoid Orazio and the guards. Attract no attention. Keep Bianca amused, put her to bed at nine and hope she fell asleep quickly.

Her palms dampened with sweat. Then she had to climb out her bedroom window and meet Pak Lam's contact. Get what she needed, run back to the house and get back into her bedroom.

So many things could go wrong. Any one of them could be deadly.

———

Resting his forearms on the railing, Orazio stood on the second deck looking down at the nanny and the kid. They were easy to spot in their silly white hats, not that he needed to worry. They weren't going anywhere, nor were Tommy and Catarina, seated in the lounge by a window, enjoying their drinks and the view. With his four companions contained, he was free to roam.

No legitimate retail store would pay cash for stolen jewelry, especially without papers, but every large city had gangsters eager to fence stolen goods. He didn't trust the blacks to keep quiet. If Tick-Tock found out about the stolen jewelry, a serious breech of family protocol, he might have someone kill him.

However, given Silvano's assessment of Vietnamese gangs, Orazio figured they would have no contact with the Rotondo Family. After the sit-down, he had driven to Saigon Canteen, a Vietnamese restaurant at one end of a strip mall on Veterans Boulevard. To the left of the door, a dozen tables filled a small dining room. Behind a takeout counter on the right, a Vietnamese punk with hooded eyes greeted him. Orazio told him he had some fine jewelry; did he know someone who might buy it? The punk told him to wait and disappeared into a back room. When he returned, they set up a meet. He'd told the punk to meet him today on the riverboat, a neutral place where he couldn't be ambushed.

As the Natchez floated past Jackson Square, Orazio noticed a large cathedral with one tall spire flanked by two shorter ones. Impressive, but it did not compare to the cathedral in Venice, not that he ever attended Mass. He'd probably rot in Hell for his many sins. If there was a Hell.

Last year during his visit to New Orleans he had contemplated living here. Now, he just wanted to complete his business and fly back to Venice. He checked the time. 2:30. The punk was probably waiting for him, but as Father always said: For important negotiations, never arrive early. Keep your adversary waiting. Make him wonder.

Enjoying the cool breeze and fresh air, he strolled past the lounge and mounted the stairway to the top deck. The wind was stronger here, whipping the canvas of the canopy that sheltered passengers. Only a handful of people stood beneath it.

His adversary was waiting in the far corner, Nguyen "Killjoy" Ng, the son of the gangster who owned the Saigon Canteen. Orazio was familiar with the colloquialism: killjoy, one who spoils the pleasure of others. A relatively benign term, but with Vietnamese gangs, it had a more dire meaning. Killjoy Ng didn't spoil the pleasure of others, he killed them.

The punk gazed at him, expressionless, as Orazio approached him.

He was only a boy, no more than twenty and a midget compared to him, almost a foot shorter. His glossy black hair was cut short, and pock-marks disfigured the cinnamon-brown skin of his cheeks. But his almond-shaped eyes reflected his calling: Killer eyes, flat and without emotion, gazing at Orazio like he was no more important than a waiter.

He'd fix that.

"You are interested in diamond jewelry," Orazio said.

"Possibly. If it is of good quality."

"You have the authority to make the deal?"

Killjoy grew still, like a cobra contemplating its next meal. "Do not insult me. You want to fence some jewelry, or not?"

The insolent swine. "Answer the question. Do you have the authority to cut a deal, or not?"

"My father will pay no more than thirty-five cents on the dollar. And only if the diamonds are good quality."

"The quality is excellent. Enough to warrant fifty cents on the dollar."

"Not gonna happen. You want that much, sell them yourself." Killjoy smiled, displaying crooked teeth. "But you want to dump them fast. They are stolen, right? No papers."

Orazio considered. Yes, he wanted to sell them fast, and yes, they were stolen. But it galled him to take so little for such fine jewelry.

"Forty cents on the dollar or no deal. I have brought a sample."

He took a drawstring bag out of his pocket and showed him the three-string diamond necklace. Even in the faint sunlight, the diamonds glittered.

"Huh," Killjoy grunted. "A fine-looking necklace. But my father will examine it more closely."

He returned the necklace to the drawstring bag and put it in his pocket. "I have more items that are equally fine. In a store, they would sell for a million dollars."

"But you did not go to a store. You came to us. My father will make the final decision. After we get off this boat, bring the jewelry you wish to sell to Saigon Canteen."

"Your father will have cash ready for me?"

"Have no fear. My father will have plenty of cash."

"Good. I need time to get the rest of the jewelry. Tell your father I will see him at five o'clock."

"Fine," Killjoy said.

Orazio looked over the rail. Two decks below them, the nanny and the kid were sitting on deck chairs. The nanny had removed her hat and turned her face up to the sun.

"See that woman down there?" he said. "Is she Vietnamese?"

Killjoy leaned over the rail. After a moment, he said, "Looks like it to me, part Vietnamese anyway. She's a looker. You know her?"

"Tell your father I will be there at five o'clock," Orazio said, and walked away.

The insolent swine asked too many questions. But he had confirmed what Orazio had suspected. Laura claimed to be Chinese-American. She wasn't. She was Vietnamese. According to Silvano, the Vietnamese were a violent people. Vicious and untrustworthy.

He'd better make sure that she never left the house. For the next few days, the treacherous Vietnamese nanny, would be his prisoner. Even if he was there, he would tell the guards to watch her, day and night.

Soon he would fly back to Venice.

Laura and the kid would not.

CHAPTER 26

SUNDAY 5:00 PM

Driving west on Veterans Boulevard, Orazio slowed as he passed the Saigon Canteen. Lights blazed in the front windows and a half-dozen cars were parked outside.

"Where you go?" Tommy said in his fractured English. "That is the restaurant, there."

"I want to see who else is around."

He pulled into the parking lot at the other end of the strip-mall and drifted past the one-story, brick-front building. The auto parts store on the end was closed. Beside it an insurance office was also closed. No lights in the store selling eyeglass frames beside the restaurant. Good.

The Smith & Wesson .22 caliber revolver inside his jacket was small and easily concealed, but deadly at close range. If he had to use it, only the people in the restaurant would hear it.

He backed Silvano's SUV into the handicapped space near the door of the Saigon Canteen, nose out for a quick getaway. Speaking Italian to make sure Tommy understood, he said, "I do not trust these Vietnamese gangsters. Be ready. If I say *Go*, shoot them, understand?"

Grim-faced, Tommy said, "What if they shoot first?"

He locked eyes with his brother. "Do as I say. You hear me say 'Go!' shoot them immediately and shoot to kill. Our lives may depend on it."

"What about you?" Tommy said, as obstinate as ever. "Are you going to shoot?"

Orazio patted his jacket. "My weapon is here. Do not worry. I will shoot and I will not miss. But perhaps this will not be necessary. Be strong, Tommy. We go inside now."

He'd known all along that using a Vietnamese gang to fence the stolen jewelry involved certain risks. Silvano said they were more vicious than the blacks, and Silvano was seldom wrong in such matters.

But during his years as enforcer for the Antonetti Family, Orazio had become skilled in his assessment of people. Only twice had he been mistaken. His body still bore the scars, but he had learned from his mistakes. The men who'd crossed him had died in excruciating pain.

A deep calm settled over him as they left the SUV and approached the Saigon Canteen. He felt confident in his assessment of Killjoy. The punk was full of bluster, but when it came to life or death, he would be no match for Orazio Antonetti. Of this he was certain.

160

Tommy opened the door and Orazio stepped inside. The aroma of garlic and hot red peppers filled the air, and voices floated through the arched doorway of the dining room to his left. Beside the doorway, a huge fish tank in the foyer held brilliantly colored tropical fish languidly swimming in the water.

To his right, dressed in a white shirt and black trousers, Killjoy stood behind the take-out counter, his face expressing confidence and arrogant disdain. His eyes flicked to Tommy and back to Orazio. "Come in the back room. We do our business there."

"No," Orazio said. "Tell your father we do the deal out here. Your customers in the dining room will see and hear nothing. Unless, of course, you try to screw us."

Killjoy frowned. "Wait here. I will speak to my father." Moving to his right behind the counter, he went to a door in the rear wall. Orazio saw no sign of a weapon, no suspicious bulge under his shirt. Killjoy opened the door and disappeared.

Orazio said in Italian, "If they insist that we go in the back room, stay alert. Be ready to shoot."

Tommy took a Beretta M9 .22LR out of his jacket and held it against his right thigh, out of sight.

The door of the back room opened. Killjoy came out first, followed by his father and two other men, small in stature but with menacing eyes and aggressive postures. Both had semiautomatics in their hands.

The father, a small man with short gray hair, displayed no weapon, but his eyes were cold. "Not do business out here. Come in back so I can examine your jewelry."

Orazio knew what this meant. The gooks were going to screw them.

Or so they thought.

In Italian he said to Tommy, "Let us see what they say. I will be right behind you."

He waited as Tommy followed the father and the two armed men into the back room. Killjoy held the door open, waiting for him.

"Want to see the rest of the jewelry?" Orazio said. "I'm sure you will be impressed."

Relaxed and confident, Killjoy said, "Sure."

With a swiftness that belied his size, Orazio put a choke-hold on him with his left arm. The punk weighed no more than a flea, stinking of hair gel, gasping for air, flailing his arms and legs.

Clamping him against his chest so his feet could not touch the floor, Orazio muscled him through the door into the back room and assessed the scene with one glance. A refrigerator-freezer on one wall, cartons of canned food stacked against the others. To his left a table with butt-filled ashtrays stood near a door marked "Kitchen."

Ahead of him, the father stood beside the two armed men. No one else. Excellent. Three against two.

Ten feet to his right, Tommy raised his Beretta.

A sudden stillness came over the room.

The only sound came from Killjoy, gagging, clawing at his arm with both hands. Orazio tightened his grip, his left forearm pressed against the punk's throat.

The father stared at him, his eyes burning with hatred. The two armed men held their fire and looked to the father for guidance.

More gagging sounds from Killjoy as he clawed at Orazio's forearm.

In Italian, he murmured to Tommy, "Be ready."

To the father, he said in English, "You value your son's life?"

"Let him go or my men will kill you," the father said.

"Shoot me and your boy is dead. You made a mistake. You intended to take the jewelry and pay us nothing. This is what happens when you fuck with the 'Netti brothers."

He clenched his forearm tighter around Killjoy's throat. Using his free hand, he gripped the punk's head, gave a sharp twist and heard the punk's neck snap.

The father gasped and his face clenched in horror.

Orazio dropped Killjoy's lifeless body on the floor. Took out his weapon. Shouted, "Go!"

Tommy shot one armed man in the chest. Orazio shot the other in the head. "To the car!" he shouted in Italian. Tommy turned and ran.

Frozen in place, slack-jawed, the father raised his hands in surrender. Orazio shot him.

The door to the kitchen opened. A man in a soiled apron looked in the room and quickly shut the door. Orazio ran to the foyer and heard frightened voices in the dining room.

To keep the diners at bay, he fired two shots into the arched doorway. Chunks of plaster showered to the floor. Inside the fish tank, the tropical fish flitted to and fro, frightened by the loud reports.

He ran outside and jumped in the passenger seat of the SUV.

Tommy floored the accelerator and the SUV rocketed out of the parking lot. "Jesus Christ! I thought we were dead!"

"Slow down. You want the cops to stop us for speeding?"

"Mother of God, you're a cold one," Tommy said, easing off the accelerator. "I don't mind taking a risk now and then, but this was crazy. Kill three guys—"

"Four. I broke the punk's neck. Did you not see me?"

Tommy mopped sweat off his forehead. "What about the jewelry? How do we get rid of it?"

"Take it back to Venice, put it in my safe and let it sit there a while."

"But that means we gotta take it through customs again."

"Catarina got away with it in New York, she can do it here."

"She won't like it, I can tell you that."

"*Make* her like it," Orazio said. "If you don't, I will."

———

5:35 PM

Frank let the hot water in Kelly's shower beat on his body. It soothed the tense knots in his muscles, but questions buzzed in his mind like angry bees at a hive. The scariest one being: What if he'd shot the girl?

It had been an exhausting day. Capturing King Rock was only the beginning. Vobitch was thrilled when he called and told him King Rock was in custody, but he'd issued a stern warning. "When you get to the station, Internal Affairs will interview you and the video cameras will be running." Vobitch said he'd back him to the hilt—King Rock had shot first—but he didn't want any lingering questions about why Frank shot the fucker.

Before he went to the station he'd called Kelly, told her King Rock was in the lockup and said he'd give her the blow-by-blow after the IAD interview. The grueling interrogation lasted more than two hours, starting with his visit to Ella Hughes, his stakeout of the B-n-L crash pad, and the minute-by-minute details of what followed. After the interview, he called Kenyon. By then it was one o'clock. Kenyon wanted him to come over and tell him about it, so he'd called Kelly back and asked her to meet him at Kenyon's house.

Why tell the story twice? Already he was sick of dealing with it.

He shut off the water, got out of the shower and toweled off. He felt better now that he'd washed the sweat off his body, but now he had to deal with Kelly. She hadn't said much at Kenyon's house. The four of them sat around the kitchen table drinking beer while he described what happened. Lots of questions from Kenyon, none from Kelly. She knew better than to yell at him in front of Kenyon and Tanya, but he'd caught the angry vibes she gave off, knowing she was pissed.

Tanya had insisted they stay for dinner. Now it was time to face the music. But he didn't want to. He wanted to sleep for a week.

No, he wanted to make love to Kelly, then sleep for a week.

When he went in the living room, she was sitting on the sofa, sipping red wine. An empty wineglass stood beside a wine bottle on the coffee table. "Why didn't you call me after you got the tip?"

Let the shit-storm begin. He sank onto the couch, poured himself some wine and took a big swallow. "No time. I wanted to grab him fast."

"You had time to call me while you waited outside the crash pad."

"He could have come out any second."

"You didn't even call for backup!"

He locked eyes with her. "That's not why you're pissed. You think I should have killed him."

"Why didn't you? I would have."

"That's why I didn't call you. Think about it. You know what would have happened then? You'd be sitting in the station with IAD, trying to justify why you killed him."

"Frank, he shot at you! If I'd been there, the bastard would have tried to kill me, too!"

"You think an IAD interrogation is fun?" he snapped. "It isn't. I've been there, more than once. You haven't. I had to make a lot of quick decisions today. What happened, happened. I don't feel like arguing. I've got enough problems as it is. IAD took my SIG and I'll be riding a desk until they complete the investigation."

Kelly put her wineglass on the table and gave him a hug. "Okay, Frank. Truce. You got the bastard, that's what's important."

Mollified, he said, "Yes, it is. Now Angelique will get the justice she deserves."

Kelly picked up the TV remote and said, "Let's see if it made the six o'clock news."

His take-down of King Rock was the top story. Worse, they ran clips from the press conference leaders of the African-American community had held at five o'clock.

First up, King Rock's attorney, an older Caucasian man with ruddy cheeks and a wimpy mustache. "Homicide Detective Frank Renzi acted with reckless disregard for my client's life. Rufus Barrett, an innocent man, is lying in a hospital bed because Detective Renzi shot him twice. Meanwhile, the *real* criminal, who murdered the mother of my client's child, is still at large."

Frank clenched his jaw. A white cop had shot a black man, hadn't killed him, but no matter. Let's hang the cop from the nearest tree. Forget about King Rock murdering the mother of his son.

"You idiot!" Kelly screamed at the TV. "These gangs are the scourge of the city, selling dope and killing anybody who gets in their way." Turning to Frank, she said, "Doesn't he know that?"

He didn't bother to answer. Potshots from lawyers and reporters were nothing new to him. He'd been through it before when he worked for Boston PD. Resigned to it, he watched two black ministers and a black councilwoman condemn Frank Renzi for his despicable act.

They didn't want to hear his side of the story. The scumbag had shot at him, with a clear intent to kill. But these days, white cops who shot black men were pariahs.

"What about Angelique?" Kelly said. "Why don't they talk about the innocent victim, instead of defending her killer?"

King Rock's attorney took the microphone again. "An NOPD officer tried to circumvent the justice system by shooting my client. Homicide Detective Frank Renzi should be fired!"

Unable to stop himself, Frank shouted, "He tried to kill me, asshole!"

"... my client is not the first person of color Detective Renzi has shot. Six months ago he shot a young Vietnamese-American. Fortunately, the man survived."

"Jesus," Frank muttered. "The guy beat a ten-year-old boy to death with a baseball bat."

"Exactly," Kelly said. "And kidnapped the boy's mother and sister."

But the attorney saved his best shot for last. "Detective Renzi has a history of violence involving minorities. Ten years ago when he worked for the Boston police department, he shot and killed a young black girl." The lawyer shook his head. "She was only nine years old."

Frank sagged back against the couch, devastated by the cruelty of the statement. What the hell did this ambulance-chasing lawyer know? Had he ever faced a gangbanger with a gun?

Kelly said, "He's an asshole, Frank. Don't let him get to you."

Soon after they got involved, he'd told her about it, the bare bones, but not the details. Not that he still woke up at night, clammy with sweat, seeing nine-year-old Janelle Robinson's face. Not that it had been, other than the death of his mother, the most painful day of his life.

What followed was equally painful, an acrimonious divorce that had poisoned his relationship with his daughter and driven him out of Boston. But what the hell. Never complain. Never explain.

He gulped some wine as the feeding frenzy continued, reporters shouting questions at King Rock's lawyer, who never mentioned the girl. Of course not. That would make his client look bad, the mother of his son dead less than two weeks and he already had a new girlfriend.

Frank had a hard time believing that King Rock's lawyer thought he was innocent. In his experience, people could spin stories and rationalize to themselves, but most of the time, it came down to *What's in it for me?*

Cui bono? as Judge Salvatore Renzi often said in his courtroom. Who benefits? King Rock's attorney, for one. King Rock's murder trial would get reams of publicity and bring him more clients. The reporters, for an-other. After chasing the Angelique murder for a week, frustration had set in. Given a new angle, they flocked to it like flies to fresh blood.

He set his wineglass on the coffee table and rose to his feet. "I'm go-ing home."

Kelly gazed at him, somber-eyed. "You can sleep here, Frank. You know that."

"I doubt I'll be sleeping much tonight." Making love to Kelly would ease his pain, inhaling her intoxicating scent, hearing her throaty voice urging him on, feeling her bare skin beneath his hand.

But she deserved his full attention and she wouldn't get it tonight.

CHAPTER 27

MONDAY December 20 – 9:20 AM

"Christ on a crutch!" Vobitch said. "We take a vicious killer off the street and everybody's up in arms because you shot him."

Frank poured himself a cup of coffee and wearily sank onto the chair beside Vobitch's desk. Last night Vobitch had watched King Rock's lawyer spout off at the press conference, which infuriated him.

This morning at 8:00 AM Vobitch had held his own press conference. Frank stayed in the D-8 break room and watched it live on TV. Vobitch issued an emphatic statement of support. Homicide Detective Renzi had worked under his command for nine years and had always acted in a professional manner. But Sunday morning, when Detective Renzi tried to serve a warrant on Rufus Barrett, a convicted felon, Barrett pulled out a gun and shot at him. NOPD had since determined that Barrett's gun was unregistered and the serial numbers had been obliterated.

"Did you like the part when I said Divine intervention saved you?" Vobitch chortled. "I figured that would impress all the Catholics. The motherfucker shot at you, and the citizens of New Orleans are fortunate to have a detective who puts his life on the line to protect them from vi-olent criminals like Barrett." Vobitch flashed his evil smile. "I phrased it a little nicer, left out the F-bomb to make sure the TV stations and the fucking local rag would run it."

Despite his bad mood, Frank had to smile. Sometimes working for Vobitch could almost be entertaining. Almost. "But I still have to go through an Internal Affairs investigation."

"I wouldn't worry about it too much if I were you. Every cop in town knows the sonofabitch shot Kenyon." Vobitch paused to sip his coffee. "The Assistant Superintendent might give us grief though. He called me at home last night."

That sounded ominous. Wendell Hicks was African-American, eager to maintain a cordial relationship with the black ministers and city coun-cil members. "What did he say?"

Vobitch smiled. "Nothing. I saw his name on the Caller-ID and didn't pick up." His phone rang and the smile disappeared. "That's probably good old Wendell now." He picked up and barked, "Vobitch." Gazing at Frank, he listened, then held up his hand, fingers crossed. "My wife and I were at a concert last night."

Unwilling to hear the conversation, Frank took his coffee in the hall, leaned against the wall and massaged his temples, trying to ease a pounding headache. After he left Kelly last night, he'd gone home and sat in his condo, brooding over the shooting, rerunning it like a video. Freeze-frame: King Rock's girlfriend aiming a gun at him, her finger on the trigger. Thinking about it made him shudder. Thinking about how close he'd come to shooting her was worse. Thinking that if someone shot his daughter, he'd be devastated. Which had caused him to pick up the phone and call Maureen, who lived in Baltimore.

He sipped some coffee, replaying the conversation in his mind.

"Hey, Dad, great to hear from you. How are things in New Orleans?"

"Same old, same old. How are you doing? How's Jeremy?"

Maureen lived with her boyfriend. She was an orthopedic surgeon. Jeremy was a dentist. They worked long hours, but still found time for their mutual passion: their love of horses and show jumping. No hints of wedding bells yet. Fine by him. He was in no hurry to walk her down the aisle and give her away to someone else.

"Jeremy's great. We're about to hit the sack and get ready for another long week. This working for a living isn't all it's cracked up to be."

Enjoying her dry humor, he smiled. Maureen had green eyes and auburn hair like her mother, had inherited her lean and lanky physique from her dad. And his sense of humor.

"Mom's coming down to spend Christmas with us. What are you doing?"

"Probably fly to Boston and spend some time with your grandfather. I haven't booked the fight yet. At this late date it'll probably cost me an arm and a leg."

"Check Priceline and Expedia. You might get a good deal."

When it came to online shopping, his daughter was an expert. "Good idea. Tell Jeremy I said hello. I'll call you on Christmas."

"Okay, Dad. Love you."

"Love you too," he'd said and ended the call. But his emotional high from talking to Maureen hadn't lasted long. Dark thoughts intruded. Accusations of professional misconduct. King Rock's lawyer digging up his past. Devastating images of nine-year-old Janelle Robinson, dead on the floor in a dingy Boston apartment. Unable to sit still, he put on his running gear and went for a run beside the Mississippi. An hour later, hot and sweaty, he took a shower, walked over to Frenchman's street and hit the clubs. The music calmed him, but when he got home he still couldn't sleep, had tossed and turned until dawn.

He massaged his bleary eyes, heard Vobitch call to him. "Frank, I'm off the phone."

When he went back in the office, Vobitch was shuffling papers around his desk. A bad sign.

"Okay," Frank said. "Lay it on me. What's the bad news?"

Vobitch gazed at him, expressionless. "Wendell wants me to fire you, but I told him to put that idea where the sun don't shine. I told him IAD had taken your service weapon and you're restricted to desk duty until the IA board renders a verdict."

Frank said nothing. That could take weeks. He hated desk duty.

"Which will free you up to grab Natalie." Vobitch took a Glock 9mm out of his desk drawer, put it on the desk and gave him a stern look. "This is between you and me. If you need a weapon to arrest Natalie, use mine. Make us all happy for Christmas."

———

9:45 AM

Natalie stood beside the coffee table, watching Bianca use bright-colored crayons to color a big Christmas wreath with ornaments and bows. But Christmas was the last thing on her mind.

This morning Orazio had left the house before breakfast. When she heard the garage door open, she'd stood by the window and watched him drive away. Alone. Earlier she had received a text from Conti: *We need to set up another meet.* Hoping to stall him, she'd texted back: *Can't get out. Guard posted at the door.* Conti's reply: *Text you later.*

The bastard didn't care if Orazio killed her. He wanted information. Information she couldn't provide. Orazio never talked to Tommy when she was around. Worse, he kept watching her, stone-faced, his eyes hard and implacable. Yesterday after they got back from the steamboat ride, he and Tommy had driven off in the black SUV and had returned two hours later. She had no idea what they were doing.

There were too many things she didn't know.

At breakfast Catarina had complained to Tommy, "We better be home before Christmas." Tommy had given her a dirty look and said, "Don't worry. We'll be home for Christmas."

Her stomach cramped. She was surrounded by enemies. Orazio. Conti. Renzi. But her biggest enemy was time. Most people began their celebrations on Christmas Eve, which was five days away. That meant the 'Netti brothers would fly back to Venice by Thursday at the latest, three days from now, two if they left on Wednesday.

She had to get away from them. Soon.

"Can I wear my pretty new dress for dinner tonight?" Bianca asked, gazing at her with imploring eyes.

"Not tonight. In a couple of days maybe. Want to go down to the kitchen and visit Annmarie?"

Bianca set aside her crayons and beamed her a big smile. "Yes!"

Natalie grabbed her purse and they went downstairs. Nicky glared at her as they passed him, but said nothing. When they entered the kitchen, Bianca said, "Hello Annmarie!"

"Hello Laura, hello Bianca," Annmarie said, smiling at them.

"You have a new friend for life," Natalie said.

Annmarie laughed. "Want a Popsicle, Bianca?"

"Yes, please. I love Popsicles!"

Annmarie took a Popsicle out of the freezer, unwrapped it and set it on a paper plate on the counter. Then she hoisted Bianca onto a wooden stool, gave her some paper napkins and said, "Let the drips fall on the plate, not on your pretty pink shirt."

"You're very good with kids," Natalie said.

"I had to be. I took care of my younger brothers and sisters. Two of each. My mother was a devout Catholic, no birth control." Annmarie shook her head. "Not me. I'm stopping after two."

"My mother stopped after one," Natalie said. She didn't explain why.

"An only child? I can't imagine it." Annmarie cocked her head, smiling at her. "You remind me of the Vietnamese girl I see at the hairdresser's every week. A lot of Vietnamese families live in New Orleans. She's gorgeous and she has beautiful shiny-black hair like yours."

Taken aback, Natalie said nothing. She had told Orazio she was Chinese-American, to match the name on her passport. If Annmarie thought she looked Vietnamese, maybe Orazio did, too.

She forced a smile. "No, I am Chinese-American." To distract her, she pointed to a door on the wall opposite the garage. "What's in there?"

Annmarie rolled her eyes. "That's where The Boss takes his ..." She glanced at Bianca, who was gazing at them, sucking on her Popsicle. Annmarie mouthed *girlfriend*. "He keeps the door locked when he's not here with her watching porn flicks. I've only been in there once. I had to sub for the girl who cleans up after them. There's a bar with all kinds of liquor and two plush sofas facing a huge screen." Annmarie grinned. "Larger than life action. And the bathroom has a Jacuzzi. I can't imagine what they do in there."

"No door to get out?" Natalie said. "In case of a fire?"

"No. Not even a window."

"And no security cameras, I bet," she said, smiling to make it seem like she was joking, watching Annmarie to see how she would react.

"If there are, The Boss is the only one who sees what's on them."

"What about the security cameras on the outside of the house?"

"You spotted them, huh? They only turn them on when The Boss is here. He's paranoid about security, brings his goons with him when he comes here to get away from his wife."

"What's his name?" If she got a name, maybe she could get Conti off her back.

Annmarie frowned, her dark eyes wary. "Everyone who works here has to sign a confidentiality agreement saying they won't talk about anything. I don't think they're talking lawsuits, you know? More like broken legs. Or worse." She ran her fingers through her short dark hair, looking anxious. "I shouldn't be telling you this."

"Don't worry," she said. "I won't tell anyone."

"What is a goon?" Bianca asked in Italian, gazing at them, her Popsicle forgotten.

She glanced at Annmarie, who met her gaze with troubled eyes.

Natalie smiled at Bianca and said, "Like a goomba. Another name for a friend, but not as nice. How do you like your Popsicle?"

"Good," Bianca said, smiling happily. "Waffles are good, too."

Natalie heard footsteps in the hall. A chill skittered down her neck. "We better go back upstairs or Nicky will get mad."

Somber-eyed, Annmarie said, "If you're thinking about sneaking out some night to meet your boyfriend, be careful."

No flies on Annmarie. Why else would she ask about the locked room and the security cameras? Forcing a smile to hide her nervousness, she said, "I'm not going to sneak out of the house. My boyfriend lives in Boston." And realized Bianca was staring at her. No happy smile now.

Damn, she had to be careful. Bianca knew what *boyfriend* meant, had used it to refer to Conti and Renzi. Ridiculous, of course.

They weren't her boyfriends. Far from it.

But she was definitely going to sneak out of the house tonight. If Bianca figured out what "sneak out of the house" meant, that might complicate matters.

CHAPTER 28

9:35 AM

Frank put Vobitch's Glock in the bottom drawer of his desk, happy to have it, but in no hurry to use it. David and Orville were out working other cases. He was stuck in the office. But forget King Rock and his asshole lawyer and the IAD investigation. As Vobitch had correctly pointed out, now he could focus on Natalie.

Few days went by when she wasn't in his thoughts. Yesterday he'd been too stressed out to think about her. Now he could work on a plan to get her out of the mob house and arrest her.

He went to the stack of directories on the file cabinet in the corner and took the directory for Metairie back to his desk. He'd used it to find out who lived in the mob house, Alma Esposito, allegedly. Now he'd use it to make a list of residents who lived near the mobsters.

Conti was paying off-duty cops to watch the house, thinking they were only reporting to him. But Frank had given Natalie's photograph to Tony Coppola so he could post it in the surveillance van with a note to call Frank's cellphone immediately if she left the house.

She had, but he didn't find out about it until this morning. Yesterday at noon, Natalie, Bianca, Catarina and the 'Netti brothers had driven off in a black SUV and hadn't returned until four-thirty. The cop who left the message said he didn't know where they went. He got paid to watch the house, not to follow the mobsters.

Where did they go? Frank wondered Maybe they went sightseeing to break the monotony. Tour the French Quarter in a mule-drawn carriage instead of stealing diamonds and killing people.

His cellphone rang. He checked the ID. John Conti. Had he watched the Sunday night massacre on TV last night? Had he heard King Rock's lawyer dump sleazy accusations on Detective Frank Renzi? He was in no mood to deal with Conti, but why postpone the inevitable? If he didn't answer, Conti would keep calling.

He punched on and said, "Renzi."

"Frank, did you find us a surveillance house?"

He didn't answer immediately. Maybe Conti hadn't seen the Renzi trial-by-media last night. Local news didn't interest him. Conti and his boss were after the American Mafia kingpin who ran the Antonetti Family in Venice, but they didn't know his name or where he lived. Rather than arrest the thugs who'd murdered Bianca's parents, Conti had forced Natalie to spy on the 'Netti brothers. They expected her to find out who the Mafia kingpin was.

"Not yet. I was working all day yesterday. Why?"

"My supervisor is concerned about the cost of watching the mob house. This morning I texted Natalie to set up another meet. She texted back saying she can't leave the house. The 'Netti brothers posted a guard to watch the door. We need to find a surveillance house soon so Natalie can make up an excuse to meet us there."

"I said I'd try to find one, but I've been busy working a murder case."

Busy getting shot at by a lowlife killer.

"We must find one as soon as possible. The 'Netti brothers won't stay here long. They will probably fly back to Venice for Christmas. That only gives us three or four days."

Frank thought about it. Conti was right, and if the mobsters had a guard posted at the door, it meant they didn't trust Natalie. Then again, she might be lying. It wouldn't be the first time.

"Give me her cellphone number."

"Why?"

"I want to text her and ask her about the guards."

"That will not be necessary."

A jolt of anger flamed his gut. Conti didn't want to give him Natalie's number. He wanted her all to himself. "Well, I guess I'll just have to go there and ring the bell and see for myself."

"Let me tell you something, Renzi. I am running this operation and you better not fuck it up. If I hadn't called you, you wouldn't even know where Natalie was."

"Let me tell *you* something, *Conti.* I was the one who got you on the plane to New Orleans, because you made the mistake of assuming the 'Netti brothers would stay in New York. Then I called my colleague and had him follow them after they landed. If I hadn't, you wouldn't know where they are. What's her cellphone number?"

Dead silence on the other end. After a moment, Conti spit out the number and Frank wrote it down.

"Call me when you get the surveillance house," Conti said, and ended the call.

In your dreams, asshole. He added Natalie's number to the contact list in his cell and leaned back in his chair. He wasn't going to text her now. He had no interest in the guards. That was just an excuse to get her number. But Conti was right about one thing. The clock was ticking.

Finding someone who'd let them use their house for a few days wouldn't be easy, but it was the safest way to get Natalie and Bianca away from the mobsters. A helluva lot better than bursting into the house, guns blazing.

Why not think positive? Lots of people went away for the holidays. He'd find someone who lived near the mobsters, text Natalie and have her bring Bianca to the surveillance house. Arrest Natalie and protect Bianca so the 'Netti brothers couldn't kill her.

Envisioning himself celebrating Christmas with his father, he opened the city directory and started flipping pages.

———

Orazio waited impatiently at a traffic light. Twenty past noon and traffic was already heavy in the French Quarter. He had completed one task but others lay ahead. The whoop of distant sirens drifted through the open window, another concern. Dead men tell no tales, but diners at the Saigon Canteen might. He didn't believe anyone had gotten a good look at him last night, but if they'd seen Silvano's SUV and described it to the cops, it could be a problem.

Unfortunately, he had intended to use the money he got for the jewelry to finance part of his real estate purchase. A half hour ago, he had finalized the deal. The property was no mansion, but a fine house nonetheless, four bedrooms, four bathrooms, an elegant library, and a kitchen with stainless steel appliances. The price was $970,000, which required a ten percent deposit. He'd given Silvano's real estate agent $97,000 in cash. An early closing date had cost him a thousand more.

At 8:30 AM on Thursday, he would sign the papers at the real estate agent's office, leaving just enough time to speed to the airport. Tommy and Catarina would meet him there. Then he would fly to Venice and keep his date with his favorite whore. She asked no questions and did whatever he asked, a pleasant companion to celebrate the successful completion of his business in New Orleans.

Now he had to talk to Tick-Tock's nephew. The fagosa. The idea of a man sucking another man's cock filled him with disgust. Angelo and his pretty-boy lover spent their vacations on the Costa del Sol in Spain, frolicking on the beach with other fagosas.

But like it or not, he had to deal with him. He would make Angelo understand the urgency. Complete his work on the uncut diamonds by Wednesday afternoon or else.

The light changed and he accelerated.

He assumed Tommy and Catarina were at the house, but he didn't trust the nanny. He punched a number into his cellphone and waited, steering with one hand as he drove down Conti Street.

"Hello." Nicky's clipped voice.

"This is Mr. Antonetti. Are Tomasso and his wife still there?"

"Yes, sir. Tomasso is in the living room watching TV. His wife is upstairs in their room."

"And the child?"

"She's upstairs in her room with the woman that cares for her."

"Good. See that they don't leave the house." He ended the call. After he finished talking to Angelo, he would devise a plan to get rid of the kid and the insolent nanny. Tomorrow perhaps. Wednesday at the latest.

He stopped at a stop sign at the intersection of Bourbon Street. The stench of beer and vomit wafted through the window. Tourists came here at night to gawk at strippers, listen to music and drink themselves into a stupor. Some called New Orleans The Big Easy. Easy to get drunk, easy to get laid and easy to get killed if they weren't careful.

He drove across Royal Street and pulled into a garage for a nearby hotel. A young man in a blue uniform shirt hurried to the SUV.

Orazio gave him a twenty. "Don't put my car upstairs. I will be back in fifteen minutes."

"Yes, sir." The kid took the twenty and said, "I'll park it here, beside the booth."

He left the keys in the SUV, took his briefcase and set out for Esposito Fine Jewelry. Royal Street was alive with people, young couples with children, women pushing strollers, older couples walking hand in hand. Many were foreigners. Some were Japanese; others were Slavic with angular faces, jutting jaws and shaggy haircuts. Each store had an enticing window display: antique furniture, rare coins, silver bowls.

Some exhibited fine art, but none could compare to the paintings in European museums. He had studied such paintings in case an opportunity arose to steal one. But after learning that they were easy to steal but difficult to sell, he had abandoned the idea.

A painting in one window caught his eye, a blue dog with beady yellow eyes sitting on a piano bench. Edward Rodrigue was the artist. Another painting featured two dogs, one blue, the other orange. The prices were ridiculous. A child could paint them and make a fortune.

A mule towing a white carriage clip-clopped by and stopped to take a dump, the driver talking to the tourists in the carriage. Careful to avoid the mule droppings, Orazio crossed the street to Esposito Fine Jewelry and studied the window display. A three-tiered diamond necklace draped over black velvet. A sparkling diamond brooch with red rubies. Several diamond earrings.

A security guard in a blue uniform stood inside the door. To keep out the riffraff one had to press a button to enter, but the guard recognized him, opened the door and said, "Good morning, Mr. Antonetti. Angelo is expecting you. He'll be right out."

There were no customers in the store. Soft music issued from a speaker in the corner, an operatic tenor with a rich voice singing a Verdi aria, elegant music to entice tourists to buy expensive jewelry. Orazio stood beside a glass case with diamond jewelry. Tick-Tock had taken four large uncut diamonds as his tribute. Would he have Angelo make him another ring to adorn his fat fingers? Or cut them and sell them to augment his fortune.

Angelo bustled out of an office at the rear of the store and said, "Sorry to keep you waiting."

Undeniably handsome—large dark eyes and thick sensuous lips—the fagosa wore blue velvet trousers and a matching jacket over a frilly white shirt open at the throat to display gold chains.

Orazio could smell his flowery perfume. Disgusting.

"You need to work quickly," he said. "I must have my diamonds by Wednesday."

Angelo frowned. "That may not be possible, I have—"

"Do not tell me what is not possible. I will be back on Wednesday at three o'clock." He opened his jacket to show the weapon in his shoulder holster. "If they are not ready, you will suffer the consequences."

Angelo's face paled. "Of course. I will put my other projects aside and do yours first."

"See you Wednesday," Orazio said. Angelo would probably call his uncle to complain, but he followed Father's dictum: Maintain control or lose the respect of others. Including Tick-Tock.

He hurried back to the SUV, tipped the valet and drove off, already focused on his next task. Last night on TV he had watched a program about a neighborhood north of the French Quarter where many African-Americans lived. New Orleans had one of the highest murder rates in America, many of them in black neighborhoods. At the next intersection, he turned left and drove north. He took the Smith & Wesson out of the holster inside his jacket and put it in his lap.

Ten minutes later, he came to a street lined with gaudily painted bungalows. Black men with hostile eyes watched as he drove by, and music drifted out of open windows, loud music with trumpets and drums. The sun was shining now, but these streets would be dark and deserted at night, perfect for his plan. Tell the nanny he was taking her and the kid Christmas shopping in the French Quarter. Drive here, find a deserted street and get them out of the car.

By the time the nanny figured out what was happening, it would be too late. Shoot them in the head and drive away.

No witnesses. No worries.

The cops would assume the blacks had killed them.

CHAPTER 29

9:40 PM

Natalie stood in the darkness, her body rigid with tension. Over the past twenty years, she had faced many life-and-death situations.

This rivaled any of them.

If Orazio caught her sneaking out of the house, he might kill her.

The bedroom was silent and still. Bianca was asleep, but she often woke during the night. Natalie had told her what to do if that happened and she wasn't there. Go across the hall and knock on Catarina's door, Catarina would help her. But if Bianca noticed the open window and told Catarina about it, Catarina might tell Orazio.

She knew he was home. Earlier he had parked the SUV in the garage. She would have heard the garage door open if he left. She had decided not to put the wedge under the door. Already Orazio didn't trust her. If he came in the room and found her missing, he would be furious. When she came back, he would be waiting, with a gun.

Orazio wasn't her only problem. At the mall on Saturday, Conti said he'd seen Orazio get into a white limousine that morning. Conti was watching the house. For all she knew Renzi might be out there, too, waiting to arrest her. Which meant she had to avoid the front of the house, climb over the fence in back and hope no one saw her.

According to Annmarie, the security cameras were only activated when the mobster that owned the house was here. And tonight he wasn't. She crept to the side window, her heart racing, her palms sweaty.

Unlike the casement window facing the street, the window above the garage was a horizontal slider. She wound the clothesline around the four-inch metal handle and knotted it tightly.

If her weight pulled the window out of the frame, Orazio and the guard would hear it and come running. Game over.

The weather hadn't cooperated either. Not a cloud in the sky. Like a round of bright yellow cheese, a full moon lit up the garage like a spotlight. She had on her black running suit, but after she climbed out the window, she had to rappel down to the two-foot-wide gutter between the house and the steep-slanted garage roof. If anyone in the house across the street looked out the window, they would see her.

What if someone walked past the house?

She had to stop worrying about all the things that could go wrong.

She looped the clothesline under her crotch, wound the cord around her palm and checked her wristwatch. 9:45. Bruce was meeting her at the hair salon at ten. Even at a dead run it would take ten minutes to get there. After she picked up the items Pak Lam had sent, she had to race back to the house before the guards changed shifts at midnight. Climb up to the roof quickly and quietly, get through the window and remove any trace of her clandestine activity.

She swung one leg over the frame of the window, then the other, sat on the frame and took a deep breath to calm herself. The gutter was ten feet below her. Gripping the frame with one hand, she pulled the cord to take up the slack. Bracing her feet against the aluminum siding, she inched her way down. Only ten feet but it seemed to take forever. Her shoulders ached with the strain.

At last, her running shoes landed on the gutter. She unwound the rope and flexed her fingers. Her palms were slick with sweat and her heart pounded a tattoo against her ribs. She unzipped her pants pocket, touched the iPhone Pak Lam had sent her for good luck, and zipped it shut. Aware of how exposed she was in the moonlight, she crept along the gutter to the front of the house. The guard's yellow Jeep was in the driveway. No one on the sidewalk in front of the house. No one on the lawn or the cement walk to the front door.

Her nostrils flared. She smelled smoke. Cigar smoke.

Her heart jolted. Twelve feet below her, Orazio was outside, smoking one of his Cuban cigars. Panic-stricken, she inched backward as quietly as she could. The scent of Orazio's cigar followed her.

Could he hear her?

Breathing silently through her mouth, she crawled to the rear of the house. The full moon illuminated the lush grass twelve feet below her. Ten feet beyond the house, a six-foot-high, wood-plank fence loomed. At one of her Taekwondo lessons she had practiced jumping from high places. But this was no practice session, this was a life-or-death leap.

She visualized what she had to do. With both hands, she pushed off from the roof. When her feet hit the ground, she tucked her legs and rolled toward the house. If Orazio or the guard heard the thump when she landed, they would come running.

She lay still, listening.

Thirty seconds passed. No running footsteps. No guard. No Orazio.

She rose to her feet and gathered her strength. Three long strides and a running leap got her to the top of the fence. Lying on her belly, she flipped one leg over, then the other, landed on thick grass and lay still.

No lights were visible in the two-story white Colonial ahead of her. She crept past the house to the street and took off running.

Transcontinental, a four-lane thoroughfare, was one block away. Then she had to run eight blocks south to Veterans Boulevard. The hair salon was one block over.

———

Seated behind the wheel of his rental car, a black Toyota Camry, Clint yawned and checked his wristwatch. 9:55. Time for his nightly patrol. Festus had an odd name and the weirdest eyes he'd ever seen, but the former PI was indispensable to his operation, sat in his shit-brown Chevy Cavalier at the far end of the block, watching the mob house.

Two sets of eyes were better than one, and it allowed them to take breaks. At 2:00 AM Clint went to the cheap motel on Vets Boulevard where he'd rented a room, slept for three hours and relieved Festus at 5:00 AM. Festus slept at the motel until 8:00 AM, and they resumed their two-man surveillance. A grueling schedule, but he wouldn't be here long. Take out the Brixton bitch, fly back to D.C. for the holidays and celebrate with a fine meal and some expensive cognac.

He got on his cell and called Festus, who said, "Yo, Boss. Wha's up?"

"I'm gonna drive around and see if I spot anything unusual. Call me immediately if anyone leaves the mob house." If it was the Brixton bitch, he wanted to know right away. He touched the Beretta on the passenger seat. This time of night most people were either asleep in bed or watching TV. It would be easy to jump her.

"Anyone leaves the house," Festus said, "I'll dial you up right away."

Clint shut the phone and started the Toyota, quiet, dependable and innocuous. Without turning on the headlights, he pulled away from the curb and slowly drove down the block. Christmas lights blinked on and off inside the home opposite the mob house.

He turned left at the next intersection. A beat-up black van was parked just beyond the corner. The same van he'd seen last night.

Red flags went off in his mind. What was a scuzzy van doing in this neighborhood two nights in a row? No one in the cab. Were there cops inside the rear compartment? After he finished his patrol, he would come back and check out the van to make sure there weren't.

Two blocks later he hooked a right on Transcontinental and turned on his headlights. He didn't want some dick-head cop stopping him for a moving violation. The thought amused him. He intended to commit a far more serious violation at his earliest opportunity.

A sudden flash of motion caught his eye. Ahead of him, a dark-clad figure darted around a corner and ran down Transcontinental. He slowed down, shut off the headlights and drifted closer.

Jesus fucking Christ, it was the serial-killer bitch! He'd know her anywhere. For months he had studied her photograph, bent on revenge, imagining the pain he would inflict upon her.

Dressed in a black running suit, Natalie Brixton was racing down the sidewalk like the harpies from hell were after her. He studied her hands. She didn't appear to be armed, but he would take no chances. His trusty Beretta had never failed him yet.

A chuckle burbled from his mouth. He could hardly believe his luck. The bitch wasn't out for her nightly run. She had a destination in mind, running hard, arms and legs pumping.

Two minutes later she dashed across the grassy median that divided the north-and-south-bound lanes of Transcontinental and ran down a side street one block north of Veterans Boulevard.

He accelerated to the next U-Turn, reversed direction, turned onto the side street and saw her run through a parking lot behind a one-story building. He killed the headlights and eased into the lot. An older model blue Mustang was the only car parked behind the building.

A sign posted on the wall said: **Parking for HIP HAIRSTYLES only.**

The bitch was meeting someone. Not for a haircut. Not at this hour.

He grabbed his Beretta and got out of the car.

———

Natalie took a moment outside the door to catch her breath. Photographs of men and women with sleek hairstyles decorated the windows on either side of the door. A sign on the door said: CLOSED. No lights in the front part of the salon, dim light in the back.

She tapped on the door. Moments later, a young Asian man opened the door, smiled at her and said, "Hello, Natalie. I am Bruce. So happy to meet you."

She stepped inside and shut the door. The faint odor of chemicals filled her nostrils. "No worries," Bruce said. "I am the only one here."

They were the same height, five-seven. A handsome man in his twenties with dark almond-shaped eyes, Bruce had styled his glossy black hair in one of the mod hairdos young men favored these days. The sides were trimmed short, the longer hair on top swept back from his forehead in a pompadour.

"Thank you so much for doing this," she said.

"No problem. My grandfather speaks very highly of Pak Lam. It is an honor for me to help you. Come in the back. I have something for you."

Beyond the reception counter, stylist chairs faced mirrors along two sides of a square room. Against the back wall on the left, a black leather chair stood in front of a sink. To the right of the sink, an arched doorway opened onto to a smaller room.

Here the chemical odor was sharper. A fluorescent ceiling light illuminated an eight-foot counter with hair-styling products in the glass case below it. Bruce gave her an envelope that lay on the counter.

"Here are the items you need."

She opened the envelope, took out a U.S. passport and a driver's license and smiled. The woman who prepared false documents for Pak Lam had used the photograph on her Liang Lam passport, the one Conti had confiscated. The name on the documents was James Wong. She would have to cut her hair again, but this was a small sacrifice if it allowed her to escape.

"When we spoke on the phone," Bruce said, "Pak Lam said you should rent a car and drive to Atlanta. His contact will meet you at the airport and give you a plane ticket to Boston."

She heard a strange sound.

A small round hole appeared in Bruce's forehead. Blood oozed from the wound. Horrified, she froze.

Gazing at her with vacant eyes, Bruce sagged like a rag doll and collapsed on the floor.

"Move and you're dead." A snarl from behind her.

Her heart beat her ribs like a wild thing. Filled with dread, she turned.

A short older man with a military buzz-cut faced her, dressed in a dark suit. His hands held a Beretta with a silencer attached to the muzzle. Aimed at her heart.

He smiled, a grotesque smile given the circumstances.

"We meet at last."

Shaken to the core, she whispered, "Who are you?"

His lips thinned in a grim line. "CIA Agent Clint Hammer, at your service. You killed my friend," he said, his pale gray eyes as cold and hard as agates.

And it all became clear. This was Oliver's CIA friend.

Bile rose in her throat, sour as swill. She swallowed it down. Her pulse pounded in her ears and her breath came in short gasps. How did he find her? Not that it mattered. CIA Agent Clint Hammer intended to avenge his friend's murder.

"You seduced Oliver with your sexy smile," he snarled. "Ambushed him in his hotel room and shot him in cold blood."

Her mind scrabbled for a way out. The man with the cold agate-eyes had already shot Bruce. Now he would shoot her. She had no weapon. A spray bottle of water stood on the counter, useless against a Beretta.

How ironic. That was her weapon of choice when she had avenged her mother's murder. When a man held a gun on her in a sleazy motel, she had done a sexy striptease to distract him. That wouldn't work with Hammer, but maybe she could goad him into a making a mistake.

"For a CIA man you're not so tough. Shooting an unarmed woman?"

"Fuck you bitch!" he said, and stepped closer.

Close enough for her to smell his sweat. But not close enough.

"Oliver told me about you. He said you were useless in a fight. He said you were a pussy."

The man's face turned crimson. He took another step closer.

"Liar! He said no such thing."

She inhaled through her nose, deep down to her diaphragm. Offered a silent prayer to the Vietnamese spirit gods. Found her center of power.

Exploding in a TKD spin move, she kicked his head with all her might. The Beretta flew out of his hands and skittered across the floor to the wall. But the blow failed to put him down.

"You fucking bitch! I'll kill you with my bare hands."

She tried to run past him, but he lashed out, a roundhouse punch to her jaw.

Stunned by the blow, she backed away and tried to clear her head.

The assassin stood between her and the front door. The Beretta lay on the floor ten feet behind him. If he grabbed the gun, she was dead.

She glanced behind her. On the wall behind the display case was another door. She darted around the display case and opened it. Inhaling the sharp odor of chemicals, she plunged inside and slammed the door.

Plunged into darkness, she groped the wall and found a light switch. She flipped it and a bare bulb in the ceiling illuminated a rectangular room with cement-block walls. The door had no lock on it.

She was trapped inside a storage room.

Soon the CIA man would open the door and shoot her.

A stack of boxes stood beside the door. She grabbed the top one and put it on the floor against the door. Added another, and another. But they wouldn't keep the assassin out for long.

She needed a weapon.

The narrow room was eight feet wide. No windows. Floor to ceiling metal shelves lined the cement-block walls. Freestanding shelves in the center held cartons labeled peroxide and bleach. Maybe she could use the chemicals to blind him.

She opened a carton and took out a large plastic bottle of bleach.

Blam! A shot pierced the wooden door.

Her heart leaped into her throat. Any second now he would break down the door and shoot her.

But not if he couldn't see her. She heaved the container of bleach at the bulb in the ceiling. The gallon jug hit the bulb and shards of broken glass clinked onto the cement floor. The jug bounced off a metal shelf and landed on the cement floor with a thump.

Now the room was completely dark.

But darkness was her friend. She waited.

CHAPTER 30

The instant he shut the door Clint knew he'd made a mistake. The room was dark as pitch and reeked of chemicals. Worse, he could feel her presence, lurking in the darkness. The Vietnamese bitch was going to ambush him like the gooks in 'Nam, hiding in the jungle, waiting for GIs to walk down a path and hit a tripwire that set off an explosion that blew off their legs.

The room was so quiet he could hear himself breathe. His sweat-soaked shirt clung to his back and droplets of perspiration ran down his forehead into his eyes. Jesus Christ! Forty degrees in D.C., sixty-five in New Orleans, the city he detested and hoped never to visit again.

His head throbbed where the bitch had kicked him, and she was going to pay for it. Holding the Beretta in his right hand, he groped the wall with his left. His fingertips found a light switch and flicked it.

Nothing happened. What the fuck?

Panic hit him like a fist, the nightmare that woke him night after night and sent his heart racing out of control as he lay still in the dark. The dreaded fear that had tormented him for years. Not just fear of the dark, the belief that he would die like Oliver. Alone and helpless.

A sound.

Terror froze him to the spot like a prisoner shackled to a stake.

He gripped the Beretta in his sweaty hands. Smelled the sweat-stink of fear issuing from his armpits. He set his finger on the trigger and aimed the weapon in the direction of the sound.

A sharp intake of breath. The sound was close. Too close. Terrifying.

If she was this close, he would have only a fraction of a second to locate her and fire. Did the bitch have a gun? If he fired and missed, the muzzle blast would reveal his position. On the other hand, if he hit her, she might cry out and give her position away.

Then he could finish her off.

He clenched his teeth to keep them from chattering. If only the room wasn't so dark and claustrophobic. His chest heaved, his lungs seeking the oxygen he so desperately needed. But his shallow rapid breaths failed to slow his galloping heart. He was no longer the powerful man who tormented others, he was a pathetic piece of shit, shaking with fear, unable to defend himself from his enemy. No one would save him.

If he didn't conquer his fear, the serial-killer bitch would kill him.

———

She heard panting, the sounds dogs made after they chased each other around a field. But the sounds were only a few feet away and they didn't come from a dog. She stayed in a crouch, one knee on the cement floor, ready to leap at him if he attacked her.

Nostrils flared, she inhaled deep through her nose and slowly released the breath, seeking the center of calm deep within her. For many years she had worked hard to achieve this, practicing her Taekwondo skills. Now the calm she so desperately needed eluded her.

A chill rippled through her. Were the ancestor spirits of the men she had killed punishing her?

Now she might have to kill again.

Did the spirits of his victims haunt Frank Renzi? Probably not. Four months ago he had captured her, handcuffed her and put her in a cruiser to question her. When she spoke of the obligation she'd felt to avenge her mother's murder, she had seen the unforgiving look in his dark penetrating eyes. He didn't understand.

He was on the right side of the law, a virtuous cop doing his best to protect honest citizens. She was a criminal.

She had tried to escape her life of crime.

Now it had come back to haunt her.

A shot whizzed past her shoulder. A split second later she heard the spit of the silenced Beretta. For an instant, the muzzle flash lit up her assassin, a lightning strike in the pitch black room.

Instinctively, she fell to the floor and rolled.

When her forearm touched the wall, she rose to her knees. Instinct and quick reflexes had saved her, but they wouldn't get her out of the storeroom. She was trapped.

She didn't want to think about what would happen if she died here.

Didn't want to think about what Orazio might do to Bianca.

Didn't want to think. Period.

———

After he fired, he quick-stepped left, an evasive tactic in case she had a weapon. He knew he'd missed. In the darkness, he heard a scuffling sound and fired again.

The bullet ricocheted, glanced off the metal shelves, slammed into the concrete floor beside him, then off a shelf inches from his head.

The Beretta was useless in here. He could as easily kill himself as the Brixton bitch, the slug rattling around the claustrophobic space like a marble in a shoe box.

He jammed the Beretta into the shoulder holster inside his jacket and inched toward the door with his hands in front of him like a blind man. When his fingers touched the wall, he groped for the doorknob. He would run out the door, crouch on the other side and shoot the bitch when she came through the door, her only escape route.

It would be over in seconds.

The faint scent of deodorant warned of her presence. He lashed out blindly with his fists. He hit nothing, but he knew she was there. Every nerve in his body vibrated, signaling her presence. But the inky darkness paralyzed him. Rendered him impotent. He pictured the bitch, just beyond his reach, poised and ready to pounce.

In the silence, he heard his raspy breathing. It was only a matter of time before she zeroed in on him. His bladder betrayed him. A trickle of urine dribbled into his jockey shorts.

The bitch grabbed his legs and yanked. With a muffled cry, he fell to the floor, his head bouncing off the concrete. Pinpoints of light danced across his vision from the shock of hitting the floor.

He rolled onto his stomach. Where was she?

Battling dizziness, fearing another blow, he struggled to his knees.

Nothing happened. He listened hard.

Heard only his own terrified breathing.

He felt like a mouse in a trap. Each attack diminished his strength and left him in pain. He had to do something. Fighting the pain, he grabbed onto a metal shelf and hauled himself to his feet.

She kicked his right knee, a painful blow that made him groan. Blindly, he lunged for the door. His knee gave out and he collapsed on the floor. Jesus! Could the bitch see in the dark?

No, she was listening to his movements.

His only option was to stay quiet where he'd fallen. His knee ached and the Beretta dug into his gut. Even if it jeopardized his own safety, he would have to use it. But first he would lie absolutely still. Play dead.

Let her come to him. Whip out his Beretta and shoot her.

"Why did you kill Bruce?" snarled a venomous voice.

Her words enraged him. *Why did you kill Oliver?* he wanted to scream. But fear sealed his lips. Jesus Christ, he'd strangle the bitch with his own hands, wring her neck like a chicken.

A sound nearby. He struggled to his feet and extended his hands.

His fingers touched her shirt. He grabbed it and pulled her to him. Her knee slammed into his groin. Agonizing pain, crushing his nuts. He screamed. Words of self-preservation in his mind said, *Shoot the bitch!*

He took out the Beretta and fired blindly. In the muzzle flash he saw no one. The last thing he felt was her breath on the back of his neck.

———

Breathing hard, she chopped his wrist with her hand. The Beretta clattered to the floor. Now was the time to go for the kill, while he was weak, injured by her previous blows.

But she didn't want to kill him.

Better to incapacitate him with a Taekwondo move. Extending her fingers, she stiffened her right hand into a blade. One blow with the bony edge would disable him long enough for her to run out the door.

His foot lashed out, a glancing blow that struck her leg. Instinctively, she swung her arm as hard as she could, aiming for his jaw. But her stiffened right hand connected with the flesh of his neck.

 She heard his head strike something and he fell to the floor with a thump. She inched toward the door, reached for the knob and jerked back her hand. *No! Leave no fingerprints!*

Using the front of her shirt, she turned the knob, opened the door and lunged through it. The bright light above the display case made her blink. She turned and looked into the storage room.

Clint Hammer, the CIA agent intent on killing her, lay on the floor, motionless, his head tilted at an odd angle. His pale gray eyes were open, sightless and staring. Jesus! He was dead! When he fell, his head must have hit the metal shelf hard enough to break his neck.

Panic sent her into survival mode. She had to get out of here.

She paused beside Bruce's body, overwhelmed with grief and a deep sense of shame. At Pak Lam's request Bruce had come here to help her. Now he was dead. This would sully Pak Lam's reputation. And hers.

Sooner or later she would have to tell him what had happened. But she couldn't think about that now. When workers came here tomorrow morning, they would find two dead men and call the police. She had to eliminate any trace of her presence.

She ran to the styling area and grabbed a towel and a pair of latex gloves from a shelf above the sink. She put on the gloves and ran back to the storeroom. Disgusted by the stench, she grasped the CIA agent's arms, dragged him out of the storeroom and left him on the floor beside Bruce's body.

In the shadowy storage room she found the jug of bleach she'd thrown at the ceiling bulb. She poured bleach on the towel, wiped the doorknob, then the bleach container to erase her fingerprints. Partials might remain on the metal shelves or the concrete walls, but she had no time to deal with that. Now it was 11:05. She had to get back to the house before relief guard arrived at midnight.

Should she take the Beretta? Armed with a weapon, she could protect herself from Orazio. No. Better to leave it here. She took a ballpoint pen off the display counter, returned to the storeroom and located the Beretta. Emulating the detectives on TV shows, she stuck the pen into the trigger guard, picked up the gun and dropped it on the floor beside the CIA agent.

Sooner or later, the cops would identify the owner of the weapon that had killed Bruce. But Clint Hammer was dead, too. The cops would know someone else had killed him.

She knelt beside his body and searched his pockets. She found a cell-phone and a set of car keys in one, a wallet with a driver's license and a wad of cash in another. She rose to her feet.

Only Bruce and Pak Lam knew she was here. She had a new passport and driver's license. Why go back to the house? Why not go to the train station, board the next available train and get out of New Orleans.

But what about Bianca?

Catarina would care for her, but she couldn't prevent Orazio from killing her.

For precious seconds she stood there, paralyzed, torn by her dilemma.

Self-preservation jolted her into action. Now it was 11:15. Any minute now a security patrol might drive by the salon and wonder why a light was on in the back. She had to get out now.

She jammed Hammer's wallet and car keys in her pocket and opened his cellphone. He had shut it off to keep it from ringing while he crept inside to kill her. The latex gloves made it awkward, but she managed to remove the SIM card from the phone.

Standing beside Bruce's body, she murmured a sorrowful goodbye. She would deal with her sorrow and shame later. She shut out the light and crept to the front door. Street lights illuminated Veterans Boulevard. Not much traffic at this hour. She waited for two cars to pass, opened the door and slipped out into the night.

Hugging the side of the building, she went around back. A black Toy-ota Camry was parked beside Bruce's Mustang. She had the keys. How easy it would be to hop in the Camry and drive to Atlanta.

No. She had to protect Bianca.

But she'd better dump the Toyota somewhere so the cops wouldn't find it for a while. She unlocked the door, got behind the wheel and drove out of the parking lot without turning on the lights. Four blocks away, she parked the Toyota on a side street outside a darkened house, got out and walked away. One task accomplished, but now it was 11:25.

She turned the corner and began to run. One block later she stopped at a storm drain and dropped the car keys and the SIM card down the drain. Two blocks later she put Hammer's license down another. On the next side street she dropped his cellphone into another drain.

Now she was only three blocks from the mob house, but it was 11:45.

In fifteen minutes the relief guard would arrive.

She set off at a dead run.

———

Festus yawned and checked his watch. 11:45.

Usually when Clint went on his ten o'clock patrol he came back thirty minutes later, gave him a call and said, "All quiet on the western front." Some smart ass shit like that. Not tonight.

No black Toyota Camry parked at the other end of the block.

He'd called Clint three times since eleven o'clock, got no answer.

Clint was paranoid about leaving his cellphone on. "Call me no matter what if that bitch leaves the house," he'd said.

Dammit to hell! Where was he?

His stomach rumbled with hunger, an acid fizz that aggravated his ulcer. Man, he had to eat something. Usually Clint brought him a steak-and-cheese from Subway after his patrol. Seemed like his anal-retentive boss had forgotten about him, might have gone to the motel to catch some extra winks.

He cranked his Chevy Cavalier. Almost midnight, all the Christmas lights were off on the homes along the street, folks tucked into their comfy beds. The only people who left the target house at this time of night were hard-eyed men with bulges under their jackets, one coming, one going. He figured they were mobsters guarding the house.

Fuck it. The asshole wasn't paying him enough to put up with this bullshit. He'd grab something to eat, drive to the motel and see if Clint's Toyota was there.

CHAPTER 31

TUESDAY December 21   8:30 AM

"If you hadn't called me last night, you'd have been out of luck," said Mary Hogan. Sixty-six years old and still attractive, slim and trim in a royal-blue pantsuit, she had Irish-blue eyes and wavy auburn hair.

"Glad I caught you," Frank said. Glad? Thrilled was more like it. They were in her guest room on the second-floor. Beyond a double bed facing a small TV on a chest of drawers, a window yielded a clear view of the mob house in the next block. Use binoculars, he could see even better.

"I really appreciate your letting us use the house. We've gotten reports about suspicious activity in one of the houses down the street."

Mary Hogan frowned. "There won't be any shooting, will there?"

He sure as hell hoped not. "No, nothing like that. We just want to monitor the house."

She gave him a sharp look. "Drugs? Prostitution?"

"I can't get into the details, but don't worry, we'll take good care of your house. Is your luggage up here? I can take it downstairs for you."

"Thanks, that would be great. It's down the hall in my room."

The master bedroom was larger than the guest room and had its own bathroom. A single suitcase stood by the double bed.

"Only the one?" he asked.

"Yes," she said wistfully. "Only one this year. Howard passed away in February. This will be my first Christmas without him."

"I'm sorry to hear that. Holidays are difficult when you lose someone you love. My mother died ten years ago and I still miss her." He loved his father and admired him greatly, but emotionally he'd been closer to his mother. Mary Hogan was flying to Phoenix to spend Christmas with her daughter, but he still hadn't bought a plane ticket to Boston. Not with Natalie still free, no doubt plotting her escape this very minute.

"I'm grateful for all the years we had together," Mary said. "We had some wonderful times, but you can't live in the past. Go ahead downstairs while I freshen up."

He carried the suitcase downstairs and rolled it into the kitchen, neat and tidy, no dirty dishes, just a coffee mug in the sink. He had offered to drive Mary to the airport. It was the least he could do. Setting up their surveillance in her house would allow him to accomplish his goal.

Arrest Natalie Brixton and put her in jail.

Mary entered the kitchen, went to the counter and opened her purse. "Let me check to make sure I've got everything before we leave." She flashed a smile. "Do I sound paranoid?"

"Not at all. It's easy to forget something."

She closed her purse, took a set of keys off the counter and gave them to him. "No one will be smoking inside the house will they? I hate the smell of cigarettes."

"No worries. No one on my team smokes." He waited a beat and said, "But is it okay if we put a six-pack in the refrigerator?" Jiving her to see what she'd say.

Her Irish-blue eyes widened. Then she laughed. "You're a rascal, Detective Renzi. I like your style." Her smile faded and she heaved a sigh. "I'm not looking forward to Phoenix."

"Why not?"

"Have you ever been there?"

"No."

She made a face. "Hot as hell and dull as dishwater. Pam wants me to move there and live with her and the kids. But all my friends are here." She paused. "One friend in particular."

He got the picture. "And you'd rather spend the holiday with him?"

"I love my daughter and I'm crazy about the little darlin's, but I'm not moving to Phoenix."

A decisive woman. He liked that. "Just kidding about the beer, but could we put our lunches in the refrigerator? We'll be working long shifts, one person in the guest room, one down here."

"Of course," she said and gestured at the counter. "Feel free to use the coffeemaker."

"When you get back, we'll compensate you for the use of your house." He took out his wallet and gave her a hundred dollars. "Treat Pam to a nice dinner. I took this out of petty cash." Actually it was his money, but he wanted her to feel good about letting them use the house.

Her face lit up in a smile. "That's very kind. Thank you."

He checked his watch. 8:40. "We better go. I wouldn't want you to miss your flight."

And he wanted to complete the setup here. Conti didn't know about it. Last night he'd called Conti at five, saying he'd had no luck so far. True at the time. He'd called Mary Hogan later.

All he had to do was get Natalie and Bianca to come to Mary Hogan's house and bingo. Mission accomplished. Conti would be pissed, but so what? Once Natalie was locked up, he could fly to Boston and celebrate the holiday with his father.

————

9:35 AM

Natalie took a bite of her blueberry muffin. Her stomach revolted. Nauseated, she spit the morsel into a napkin and massaged her throbbing temples. Her jaw still ached where Hammer had punched her. Seated beside Catarina on the other side of the table, Bianca wasn't eating either, picking her muffin apart and leaving crumbs on her plate. The girl seemed to have an uncanny ability to decipher her moods. Happy when she was happy, upset when she was worried. Like now.

Last night she'd managed to get back into her room undetected. Physically and emotionally exhausted, she'd run a bath and soaked in the steamy water, recalling the ugly hole in Bruce's forehead. The CIA agent's twisted neck. Their sightless vacant eyes. She crawled into bed but she hadn't slept, thanks to the hideous images in her mind.

This morning Bianca had woken at seven, cranky and uncooperative. She wanted to go downstairs for breakfast. Natalie wanted to find out if the cops had found the bodies in the hair salon. She told Bianca to color a pretty picture in the coloring book and put on the local news. The lead story was about a shooting at a Vietnamese restaurant in Metairie. She tuned it out, ruminating about last night's disaster.

A news jingle cut into her thoughts. A bulletin flashed on the screen: **Two Men Found Dead in Hair Salon.** "This just in," said the newswoman. "Detectives from the Jefferson Parish Sheriff's office are investigating a double murder in Metairie. The manager of Hip Hairstyles opened the shop at seven-thirty and found two bodies, one shot execution-style in the head. A possible murder weapon was found on the floor near the second man. Detectives have identified one man but won't release his name until his next of kin are notified. No identification was found on the other man. Detectives believe the men were murdered sometime after the salon closed at nine o'clock last night. They ask anyone with information to call Crime Stoppers."

Natalie set her plate aside and sipped her tea. The bulletin had reassured her up to a point. No mention of suspects. No questions raised about who killed the second man. But soon there would be.

And Orazio was acting strange. A half hour ago when the newspaper was delivered, he took it in the sitting room to read it. A minute later, he called Tommy over and showed him something in the newspaper. Then they had gone upstairs, visibly concerned.

What had Orazio seen in the newspaper?

She rose to her feet and said to Catarina, "I'm going to take my tea in the sitting room and read the newspaper."

Impeccably dressed in one of her new outfits, Catarina smiled and said, "I miss reading my newspaper in the morning, especially the fashion section. But we'll be home in a few days."

She forced a smile. "Yes, just in time for Christmas. How nice."

Nice for Catarina, but she didn't intend to be on the plane with her. By then she and Bianca would be gone. If Orazio hadn't killed them.

She set her tea on the table beside the wing chair and picked up the *Times-Picayune*. A headline in the Metro section caught her eye. **No Leads in Restaurant Massacre.** Beside the article was a photo of a restaurant surrounded by police vehicles and yellow crime scene tape.

But she had no interest in that. The newswoman's words flashed into in her mind. *Detectives have identified one man but won't release his name until his next of kin are notified.*

Tears misted her eyes. Bruce's family would be devastated, especially his grandfather, who had sent him to meet her at Pak Lam's request. Last night she'd been too exhausted to call Pak Lam, but she could no longer avoid it. She had to call him before Bruce's grandfather did.

She finished her tea and set the mug on the table beside the newspaper. The other headline drew her eye. **No Leads in Restaurant Massacre.** She skimmed the article.

The Saigon Canteen remains closed as homicide detectives seek clues to what happened there Sunday night. Witnesses say two men entered the Vietnamese restaurant shortly after five o'clock. Detectives believe they shot the owner, Bao Ng, 64, and his nephews, Chien Ng, 24, and Dung Ng, 26, in a storeroom at the rear of the restaurant. The owner's son, Nguyen Ng, 23, also died, apparently from a broken neck.

The Ng family is well-known to police. Two months ago the nephews were arrested in connection with a home invasion in which a Vietnamese family was viciously beaten and robbed of money and jewelry. At the time of the massacre the nephews were free on bail. Witnesses have been reluctant to talk to police. Detectives ask anyone with information to call the Jefferson Parish Sheriff's office.

She rubbed her swollen jaw, thinking: *Five o'clock Sunday night. Four men dead.* Was that where Orazio and Tommy went after the steamboat ride? Was that why Orazio showed Tommy the newspaper? An icy chill prickled her neck. She had no proof that they were at the restaurant Sunday night, but it seemed like a reasonable assumption. Not that she was going to call the detectives and tell them.

She had to escape. Human life meant nothing to these monsters.

She returned to the table and said to Catarina in Italian, "I need to talk to the woman who cooks lunch. I'm not feeling well. I want to ask her to make me some soup."

"I want to come with you!" Bianca said, pouting.

Her stomach clenched in a knot. If Bianca pitched a fit, Orazio might hear it and come downstairs. "Not now. I'll bring you down later for a Popsicle."

"No. I want one now!"

Catarina came to her rescue. "Settle down, Bianca. Laura doesn't feel well. Stay here with me while she talks to the cook."

Dreading the phone call she had to make, she hurried to the kitchen. Annmarie wasn't there, but the door to the garage was open. When she stepped into the garage, Annmarie was coming out of the laundry room.

"Hi, Laura, how ya doing?"

"I need to call my boyfriend in Boston, but I'm afraid Nicky will come looking for me. Can you warn me if he does?"

Annmarie frowned. "What happened? Your jaw looks like it's swollen. Did someone hit you?"

"No. I need to make my phone call. Can you help me?"

Still frowning, Annmarie said, "Okay, but you need to put ice on your jaw. I'll shut the door to the garage while you make your call. If anyone comes looking for you, I'll rap on the door."

"Thank you." She took out her iPhone and punched in a number.

Pak Lam answered right away. "Natalie, I've been so worried. Why didn't you call me last night?"

"Something terrible happened." Her heart pounded and her mouth felt drier than burnt toast. What would Pak Lam say when she told him Bruce was dead?

"I managed to get out of the house, but someone followed me. The CIA agent who's been hunting for me because I killed his friend in Boston. I don't know how he found me."

"Tell me what happened."

"We should have locked the door, but we didn't. Bruce told me you know his grandfather. While we were talking in the back room, the CIA agent came inside, but we didn't hear him. He shot Bruce."

A sharp intake of breath. "That is terrible! Is he badly hurt?"

She clenched the phone in her sweaty hands. "It pains me to tell you this. I'm so ashamed. I know this will bring dishonor to you. Bruce is dead. I should not have allowed this to happen."

Silence on the other end. She waited.

At last Pak Lam said, "You could not foresee that this would happen. Tell me the rest of it."

She glanced at the door to the kitchen. "I can't talk long. I'm hiding in the garage. The mobsters might come in and find me. The CIA agent tried to kill me, too, but I kicked him in the head and ran in a storage closet." She paused and took a deep breath. "I killed him."

"Good. I would expect nothing less from my esteemed daughter. When I speak with Bruce's grandfather, I will tell him you have avenged his grandson's murder. But why did you not leave New Orleans immediately? Did Bruce give you the documents?"

"Yes, but I'm worried about Bianca. If I leave her with these mobsters, they will kill her. She's only five years old."

"You want to take her with you."

"Yes. I know it will be complicated, but—" A sharp rap sounded on the door to the kitchen. "Someone's coming. Call you later."

She jammed the iPhone into her purse and lunged into the laundry room. She heard the kitchen door open, then footsteps.

Orazio appeared in the doorway of the laundry room.

"What are you doing in here?" he said, glaring at her.

"I want to hand wash some clothes and I need detergent," she said, angling her face away from him so he wouldn't see her swollen jaw.

His relentless eyes locked onto hers, hard as granite. "After dinner I will take you and the girl Christmas shopping. That should make you happy."

"Tonight?" she said stupidly, the headache pounding her temples like a sledgehammer.

"Yes, tonight. Did I not say after dinner? Make sure she is dressed and ready to go." Orazio punched the button to open the garage door and climbed into the black SUV.

Filled with despair, she went in the kitchen.

Orazio had just given her a death sentence.

Annmarie handed her a towel wrapped around a bag of frozen peas. "I don't know what's going on, Laura, but remember what I said. These guys don't mess around."

"Thanks for the warning, and the frozen peas." She forced a smile. "I promised Bianca I'd bring her down for a Popsicle later. See you then."

That would make Bianca happy, but it would take a lot more than a Popsicle to make her happy.

Delivering the bad news to Pak Lam was bad enough.

After dinner Orazio was taking her and Bianca Christmas shopping.

Nonsense. He was going to take them somewhere and kill them.

CHAPTER 32

TUESDAY 10:15 AM

Orazio leaned against the redwood railing behind the seafood restaurant, puffing his cigar. Leaden clouds filled the darkening sky. A storm was brewing over Lake Pontchartrain, like the problems festering in his mind. What was the nanny doing in the garage this morning?

He didn't believe her bullshit excuse about washing clothes. She was up to something. When he said he would take her and the kid shopping after dinner tonight, he had seen the anxious look on her face. Almost as though she suspected what might happen.

On his way to the restaurant he had driven past the elegant property that would soon be his, but this failed to ease his black mood. Thursday morning he would sign the papers, launder close to million dollars in cash and acquire a fine piece of real estate. His ownership would be hidden in the LLC trust Silvano had created many years ago for Father. The one satisfactory part of his stay here.

The matter at the Vietnamese restaurant worried him. Thanks to the sensational article in today's newspaper, the cops would be under pressure to solve the crime. The article said the Ng family was known to the cops. If Silvano saw the article, would he recall the comment he'd made at the sit-down about Vietnamese gangs?

Orazio puffed his cigar. The SUV was the problem. In his haste to escape from the Saigon Canteen, Tommy had turned right on Veterans Boulevard, which took them past the restaurant. What if someone saw them and described the vehicle to the cops? There were plenty of black SUVs around, but cops had ways to identify the owners.

And the black SUV belonged to Silvano.

Dread pierced his gut like a corkscrew ripped into a piece of cork. If the cops questioned Silvano as to the whereabouts of his Toyota Sequoia on Sunday night, the consequences would be catastrophic. Silvano was no fool. He knew Orazio had stolen diamonds from a jewelry store in Venice. Would he now suspect that Orazio had gone to the Saigon Canteen to fence stolen jewelry? Valuable jewelry he had not reported to Tick-Tock, denying him the tribute he rightfully deserved.

Now Silvano's SUV was parked behind the restaurant where the cops wouldn't see it. And it was safe enough parked in the garage where they were staying. But tonight after dinner when he got rid of the kid and the nanny, he couldn't use Silvano's SUV. That would be foolhardy.

Tommy's pain-in-the-ass wife was another problem. Catarina wanted to go shopping this afternoon. To quiet her incessant demands, he had agreed to drive her and Tommy to Canal Place, a ritzy shopping mall in the French Quarter, at two o'clock. Using the black SUV to get there would be a huge risk. The cops might already be looking for it.

He drew on his cigar, a fine Montecristo imported from Cuba. The distinctive aroma reminded him of his father. What would Father do? At certain times, he felt Father's presence, swirling around him like smoke from a cigar. Times when danger lurked on all sides.

A piercing screech distracted him. Seagulls hovering over a nearby dumpster flapped their wings and emitted raucous calls, fighting over discarded scraps from the seafood restaurant. Rolling thunder drew his attention to the sky, black with clouds now.

Perhaps this was an omen.

The gulls knew a storm was approaching. Trolling the lake for fish during a violent storm would expose them to danger, so they settled for less, the entrails of fish from the restaurant kitchen.

He puffed his cigar and blew a smoke ring, just as Father used to do so many years ago.

What would Father do?

Like a puff of smoke, the solution came to him. He would drive to the airport, park Silvano's SUV in the garage and ride a shuttle bus to a rental car agency. There he would rent another SUV, a different make and model, and not black. Tommy and Catarina might wonder about this, but to hell with them.

He would need a credit card to rent a car. Maybe he would ask Laura for hers. The thought amused him. He wouldn't, of course.

That would lead to bigger problems when her body was found and the cops identified her.

Drops of rain spattered the redwood deck. He tossed his cigar in the water and headed for the SUV. He would use one of his own credit cards to rent another SUV.

No worries. His name wasn't on the card.

———

10:35 AM

Frank hustled into the homicide office, finger-combed his damp hair and sat down at his desk. After he dropped Mary Hogan at the airport, a downpour had snarled traffic and delayed him. David and Orville were out working cases. Perfect.

He punched Kelly's number into his cellphone.

She answered right away. "Kelly O'Neil." That meant she was in her office. She knew it was him, but that's how she answered when other people were around.

"Kelly, I need your help."

"What's going on?"

"Now that King Rock's locked up, I want to serve the murder warrants on Natalie."

He told her about the surveillance house and ended by saying, "Natalie needs an excuse to leave the mob house with Bianca. Can you bring Jacques to the Hogan house this afternoon? Maybe take him outside, make it look like the kids want to play with each other."

"Difficult. My supervisor called a department meeting at two."

"Make it work, Kelly. This might be my only chance to grab Natalie. The kids won't be in any danger. David will be there. We'll handle the arrest."

"Okay. I'll think of something. I'll call the social worker and call you back."

"Thanks, Kelly. You're the best." He ended the call, and pumped his fist. Arrest Natalie, put her in the lockup and everyone would be happy.

Well, he and Vobitch would. Natalie, not so much.

His cellphone rang. When he answered, Vobitch said, "Frank, where are you?"

"Just got back to the office. I lined up a surveillance house near the mob house, just drove the owner to the airport. She few to Phoenix to spend Christmas with her daughter. I'm going to text Natalie and get her to bring Bianca to the house this afternoon."

"What if the wiseguys won't let her leave?"

Trust Vobitch to zero in on the problem. "I asked Kelly to bring Jacques to the house and play with him outside. That will give Natalie an excuse to bring Bianca over there to play with him."

"Good plan, but our gal Natalie knows we got outstanding murder warrants on her. Why go there and risk getting arrested?"

He didn't have an answer for that one. "What else can I do? It's too dangerous to try and get into the mob house to arrest her. Conti figures they'll fly back to Venice for Christmas. Thursday at the latest. That leaves today and tomorrow. Maybe Natalie will decide the mobsters are more dangerous than I am. Sitting in jail is better than getting shot."

"You think she'll go down without a fight? I don't."

"David will be there and so will Kelly. Natalie's not armed. Not that I plan on using a gun with kids around. I put Natalie in the lockup. Kelly brings Bianca to the social services people."

"What about your pal Conti?"

"He won't be there. I didn't tell him about the surveillance house."

"Okay, but be careful. Kids involved, we don't want any shooting. Speaking of which, IAD called me this morning and said they'd postpone your hearing until after the holidays."

"That's good. Is King Rock still in the lockup?"

"Yes. They're holding him on the witness intimidation warrant. The DA needs more time to indict him for Angelique's murder. I told him to charge the scumbag with resisting arrest, shooting at you and a few other things. Christ, he's a convicted felon, unlawfully carrying a firearm."

"What about his fifteen-year-old girlfriend?"

"They're holding her in juvenile detention. Her mother can't raise the money to bail her out." And after a pause, "Did you hear about the murders at the hair salon in Metairie? Manager opens up yesterday morning and finds two corpses?"

"No. I didn't have time to watch TV this morning."

"Jefferson Parish Sheriff's office called me a half hour ago. They ID'd one victim, a hair stylist who worked there. No ID on the other guy, but their detective ran his prints. Dig this. It was our racist prick CIA agent, Clint Hammer."

Frank sat bolt upright in his chair. "Hammer? Damn! There's only one reason for him to be in New Orleans. He's after Natalie."

"That's what I figure, but now he's dead. Looks like his Beretta killed the hair stylist, one shot to the head. So. Who killed Hammer?"

"Not Natalie. She's been in the mob house since Sunday afternoon at four-thirty."

"Don't underestimate her, Frank. You may think she was in there, but maybe she wasn't. Two years ago she murdered three men here and got away. In September she escaped from Boston after she stole paintings from the Gardner Museum. Only reason we know she's here is because Conti called you."

He hated to admit it, but Vobitch was right.

"How did Hammer find her?"

"The fucking asshole probably used that face-recognition software he was always bragging about. Good luck with your plan to grab Natalie. Keep me posted."

"Don't worry," Frank said. "When I arrest her, you'll be the first to know."

————

Festus poured himself a mug of black coffee, sat down at his kitchen table and rubbed his bleary eyes. He'd slept late but he still felt sleep deprived. Last night he'd driven to Subway, devoured a steak-and-cheese and called Clint again. No answer. When he drove to the motel on Vets Boulevard, Clint's rented Toyota Camry wasn't there, so he drove back to the mob house. The Camry wasn't there either, so he had driven home and fallen into bed.

He sipped his coffee. Clint already owed him for two days of surveillance. Damned if he'd keep working for him. If the asshole called today, he'd tell him to piss off. He'd already called his boss at Louisiana Livery, said he was feeling better and was ready to get back to work.

He glanced at the *Times-Picayune* on the table and skimmed the lead story. A local politician in trouble for skimming money from some fund or other. Nothing new there. He opened the Metro Section and a headline jumped out at him. **Sunday Night Massacre at Vietnamese Restaurant**. Nothing new there, either. These Vietnamese gangsters were beyond vicious.

Below the fold another headline caught his eye. **Two Men Found Dead in Hair Salon.** He skimmed the article. The cops had identified one man but not the other. They believed the men had been murdered after the salon closed at nine Sunday night.

Festus scratched the stubble on his chin. Clint had hired him to watch a mob house but wouldn't tell him his last name. At the time, he'd figured the guy was just a dry-fart, didn't want to reveal his full name. But two multiple murders had gone down within two miles of the mob house Clint had hired him to watch. He'd been a PI for several years and he didn't believe in coincidences.

Clint had to be involved. The cops hadn't identified one victim at the hair salon. Maybe that's why Clint hadn't called. Maybe he was dead.

Not that he was going to do anything about it. At least not right away.

He got up and put two frozen waffles in the toaster. Better stoke the furnace while he could. Any minute now his boss at Louisiana Livery might call him.

————

Natalie gazed into the bathroom mirror, dabbing skin-colored makeup on her jaw. The ice Annmarie gave her had eased the pain, but now there was a yellowish bruise. Orazio didn't seem to notice it when he caught her in the garage. He was too angry. But if the yellowish bruise turned purple, Catarina would notice and ask her about it.

"Laura," Bianca called through the door. "Will you read me a story?"

"I'll be right out." She put the makeup kit in her purse and took out her iPhone. No text. She checked the other phone. No text from Conti. She put them in her pants pockets, one on the left, one on the right. She didn't want to deal with Conti, but she was desperate to talk to Pak Lam.

After dinner tonight I will take you and the girl Christmas shopping.

Orazio's chilling words.

He wasn't going to take them shopping. He was going to kill them.

She had to get away, but how? Orazio wasn't here, but the guard was and so was Tommy. Too bad she hadn't kept Hammer's Beretta. At least she would have a fighting chance.

When she opened the bathroom door, Bianca was curled up on a chair beside the coffee table. She held up the Mother Goose book and said, "Rumpelstiltskin!"

"Rumpelstiltskin it is," Natalie said. Maybe a fairy tale would take her mind off her worries. She sat in the other chair and Bianca climbed into her lap. She knew the Rumpelstiltskin fairy tale, a girl locked in a tower because the king expected her to spin straw into gold.

A bit like her situation, but hers was far worse. Imprisoned in a house with vicious mobsters, because Europol agent John Conti had black-mailed her. Forget spinning straw into gold. Conti wanted the name of a Mafia kingpin. But one of the mobsters was going to kill her.

A vibration came from one of her pockets. Hoping it was Pak Lam, she said, "Hold on, Bianca. Let me get up so I can answer my phone."

Bianca slid off her lap and put the book on the chair. Natalie stood up and checked her cellphones. Her heart sank. It wasn't Pak Lam. It was a text on her Conti phone, but wasn't from Conti. *Natalie, it's Frank. You and Bianca aren't safe in that house. I can help you. Bring Bianca to the house down the street this afternoon at two o'clock. Conti won't be there.*

Her heart pounded. She was desperate to get out of the house, but Renzi wanted to arrest her. Still, if she managed to get out of the house, she might be able to escape.

She texted back: *Dangerous. Guard may not let me.*

His reply came immediately. *A woman and a little boy will be outside the green house down the street to your left. The one with a fake snowman and a reindeer on the lawn.*

She texted *I will try.* And closed the phone.

"Who was that?" Bianca asked, gazing at her.

"Just a friend. Let's finish the story." She put the cellphone in her pocket and sat down. But as she read Rumpelstiltskin part of her mind was in planning mode.

Put everything she needed to escape in her leather purse.

Hope and pray that Orazio didn't come home.

Sneak out without the guard knowing it.

She had no idea what would happen then. A woman and a child would be at the house down the street. But Frank Renzi would be there, armed and dangerous, packing a gun and three arrest warrants.

He wouldn't let her go without a fight. Maybe she could distract him.

Overpower him with a Taekwondo move, grab his gun and escape. A long shot, but she had no choice.

If she didn't get out of the house before dinner, Orazio would kill her.

CHAPTER 33

1:45 PM

Plagued by doubt, Frank chugged some water and set the bottle on Mary Hogan's kitchen counter. Bianca was an orphan and Jacques might as well be. Now, driven by his desire to arrest Natalie, he was using them, putting the lives of two innocent children in jeopardy.

His plan was a high-stakes gamble, a complicated scheme that involved mobsters, a traumatized boy, an arrogant Europol agent and Natalie, a woman he didn't trust. If it worked, he might save Bianca's life. He didn't want to think about what might happen if it didn't.

He peered out the window above the sink. Kelly should have been here fifteen minutes ago. Where the hell was she? At least the weather had cooperated. The torrential rain had stopped and the sun was shining. But would Jacques cooperate?

The boy still wouldn't talk and was prone to violent temper tantrums, screaming and throwing things. What if he had a meltdown when Kelly took him outside to play? Would Bianca throw a tantrum too? If the mob guard saw them, all hell might break loose. Bullets flying at Mary Hogan's house with two kids in the line of fire.

No way could he allow that to happen.

Conti was another problem. Tony Coppola was working the NOPD surveillance van today. Tony knew he was in the Hogan house, but Conti didn't. A while ago Tony had called and told Conti was following Orazio, who'd driven off in his SUV. Frank told Tony to call immediately if Conti came back. With Conti and Orazio out of the way, fewer things could go wrong. But if Orazio came back before Natalie and Bianca got here at two, he'd never let them leave the house. Hell, the mob guard might not let them leave either.

"Kelly's car just came around the corner!" David yelled from upstairs, watching the mob house from the window in the guest room.

"About time," Frank muttered. He went to the hall doorway and shouted, "Thanks, David. Tell me immediately when Natalie and Bianca leave the house." Provided they managed to get out.

He went in the mudroom off the kitchen. One door led to the garage, the other opened onto the driveway. He opened the entry door and watched Kelly walk up the driveway with Jacques, who was screaming and dragging his feet. Grasping a plastic shopping bag in one hand,

Kelly picked him up with the other and carried him through the mud-room into the kitchen. "Sorry, Frank. Traffic delay. Now that the sun is out everybody's going somewhere."

She huffed a wisp of dark hair off her sweaty forehead and put Jacques down. The boy sank onto his butt and drummed his heels on the floor, a three-year-old throwing a major temper tantrum. Dressed in jeans and a royal-blue T-shirt, Jacques had the cutest button nose you'd ever see, but a river of tears was leaking from his big brown eyes and running down his cafe-au-lait cheeks.

Kelly had on her take-down outfit, a navy sweatshirt and navy pants. The bulge under her shirt told him she was packing. Frank was, too. Nestled against his spine, Vobitch's Glock was tucked into the waistband of his pants, hidden by his loose-fitting sweatshirt.

"Will he be okay?" Frank said. "I need you to take him outside soon."

She gave him an arch look. "Does the Master Detective think I am without talent? Does he not appreciate the consummate acting skills I had to employ to get out of a meeting?"

Frank laughed. "What did you do? Use the girly excuse?"

"No, but my boss wasn't happy, I can tell you that. However, pursuant to your plan, I stopped to buy some toys." She took a softball-sized orange Nerf out of the shopping bag and tossed it to Jacques. Squalling wordlessly, he flung it back at her and hit her in the head.

"That went well," she said, bending down to retrieve the Nerf.

His cellphone vibrated against his leg. He took it out of his pocket and checked the ID. "Damn it to hell!"

Jacques went quiet, wrapped his arms around Kelly's legs and hid his face.

Using her warning voice, Kelly said sternly, "You're scaring him."

He held up his cellphone. "It's Conti."

She frowned. "Don't answer it. Let him leave a message."

"Okay, but there'll be hell to pay if he drives by and sees Natalie and Bianca." He checked the time. 1:55. "You need to take Jacques outside so Natalie will see you when she comes down the street. Can you quiet him down?"

"This might do it." She reached into the shopping bag and took out large Snickers bar.

She pried the boy's arms from her legs, knelt down and said, "Want a Snickers bar?"

Jacques reached for it, but Kelly pulled it away. "Let's go outside and eat it. Maybe we'll let the snowman and the reindeer have a bite."

The boy wiped tears off his face and rose to his feet.

"For someone who's never had kids," Frank said, "you've got good instincts."

Kelly shrugged. "Maybe. But I can't get him to talk. He still won't say a word."

————

Natalie stood at the window, reviewing the items she'd stuffed into her big leather purse. Her new passport, driver's license, credit card and all her cash. A small box of crayons and a notepad to entertain Bianca. Her iPhone and Conti's cellphone. After she escaped she would dump that one. Good riddance to Conti.

Failure was not an option. This was her only chance to escape.

She had dressed Bianca in jeans and a blue T-shirt with a little alligator on it. Bianca wanted to wear shorts, but she wouldn't let her. It would be cold in Boston. Before they got there she would have to stop and buy her a windbreaker.

She checked her wristwatch. 1:56. Time to go. Her stomach clenched in a hard knot. Turning away from the window, she said, "Let's take a walk, Bianca. Now that it stopped raining, it's a beautiful day. There's a little boy playing outside a house down the street."

Bianca's face lit up in a smile. "Can I play with him?"

"Maybe. We'll see." She went to the door. Her heart pounded, sending pain down her jaw. Now the bruise was turning purple. To hide it, she had slathered more makeup over it.

"Be quiet when we go past Catarina's room, okay?"

Bianca nodded. "So Tommy won't hear us."

She smiled. "Exactly. We'll go out through the door off the kitchen. Annmarie won't mind."

"Can I have a Popsicle?"

"No. You had one this morning." She opened the bedroom door and they tiptoed past Catarina's room. Orazio still hadn't returned. If he came back now, she was doomed. And she still had to get past the guard. She paused at the landing halfway down the stairs. Her heart beat her ribs like a wild thing. Nicky sat in the chair beside the foyer.

She put on her stone face and started down the stairs.

He looked up, scowling at her. "Where you going?"

"To see Annmarie in the kitchen."

Bianca squeezed her hand. She wanted to hug her.

Did Bianca know how frightened she was? Maybe not. To her this was probably an exciting adventure.

When they entered the kitchen, Annmarie said, "Hi Laura. Hi Bianca."

"We're going for a walk," she said. "It's too nice to stay inside."

"It sure is. If I didn't have to prep these vegetables for dinner, I'd go with you."

"Can I have a Popsicle when we come back?" Bianca asked.

"If Laura says it's okay," Annmarie said. "Have a nice walk."

"See you in a while," Natalie said, desperately hoping she wouldn't.

If all went well, she would never set foot in this house again.

She looked in the garage and breathed a sigh of relief. No black SUV. She opened the side door. Nicky's yellow Jeep stood in the driveway.

She wanted to take Bianca's hand and run down the street to the green house. But if Nicky saw them, he'd be after them like a shot.

Would he shoot them? Not in broad daylight on a street where any-one could see them probably. Not even Orazio would dare to do that.

But she had to play the part. Just a nanny taking her charge for a walk in the sunshine. She slung the strap of her purse over her shoulder and took Bianca outside. The fresh air felt marvelous.

A strange calm settled over her.

Renzi wanted to arrest her. Maybe this was a just ploy to get her away from the mobsters. In his text he'd said Conti wouldn't be there, but cops lied all the time.

Conti was the biggest liar of all, lying beside her in bed after sex, say-ing he loved her. The prick.

Conti had forced her to make a deal with the devil. A deal with no good outcomes. Risk her life by infiltrating a murderous Mafia gang to get information for him, or face three murder charges in New Orleans.

Where would she be two hours from now?

Driving to Boston or sitting in a jail cell?

She had no control over what would happen. Fate would decide.

———

Frank stood at Mary Hogan's front door, watching Kelly and Jacques pretend-feed bits of the Snickers bar to a Styrofoam snowman with a carrot nose, and a small brown-plastic reindeer.

Now it was 2:02. No sign of Natalie and Bianca.

"They just came out of the house!" David yelled from upstairs. "Walking down the driveway."

He tapped the storm door to signal Kelly. She nodded, took the orange Nerf out of her pocket and tossed it to Jacques. He got a hand on it, but the Nerf bounced on the grass and rolled toward the sidewalk. Kelly dashed after the ball and caught it before it rolled into the street.

Now he could see Natalie and Bianca walking down the sidewalk on the other side of the street. When they reached the corner, Kelly waved and called to her. Natalie took Bianca's hand and they crossed the street.

So far so good. Bianca went over to Jacques and said something. She was three years older than Jacques, but only an inch or two taller. Kelly gave the Nerf to Bianca and spoke to Natalie.

Watching anxiously, Frank thought, *Get her in the house!*

Bianca tossed the Nerf to Jacques. He caught it but he didn't seem to know what to do, just stood there with the Nerf, staring at Bianca.

Natalie spoke to Bianca and they came up the walk to the front door.

Frank opened it and let out a sigh of relief as Natalie brought Bianca inside. Maybe his plan would work after all.

Natalie looked at him, stone-faced. "Is Conti here?"

"No. He doesn't know I'm here. I didn't tell him about this house."

Wide-eyed and silent, Bianca looked at him, then at Natalie.

When Kelly came inside with Jacques, Frank shut the door, gave her a look and said, "Treats for the kids in the kitchen."

He wanted to talk to Natalie alone. She seemed tense, her expression strained, her eyes wary, and her jaw was swollen.

He waited until Kelly took the kids to the kitchen, then said, "Your jaw is swollen. Did someone hit you?"

She raised her chin, challenging him. "Orazio is going to kill us."

"He threatened you?"

Her lips tightened. "Nothing so obvious. This morning he said he would take me and Bianca Christmas shopping after dinner tonight. I don't think shopping is part of his plan."

He didn't like the sound of that. Maybe he'd gotten them out of the house in the nick of time.

209

To allay her fears, he said, "We can protect you." *Put you in a jail cell, Orazio won't get near you.*

She gazed at him, skepticism visible in her almond-shaped eyes. Could she read his mind?

He pointed her toward the kitchen and followed her. When they entered the room, Bianca said in English, "Can I have a Popsicle?"

Natalie smiled and said to Kelly, "She already had one today, but I guess it's okay if she has another one. Bianca loves Popsicles."

"I'm not sure we have any," Kelly said. "Jacques, do you want a Popsicle?"

The boy sank to the floor beside the kitchen table and began kicking his feet and screaming. Bianca stared at him, frowning. In English she said, "Why he do that? He's not nice."

Natalie shushed her and said to Frank, "What's wrong? The boy seems very unhappy."

"His mother died recently," Frank said quietly. "Murdered. Jacques isn't over it yet."

Natalie said something in Italian to Bianca. Now Bianca looked sad, too. Natalie knelt down beside Jacques. "What's wrong, Jacques? Such a beautiful boy. I love your name."

Jacques stopped screaming and kicking his feet.

"Your name reminds me of a song I know." In a soft voice, she began to sing. *Frère Jacques, Frère Jacques, Dormez-vous? Dormez-vous? Sonnez les matines, sonnez les matines Ding ding dong, ding ding dong.*

Jacques sat up, staring at Natalie, and she sang the song again. When she finished Jacques said, "Mama used to sing that song to me."

Kelly gasped. Equally stunned, Frank watched as Natalie sat on the floor and rubbed the boy's back. "A beautiful song for a beautiful boy. You miss Mama?"

"Mama," he said, gazing at Natalie with doleful eyes.

"You have a big pain in your heart," she said. "Shall we draw a picture of it?"

She opened her leather handbag and took out a small box of crayons and a notepad. Using a red crayon, she drew a big sad face. Then she handed the box of crayons to Jacques.

"Show me where it hurts, Jacques. Draw me a picture of your heart."

Jacques took out a blue crayon and drew a lopsided heart. "Mama's heart."

Natalie hugged him. "Very good, Jacques. You miss Mama and Mama misses you."

"Sing the reindeer song," Bianca said. "A happy song."

Natalie looked up and smiled at her. "Okay."

But then David called from upstairs, "Blonde woman incoming from the mob house."

"Catarina," Frank said. "Go talk to her, Kelly. I'll keep everyone in the kitchen."

The front doorbell rang. Natalie scrambled to her feet and grabbed her leather purse. "No. I'll talk to her."

Before he could stop her, Natalie bolted out of the kitchen and ran toward the front door.

"Don't leave me!" Bianca screamed, and ran after her.

With an ear-splitting wail, Jacques ran after Natalie and Bianca.

"Kelly!" Frank said, "make up a story and get them in here. Catarina, too." Hell, he'd take her into custody along with Natalie.

But by the time Kelly caught up to Jacques, Natalie had opened the front door. She grabbed Bianca's hand and took her outside.

Jacques kept on wailing.

Kelly scooped him up and stepped outside.

Cursing under his breath, Frank waited. A minute passed.

The storm door opened and Kelly came back inside, clutching Jacques, who was wailing and kicking his feet.

She grimaced at Frank and said, "They're going back to the house."

CHAPTER 34

"Orazio is very angry," Catarina said, avoiding her eyes as they walked down sidewalk.

Sick with despair, Natalie didn't answer, focused on putting one foot in front of the other, taking tiny gasps of air through her mouth, tasting the sour bile in her throat. Any second she might drop to her knees and vomit in the gutter. *Don't think about Orazio. Prepare your story.*

Bianca squeezed her hand, anxiously looking up at her. The girl was frightened. Not half as frightened as she was. *We'll protect you,* Renzi had said. Empty words. He didn't have to face Orazio.

Her only chance to escape was gone. The woman with Jacques was a cop—she'd seen the bulge under her sweatshirt—and another cop was upstairs. Three armed cops in a so-called safe house.

Renzi had lured her there so he could arrest her.

How stupid of her to think that she might escape from him. She'd be lucky to escape with her life.

When they reached the driveway, a dark blue SUV was parked beside Nicky's yellow Jeep. Orazio stood at the front door, glaring at them. She tried to quell her mounting sense of desperation, her heart racing, her shirt clammy with sweat. Orazio was going to kill her.

If he didn't do it now, he would do it later.

She and Bianca followed Catarina into the house. Bianca gripped her hand tighter. Nicky was sitting in his usual spot beside the foyer. She refused to look at him.

"Take the girl up to your room," Orazio said to Catarina. "Wait there until I call you."

Without a word, Catarina took Bianca's hand. As they mounted the stairs, Bianca turned, gazing at her with terrified eyes.

Orazio motioned her into the dining room. The table was already set for dinner, porcelain place-settings, gleaming silverware, linen napkins folded just so. She had an overpowering urge to laugh. The condemned woman would sit at an elegant dinner table to eat her last meal.

"Why were you in that house?" Orazio said in a quiet voice. Which made it all the more sinister.

She dug her fingernails into her palms. "It's a nice day. Bianca can't stay inside all the time. She needs to get some fresh air and a bit of sun."

"After you went shopping with Catarina, did I not tell you never to leave the house?"

"Yes, but—"

Orazio slapped her, a vicious blow to her cheek. She recoiled and backed away. Shooting stars danced before her eyes. She shook her head and blinked rapidly to clear her vision.

Nicky was watching her from the foyer with a smug smile on his face. The bastard.

Orazio stepped closer, looming over her in his business suit, so close she could smell his spicy aftershave. "Why do you not listen, Laura? I made it very clear that you are not to leave the house."

She said nothing, resisting an urge to rub her cheek where he'd slapped her. *Don't let him intimidate you. Show no fear. If you do, he'll come after you like a lion pouncing on a gazelle.*

"You women are impossible. We stay in an elegant house and eat home-cooked meals, but are you happy? No. Catarina constantly complains that she is bored. Now I must take her and Tomasso shopping. Go tell them I am ready to leave. Take the girl to your room and stay there until it is time for dinner." His implacable eyes bored into her. "Do not leave your room. If you do, Nicky will shoot you."

The words chilled her. No more subtle threats.

If she tried to escape, she would die.

Shaken, she left the dining room and approached the stairs. Her legs felt weak and shaky, and she could barely breathe. Gripping the banister with one hand, she climbed the stairs, went to Catarina's room and tapped on the door.

Catarina opened it immediately. Her eyes widened as she stared at Natalie's cheek. "My God, he hit you," she whispered. "I'm so sorry."

"Orazio is ready to take you shopping now. He told me to stay in my room with Bianca."

"Tommy," Catarina called over her shoulder, "Orazio will take us shopping now." To Natalie she whispered, "Be careful. I do not trust this guard."

Natalie didn't either, nor did she trust Catarina. When the chips were down, Catarina's allegiance would be with Tommy and Orazio.

"Where's Bianca?"

"Watching TV. Wait here, I will get her."

Tears misted her eyes, but she blinked them away.

She had to stay strong for Bianca.

Bianca came to the door, smiled and said, "I'm watching a TV show. The Muppets."

"That's good. Let's go in our room and I'll put it on for you."

If only she could be like Bianca. The girl had witnessed a sad scene at the house Renzi was using to spy on the mobsters, but she seemed to have forgotten the little boy who was devastated about losing his mother. His murdered mother.

A simple folk song had soothed him.

A show about puppets on TV had distracted Bianca.

But nothing could quell her fears about what would happen after dinner. Orazio was taking Catarina and Tommy shopping. If she didn't find a way to escape before he came back, she and Bianca were as good as dead.

———

Frank stood beside David at the second floor window, unable to contain his fury. His plan to grab Natalie and Bianca had failed. Natalie had thwarted him again. She might not have suspected that Kelly was a cop, but hearing David warn them that Catarina was coming had put Natalie on full alert. She knew he wanted to arrest her.

Maybe Orazio had threatened to kill her and maybe he hadn't. Either way, Natalie preferred to take her chances with the mobsters.

"Whose SUV is parked beside the yellow Jeep?" he said.

"I don't know," David said. "Orazio drove it in the driveway two minutes after Natalie brought Bianca in here. I didn't want to interrupt at a crucial moment, so I didn't say anything." David turned to him with a worried frown. "Should I have told you then?"

"Doesn't matter. Either way, we're screwed. Keep watching the house. If Orazio comes out with Natalie and Bianca, tell me right away. Natalie claims he's going to kill them tonight."

"Jesus!" David said. "What do we do then?"

"Stop him," Frank snapped. "I'm going down and talk to Kelly."

When he entered the kitchen, Kelly was trying to comfort Jacques, who was sobbing as though his heart would break.

"David says Orazio came home right after Natalie got here. Not in the black SUV. Now he's got a blue one. What did the blonde woman say? Catarina."

"She seemed scared. She told Natalie to bring Bianca home right away. I played dumb and told her Bianca could come over anytime and play with Jacques, and they left." Massaging the sobbing boy's back, Kelly said, "What could I do? Whip out my Glock and make them stay?"

"You did the right thing, but I'm worried about Natalie. This might have been our only chance to grab her and put Bianca in a safe place."

"I know you want to arrest her, but did you see how good she was with Jacques? Singing to him? Comforting him? She's not all bad."

"Maybe not, but she killed people."

"True, but you showed me her diary. Natalie's mother was murdered, too. Maybe that's why she can relate to the pain Bianca and Jacques are feeling."

Irritated, he said, "She shot me. At the time, you were pissed off about it. Now you want to give her a pass?"

A nasty gleam appeared in Kelly's sea-green eyes, a look he knew well. "No, but I think you need to cut her some slack."

Jacques flailed his arms and squirmed, trying to get down. When Kelly set him on his feet, he looked at Frank and said, "Mama."

Locking eyes with the boy, he said, "What happened to Mama?"

"Frank," Kelly said sharply. "Not now."

"You want to put King Rock away for killing Angelique, don't you?"

At the sound of his mother's name, Jacques began crying again.

"Frank, don't push him. Give it a few days. I can't wait to tell the social worker how Natalie got him to talk."

"I'm glad she did, but you're right. It's better to wait. Right now, arresting Natalie isn't my biggest concern. She says Orazio is planning to kill her and Bianca."

Kelly's eyes widened in horror. "Kill them? Frank, we have to get them out of there!"

"Yes, but marching up to the door to get them will get us nowhere. Orazio told her he'd take them shopping tonight after dinner. That might be a plus. If he does, we'll ambush him. Tony's in the surveillance van. He can cut Orazio off so David and I can capture him. Or kill him if he shoots at us. I'm sure he'll be armed. Either way, we've got a better chance of rescuing Natalie and Bianca if they're out of the house."

"Okay. I'll take Jacques back to the social worker and come back and help you."

His cellphone rang. He checked the ID and answered.

"Why didn't you tell me you found a surveillance house?" Conti screamed. "I just found out Natalie and the girl took a walk and went in a house down the street. Are you there now?"

Frank massaged his temples. What else could go wrong?

"Yes, but Natalie isn't."

"Stay where you are. I'll be there soon."

He ended the call and said to Kelly, "That was Conti. You better get Jacques out of here. Conti's coming here, loaded for bear. It ain't gonna be pretty."

———

Bianca perched on the chair, staring at the TV screen. The Muppets were doing silly things and laughing. She wasn't. When Catwoman turned on the show in her bedroom, she had pretended to like it so Cat-woman wouldn't get mad.

Owl was already mad at her. Glaring at her with his hateful eyes. Just thinking about them made her tummy hurt. Her eyes filled with tears. Laura had a big red mark on her cheek. Owl must have hit her. Now she was in the bathroom with the door shut.

Why was Owl so angry? All they did was take a walk. She hated stay-ing inside all the time. Then the lady who lived in the green house in-vited them to come over so she could play with the little boy. The lady gave her an orange Nerf ball. She tried to play catch with the little boy but he wasn't much fun and then Laura said they had to go in the house.

Laura's boyfriend was there, the one that looked like Papà, except for the scar on his chin. The lady called him Frank.

She thought about Papà. She hadn't seen him for so long, it was hard to remember what he looked like.

Then the little boy threw a tantrum. When she said he wasn't nice, Laura whispered to her in Italian, saying not to be rude. Then Frank talked to Laura in English. He said the little boy's mother had died. She got that part of it, but then he said another word.

It sounded a little bit like *merda*, but different.

She didn't know what it meant.

When Laura sang *Frere Jacques,* the little boy stopped crying. Laura let him use her crayons to draw a picture of his mother's heart, saying he missed his mother and his mother missed him, too.

Her eyes brimmed with tears. She missed Mama a lot.

Did Mama miss her?

The bathroom door opened. Laura came out and gave her one of her happy smiles, but that didn't fool her. Laura wasn't any happier than she was. She hated living here. Christmas was coming. When she and Laura stood at the window after it got dark, all the houses on the street had pretty decorations that lit up in different colors, red and white or green and gold.

Laura sank onto the chair beside hers. "How's the Muppet show? Is it good?"

She looked at the TV. Now the purple Muppet was dancing around and singing. "No. Turn it off." She left her chair and climbed into Laura's lap. "I'm scared of Owl."

Laura hugged her and said, "Don't be scared. I'll protect you."

She touched the red place on Laura's cheek with her finger. "He hit you."

"Yes." Laura heaved a sigh. "He's a very bad man, I told you that. If you promise not to tell anyone, I'll tell you a secret."

She didn't want to hear any more secrets. Last time Laura told her a secret, she said her mother died when she was ten. Maybe that's why she felt sorry for the little boy.

But *her* mother was dead, too.

Maybe Laura was going to live with her boyfriend and leave her here with Owl. Then she would never see Laura again.

She put her arms around Laura's neck and sobbed, "Don't leave me, Laura."

"I won't leave you," Laura whispered, rubbing her back. "I promise."

CHAPTER 35

Orazio stopped at the gate inside the Canal Place garage, pressed the button and took a ticket. The gate lifted and he drove up the ramp.

Dead silence in the SUV. He glanced at Catarina in the rearview mirror, sitting in back, too frightened to talk. Beside him, Tommy wasn't talking either. His brother knew he was furious, knew enough to keep his mouth shut.

He rounded the turn and drove up to the next level. No vacant spaces. The multilevel cement structure was full of cars, moviegoers and shoppers buying last-minute Christmas gifts.

"Why are you driving a different SUV?" Tommy asked. "Where's the black one?"

"Quiet," Orazio hissed. His brother had the brains of a flea. When too many people knew a secret, it was no longer a secret. Catarina knew about the stolen jewelry, but not about their attempt to fence it at the Vietnamese restaurant. Or the murders.

"Why did you let the nanny leave the house, Catarina?"

Her frightened eyes met his in the rearview. "I didn't. Tommy and I were in our room."

He continued up the ramp past vehicles parked on both sides. "Why did she take the girl in that house? Who else was there?"

"A woman and her little boy. She was very nice. She said Bianca could come over and play with the boy anytime she wanted."

"No one else was in the house?"

"Not that I saw."

"This woman is the boy's mother?"

Catarina didn't answer, avoiding his eyes in the mirror.

"Look at me! I asked you a question. Did you not hear me?"

"I'm not sure," Catarina said, reluctantly meeting his eyes in the mirror. "The woman was white, but … the boy was black."

Merda! He knew it. The woman was a cop!

He continued to the rooftop level and found a vacant space. In stony silence they rode the elevator down to Level Three where the cinema and the food stalls were located. Most of the tables in front of the food vendors were empty. People were in the theater or downstairs shopping.

"Meet us here at four o'clock," he said to Catarina. "Don't be late."

She managed a fake smile. "Don't worry, I won't. Thank you for taking us shopping."

"Go find your precious Saks Fifth Avenue. I need to talk to Tommy."

As Catarina hurried to the escalator Orazio sat in a molded-plastic chair at a vacant table. Tommy took the seat opposite him. Odors from a nearby pizza shop filled the air, but American pizza couldn't compare to Italian pizza: crust slathered with tomato gravy, layers of mozzarella and Parmesan cheese, topped with slices of fresh-cooked sausage.

"I didn't hear them go out," Tommy said in Italian. "We were in our room. I thought the guard was supposed to make sure they didn't leave the house."

"The woman in that house was a cop."

Tommy's eyes widened. "How do you know this?"

"I know this because white women do not have black babies."

"Maybe her husband is black."

He slammed his palm on the table. "In that neighborhood? Don't be stupid."

Visibly angry, Tommy glared at him but said nothing.

"I will get rid of them tonight. The girl and the nanny."

A frown creased Tommy's forehead. "Why?"

He took a deep breath to calm himself. "Did you forget that the girl witnessed what happened in Venice? Her parents are dead, but if that cop had taken custody of her, she could testify against us."

Tommy puffed his cheeks. "How will you do it?"

"Never mind. Don't tell Catarina. If you do, I will make you wish you had never been born."

Avoiding his gaze, Tommy muttered, "I won't."

"I need to think. Go downstairs and buy your wife something nice for Christmas."

As soon as Tommy got on the escalator Orazio reached inside his jacket and took out a cigar. And put it back. These stupid Americans did not allow smoking inside public buildings.

He thought about what Catarina said. If the woman in the green house down the street was a cop, maybe there were others, spying on Tick-Tock's house. How long had they been watching?

The publicity about the murders at the Saigon Canteen worried him. He should have made it look like a fucked-up robbery, but he hadn't. His clueless brother wanted to know where the black SUV was. Earlier he had parked it at the airport and rented another one.

His cellphone rang. *Merda!* Another problem.

He punched on and said, "Hello Silvano, how are you?"

"Where are you?" Silvano said, ignoring his pleasantry, a sure sign of displeasure.

"At Canal Place in the French Quarter. Catarina and Tommy are Christmas shopping."

"A detective came to my home today, asking about my Toyota Sequoia SUV. He wanted to know where it was Sunday night."

An ice pick of fear pierced his heart. Someone had seen the SUV outside the Vietnamese restaurant, just as he'd feared.

"What did you tell him?"

"I said it was in my garage." And after a pause, "But you and I both know it wasn't. Where was it?"

"Parked in the garage at Tick-Tock's house. Sunday afternoon I took Tommy and his wife for a steamboat ride along the river. We came home at four-thirty."

Silence on the other end.

He wiped his sweaty palms on his trousers and waited.

"Did you see the newspaper article about these murders at the Vietnamese restaurant?"

"No. What happened?" When difficult questions arise, admit nothing. But his worst fear had come true. Silvano had read the article, and a cop had questioned him about the SUV.

"Someone whacked four Vietnamese gangsters. It did not appear to be a robbery."

"Perhaps another Vietnamese gang was responsible."

"Perhaps," Silvano said.

Orazio said nothing, growing more and more apprehensive during the extended silence. Did Silvano recall the comment he'd made about the Vietnamese gangs that stole cash and jewelry? If Silvano knew the Ng Family bought certain items for cash, he might conclude that Orazio had tried to fence jewelry at the Saigon Cafe Sunday night. Diamond jewelry worth many thousands of dollars that he had not reported to Tick-Tock.

Silvano might also surmise that the deal fell apart, which necessitated the murders that had drawn so much attention.

At last, Silvano said, "Your business will soon be finished here."

"Yes, thanks to you, and I appreciate it. Angelo will have those items ready for me on Wednesday afternoon."

"Good. Meet me at the real estate agent's office at eight-thirty on Thursday. Leave my SUV in Tick-Tock's garage. I will drive you to the airport."

The hairs on the back of his neck prickled.

"That is very kind of you." *No it wasn't. It was terrifying.*

"See you Thursday," Silvano said, and ended the call.

Orazio hurried to the elevator and rode it to the rooftop garage. The air was hot and humid. He mopped sweat from his forehead. His hand trembled as he held his lighter to his cigar and puffed to get it going.

The aroma of a fine cigar usually settled his nerves, but not today.

When he was seven, Father had taught him to play chess, an enjoyable game but also designed to be instructive. The first thing Father taught him: a chess match might be decided because of one bad move, a move that—once made—set the player on a certain path to destruction. And in chess, as in life, such a move could never be taken back.

Snippets of Silvano's words echoed in his mind. *I told him the SUV was in my garage. But you and I both know it wasn't. Someone whacked four Vietnamese gangsters. Leave my SUV in Tick-Tock's garage.*

Most alarming of all: *I will drive you to the airport.*

Silvano's SUV was not parked in Tick-Tock's garage. This was easily remedied. But Silvano's offer to drive him to the airport was ominous. If a made man, especially a close confidant of The Boss, said he was taking you for a ride, it was definitely not good news. Orazio shuddered.

When he arrived at the real estate office on Thursday, a bullet might be waiting for him.

———

3:15 PM

Frank trained the binoculars on the mob house. David was downstairs taking a break. An hour ago Orazio, Tomasso and Catarina had left in the dark blue SUV and hadn't returned. No sign of Natalie and Bianca. He was pissed that his plan had failed, but he was also worried. What happened after they returned to the house?

He doubted that Orazio would kill them there. But Natalie seemed certain he would kill them tonight, and he believed her.

He got on his cellphone and called Tony Coppola in the surveillance van. "Tony, it's Frank. Is Conti there?"

"No. I haven't seen him for quite a while."

"I'm still at the Hogan house. Conti's pissed that I didn't tell him about it. But here's the big problem. Natalie thinks Orazio is going to kill her and Bianca. He said he'd take them shopping after dinner. If he does, be ready to stop the SUV."

"Will do, but what if Conti comes back?"

"Screw Conti. He's focused on the mobsters. He doesn't give a shit about Natalie and the girl."

"Whatever you say, Frank. I'm with you."

"Thanks, Tony." He ended the call and spotted Kelly walking toward the side entrance of the Hogan house, carrying two plastic bags.

He yelled to David, "Kelly's here with the take-out." He hadn't eaten since breakfast, but he wasn't hungry. Acid was eating a hole in his gut.

A minute later he heard footsteps on the stairs and Kelly entered the guest room. "What's going on?"

"Orazio, Tomasso and Catarina drove off in the dark blue SUV an hour ago and haven't come back. Natalie and Bianca weren't with them. How's Jacques?"

"Okay. Better than he was, anyway. When I told the social worker how he responded when Natalie sang to him, she was thrilled. She said she'd tell the speech therapist to try that."

Frank saw Conti pull into the driveway. Silently cursing, he got on his cellphone, called Conti and said, "Get your car out of the driveway! You want the mobsters to see you?"

"Don't tell me what to do," Conti snarled.

"Move it now! Park on the side street and come in the door beside the garage," he said and ended the call.

"Asshole," Kelly said. "What is he thinking?"

"He's not thinking. He's too pissed. I better go down and talk to him. Stay here for a minute. I'll send David up to stand watch."

When he entered the kitchen, the spicy aroma of Kung Pao Chicken filled the air as David spooned some onto a plate.

"Conti's here," Frank said, "and he's loaded for bear. Can you go up-stairs and watch the mob house?"

"Aw shucks, and miss all the excitement?" David flashed a broad grin and headed for the stairs with his plate of Chinese take-out.

Frank went in the mudroom. Conti stood outside the door with the mother of all frowns on his face. When Frank opened the door, Conti brushed past him and entered the kitchen.

"Jesus Christ, Renzi. Last night you told me you didn't find a surveillance house. But I drove by the mob house this afternoon and saw Natalie and the girl come out of this one."

"I have warrants for Natalie's arrest. And I'm worried about the girl."

"You never intended to tell me." Conti glared at Kelly as she entered the room. "Who's this? Another NOPD cop to help you arrest Natalie?"

"Detective Kelly O'Neil," she said, matching Conti's nasty look. "I'm worried about Bianca. Why aren't you?"

"If you're so worried," Conti snapped, "why did you let her go back to the house?"

"They sent Catarina to get them," Frank said. "If we hadn't let them go, Orazio might have come over here with a gun. We had two kids here. I didn't want to endanger their lives."

"I just came from the local FBI office," Conti said. "When I told the Special Agent in Charge about the 'Netti brothers, he was very appreciative. He's been trying to identify the man who runs the Mafia gang in New Orleans. He's mobilizing a SWAT team to arrest them."

"A SWAT team?" Frank said. "Are you crazy? Two women and a five-year-old girl are in that house. Once the FBI takes over, you'll have no control over what happens."

"They know what they're doing. The SWAT team will order them to come out of the house. If they don't, SWAT will make a forced entry and take the 'Netti brothers into custody." Conti smiled, thrilled with his new-found power. "We'll take them to the FBI office and interrogate them, maybe cut them a deal if they give up the name of the Mafia kingpin who runs the local gang and the Antonetti Family in Venice."

Frank wanted to strangle him. If a SWAT team went in guns blazing, the mobsters wouldn't go down without a fight. Hell, they might even use Natalie and Bianca as shields. Even if they didn't, there was no way to guarantee the safety of anyone inside the house, least of all Natalie and Bianca. A sick feeling invaded his gut.

"How soon will the SWAT team be here?"

Conti smiled tightly. "I'm not sure. But it shouldn't be long."

CHAPTER 36

6:15 PM

Natalie dried her sweaty palms on the napkin in her lap. The odor rising from the Veal Alfredo on her plate—veal fried in a spicy batter and the thick creamy sauce coating the noodles—nauseated her.

She knew she should eat to keep up her strength. After dinner Orazio was going to take her and Bianca somewhere and kill them.

The guard was eating in the kitchen. No need to watch the door, not with Orazio seated at the head of the table in an expensive business suit like the Mafia kingpin he was. He'd made Bianca sit on the chair to his right and told her sit beside Bianca. Tommy sat to Orazio's left, facing Bianca. Beside him, Catarina sat in the chair opposite hers.

Just a happy Italian family eating a home-cooked meal.

It might be her last.

Every muscle in her body was knotted with tension. Orazio, Tommy and Catarina were drinking wine. She didn't dare touch hers. She needed to stay alert. What she needed most of all was a way to escape from Orazio before he executed his murderous plan.

Catarina was in a festive mood. Apparently she had forgotten the nasty scene when they returned from the house down the street, prattling about the fabulous silk dress she'd bought at Saks. It was the perfect shade of red. All her friends in Venice would be jealous. Tommy seemed strangely subdued, silently wolfing down fried veal and noodles.

"I saw a notice posted in Saks," Catarina said to Orazio. "There will be fireworks at nine o'clock tonight in the Spanish Plaza. Maybe we can take Bianca—"

"No." Orazio put down his fork and glared at Catarina.

"But Bianca would enjoy the fireworks—"

"Did you not hear me?" Orazio snapped. "I said no."

Natalie tried to get her attention: *Don't make him angry.* But Catarina just drank some wine and sliced off a bite of veal.

Bianca began swinging her legs back and forth, faster and faster. She might not have understood the exchange between Orazio and Catarina, but she knew Orazio was angry. Natalie put a hand on her leg. This was the worst possible time for Bianca to throw a tantrum.

Bianca stopped swinging her legs and stuck out her lower lip in a pout. She picked up her fork, twirled strands of noodles around it and let them fall to her plate.

Orazio frowned at her. "Stop playing with your food."

Bianca went still and stared at her plate.

Do what he says, Natalie silently pleaded. *Don't make him angry.*

"Eat your dinner!" Orazio commanded.

Bianca grabbed her plate with both hands and shoved it off the table.

The plate fell to the floor with a clatter, scattering pieces of porcelain, bite-sized chunks of veal and clumps of noodles over the polished wood floor.

Dead silence in the room. Everyone stared at Bianca.

"That's rude!" Orazio said in Italian. "Clean up the mess you made!"

Bianca screwed up her face and began to cry. Orazio grasped her forearm, pulled her off the chair and dragged her closer. Bianca wailed in fright. He released her arm and took hold of her chin.

"Stop crying and clean up the mess you made!"

Recognizing the murderous look in his eyes, Natalie rose from her chair. "I'll help you, Bianca."

Avoiding the gooey mess on the floor, she hurried to the sideboard, returned with an empty serving platter and put it on her chair. Hiccoughing sobs, Bianca looked up at her with mournful eyes. She used a linen napkin to wipe away her tears. "Put the broken pieces on the serving platter, Bianca. I'll wet a towel and clean up the noodles."

Without looking at Orazio, she hurried to the powder room below the staircase, a cramped space with a steep-slanted ceiling, a toilet and a small sink. She took a towel off a metal rod, wet it and returned to the table. Two large pieces of broken porcelain sat on the serving platter. Bianca stood by her chair, silently staring at the mess on the floor.

"The maid could do it faster," Tommy said. "Probably got a mop in the kitchen."

"No," Orazio snapped. "The girl made the mess. Let her clean it up."

Filled with an icy rage, Natalie clenched her jaw. Orazio was heartless, yelling at a defenseless five-year-old girl, displaying his power over her.

But this was only a prelude. Soon he would kill her.

She had to get Bianca out of here. Her heart hammered her chest as she put the broken porcelain on the serving platter, scooped up pieces of veal and noodles with the towel and dumped them on the platter.

An ominous silence filled the room, interrupted only by the clink of silverware as Tommy attacked his veal. Catarina was gulping wine like an alcoholic who hadn't had a drop in weeks.

Bianca was picking noodles off her jeans. Natalie tried to assess her mood. Frightened yes, but angry, too. Dumping her plate on the floor had been a deliberate act. Bianca had to know there would be consequences. Why was she so angry? Missing the fireworks? Doubtful. Something else was bothering her.

She finished mopping the floor, tossed the filthy towel on the serving platter and rose to her feet, intending to take the platter to the kitchen.

"Leave it," Orazio said. "Take the girl to her room and stay there."

"But Natalie didn't eat her dinner," Catarina said. "She must be hungry—"

"Silencio!" Orazio thundered. "Or I'll send you to your room too."

Tommy glowered at him, but said nothing.

Gripping Bianca's hand, Natalie went to the staircase. She squeezed Bianca's hand, but Bianca didn't squeeze back. The girl was terrified. So was she, but as they mounted the stairs the rage that she'd felt moments ago returned. No way would she allow Orazio to kill Bianca.

When they entered their room, Bianca ran to the table near the TV set, opened the coloring book and scribbled furiously on it with a black crayon. Natalie went into the bathroom, shut the door and massaged her throbbing temples. She and Bianca were trapped inside a house with a madman bent on killing them. A hopeless situation.

Then she recalled her mother's words, spoken more than twenty years ago, but she'd never forgotten them. "Never give up, Natalie."

Setting her jaw, she took the cloth pouch that held her makeup kit off the shelf beside the tub, unzipped the pouch and took out her iPhone. No messages. Not that it mattered. Pak Lam was too far away to help her. But a red light was flashing on her Conti phone.

She had a text message. Not from Conti, from Frank Renzi. *R U OK? I am in the house down the street. My teams are stationed at both ends of the block. If O takes you and B out in the SUV, we will stop him.*

Tears misted her eyes. Help from an unexpected quarter. Frank was worried about her.

"Laura," Bianca called from outside the door. "I have to pee."

"Okay, I'm coming." She put the iPhone in the makeup bag, zipped it shut and put it back on the shelf. She stuck the Conti cellphone in her pocket and opened the door.

Bianca was kneeling at the table, scribbling on another picture.

She took out the Conti phone, accessed Frank's text, hit Reply and typed: *Not OK. B threw tantrum. O sent us upstairs to our bedroom.*

Her heart jolted. Voices outside the door. Tommy and Orazio.

She hit Send and jammed the cellphone in her pocket.

———

6:30 PM

Unable to sit still, Frank did another circuit around Mary Hogan's kitchen table and perched on a chair opposite Kelly. "I texted Natalie a half hour ago but she never answered."

Kelly looked at him, somber-eyed. "You don't think Orazio killed them already, do you?"

"I don't know. He killed a lot of people in Venice. Why worry about two more?"

Kelly had on her take-down outfit and her game-face. Her Glock 9mm lay on the table in front of her. "Where's Conti?"

"Hell if I know. I called Vobitch and laid out the situation. But when I asked him to call the SAC and ask about the SWAT team, he said he did-n't think the SAC would tell him anything."

But Vobitch would monitor the situation with his radio handset and had sent reinforcements. Now Orville and David were in a squad car at the far end of the block north of the mob house, ready to stop Orazio if he drove in their direction with Natalie and Bianca.

Frank massaged his eyes, then his aching temples. He'd done what he could to protect them. Now it was a waiting game. He hated waiting.

The odor of Kung Pao Chicken lingered in the air. He hadn't eaten any. He'd run out of Rolaids hours ago, not that they did much to relieve the acid in his gut.

His cellphone was on the table beside Vobitch's Glock. Not as good as the SIG-Sauer that IAD had confiscated, but better than nothing.

He checked the phone. No messages.

Kelly gulped some bottled water. "Conti's a heartless bastard. How can he think about letting a SWAT team go into the house? All hell could break loose. Doesn't he care about Bianca?"

"Hell, no. He's like a bulldog on a bone, got one thing on his mind. Grab the 'Netti brothers and make them talk. No telling what's going on inside that house right now."

He got on his cellphone and called Tony Coppola in the surveillance van. If he used his radio, everyone would hear their conversation, including some things that were better not spoken aloud.

"Hey, Frank, what's up?" Tony said.

"Nothing doing at the mob house?"

"Nope. Quiet as a cemetery in a fucking snow storm."

Frank grinned. Man, he loved this guy. Tony could sling some zingers. "Any sign of Conti?"

"No, which is fine by me. That guy's a major pain in the ass."

"If you see him, tell him to call me. In the meantime, be ready. If Orazio takes Natalie and Bianca out of the house and drives your way, block the intersection with the van."

"Damn straight," Tony said. "Grab the scumbag before he hurts anybody."

Frank closed his cell and it immediately vibrated. He checked it and said, "Great! I just got a text from Natalie." He read it to Kelly: *Not OK. B threw tantrum. O sent us upstairs to our bedroom.*

"What an asshole," Kelly said. "But at least we know they're alive."

"For now they are. Go upstairs and keep me posted on what's happening."

"Why? Tony's watching the house and so are David and Orville. What are you going to do?"

He picked up the Glock. "Wait by the front door. If Orazio comes out of that house, I'll be ready."

"You are not! You're gonna get a vest out of your car and put it on!"

From the look of fury in her eyes, he knew better than to argue, and she was right. If Orazio left the house with Natalie and Bianca, he'd be packing. A Kevlar vest wouldn't guarantee his survival, but it would protect his vital organs. Take a bullet in the head and it was all over.

He went to Kelly, put his arm around her and pulled her close. "Okay, but you're wearing one, too. There's an extra one in my trunk. Keep an eye on the house while I get them."

He went out the side door, jogged down the side street to his Dodge Charger and opened the trunk. And closed it. Why leave the car here? If something happened—and he had the feeling it might—he would need the car. He got in the Dodge and drove into Mary Hogan's driveway.

Someone in the mob house might see it, but so what?

Situation critical.

He took two vests out of the trunk, went in the side door, put the vests on the counter and took off his sweatshirt. He strapped the larger vest over his T-shirt and heard footsteps on the stairs.

Kelly hurried into the kitchen. About to give her the smaller vest, he noticed her stricken expression. "What's wrong?"

"An FBI Hummer just drove past the mob house. The SWAT team has arrived."

CHAPTER 37

6:50 PM

She braced herself against the wall between the front window and her bed, staring at the door. No voices in the hall now, only footsteps.

They stopped outside the door.

Her heart pounded like a runaway freight train.

The door flew open and Orazio strode into the room, his eyes cold and hard. Eyes without mercy. Eyes from hell.

"Ready to go shopping?" he said.

She gritted her teeth and put on her stone-face. Damned if she'd let Orazio see how terrified she was. Frank's text had given her a sliver of hope. But if she and Bianca got into a car with Orazio, there was no guarantee Frank could save them.

Should she put up a fight? Refuse to go with him?

Orazio crossed the room to Bianca, who stood by the table in front of the TV set. "Laura," he said, "her pants are stained with food. Why didn't you change them? I told you I would take you Christmas shopping after dinner."

Bianca yelled in Italian, "I don't want to go shopping with you! You killed Mamma! I hate you!"

Orazio smiled, seemingly amused. "You're quite the little spitfire."

"I hate you too!" Bianca screamed at Natalie. "You don't care about me. All you do is talk to your boyfriends on the phone."

Her heart slammed her ribs in a frenzy of fear. Bianca had uttered the worst possible words at the worst possible time.

Orazio turned, his face livid with fury. "Who are these boyfriends you talk to?"

"I don't have any boyfriends."

Orazio grabbed Bianca's arm. "Did you lie to me?" When Bianca started to cry, Orazio shouted, "Stop crying!"

To Natalie he said, "You have a cellphone?"

"Where would I get a cellphone?"

He crossed the room in two strides and slapped her. "Where is it?"

Stunned by the force of the blow, she struggled to catch her breath, finally managed to say, "I don't have one. I told you."

"You lie," he said, looming over her. "You are *una senora cattiva*. Treacherous and deceitful."

230

Like an enraged bull, he began to search the room. He put her suitcase on her bed and opened it. She had unpacked her clothes so it was empty, but Orazio searched each pocket. Finding nothing, he went to the table between the beds and opened the drawer. No cellphone.

Disgusted, he slammed the drawer shut. It sounded like a gunshot.

Bianca screamed and ran to the bathroom door beyond her bed, her eyes brimming with tears, watching Orazio.

With grim determination, he searched Bianca's suitcase, then crossed the room to the dresser that held the TV set. One by one he yanked open the drawers and pawed through their clothes.

Filled with despair, Natalie watched him with mounting desperation. If he searched her pockets and found the Conti cellphone, he would kill her. He was in such a rage, he might kill Bianca, too.

After a cursory glance at the coloring book on the table, he checked the box of crayons and dropped it on the table. Continuing his methodical search, he raised the cushions of both easy chairs and found no cellphone. His movements grew more agitated. He raised the mattress on Bianca's bed, first the foot, then the head. Finding nothing, he repeated the process with her bed. And found nothing.

He slowly approached her and removed a cigar from his shirt pocket. Gazing at her, he took out a lighter, flicked it, held the flame to the tip of the cigar and puffed. And puffed and puffed. A pungent aroma filled the air. When the cigar was lighted to his satisfaction, he smiled at her, his eyes gleaming with demonic zeal. "Tell me where is this cellphone."

Her stomach clenched like a fist. "There is no cellphone."

He grabbed her left forearm and touched the flame-red end of the cigar to it.

Shocked by the pain, she cried out. The sickening odor of burnt flesh filled the air. He released her arm.

She staggered backward and sank onto her bed.

"Where is the cellphone? Tell me or I will burn you again."

Bianca screamed, "Stop! Stop! It's in her pocket."

The air left her lungs in a whoosh. Natalie clenched her teeth in despair. Game over.

Orazio yanked her to her feet. Searched one pocket and found nothing. Searched the other pocket and took out her Conti phone.

"You lied to me, and not for the first time. Who is this woman in that house down the street?"

When she didn't answer, he said, "Who else was in the house?"

"No one."

Orazio puffed his cigar. "Who are these boyfriends you talk to?"

She raised her chin and glared at him. "I don't have any boyfriends."

"You want me to burn the other arm?"

"No!" Bianca shrieked and ran into the bathroom and slammed the door.

Orazio rushed to the bathroom and tried to open the door, but Bianca had locked it. Visibly angry, he kicked the door.

"Come out here, you little vixen!" The door didn't open. Silence in the bathroom.

He turned and approached her. But this time she was ready, poised in her Taekwondo fighter stance, legs apart, balanced on the balls of her feet, her arms by her sides, ready to strike.

Surprise registered on his face. "What, you want to fight me with karate? Judo? Kung Fu? You call yourself Laura Lam and claim to be Chinese, but you are not." His eyes bored into hers. "You lied to me. You are Vietnamese. Admit it."

"I admit nothing," she said, spitting the words at him. "You are despicable, a ruthless murderer who kills innocent people."

With no discernible reaction, he drew on the cigar and blew a plume of smoke. Set the cigar on the front windowsill, careful to leave the lighted end beyond the edge. Silently and methodically, he removed his jacket and laid it on her bed. Her heart jolted in fear.

In a suit, he looked like a businessman. In shirtsleeves, his powerful physique was unmistakable, massive shoulders and muscular arms that strained the fabric of his white shirt. She tried to calm herself. He outweighed her by a hundred pounds, but she was quicker, more agile.

"You want to fight me with your Asian martial arts? Go ahead." He assumed a boxer's stance, his left fist tucked below his chin, his right fist clenched below it, ready to strike.

Poised on the balls of her feet, she stepped to her left. His left fist jabbed at her. She dodged it easily and kept circling left. He mirrored her move, his implacable gaze locked on her face. Now he was between her and the door. She was trapped.

She pictured Clint Hammer dead on the salon floor, the man who'd killed Bruce. Orazio had killed Bianca's mother. Now he wanted to kill Bianca. She had to stop him. The odds were against her, but at least she would go down fighting.

He swung his right fist, a knock-out punch had it landed, but she ducked and danced away, breathing hard, inhaling the smoke from his smoldering cigar on the windowsill. The pungent aroma inspired her.

She grabbed the cigar and threw it at his eyes. The cigar hit his fore-head and fell on the floor. Unfazed, he brushed ash off his forehead with one hand and stepped on the cigar, grinding it out in the rug, send-ing pungent smoke spiraling into the air.

"You are no university student," he said calmly. "You are a spy. Who sent you to us?"

She kept circling left, watching his granite-hard eyes, watching for a signal that would reveal his next move. He blinked. Cocked his right fist.

Gathering her energy, she breathed deep to her diaphragm. Found her center of energy. Focused.

Exploding in a Taekwondo spin move, she leaped and kicked him in the head.

With a loud grunt, he staggered and fell to one knee, planting his other foot on the floor.

Her heart catapulted into her throat. She had landed a solid blow, one that would have felled most men, but Orazio seemed impervious to it.

Desperate, she leaped again and kicked at his head, but he dodged her foot. His right hand snaked out and locked onto her ankle.

Off balance and panting with exertion, she hopped on one foot. In-exorably, his powerful arms pulled her closer. She pummeled him with her fists, boxing his ear. He grabbed her forearm where he'd burned her and squeezed. Pain shot up her arm.

Before she could recover, his fist slammed the side of her face. She fell to the floor, gasping with pain.

Breathing hard, Orazio rose to his feet and stood over her. "My father warned me about you Asians. You are treacherous and deceitful."

A voice called from downstairs. "Mr. Antonetti, come quick. I need to talk to you!"

"Just a moment," Orazio called. He yanked her to her feet and sat her on the bed, glowering at her. "But first I will make sure my deceitful Vietnamese spy does not leave this room."

He turned and spotted the clothesline on the floor below the side window. As quick as a cat, he grabbed the clothesline and brought it to the bed. "Hold out your wrists. If you do not, I will punch you harder than before."

Knowing it was useless to resist, she held out her wrists. Quickly and efficiently, he bound them together, yanked her to her feet and hauled her to the side window. "Sit on the floor under the window."

Exhausted, she sank onto the floor. He wound the other end of the cord around the handle of the side window and tied it in a tight knot.

"Mr. Antonetti!" called the guard, more urgently than before.

"I'm coming," Orazio yelled. He put on his jacket and stood over her, his eyes fixed on hers. His expression sent shivers down her spine.

"Stay there and behave yourself," he said in a quiet voice. "If you do not, I will come back and kill both of you. Believe it."

She had no doubt that he would.

———

Orazio paused outside the door, fingering the lump on the side of his head. The treacherous Vietnamese spy had kicked him in the head and punched his ear, painful blows, but not powerful enough to defeat him. In the end, he had prevailed, but his head felt woozy. Blindsided by a fucking nanny who lied to appear innocent. He drew several deep breaths.

Rocco wanted to talk to him, but he could not allow the guard to see him in a moment of weakness. When dealing with underlings, always show strength. When his head cleared, he descended the stairs to the landing at the halfway point. It required all of his deceptive skills to mask his rage.

"Rocco," he called. "What is the problem?"

He heard rapid footsteps and Rocco appeared at the foot of the stairs, wide-eyed and agitated. "A big black Hummer drove by the house with men in FBI jackets! Looked like the SWAT teams you see on TV. Helmets and automatic rifles. I never seen anything like it."

His heart began to race. FBI? SWAT teams? He maintained a calm expression, but murderous thoughts rampaged in his mind, the first being: Silvano had ratted him out to the cops. No. Silvano would never send FBI agents to Tick-Tock's house. Maybe they were on this street to resolve a different matter. And maybe they weren't.

When in doubt, prepare for the worst. "Who else is downstairs?"

"Just the maid," Rocco said. "She's in the kitchen, cleaning up."

"Tell her to finish up and go home."

"Yes, sir." Rocco turned and ran down the hall toward the kitchen.

Orazio went in his bedroom and looked out the front window. No sign of the Hummer.

His head throbbed, a steady pain that distracted him. He touched the lump where the deceitful nanny had kicked him. Soon there would be swelling and a bruise. Fortunately, his hair would hide this. He studied himself in the mirror above the dresser. His ear was sore, but not red or inflamed. Nothing that Tommy or Catarina would notice.

He took out his cellphone and called Silvano, who answered right away. "Hello, Orazio. How are you?"

"Did you tell the cops your SUV was here?" This was no time for polite chit-chat. Be direct. Let the chips fall where they may.

"Of course not. Why would I?"

"The guard saw a SWAT team with FBI agents drive by Tick-Tock's house in a Hummer."

"Where are they now?" Silvano said sharply.

"I don't know. I can't see them from the window in my room."

"Where is my SUV?"

"In the garage," he said, relieved that he'd gone to the airport parking garage after leaving Canal Place and had Tommy drive Silvano's SUV back to Tick-Tock's house.

"Tell the maid to drive it to my house." A pause. "Donna knows where I live."

Of course, Orazio thought. Silvano's wife had passed five years ago and a man had his needs.

"I will send two cars, with eight of my best soldiers to help you. Here is the code to get into the room off the kitchen. In the closet you will find all the weapons you need."

He memorized the code, thanked Silvano and ended the call. He went to the dresser, grabbed the keys to Silvano's SUV and the rented SUV and ran to the stairs. "Rocco! Tell Donna to wait."

When he entered the kitchen, Donna, voluptuous and sexy even in her maid's uniform, looked at him with frightened eyes. He gave her the keys and said, "Drive Silvano's SUV to his house."

Without a word, she went into the garage. He gave the other set of keys to Rocco. "Back your car and the other SUV into the garage, nose out, and shut the garage door."

"Yes, sir," Rocco said, already heading for the garage.

Orazio strode to the door on the opposite side of the kitchen and punched in the code. A green light appeared on the keypad. He went inside and turned on the lights. No windows, no exit door. Two plush sofas faced a large movie screen. Behind them, a wet-bar with shelves of bottled liquor. Beside the bar was a gray-steel door. He opened it and stepped into a walk-in closet. A gun rack held two Remington shotguns and four Uzis. Beside it, a metal shelf held assorted handguns. The shelf above them held boxes of ammunition and spare magazines for the Uzis.

He decided the Uzis would be the most useful and carried three of them into the kitchen.

When Rocco came in from the garage, Orazio gave him one of the Uzis. Rocco smiled. "This will take out a few feds."

"Let us hope this will not be necessary." Rocco wasn't too bright, but he knew how to handle a gun. "Stay in the dining room at the front windows. Alert me if you see the Hummer or a SWAT team."

Carrying the other two Uzis, he followed Rocco down the hall toward the front door. Catarina was useless when it came to guns, but she could stand at her bedroom window and watch the back of the house.

As he went upstairs to his bedroom his thoughts returned to Laura. Who had she been talking to? Not boyfriends. Of this he was certain.

He took her cellphone out of his pocket, a cheap model with a primitive keyboard. He powered it on and opened the contact list. Only two numbers, one for JC, another for F. He called the number for JC.

A male voice with a foreign accent said, "'Allo?"

Orazio said nothing.

"Natalie, is that you?"

The man's accent sounded European. But who was Natalie?

"Who are you?" Orazio said.

After a brief silence, "Agent John Conti. Who are you?"

He ended the call. Agent John Conti. Interpol or Europol probably. The thought made him shudder.

Forget the murders at the Vietnamese restaurant. This was about the carnage in Venice. Conti knew Laura, but called her Natalie, a common tactic when agents infiltrated Mafia gangs. FBI Agent Joe Pistone had done this in New York, masquerading as Donnie Brasco.

Who was F, he wondered.

But he had no time to find out. He had to prepare for the attack.

Agent John Conti had sent a team of FBI agents here to arrest them.

CHAPTER 38

Frantic with worry, desperate to escape, Natalie tensed her muscles, straining against the clothesline that imprisoned her wrists. But the cord didn't give. It only made the pain worse where Orazio had burned her. Exhausted, she sank back against the wall below the windowsill.

Orazio had called her a Vietnamese spy. Her cover was blown. Worse, he had her Conti cellphone. She had deleted any texts she'd sent or received, but Conti's number was in it and so was Frank's.

If Orazio called Conti, Conti would know someone had taken the phone from her, but he would do nothing to save her. If Orazio called Frank, Frank would know she was in trouble, but what good would that do? He knew she and Bianca were upstairs in her bedroom, but he didn't know she was a prisoner, shackled and unable to move.

She heard the bathroom door open. Bianca saw her hunched on the floor with her wrists bound together and shut the door.

"Bianca," she called softly. "It's okay to come out. He's gone."

After a moment the door opened again. Clutching a small first aid kit, Bianca ran across the room, sobbing as if her heart would break. "I'm sorry I got you in trouble, Laura. I didn't mean to."

"I know you didn't. You miss your mama and you were upset."

"I'm afraid of Owl."

"So am I. He's a very bad man."

"Your arm must hurt. Maybe I can make it better." Bianca put the blue-plastic first aid kit on the bed nearest the window, opened it and held up a packet of band-aids. "Will this help?"

"Maybe. Show me what else is in it."

Bianca brought it over and held it so she could see the contents. More band-aids, antiseptic wipes, a small tube of antibiotic ointment, sterile gauze pads, a roll of adhesive tape, and a small pair of scissors.

"Open the little tube and squeeze some ointment onto a gauze pad."

Bianca took out the tube and unscrewed the cap. A blob of white ointment oozed onto her finger. She put her finger over the burn.

"No, don't do that. Open one of those little square packets and squeeze some ointment on the pad. Then put it over the burn."

Frowning in concentration, Bianca tore open the packet, squeezed ointment onto the gauze pad, and pressed it against the quarter-sized burn. The pad was just large enough to cover it. "Perfect," Natalie said. "But we have to get out of here before Orazio comes back."

237

"Why don't you call your boyfriend? Maybe he can help us." Bianca raised the front of her shirt.

The iPhone was tucked into the waistband of her jeans.

Stunned speechless, she stared at her lifeline to Pak Lam. And now, though she hated to admit it, to Frank Renzi.

"How did you find it?" she said.

"When I was in the bathroom, I looked in your makeup bag and saw it. Call the man who lives in that house with the little boy. The one who looks a little bit like Papa. He's a nice man."

A nice man. Well, Frank could be nice when he wanted to be. Bianca didn't know he wanted to arrest her. But that didn't matter now. If they didn't get out of here, Orazio would kill them.

"Okay, push the long button on the top to turn it on."

But Frank's number was in her Conti phone, she realized, not her iPhone contact list. The area code was easy. She remembered the next three digits, but the last four were hazy. She closed her eyes and concentrated. Was the last digit a three or an eight?

When the iPhone screen lit up, Bianca said, "What do I do now?"

"Press on the picture of the telephone."

When the next screen opened, Natalie said, "Okay, do you know your numbers?"

Bianca smiled. "Yes! All the way up to twenty!"

"Good. I'll tell you three numbers and you punch them in, okay?"

"Okay," Bianca said, her tiny finger poised over the buttons.

She recited the area code one digit at a time and watched to make sure Bianca hit the correct buttons. Then she gave her the next three digits.

Bianca happily poked the buttons.

She recited the next three numbers and stopped. She still wasn't sure about the last one.

"Hit three, push the green button and hold the phone to my ear."

Bianca followed instructions and held the phone to her ear. She heard it ring. Once. Twice.

"Hello?" said a female voice. Her heart sank. Had she dialed the wrong number? Wait. Maybe it was Kelly.

"Hi, Kelly?" she said.

"There's no Kelly here." A click and the line went dead.

She wanted to scream. Now she had to go through the whole process again. And the clock was ticking. Any minute Orazio might come back.

Frowning, Bianca said, "What's wrong? Did I make a mistake?"

"No. It's my fault. The last number I gave you was wrong." She forced a smile. "Can you enter that many numbers again?"

Bianca looked like she'd just given her a Christmas present. "Yes! Tell me the numbers!"

————

Frank stood at the open front door of the Hogan house, tensely peering out the storm door. Sweat dripped down his forehead. He felt like he was in a sauna, layered with clothes, his sweat-soaked T-shirt clammy against his skin, then an insulated Kevlar vest, which he'd concealed beneath his long-sleeved sweatshirt.

"What are they doing?" he said, speaking into his cellphone. David had just called to tell him the FBI Hummer with the SWAT team had parked on the side street north of the mob house where David and Orville were stationed.

"Nothing," David said. "You want me to go talk to them?"

"No. Sit tight. Call me right away if they make a move."

He shut his cellphone and yelled to Kelly, who was upstairs watching the mob house. "David says the Hummer is parked down the street from him. Ten to one, Conti is with them. I'm going to drive my car around the block and talk to him."

"Okay," Kelly called, "but be careful."

"I will." He'd be careful all right, careful he didn't kill Conti.

He ran down the hall to the kitchen. As he opened the door to the mudroom his cellphone rang. He checked the ID. Unknown Caller.

He punched on and said, "Renzi."

"Frank! Orazio found my Conti cellphone and he's furious."

Blown away, it took him a second to respond. "Natalie? Where's Bianca?"

"Here in the room with me. She dialed the number."

"You've got another cellphone?"

A brief silence, then, "The man who guards the front door called Orazio downstairs. Before he left, he bound my wrists with a cord and tied the other end to the window fixture. He said if we tried to get away, he would … hurt us."

Kill us, Frank thought. But Natalie didn't want to say that in front of Bianca.

"Hold on a second." He charged down the hall to the front door and studied the mob house. "Which room? Which window?"

"The corner room on the second floor. The side window above the garage."

"Can you and Bianca climb out the window?"

"No. I can't move!"

"Okay, listen carefully. Find a way to get free of the cord so you can climb out the window. Get Bianca to help you." He decided not to mention the SWAT team. She was already terrified. Why make it worse? "Call me when you get free. I'll park my car in the driveway, stand beside the garage and help you and Bianca get off the roof."

"Okay, Frank. I'll try." But she didn't sound hopeful.

"You can do it." Hoping she could, he ended the call.

He ran back to the kitchen, went out through the mudroom and jumped in his car. He backed out of the driveway, drove around the corner and paused beside the NOPD van. Tony Coppola lowered the window and said, "I saw the FBI SWAT team. That sucks. Mobsters are bad enough. Now we gotta deal with the fibbies?"

"Yes, thanks to Conti. Natalie and Bianca are trapped in a room on the second floor. If SWAT tries to enter the house, they're toast. Conti's probably with the SWAT team. I'm going there now."

Tony grimaced. "Good luck with that. Keep me posted, but don't use your radio. Too many people listening. Cellphones are better."

"Exactly," Frank said, and sped off. He turned the next corner, zoomed down the street and rounded the next corner. A large rectangular Hummer H2 with a flat roof and dark-tinted windows was parked twenty yards away. Standing beside it, Conti was talking to a short stocky man with FBI stenciled on the back of his jacket.

The SWAT team, a dozen or so men in camo outfits, stood beside the Hummer. Two of them were smoking, gearing up for the action. Frank knew the feeling: grab a nicotine hit before the shooting starts. The others were checking their weapons: handguns and automatic rifles.

He parked beyond the Hummer and approached the FBI agent. Ignoring Conti, he flashed his ID and said, "Frank Renzi, NOPD. We've got a critical situation in the mob house."

"Stay out of this, Renzi," Conti said. "Everything is under control."

"Like hell it is! Natalie and Bianca are prisoners in a second-floor bedroom. Make a move on the house, Orazio will kill them."

The FBI agent, a chunky man with a bullet head, graying hair and steely eyes, scowled at him. "This isn't your jurisdiction," he said in a gravelly voice. "The SAC already notified the Jefferson Parish Sheriff's Department about possible police action in this area. I'm in charge of this operation. Assistant Special Agent in Charge Ezra Wyner. What's your interest in the case?"

"I have arrest warrants for Natalie Brixton. Agent Conti persuaded her to infiltrate the Mafia gang, but he doesn't seem too worried about her welfare."

"How do you know what's going on in the house?" Wyner said.

"I just talked to Natalie."

"Talked to her?" Conti said. "How?"

"Listen, Conti, there are three women in that house, including a five-year-old girl. You want to arrest the mafiosos? Show me how brave you are. Go on up to the front door and ring the bell."

Conti's cheeks flamed red. He shut his mouth and said nothing.

Frank turned to Wyner and said, "You want this to turn into another Ruby Ridge? Waco?" Deliberately citing two cases that had sullied the Bureau's reputation—one in 1992, the other in 1993—when several women and children died during armed sieges by FBI and ATF agents.

Judging by the pained look on Wyner's face, he didn't.

"Call the SAC," Frank said. "Ask him if it's worth endangering the lives of innocent women and children to arrest these mobsters."

"Okay," Wyner said. "But you need to understand who's in charge of this operation."

"And you need to understand that the lives of innocent people are at stake," he said. "If something happens to them, don't say I didn't warn you."

CHAPTER 39

Steeling himself, Orazio strode to his bedroom window and studied the street. No Hummer. No SWAT team with assault rifles. He circled the king-sized bed, went to the side window and studied the adjacent yard beyond the six-foot fence. In the fading light, holiday lights decorating the exterior of the house blinked off and on, no lights inside. And no FBI agents lurking near the fence, about to climb over it.

No telling how many there were. Plenty of firepower in the room downstairs, but he had only two soldiers. Silvano had said he would send reinforcements, but that might take a while.

He picked up one of the Uzis that lay on his bed. His gang in Venice used them. It was a fine weapon. He thought of it as an extension6 of himself. He controlled the Uzi; his reflexes and judgment told him when to shoot. Others might question his orders, might even fail him in the end. His weapon never did. But if an Uzi wasn't cleaned regularly, it tended to jam. Not what he wanted if a SWAT team attacked the house.

Due to its open-bolt mechanism the Uzi was easily disassembled. Quickly and efficiently, he field-stripped it and laid the components out on the bed, each precision-made part designed to fit another. He was pleased to find them clean and well-oiled. Reassured, he reassembled the Uzi. The magazine held the standard 32-rounds, this one 9mm Parabellum cartridges. A pity. Such rounds would not penetrate body armor, but now that he knew this he would aim accordingly.

He slammed the magazine into the Uzi. Where the hell was Tommy? All this activity—the guard calling him, footsteps running up and downstairs—and Tommy remained in his room, oblivious. Agitated, he took a cigar off the top of his dresser, unwrapped it and held it beneath his nose. The robust aroma calmed him. He could almost feel Father's presence. In every mafia family there were those who envied the leader, men like Tommy. They saw only the money and power that came with the position, not the burdensome responsibilities.

Where would the FBI agents attack first? The back of the house? The front? Or would it be the doomsday scenario? If they split up into teams and swarmed all sides of the house at once, he and Tommy and Catarina and Rocco would die. His reputation as a strong leader would be ruined. Forever after, everyone would know Orazio had failed to protect the Antonetti Family, bringing shame upon him. This he could not allow.

He took a final sniff of the cigar and put it in his shirt pocket. The obstacles he faced were difficult, but not insurmountable. The house was well-protected. A six-foot fence guarded three sides. Position was the key to defense. He had to think like a general and position his troops carefully. Unfortunately Rocco and Tomasso were his only soldiers.

He stood at the front window and brought the Uzi to his shoulder in the firing position. He was a fine marksman, but he was surrounded by many enemies. Last Saturday when Silvano showed him around this house, he had marveled at how spacious it was.

Now it felt claustrophobic. He was trapped.

Dire images crept into his mind: men wearing body armor and helmets, wielding assault weapons, attacking the house.

But which part of the house? He couldn't be everywhere at once.

Wait. The surveillance cameras! The only time they were turned on was when Tick-Tock came here to conduct important business or screw the whores he didn't want his wife to know about.

He bolted from the room and ran downstairs. Rocco had put his Uzi on the dining room table and was dragging one of the sideboards into the foyer to barricade the front door. "Rocco, do you know how to turn on the surveillance cameras?"

"Yes, sir. The switch is in the movie room off the kitchen."

"Where are the monitors?"

"In the utility room at the top of the stairs opposite your bedroom." Rocco smiled. "The Boss don't want nobody in the movie room while he's in there with his girlfriends."

"Excellent idea, blocking the door," Orazio said, a good general keeping his soldier happy. "Go turn on the cameras. Then come upstairs to the utility room."

Rocco ran down the hall toward the kitchen. Orazio mounted the stairs two at a time. The utility room was beside the staircase, directly above the room with the weapons. He opened the door, flicked a light switch and stepped inside. Like many homes in New Orleans, essential equipment—electricity, heating and cooling—had been installed on the second floor to guard against destructive flooding from torrential rains or the hurricanes that often threatened the area.

The right half of the room held the utility equipment, but along the left-hand wall, five closed circuit TV monitors sat on a wide metal shelf. All the screens were blank. And then they weren't. He studied the black-and-white images.

One monitor showed the backyard and the fence behind the house. Another displayed the narrow area between the north side of the house and the fence. A third showed the front of the house, including the front door. A fourth showed the narrow strip of land between the fence and the garage. The fifth monitor displayed the garage, the side door and the driveway.

Perfect. He would have Catarina watch the monitors and alert him when the FBI agents attacked the house.

Rocco rushed into the room, out of breath, clutching his Uzi.

"Wait here," Orazio said. "I will send Catarina to watch the monitors. Show her how to operate the controls. Then go downstairs and guard the front of the house."

He went across the hall to his room, grabbed the two Uzis and hurried down the hall. At the far end, he put his ear to the door of the nanny's room. He heard nothing. Should he check to make sure she was behaving? No. First he had to get Tommy into position.

He rapped on the door across the hall and stepped inside. A blast of sound greeted him, a soccer match on television. Standing beside the double bed, Catarina saw the Uzis in his hands and looked at him fearfully. Several outfits were laid out on her side of the bed. Jesus! How could she think about clothes now? On Tommy's side of the bed, two pillows were propped against the headboard.

He shut off the television set. "Where is Tommy?"

Catarina nervously licked her lips. "In the bathroom."

He strode to the bathroom door. "Tommy, come out here!"

In the silence, he heard water running. Moments later, the door opened and Tommy came out, drying his hands on a towel. He saw the Uzis and said, "What is wrong?"

Fury rose inside him like an oil gusher. In the midst of this crisis, Tommy had been lying in bed watching a soccer match on TV.

"There are FBI agents outside the house. A SWAT team in a Hummer."

Catarina gasped. Tommy just stared at him.

He thrust the spare Uzi at Tommy. "Stand at your window and guard the back fence. If anyone climbs over it, shoot them."

Tommy took the Uzi. "What do we do if they get in the house?"

"Make sure they don't. Shoot to kill. Our lives depend on it. Rocco turned on the surveillance cameras. Catarina will watch the monitors."

He took her to the utility room, returned to his bedroom and stood at the window with the Uzi.

All quiet in the room next door. No shopping for the girl and the deceitful Vietnamese spy tonight, not with a Hummer full of FBI agents outside. He would have to kill them here.

———

Natalie watched helplessly as Bianca tried to cut the clothesline with the tiny scissors. The muscles in her hands just weren't strong enough. Whenever she managed to get the blades around one strand of the cord and tried to cut it, the scissors turned sideways and jammed. Each time it happened, Bianca grew more frustrated. She'd been happy punching numbers into the iPhone, thrilled when the call to Frank went through.

Now the girl was close to tears. So was she.

She was a prisoner, as trapped here as she would be in a jail cell. Except that in a jail cell, Orazio couldn't walk in and kill her.

"Stop and rest, Bianca. You're tired."

Bianca stuck out her lower lip. "Why can't I go down to the kitchen and get a sharp knife?"

"It's too dangerous." If you try to leave the room, I will kill you both.

She had no idea where Orazio was or what he was doing. Earlier when the guard called to him, he'd sounded agitated.

"Call your friend again," Bianca said. "Maybe he'll know what to do."

"Not yet. He's counting on us to get the cord off my wrists. Let's try something else. Open the scissors and hold the handles near my fingers."

Bianca opened the scissors and held out the handles. Natalie inserted the middle finger of her right hand into one ring, the middle finger of her left into the other. A tiny screw held the two halves together. Focusing her energy, she tried to pull the scissors apart.

The metal rings cut into her fingers. Ignoring the pain, she gritted her teeth and pulled harder. Sweat dripped down her forehead. She relaxed her muscles and tried again, straining as hard as she could. At last the scissors came apart, but the point of one blade stabbed her hand.

"You're bleeding!" Bianca said.

"Never mind." She slid her fingers out of the rings. "Take one half and use it like a saw. Put the sharp edge against the cord and pull it back and forth like you're cutting wood."

Bianca's face lit up in a smile. "Like Papa used to do when he cut wood for the fireplace?"

"Exactly. Work on one strand at a time." Conscious of the passing minutes, she smiled to encourage her.

"Let's see how fast you can do it." As fast as possible.

A few minutes ago she'd heard rapid footsteps on the stairs down the hall. She had the feeling something bad was happening, but she didn't know what. Rays of the setting sun slanted through the window overlooking the street. An hour from now it would be dark.

The perfect time to escape, if Orazio didn't come back.

Bianca set the sharp edge of the blade against one piece of cord and began sawing. Natalie glanced at her iPhone lying on the floor, partially hidden by her left thigh. If Orazio came in and saw it, she was done for, but she wanted to keep track of the time. Now it was 7:44.

At 7:45 Bianca sawed through the first piece of cord.

"Fantastic!" Natalie said. "Only three more to go."

"Can we call Mr. Frank now?"

Natalie frowned. How did Bianca know his name? Then she remembered: Kelly, the other cop in the house down the street, had called him by name. "Not yet. Cut another one."

Bianca pulled another strand of cord away from her wrists and began sawing. At 7:47 the cord separated and fell away from her wrists. This time Bianca didn't ask her to call Mr. Frank, she started sawing the next strand of cord.

When that one separated, Natalie said, "That's enough. I think I can slide my hands through the last piece." Grasping the cord with the fingers of her left hand, she narrowed her right hand as much as possible and pulled it free. Then she did the same with her left hand.

"Yeaah!" Bianca exclaimed, all smiles now. "Can we call Mr. Frank now?"

Gunfire sounded from down the hall, a deafening explosion of rat-a-tat-tats.

Natalie flinched. That was no handgun. It was an assault weapon set to rapid-fire bursts.

Bianca screamed, climbed onto her lap and wrapped her arms around her neck, clinging to her.

She felt the girl's rapid heartbeat through her shirt.

Bianca was terrified. So was she.

CHAPTER 40

8:10 PM

Orazio heard gunfire down the hall, a three-shot burst, then another. He rushed to the side window. No FBI agents beyond the fence. He checked the front window. None there either.

With his Uzi in hand, he ran to Tommy's room. Tommy stood at the open window, holding his Uzi, his feet braced. The acrid odor of gunpowder hung in the air.

"What are you shooting at?" Orazio said in Italian.

Smiling proudly, Tommy said, "A guy tried to climb over the fence. I shot the fucker."

Orazio peered out the window. A man in combat fatigues lay on his back near the fence, one hand clutching his chest, his right arm flung out to the side as though reaching for the assault rifle on the ground. His helmet lay on the grass beside what was left of his bloody head.

"Good job, Tommy, " he said. His brother was hyped up and he wanted him to stay that way.

A helmeted-head popped up at the top of the fence.

Tommy raised his Uzi, but Orazio grabbed his arm. "No. There may be more. They want to rescue their buddy. Wait until they try to climb over the fence. Then blow them away."

Tommy flashed a cocky smile. "Like shooting ducks in a gallery."

"Ducks don't shoot back," he snapped. And they don't wear body armor. Unfortunately, the room downstairs had plenty of guns and ammo but no protective vests. "Guard the fence. Rocco and I will make sure they don't get in through the front door."

"Mr. Antonetti," Rocco yelled from the staircase. "What's happening?"

Merda! Another soldier needed a dose of courage. He turned and ran down the hall, cursing in frustration. He was a general without an army, racing from one flashpoint to another, commanding his soldiers. All two of them. Where the hell were Silvano's men?

He paused at the door of the utility room. Seated in front of the monitors, Catarina turned and looked at him, her face a mask of fear. "What is Tommy shooting at?"

Irritated, he snapped, "Polizia! Did you not see them on the monitors? Do your job! If you see any more cops, open your pretty little mouth and tell me, loud and clear, understand?"

Without a word, she turned back to the monitors.

When Orazio reached the staircase, Rocco stood on the landing at the halfway point. "Stay at your post," Orazio said. "An FBI agent tried to get over the fence. Tommy killed him."

"But we're outnumbered" Rocco said. "If a bunch of cops rush the front door—"

"Shoot them!" Orazio thundered. Merda! His soldiers were useless. Rocco had no balls, and Tommy was a complacent fool, acting like he'd vanquished an entire army by killing one FBI agent.

He ran to his bedroom and checked the windows. No armed men in sight. The light was fading. Soon it would be dark.

More gunfire from Tommy's room. Orazio set the Uzi on his bed and took out his snub-nosed Smith & Wesson. This might be the perfect time to get rid of the girl and the deceitful Vietnamese woman.

The spy who was working for that miserable Europol agent, John Conti.

———

Frank heard distant gunfire and stuck his head out the Hogan front door. No SWAT team in front of the mob house. Relieved, he yelled up the staircase to Kelly, "Can you tell where those shots came from?"

"I'm not sure, but I think they came from the mob house."

"I'm going there in my car."

"I thought you were waiting for Natalie to call you."

"Fuck waiting. We need to get Natalie and Bianca out of there now! Wyner might have his agents drive the Hummer around the corner, park in front of the house and have a SWAT team blitz the front door. Get your gear and meet me at my car."

He ran to the kitchen, burst out the side door, jumped in his Dodge Charger and got on his cellphone. When Conti answered he said, "Put Wyner on the phone. I need to talk to him."

"I can't," Conti said. "He's busy. Three of his men tried to get over the fence in back of the house, and someone shot them."

"Tell him to call me!" Frank said and ended the call.

Kelly opened the door and jumped in the passenger seat. "Did you call Natalie?"

"No. Conti." He backed out of the driveway and headed for the mob house. "He said a SWAT team unit took fire when they tried to get over the fence behind the house."

"It sounded like automatic weapon fire to me," Kelly said. "People must have heard it. Someone will call the cops."

He studied the houses along the street as he passed them. No lights in some homes, Christmas lights flashing on others. No pedestrians on the sidewalks, nobody outside checking to see where the shots had come from, no cars driving down the street. And no Hummer.

"The mobsters must have seen the Hummer go by the house," he said. "If they've got assault weapons, we're in trouble."

He jolted to a stop in front of the mob house, backed into the driveway, then pulled forward, angling the Dodge diagonally across the driveway, nose out, aimed at the Hogan house down the street.

"Frank, look out!" Kelly yelled. "Someone's at the first floor window with a gun."

A burst of gunfire shattered the back window, spraying cubes of glass over the back seat.

———

Crouched in the gutter below her bedroom window, Natalie heard more gunshots and flinched. Sobbing, Bianca clamped her arms around her neck and buried her face against her neck. "Owl will shoot us," Bianca whimpered.

"No he won't," she whispered. A lie. That's exactly what he would do if he got the chance. And in her frantic haste to get Bianca out of the house, she'd left her purse on the bed, a disastrous mistake. She had to go back and get it.

"In a minute we'll be safe. Mr. Frank is going to help us. We have to be very quiet and crawl along the gutter to the front of the house."

Bianca gazed at her fearfully. "You're not going to leave me, are you?"

"No." Not until Frank took charge of her, anyway. He'd make sure Bianca was safe.

After she climbed out the window with Bianca, she'd called Frank and told him they were outside, waiting in the gutter. He said he would park his car in the driveway and stand beside the garage so she could drop Bianca to him. "Won't they shoot at you?" she asked.

"Just do it. An FBI SWAT team is here. Hurry," he'd said.

She didn't like the sound of that. More armed men looking for her. On the other hand, a shootout might provide the distraction she needed to escape. It wasn't completely dark, but the light was fading fast. Under the cover of darkness, she could disappear.

But first she had to get back into her room and take the items she needed out of her purse.

Bianca kissed her cheek. "I love you, Laura."

Overcome with emotion, Natalie hugged her close so she wouldn't see the tears in her eyes. "I love you too, Bianca, with all my heart. Always remember that. But we need to hurry. Get in front of me and crawl toward the front of the house."

Bianca got on her knees and crept forward. Natalie crawled after her. When Bianca reached the front edge, Natalie grabbed her foot.

"Wait," she whispered, and crawled around her. She saw Frank's car in the driveway. Her stomach clenched. The back window had been shot out. Where was Frank? She peeked over the edge of the roof. Frank stood with his back pressed against the garage.

He saw her and held out his arms. "Drop Bianca to me."

She hugged Bianca and whispered, "Mr. Frank will catch you."

Gripping Bianca by her armpits, she eased her over the side and let go. Frank staggered momentarily when he caught her. Then, clutching her to his chest, he ran across the driveway and ducked around the fence beyond the garage.

Natalie breathed a sigh of relief. Finally, Bianca was safe. But she wasn't.

———

Clamping Bianca to his chest, Frank sprinted to the fence between the garage and the house next door. When he ducked around the fence, Kelly was crouched beside it, her Glock in one hand, her cellphone in the other. Her face registered relief. "Good going, Frank! You got her!"

"Yeah. The guy on the first floor must be on break." The guy with the assault rifle. Nothing like a bit of levity during a dangerous situation.

"I called Dispatch," Kelly said. "They're sending four squad cars."

More gunfire at the rear of the house. Bianca flinched. "It's okay," he said. "You're safe now."

"No!" Bianca said. "Put me down! You have to get Laura!"

"Don't worry I'll get her." He set Bianca on her feet. "But you need to stay with Kelly."

"Bring her in here!" called a woman's voice.

He turned and saw a red-haired woman standing outside the front door of the lavender ranch house.

"Go inside and stay there!" he called. "NOPD orders."

Frowning, the woman turned and went inside.

Kelly rolled her eyes. "Just what we need, a civilian in the mix."

"Not to mention certain other issues. After you take Bianca to the Hogan house, make some calls. I need to get someone to the station."

No need to say who. Kelly knew he wanted to book Natalie on the outstanding murder warrants. Bianca would be safe in the Hogan house for the moment, but not for long. Shots erupting from the mob house, SWAT teams with assault weapons poised to strike, and more cops on the way, he didn't want Bianca anywhere near this neighborhood.

"Where's Laura?" Bianca wailed. "I want Laura to take me!"

He rubbed her back and whispered, "I'm going to get her right now. I'll bring her to the house so you'll both be safe."

"Be careful," Kelly warned. "Don't forget the guy on the first floor."

"I won't." He wouldn't forget the guy on the second floor, either. Orazio, the Mafia thug hellbent on killing Bianca and Natalie.

"I don't want to go to that house," Bianca declared. "I want to wait here for Laura."

Frank jerked his head at Kelly. Get her out of here.

Kelly holstered her Glock, stuck her cellphone in her pocket, scooped up Bianca with both hands, and jogged across the lawn toward the Hogan house down the street.

―――――

Natalie crawled back to the clothesline that dangled from the window of her bedroom. She had used it to lower herself and Bianca to the gutter. Now she would use it to climb back to her room. Her forearm hurt where Orazio had burned her. Maybe she'd bring the tube of antibiotic ointment with her. But that wasn't her main concern.

A new passport, driver's license and cash were in her wallet, items she would need to escape from Frank.

No way was she going to let him arrest her. If he did, she would spend the rest of her life in a jail cell. Never again would she see the mountains or the ocean or a beautiful sunset. Never again would she hear beautiful bird songs. Never again would she feel a man's touch on her body.

With grim determination, she wrapped the cord around her hand. Bianca thought Frank was nice. Up to a point, he was. He wanted to protect Bianca, but he had three murder warrants for her arrest. His main goal was to take her into custody.

Not if she could help it.

In the darkness, the house remained eerily silent. No gunfire, but any minute there might be.

Hand over hand, she climbed up to the window and hooked her elbows over the frame.

Panting for breath, she paused to rest. But she had no time to rest. Get what you need and get out!

Using her elbows, she hauled herself into the room, arms extended, and lowered herself to the floor.

Breathing hard, she rose to a crouch and froze.

Voices in the hall. Male voices.

Her heart slammed her chest.

Her leather purse with her wallet was on her bed ten feet away. Maybe she could still get it.

Then she heard footsteps. Heavy footsteps, dangerously close.

If it was Orazio, he would kill her.

Terrified, she sprang to her feet, ran to the window, stuck one leg out, then the other and perched on the window frame.

Please don't come in the room.

The door opened. Orazio stood in the doorway.

His eyes, cold and hard and merciless, swept the room.

In his hand was a snub-nosed revolver.

CHAPTER 41

Intent on his mission, Orazio paused in the doorway, planning his moves. Unlike the cumbersome Uzi, the snub-nosed Smith & Wesson fit neatly in the palm of his right hand. He would shoot the girl first, then the spy. Was she cowering in despair the way he'd left her? Or plotting some new treachery?

The room was silent and still. Too silent. Something was wrong.

His gaze swept the room. Where was the girl? Hiding in the bathroom?

No. The bathroom door was open. And the nanny wasn't cowering on the floor.

Stunned, he stood there, unable to believe his eyes. The treacherous Vietnamese spy sat on the window frame, with her legs dangling outside.

For an instant, she met his gaze. Then she disappeared.

Too shocked to move, he stared at the window.

How could this be? He had bound her wrists together and secured her to the window with the cord.

Then he saw the tiny metal scissors on the floor. What was left of them. They were broken in two.

But to hell with that. He could not allow her to escape!

He ran to the window and stuck his head through the opening.

In the drainage gutter ten feet below him, she was scrambling toward the front of the house. Then he saw the car.

Parked diagonally across the driveway, the dark sedan had no markings, but three antennas sprouted from the roof. It had to be a police car. No one was in it, but the car blocked the driveway, preventing any vehicles from leaving the garage.

Merda! Were the cops helping this devious Vietnamese woman?

Rage sent his heart rate soaring. But he couldn't afford to lose control. Now the woman was at the end of gutter.

He raised the revolver. Too late. She thrust herself forward and jumped off the roof.

This cursed woman was as slippery as an eel. Slippery as an eel, but sooner or later she had to show herself.

Would she get in the police car? No. The car was empty, the back window shot out. She would run to the green house down the street, the one with the cops.

He waited, gripping the revolver.

And then he saw her. Bent over in a crouch, she was limping across the driveway. Maybe she had broken a leg when she jumped off the roof.

It served her right. He raised the revolver. The light was so poor he could barely see her in the darkness.

He took careful aim. Held his breath. Pulled the trigger.

She sprawled headfirst on the ground and lay still on the grass beyond the driveway. After a moment she raised her head. Put her forearms on the grass and struggled to her knees. The treacherous Vietnamese nanny refused to die!

He raised the revolver.

"Orazio, come quick!" Catarina yelled, her voice shrill.

Startled, he almost dropped the revolver. "What is it?" he called.

"The Hummer is coming down the street toward the house!"

———

Crouched beside the fence, Frank heard a gunshot. Not the rat-tat-tat of automatic gunfire, a single shot. The light was fading, and the moon was hidden behind banks of clouds.

He turned and breathed a sigh of relief when he saw Kelly carry Bianca through the front door of the Hogan house.

Then he heard the roar of a high-powered engine. He peeked around the fence. The FBI Hummer was barreling down the street toward the mob house. Damn it to hell! Wyner wasn't going to call him. The FBI agent was going to order a full-scale assault on the house.

He had to get Natalie off the roof before the SWAT team deployed.

But she wasn't on the roof, he realized. She was sitting on the grass beside the driveway twenty feet away.

"Natalie," he called. "Come over here to the fence!"

Seemingly dazed, she just looked at him.

The Hummer ground to a halt in front of the mob house. Deafening blasts of automatic gunfire erupted from the first floor windows. But they weren't shooting at Natalie. They were shooting at the Hummer. He darted around the fence and ran to her.

"My ankle," she said. "I think it's broken."

Sporadic gunfire came from the house. None from the Hummer, but any second Wyner's SWAT team might start shooting. Grasping Natalie by the armpits, he dragged her around the fence to get her out of the line of fire. She moaned as he lowered her to the ground.

His hands felt sticky. He looked at them and saw blood. His stomach lurched. Aghast, he said, "What happened?"

"Orazio," she said, breathing in shallow gasps. "He shot me."

He wiped his hands on his running pants. "Don't try to talk. I'll call an ambulance." He got on his cellphone, called Dispatch and said, "This is Renzi. I'm at the mob house in Metairie. A woman's been shot. Get an ambulance over here." He recited the address and ended the call.

Natalie lay on the ground with her eyes closed. She didn't look good, her face pale, her breathing shallow and labored.

He touched her arm and her eyes opened. "An ambulance is on the way. Are you pain? Where did he hit you?"

"My back. It feels like it's on fire." Her attempted smile morphed into a grimace. "Now I know how you felt when I shot you."

Amazed, he stared at her. How could she talk about something that happened two years ago at a time like this? Shot in the back, obviously in pain, surrounded by the din of gunfire.

"Well," he said, "I didn't die, and you're not going to die either."

She gripped his arm and gazed at him intently. "Where is Bianca?"

"Kelly took her to the house down the street. She'll be safe there."

Natalie closed her eyes. "Good. At least I did something right."

———

From the top of the stairs, Orazio yelled, "Rocco, don't waste your ammo! Don't shoot until they leave the Hummer."

He ran back to his room and warily approached the front window. A faint breeze failed to disperse the odor of gunpowder that hung in the air. He raised the Uzi, set his finger on the trigger and waited.

Now that the attack had begun, he felt utterly calm. In the heat of battle, action and steely resolve steadied his nerves.

He focused on the Hummer, a dark presence in the fast-dying light, just beyond the glow of the streetlight across the street.

Nothing happened for more than a minute. Then three men in full riot gear jumped out of the back. Protected by Plexiglas shields, they ran toward the front door in a V-formation.

Rocco began firing in short bursts, but the riot shields deflected the bullets, emitting high-pitched pings as the rounds bounced off the thick plastic shields and ricocheted onto the lawn.

Orazio set his finger on the trigger. The view from his second floor window provided a better angle. The rectangular shields protected only part of their bodies. Below the knees their legs were exposed and if they turned a certain way, their heads and necks.

He took deliberate aim and fired three bursts at their necks. One man crumpled to the ground like a puppet with cut strings. The others picked him up and rushed back to the Hummer. Intent on saving their comrade, they hoisted him into the back and climbed in after him.

Silence, but for how long? It was only a matter of time before they attacked again. He mopped sweat off his forehead. They were badly outnumbered. Three shooters against how many? Three dead in the backyard, thanks to Tommy. He had just wounded another, but he had no idea how many more were inside the Hummer.

Maybe he would die in this house after all.

Just as one bad move could decide a chess game, one bad decision could end a life. He hadn't told Tick-Tock about the stolen jewelry. Not out of greed, for the challenge of it. It pained him to admit it, but this had been a mistake, one that might ultimately defeat him.

Like nails hammered into a coffin, other disasters had followed. The treacherous Vietnamese gang. The massacre at the restaurant. The cops, armed with a description of Silvano's SUV, questioning Silvano.

He took a cigar out of his shirt pocket and sniffed it, savoring the aroma, recalling what Father had told him long ago: Trust no one, not even those who appear to be allies.

Maybe Silvano lied. Maybe Silvano wasn't sending any soldiers to help defend the house. And now the cops had the girl. The last living witness to the slaughter in Venice, and this Europol agent, John Conti, would question her.

He clamped his teeth together, seething with fury.

Because the treacherous Vietnamese woman who called herself Laura, the one Conti called Natalie, had lied to him.

Merda! He should have killed her and the girl after dinner when he had the chance.

Another whiff of the cigar brought a flash of inspiration.

A new plan took shape in his mind. The cops had the girl.

But he had the diamonds and the stolen jewelry.

———

Bianca sat at the kitchen table, trying not to cry.

After they came in the house, Kelly told her not to worry, they were safe now. But when she asked about Laura, Kelly had turned on the little TV set on the kitchen counter, sat her in a chair, put a paper plate with a Snickers bar in front of her and told her to stay here.

But she didn't want a Snickers bar. If she ate it she would throw up. Her tummy hurt, worse than it did when Owl and Tommy and Catwoman took her on that boat and they raced down the Grand Canal. Away from Mama and Papà.

Where was Laura?

How could she watch a stupid TV show with all those guns shooting? It was just like Venice. Owl came out of Papà's store and shot Mama. Now Mama was dead. She would never see her again, never hold her close and smell her perfume, never hear her read another bedtime story.

After Owl shot Mama with the little gun, he shot a lot of other people with a big gun.

Her stomach cramped. What if he shot Laura?

She slid off the chair, went to the doorway and looked down the hall. The front door was shut, but she could still hear the guns. She tiptoed down the hall to the living room. Kelly stood at the window, peeking around the curtain.

"Where's Laura?"

Startled, Kelly turned. "She's with Frank. He's helping her."

"Why are they shooting? It hurts my ears."

Kelly came to her, knelt down and hugged her. "It hurts my ears too, Bianca, but we're safe here. Go sit in the kitchen and have your snack while you watch TV."

"I don't want to. What if Owl shot Laura?"

"Owl? Who's that?"

"He shot my mother. And he hurt Laura. Tonight he came in our room and burned her arm with his cigar!"

Kelly gasped. "That's awful. Why did he do that?"

"Because he's bad!" she screamed. "Laura said so. I want Laura to stay with me!"

"Hold on while I call Frank." Kelly took out a cellphone and punched in a number. After a moment she said, "Frank, what's your status? I saw the Hummer park in front of the house." She listened for a while, then frowned. "No, we're fine, but Bianca is worried about … Laura."

And after a moment, "Okay. Be careful." Kelly put the cellphone in her pocket and said, "Laura hurt her ankle when she jumped off the roof, but Frank took her around the fence to the neighbor's yard."

"Why doesn't he bring her over here?"

"I'm very thirsty," Kelly said. "There's cold water in the refrigerator. Let's go get some."

Her eyes filled with tears. Kelly was just like Catwoman.

When Catwoman didn't want to answer her question, she talked about something else. Or fed her ice cream.

She didn't want water. She wanted Laura.

Kelly said Laura hurt her ankle. She didn't believe it.

Laura had promised not to leave her.

The tears overflowed and ran down her cheeks.

Something really bad had happened to Laura. She was certain of it.

CHAPTER 42

Frank felt like he was in a war zone, not a tree-lined street in suburbia. Ten minutes ago Kelly had taken Bianca to the Hogan house, but that seemed like an eternity ago. Every time a burst of gunfire came from the mob house, Natalie flinched and shut her eyes, her face sweaty and pale.

"I want to move you away from the sidewalk," he said.

Her eyes opened. Grasping her arms, he helped her sit up and crawled behind her. His gut churned with acid. The back of her shirt was soaked with blood. He put his hands under her armpits. "Lift your butt."

She did and they scooted back ten feet. He helped her lie down. "The woman who lives in this house offered to help. I want to get you a blanket and a pillow and something for the pain. Will you be okay for a minute?"

"Okay," she said in a dreamy voice. "Orazio is shooting at someone else now. Not me."

He ran to the door of the one-story ranch with the bright lavender siding. Before he could ring the bell, the red-haired woman opened the door. "Sorry to bother you, ma'am," he said.

"Forget the ma'am stuff," she said. "The name's Vivian. What do you need?" Barking at him like a moll in a thirties gangster film.

Despite his concerns, he had to smile. Vivian had sky-blue eyes and red hair like Lucille Ball's—from a bottle maybe—but cut shorter. He guessed she was in her fifties, athletic and fit in Bermuda shorts and a V-neck polo shirt.

"The woman is injured. Could you lend me a blanket and a pillow?"

"Why don't you bring her in here?"

"I don't want to move her."

"Suit yourself." She took him down a hall to a bathroom. When he opened the medicine cabinet, she said, "I knew this would happen sooner or later. Mobsters own that house. The fat one brings his whores there. And the skinny one is screwing one of the maids."

He didn't ask how she knew this. Vivian seemed like the talkative type and he had no time to waste. "Mind if I take a hand towel?"

"Not at all." She held out a plastic bag. "Put what you need in this. I'll get a blanket and some bottled water, meet you at the front door."

He dropped extra strength Excedrin, sterile bandages and antibiotic ointment into the plastic bag. When he went back to the front door, Vivian gave him a lightweight blanket, a pillow, and two bottles of water.

"You need anything else, just come to the door and ask," she said. "I'm not going anywhere."

"Okay, but stay inside. It's not safe out there."

"Are you going to arrest those hoodlums?"

Ignoring the question, he opened the door. "Thanks for your help, Vivian."

"I didn't take offense when you yelled at me before," Vivian said, grinning at him. "That's your job."

Amused, he said, "That's one of the things I do best. Yell at people." He didn't wait for her reply.

When he got back to Natalie, he dropped the blanket and the pillow on the ground. "I got you some pain meds. Let's sit you up again."

Grimacing in pain, she managed to sit up. He opened the bottled water and shook two Excedrin into her hand. While she swallowed the Excedrin, he studied her blood-soaked shirt. Bandages and antibiotic ointment weren't going to help a gunshot wound.

Where the hell was the ambulance?

Natalie drank deeply from the bottled water, then offered it to him. "Want some?"

"No thanks. You're bleeding pretty bad. I think you should lie down."

He helped her lie flat on the blanket and put the pillow under her head. She gazed at him, her almond-shaped eyes somber. "So many sad memories in New Orleans. I don't want to die here like my mother."

Touched by the poignant comment, he felt a deep sadness well up inside him.

Uttering the first thing that entered his mind, he said, "Your mother was beautiful."

"How you know?"

He hesitated, then said, "I saw the crime scene photos. She didn't deserve to die that way."

"No, she didn't. I still miss her. When I was little she'd buy us ice cream cones and we'd walk along the river. We had some wonderful times." Her lips tightened. "Yes, my mother was beautiful and she didn't deserve to die, period. Conti took my only picture of her."

He tried to imagine how Natalie must have felt. Ten years old, no father around, her mother murdered. And Conti had taken her only picture of her mother. "I'll get it back for you."

Natalie smiled and squeezed his hand. "I always fall in love with the wrong men."

He couldn't believe she'd said it, acting like they were best friends. Maybe they were. Love and hate were flip sides of the same coin.

"Like Oliver James?"

Her smile faded. "Yes. Ironic isn't it? I meet a former CIA agent in Boston while I'm planning to avenge Mom's murder and fall for him."

"But you shot him."

"I didn't want to, but he found out who I was. Who I really was. I was so close to settling the score with Mom's killer, fulfilling my promise to her. I couldn't let Oliver stop me." She locked eyes with him. "I couldn't let anything stop me."

"Did you climb out your bedroom window last Friday night?"

Her eyes widened in surprise. "Yes."

"Did you kill Hammer?"

"I didn't want to, but he shot Bruce and then he tried to kill me."

"Who's Bruce?"

Natalie closed her eyes. "Just a friend."

A burst of gunfire shattered the silence, but it wasn't coming from the mob house.

Frank looked down the street. A brown Range Rover was parked diagonally across the street, blocking the intersection near the Hogan house. He couldn't see who was in it, but he could see automatic weapons poking out the windows.

He took out his cellphone and called Kelly.

———

Bianca perched on the foot of the bed opposite the TV set. Beside her on a plaid bedspread, a peanut butter sandwich sat on a paper plate, cut into quarters. Kelly had made it for her before they came upstairs. She didn't want it.

She didn't want to watch Big Bird and Elmo on Sesame Street, either.

Where was Laura? Why didn't Mr. Frank bring her here?

Kelly was standing at the window with spyglasses in her hand.

The sound of gunshots startled her.

She jumped off the bed and ran to Kelly. "Did they shoot Laura?"

"No," Kelly said. "Get away from the window. Go sit on the bed."

"I don't want to sit on the bed! I want Laura! You lied. You said Mr. Frank was going to bring her here, but he didn't."

Kelly squatted and gripped her shoulders. "I didn't lie, Bianca. Mr. Frank will bring her here as soon as he can. Go sit on the bed."

She backed away, but she didn't sit on the bed. Big Bird wasn't on the TV anymore. A loud song played for a second and stopped.

Kelly heard it, grabbed the remote and upped the volume.

Now a pretty woman was saying something on the TV. She couldn't understand what the woman said, but Kelly had a worried look on her face. Then Big Bird and Elmo came back on.

Kelly's cellphone rang and she answered right away. "Frank, I just saw a bulletin on TV. The Jefferson Parrish Sheriff's Department said there's police activity in Metairie. They put up a map of this neighborhood and advised residents to shelter in place." After a moment she said, "I don't think the men in the Range Rover are friendlies."

Bianca frowned. She didn't know what that meant.

Then Kelly said, "But you don't know how many men there are in the house."

She ran over to Kelly. "I do!"

Kelly told Mr. Frank to hold on and said, "How many men are there?"

She held out her hand. "Let me tell Mr. Frank."

"Bianca wants to tell you something," Kelly said, and gave her the phone.

She held it to her ear like Laura did and said, "Hello, Mr. Frank?"

"Hi Bianca. What did you want to tell me?"

"About the men in the house. First there's Owl. He's a bad man. Laura said so. He burned her arm with a cigar."

"I'd say that makes him a very bad man. Who else is in the house?"

"His brother Tommy. And Catwoman. They're married."

"Is anyone else in the house?"

"Yes, another man, but I don't know his name. He sits downstairs and watches the door."

"Nobody else?"

"Nobody else. When are you going to bring Laura here?"

"I'm not sure. As soon as I can. Don't worry, you're safe with Kelly."

"But I miss Laura. Can I talk to her?"

"Not now. But I'll tell her you miss her. She misses you, too."

"She promised she wouldn't leave me."

After a pause, Mr. Frank said, "Say goodbye to Kelly for me, I have to go."

She gave the phone to Kelly and started to cry. First Mama died. Then the bad men put her on an airplane and took her far away. She didn't know where Papà was. When she asked Catwoman, Catwoman talked about something else or fed her ice cream. Laura wouldn't tell her either. She just looked sad and said, "I don't know."

Laura had promised not to leave her. Something terrible must have happened.

Tears ran down her cheeks. What if Laura was dead?

Then she would be all alone.

―――――

Frank put the cellphone in his pocket, processing what Bianca had said. Three mobsters in the house with assault weapons in a standoff with a SWAT team, and mobster reinforcements parked down the street. Worse, now that word of "police action" was on the tube, reporters and TV crews would descend on the neighborhood any minute.

But his biggest worry was Natalie, lying on a blanket with a bullet in her back, bleeding.

"Bianca said to tell you she misses you."

"She's afraid of Orazio. She saw him kill her mother. She's afraid he'll kill her too. But now she's safe."

"You will be too as soon as the ambulance gets here."

She closed her eyes. Her chest rose and fell rapidly as she struggled to breathe. She coughed and a string of bloody sputum dribbled from her lips. He wiped it away with the towel and tucked the blanket around her. Her face was pale and sweaty, and she was shivering. Damn! It looked like she was about to go into shock. He got on his cellphone and called Dispatch.

"This is Renzi up on Mobster Lane. Where the hell is the ambulance?"

"They took fire from armed men at the end of block," said the dispatcher. "They can't go in. It's too dangerous. I sent two NOPD squads up there. Not our territory, but you need backup, right?"

"Right. Patch me through to the EMT." He waited, heard the dispatcher tell the EMT that Frank Renzi needed to talk to them.

"Go ahead," the dispatcher said.

He turned away from Natalie and said in a low voice, "What do I do for a GSW in the back?"

"Is it through and through?"

"I don't think so."

"The slug could be anywhere. Is she breathing okay?"

"Difficult. Bloody sputum."

"Best thing would be to get her to the hospital. We'd take her if we could, but our orders are to stay out of harms way. We're over on the next block."

"Okay, thanks," Frank said and ended the call.

"Mobster Lane," Natalie said. "I like your sense of humor."

"Don't talk. Just rest."

"No. If I don't keep talking, I'll fall asleep."

But he knew she wasn't worried about falling asleep. She was afraid she was going to die. And she might, if he didn't get her to a hospital. He felt utterly helpless. To keep her talking he said, "Where did you go after I called you in Chicago last year?"

"Got on a plane and flew to Italy."

"How? Every TSA agent in the country had your passport number and description."

"I used Liang Lam's passport. He is the brother of Ling Lam, the passport I'm using now." Her hand fluttered to her hair. "I had to cut off most of my hair. But it grew back."

"Where'd you get the passports?"

"From the Mountain Man." She looked at him, dreamy-eyed. "When I was a teenager I thought mountains and birds would protect me. But I was wrong." A spasm of pain made her grimace. Then she muttered, "Willem loved me, I think." She gripped his hand. "Please don't leave me."

He squeezed her hand and his throat thickened. Two days ago his only goal was to arrest Natalie and put her in jail. Now he was afraid she was going to die, desperate to get her to a hospital so the doctors could save her. Fighting the lump in his throat, he said, "I won't leave you. Hell, the Budweiser Clydesdales couldn't drag me away."

Natalie smiled faintly. "You watch too many commercials."

A sharp voice behind him said, "She's bleeding! She needs to go to the hospital."

When he turned, Vivian stood over them, pointing at the blanket and frowning.

"I know she does, but the ambulance can't get here, complications down the street."

"More Mafia hoodlums probably. My florist's van is in the garage," Vivian said in a firm voice. "We'll use it to take her to the hospital."

Not the best solution, but what choice did he have? "Okay. Go get it ready."

He got on his cellphone and called Tony Coppola, who said, "This is a helluva mess, Frank. Four assholes with assault weapons drove by and shot at the van."

"Where are you? Are you okay?"

"Yup. I got out of there pronto. I'm parked on the next street over. Why?"

"I need to get Natalie to hospital. The woman who lives next door to the mobsters will let us use her van. Can you sneak through her back yard? We're outside, in front of the lavender house."

"Be there in a jiffy," Tony said, and ended the call.

Natalie opened her eyes and squeezed his hand. "She must be a red-head. Only a redhead could boss you around like that."

Amused, he grinned, but quickly sobered. Mob thugs were blocking the street beside the Hogan house.

The big question: Were more of them parked at the north end of the block?

CHAPTER 43

In the shadowy darkness of his bedroom Orazio stood two paces back from the front window. The gritty stink of gunpowder irritated his nostrils, and his ears hurt, a painful buzzing. He mopped sweat off his forehead and pinched his nose. Would this ordeal never end?

For ten minutes, he had fired short bursts at the FBI agents. Now that he'd hit one they weren't stupid enough to attack the front door, but every so often a helmeted man in a flak jacket and full body armor jumped out of the Hummer and fired a withering salvo at the house.

His shoes crunched on broken glass as he cautiously drew closer to the window. The glass had been shot out by his enemies, the wood frame pock-marked and splintered. He raised the Uzi, sighted on the back of the Hummer and waited.

Moments later two men jumped from the back of the Hummer and raised their weapons. Orazio raked them with a burst from his Uzi and pulled back from the window.

More gunfire from downstairs, Rocco shooting from the dining room.

Orazio checked the magazine, his last one and less than half full. A shiver ran down his spine. Faced with a well-armed enemy, nothing was worse than hearing the click of a firing pin strike an empty chamber.

He ran down the hall to Tommy's room. His brother turned from the window and flashed a self-important smile. "No one tries to get over the fence now. Not since I took out three of them."

Always the braggart. "Fine, but I need more ammo. Go get the rest of the magazines from the room downstairs. I'll hold your Uzi."

A burst of gunfire came from the street. Tommy flinched. "How many men you figure they got out there?"

"Too many," Orazio said. "Go get the ammunition. Hurry."

Tommy gave him the Uzi and ran out of the room. Orazio followed him down the hall and stopped at the utility room beside the staircase. Catarina turned from the monitors and looked at him, her face pale and drawn. She wasn't thinking about shopping now.

"Come with me," he said. "I need you in Tommy's room."

"Why?" she said, frowning. "Where's Tommy?"

"Shut up and come with me." He dragged her out of the chair, hustled her down the hall to Tommy's room and stood her at the open window. "I need you to defend the back fence."

"No," she said, shaking her head. "I can't shoot—"

He slapped her, first one cheek, then the other. "You want to die?"

Tears filled her eyes and her shoulders sagged in defeat. He placed her hands in the proper position on Tommy's Uzi and released the safety.

"Look at me! If anyone tries to climb over the fence, shoot them. Understand?"

"Yes," she whispered, her eyes wide with fear.

He heard footsteps pounding up the stairs and hurried to his room.

"I gave four to Rocco. That's all the rest," Tommy said, gesturing at the eight magazines on the bed.

"Take four for yourself and get the other Uzi in the weapon closet. Catarina is using yours to guard the back fence from your room. You and Rocco defend the front door from the dining room. I will shoot from here. This window gives me a fine view of the Hummer."

"Whose car is that in the driveway? It's blocking the garage."

Unable to suppress the fury that rose inside him, he said, "A fucking police car. Polizia!"

Tommy stared at him. "Polizia? Why?"

He glared at his brother. "Use your brain. Remember when the girl and the nanny went in that house down the street? I told you that woman was a cop."

Agitated, Tommy waved his hands in the air. "FBI agents and polizia? How can we hold out against so many men? I thought Silvano was sending his soldiers to help us."

So did I, but maybe he won't. "Go get the other Uzi and help Rocco."

Frowning, Tommy held his gaze for a moment, then turned and grudgingly left the room.

Tommy was unwilling to challenge him now, but there might come a time when he would. Orazio slid his right hand inside his jacket and touched the Smith & Wesson in the pocket below his left armpit. If Tommy did not follow orders, he would not hesitate to use it. Nor would he turn his back on his brother. Tommy knew he had the diamonds, but he didn't know where they were.

Orazio knelt beside the dresser and extended his arm underneath it. His figures touched the drawstring bags with the diamonds and the stolen jewelry he had taped underneath the dresser.

Reassured, he slammed a fresh magazine into his Uzi.

———

"Vobitch is ripshit," David said.

"About what?" Frank said, crouched by the fence with his cellphone.

"After the mobsters shot at Tony, he got on his radio and asked me how things were on my end of the block. I told him four men with as- sault rifles shot at us, but Orville took evasive action and backed the cruiser around the corner. Then Vobitch got on the radio and put out a call to you. Twice. The second time he sounded really pissed."

Frank clenched his jaw. What could he say? In his haste to rescue Na- talie and Bianca, he'd left his radio in Mary Hogan's kitchen? Bullshit. He hadn't forgotten it. If he didn't talk on the radio, nobody could tell him what to do. Or not to do.

"Bianca's with Kelly in the Hogan house, but Orazio shot Natalie. I need to get her to the hospital. Placate Vobitch, okay? Gotta go."

He ended the call just as Tony charged around the corner of Vivian's garage and loped across the lawn. Dark with sweat, a gray T-shirt clung to his barrel chest. A Gulf War veteran, Tony had joined NOPD twenty years ago after leaving the Army. His most prominent feature was his large crooked nose, a testament to his youthful boxing days when it had been broken twice. Tony had recently turned fifty but he was still in shape, brawny shoulders and thick powerful legs. He nodded at Natalie, lying on the blanket with her eyes shut. "How's she doing?"

Frank shook his head and held a finger to his lips. "We need some- thing to lift her into the van."

"I know how to do it," Tony said and headed for the house.

Natalie opened her eyes. Agitated, she grabbed Frank's hand. "Pak Lam. You have to call him. His number is in my iPhone."

He stroked her hand. "I'll call him. Don't talk now, close your eyes and rest. We're taking you to the hospital."

She met his gaze for a moment, then closed her eyes.

Tony came out of the house with a yellow bedspread, folded it in half lengthwise and put it on the ground beside Natalie. "Vivian says to bring her in the garage. Piece of cake if you know what you're doing. I did it plenty of times during the war. Grab your side of Natalie's blanket."

Tony gripped the other side. They hoisted the blanket and gently low- ered Natalie onto the bedspread.

She didn't stir, her eyes closed, her face ashen.

"Okay, "Tony said, "now we use the bedspread to carry her." With Natalie swaying between them, they lugged her into the garage.

Vivian stood at the rear of a small white van, the rear doors spread open like butterfly wings. "I put three blankets down to pad the floor," she said. "Nobody will see her. Hurry!"

Spurred by the urgency of her words, they hoisted Natalie into the van and lowered her to the floor. Not a peep from Natalie, whose eyes remained closed. They inched her forward until her head was behind the front seats and climbed out of the van.

Frank studied the lettering on the side of the van: ALPERT'S FINE FLOWERS. That explained the sweet flowery aroma in the van.

Vivian stood by the driver's door, clearly impatient, jingling the set of keys in her hand. She wasn't going to like what he was about to tell her.

"The mobsters shot at my colleagues at the north end of the block. They're okay but the mobsters are in a car blocking the intersection. Which means Tony's driving the van."

Vivian frowned and shook her head. "No. It's better if I drive."

"No. They may shoot at us. You're a civilian. We get paid to do things like this. Never put a civilian in harm's way. NOPD protocol."

"Bullshit! It's my van and I'm driving. Besides, these mobsters are idiots when it comes to women. They're less apt to shoot at me. I'll tell them I've got a delivery to make."

"She's right," Tony said. "A woman might be able to charm the goombas. Otherwise, we gotta drive past them guns blazing. And they got more powerful weapons than we do."

Clearly pleased, Vivian nodded her head emphatically.

"Maybe," Frank said, "but Vobitch will have our heads on a platter."

"We're wasting time," Vivian said. "Frank, ride in back with the woman. Big Guy can ride in front with me." She thrust a small floral arrangement with white lilies and pink peonies at Tony. "Put this in your lap and hide your gun in it."

"I don't know," Tony said dubiously. "I got allergies. Does it have pollen?"

"Of course it does! That's what flowers do. Pollinate. You'll be fine." She plucked out a white lily and gave it to Frank. "Give this to the woman. Lilies bring good luck."

Frank didn't like the way this was going, but Vivian was right. Why waste time arguing? Natalie had been shot twenty minutes ago. He took the lily, climbed in back and pulled the door shut.

He crawled forward, knelt on the blankets beside Natalie and gave her the lily. "Vivian says lilies bring good luck."

Natalie held the lily to her nose, inhaled the fragrance and laid the flower across her chest. "That's what we need. Good luck."

True, Frank thought, but he wasn't going to rely on luck. He took out his Glock and set it on the blanket beside him. Up front in the shotgun seat, Tony turned and winked at him. Everybody acting upbeat, but a lot of things could go wrong.

The thugs might shoot first, ask questions later. The windows in the cab of Vivian's van were tall and wide. If the thugs stopped them and looked inside the van, they would see him behind the front seats.

Then he remembered the SWAT team in the Hummer. But there was no time to call Agent Wyner. Would the FBI agents shoot at a civilian vehicle? Maybe not, if an NOPD cop was in it.

"Tony, when we approach the Hummer, flash your badge at them."

Vivian backed out of the garage, wheeled the van into the street, jerked to a stop and accelerated. The Hummer was parked thirty yards away in front of the mob house. All quiet at the moment, no gunfire from the house, none from the Hummer.

"Slow down," Tony said to Vivian as they neared the Hummer. He lowered his window, flashed his NOPD badge and said, "I got orders to escort this woman out of the neighborhood."

Frank smiled. Trust Tony to come up with a legit-sounding excuse.

"Okay, but be careful," a grim-faced FBI agent said. "We can't be held responsible if you get shot at." The agent waved them along.

So far so good, but getting past the thugs wouldn't be so easy. Frank bent closer to Natalie and whispered, "Quiet. No talking."

The van slowed and came to a stop beside the mob car. Vivian lowered her window and called, "Could you folks move your car please? I have to deliver some flowers to a wedding."

"A little late for a wedding, ain't it?" a surly voice called. "Almost nine o'clock."

Frank waited tensely, sweating it out, gripping the Glock in both hands. Tony had his Glock in his hands too, hiding it behind the flower arrangement in his lap.

"Not really," Vivian said. "It's a candlelight service."

"What kinda people get married on a Tuesday? They ain't Catholic, that's for sure."

"No, but they're important clients and they're paying us a boatload of money. Could you please move the car? We're already late!"

Frank held his breath. The woman had balls, he'd give her that.

Seconds passed. Not a peep out of Vivian gripping the wheel, or Tony gripping his Glock.

In the distance Frank heard sirens approaching. NOPD squad cars or Jefferson Parish deputies. If they got here before Vivian drove past the mobsters, all hell might break loose.

"What's in the back?" said the thug.

"Flowers," Vivian said. She plucked a lily from the arrangement on Tony's lap and held it out the window. "Take this with my compliments. Lilies bring good luck." Without waiting for a reply, she drove forward, slowly at first, second by agonizing second.

No gunfire from the mobsters, who pulled their car forward.

Vivian inched the van around it, turned the corner and accelerated.

"Hah ... hah ..." Tony shuddered and let out a violent sneeze. "Hah-chooooo!" After a moment, he said, "Sorry about that. I held it as long as I could. Good going, Viv! You got nerves of steel. The NOPD could use a woman like you."

CHAPTER 44

Natalie closed her eyes and pressed her lips together, fighting the pain. The woman had given her a white lily for good luck, but it wasn't helping. It was harder to breathe now, and the pain was worse than before. Her back was on fire, and the fire was spreading.

Frank was taking her to a hospital. He seemed worried about her.

Strange. For a long time, she had thought of him as her enemy. Now he seemed more like a friend.

During her life's journey, she had cared deeply for only a handful of people. Mom had been the center of her world until she was ten, and then Mom was gone, brutally beaten to death.

After that her heart was an iceberg inside her chest. Later that year, the ice thawed a bit when she adopted a stray kitten. She loved petting Muffy's soft fur and hearing her purr after she lapped up milk with her little pink tongue. When her cousin killed Muffy, she knew hate for the first time, a deep loathing that inspired her first urge to kill.

Years later in high school, she had studied her heritage. Guided by the Vietnamese spirit gods, she made a solemn vow to avenge her mother's murder. Taekwondo lessons, acting in drama club and befriending Gabe sustained her through high school. She tried to picture Gabe's face. It had been so long since she'd seen him. He and his wife had twin sons.

She tried to figure out how old they must be, but her brain refused to cooperate. The pain was worse now, agonizing when the van jolted to a stop and started up again.

After high school she set out to avenge her mother's murder, her heart set in stone. Until she met Willem and fell in love with him. He thawed her frozen heart, but in the end he had abandoned her. Years later she'd found momentary happiness with Oliver, but he betrayed her too. When it came down to it, other than Mom and Gabe and Pak Lam, everyone she had ever cared about had betrayed her.

Even Bianca. Not intentionally, but when Bianca told Orazio that she had talked to Frank on the phone, it had sealed her fate.

She opened her eyes and studied Frank, kneeling beside her, grim-faced, his eyes fixed on the front windows of the van.

Would Frank betray her? In Boston she had read news articles about him. He had suffered his own betrayals. Maybe they were kindred spirits after all. If she hadn't killed three men in New Orleans, she would never have met him.

Was that what the Vietnamese spirit gods had intended all along?

A spasm of coughing consumed her. She had no strength left.

Not even a good-luck lily and the Mountain Man could save her this time.

———

Tony's monumental sneeze gave them a good laugh—Vivian said it should go in the Guinness Book of World Records—but Frank urged her to drive faster. Natalie's face had a grayish pallor and her breathing was labored, her chest rising and falling.

"Screw the traffic lights," he said. "East Jefferson Hospital is only five minutes away."

When he told Natalie it was safe to talk, her eyes opened. "I didn't tell Bianca about her father. Bad enough that she lost her mother. How is Jacques? Such a sad little boy. Who killed his mother?"

"He's not doing too well, but you got him to talk when you sang to him. The man who shot his mother is in jail, awaiting trial." He didn't see any point in telling her who'd shot Jacques' mother.

And then they were at East Jefferson Hospital. Frank had called ahead so when Vivian pulled the van under the canopy in front of the emergency room entrance, two men in green scrubs were waiting.

Now that they were finally here, he was reluctant to leave her.

Natalie gripped his hand and locked eyes with him. "Promise me you will talk to Pak Lam."

"I will," he said. "I promise."

"He will be worried about me. Do you have my iPhone? His number is in it."

"Where's your iPhone?"

"In my leather handbag. On the bed in my room."

"Okay. After we get you into the hospital, I'll go get it. Don't worry, I'll call him." After he captured the bastard who'd shot her.

"Thank you," she whispered. "For a long time I considered you an enemy. Now you seem more like a friend."

Overcome with conflicting emotions, he couldn't speak. He felt sad that she was so alone, no relatives, no friends here. Glad that she trusted him enough to ask him to call her friend in Boston. Guilty that he had to arrest her and put her in jail.

But he had no time to tell her this. The back door of the van opened and two EMTs told him to get out, they'd take it from here.

When he got out, the EMTs whisked Natalie onto a waiting gurney. And she was gone.

A security guard motioned at Vivian to move the van. She pulled forward, turned right and parked in a fire lane. ALPERT'S FINE FLOWERS was barely visible in the dim light.

Frank ran to the driver's door and said to Vivian, "You did great with the mobsters, but we need the van to get back to the house."

To his surprise, she said, "No problem. I'll take a cab to the golf course. My husband's probably in the bar by now. I'll have the bartender mix us a couple of Hurricanes. Otherwise Herb might faint when I tell him what just happened."

"Herb," he said. "Herb Alpert?"

Vivian rolled her eyes like she'd heard this before. "Yes, but not the trumpet player. Herb's got a way with flowers, though. He makes gorgeous floral arrangements."

"You need money for the cab? I'll pay for the fare."

"Are you kidding? I should pay you! This is the most excitement I've had in years. And don't fret about your boss. I'll tell him Big Guy drove and I was safe in back with you."

Frank laughed and shook his head. "You're something else, Vivian. When things calm down after the holidays, Tony and I will take you and Herb out for a drink."

He got behind the wheel, put the van in gear and said to Tony, "Let's go get the sonofabitch that shot Natalie in the back."

"Now you're talking," Tony said. "She didn't look too good, but the doctors will fix her up."

"I hope so." Frank stomped the accelerator and headed for the exit

Ten minutes later he stopped one street over, behind Vivian's house. An NOPD cruiser blocked the intersection. Two uniformed officers stood beside the cruiser.

"I know these guys, Frank. Lemme handle this." Tony jumped out and ran over to the two officers. He gestured at Vivian's van, pointed down the street, came back and jumped in the van. "I told 'em we had to get to the NOPD surveillance van down the street." Tony grinned. "I didn't tell them what we were gonna do after we got there."

Frank pulled around the NOPD cruiser and accelerated. "Park behind the van," Tony said. "We need to pick up a few essentials."

The essentials turned out to be a grappling hook with a rope line, handcuffs and a box of latex gloves. Tony gave him a pair of gloves and said, "You're already facing an IAD hearing for shooting King Rock. No sense leaving any prints while we're gunning for this Orazio prick."

They put on gloves and trotted alongside the house behind Vivian's. No lights inside the house, no gunshots from the mob house. The neighborhood was eerily quiet. Normally, in a situation like this all the looky-loos would be outside, but apparently the radio and TV bulletins warning people to stay inside had worked.

Just as they reached the wood-rail fence behind Vivian's house, Frank's cellphone rang. On their way here, they had ignored the chatter on Tony's radio, but he couldn't ignore this call. He signaled Tony to wait and answered.

"What the fuck is going on?" Vobitch said. "All hell breaks loose, not a peep from you."

"Tony and I just took Natalie to the hospital. Orazio shot her in the back."

"How bad is it?"

"She didn't look good."

"Where are you now?"

A burst of gunfire came from the mobsters. The perfect excuse to say to Vobitch, "Near the mob house. Gotta go. It's bedlam here."

He put away his cellphone and said to Tony, "Let's go."

They hopped the rail fence, ran along the south side of Vivian's ranch house and stopped beside her garage.

More gunfire from the mobsters. "Motherfuckers got automatic weapons," Tony muttered.

"Right. At least three shooters, maybe four. Orazio, Tomasso, the Mafia thug who guards the door and Tomasso's wife."

"One for each side of the house," Tony said. "So what's the plan?"

"I figured we'd climb up to the gutter between the house and the garage roof, get into the house through Natalie's bedroom window. But if the mobsters see us, we're toast."

"Maybe not," Tony said. "They're busy shooting at the FBI agents. But we gotta worry about the feds, too." He jerked his head at the fence between Vivian's property and the mob house. "Let's take a peek."

Crouched low, they sprinted across Vivian's lawn to the fence. Frank took a look and said, "Good news. When we drove past the Hummer, it was in front of the house. Now it's twenty yards farther up the street, parked beside the fence on the north side of the house."

Tony took a look and said, "Okay. The feds are focused on the thugs in the house. They won't be expecting somebody to try and get into it.

But we gotta be careful. Hard to tell where the inside shooters are. I see the gutter and the second floor window above it. There's a side door beside the garage, but it's closed. No window in the door."

"No windows on the side of the house beside the garage either."

"That's your Dodge in the driveway, right? Strategically it's in a great tactical position, halfway between us and the garage. We run to the Dodge first, then to the garage."

Gripping his Glock, Frank said, "Cover me. I'll go first."

Tony grabbed his arm. "Hold on. For all we know this Orazio prick could be in Natalie's room. But it seems like the shooters are focused on the feds in the Hummer. Next time shots are fired, you run to the Dodge. I'll cover you. If nobody shoots at you, run to the garage and cover me until I get there." Tony smiled grimly. "My urban warfare experience comes in handy sometimes."

A long minute passed. Then, a burst of shots came from the house. The agents in the Hummer returned fire. During the ear-splitting gunfire, Frank sprinted to the Dodge and crouched behind it. Tony signaled him to go. He sprinted to the garage and flattened his back against the side of the house. If anyone shot at Tony, he wouldn't be able to cover him. The Hummer was parked near the north side of the house where he couldn't see it. He could barely see Natalie's window on the second floor. The good news. Nobody could see him, either.

He waited tensely.

More gunfire, the mobsters firing at the Hummer.

Then he saw Tony run to the Dodge. Moments later Tony ran up the driveway and slapped him on the back. "So far so good, Frank. Here's what we do. I boost you up to the gutter and toss you the grappling hook. You secure the hook and I haul myself up to the gutter. Then we hunker down for a bit, see what happens."

Tony laced his fingers together. Frank holstered his Glock, put one foot in Tony's hands, and Tony thrust him upward. He grabbed the edge of the roof, chinned himself upward and scrambled onto the gutter. Tony tossed him the grappling hook with the rope.

He secured the hook and Tony hauled himself up the side of the garage onto the gutter.

"That's Natalie's window," Frank whispered, pointing. "But there's another window overlooking the street. Orazio's room is beside hers."

"Could be dicey," Tony muttered. "What if he's in her room?"

Frank took out his Glock. "I'll shoot the fucker."

"Like hell. He sees you, you're dead. Here's what we do. I kneel down under the window and make like a fucking camel. Hold your Glock in one hand, ready to shoot, and stand on my back. Take a quick peek in the window. If you see the bastard, jump off my back. He comes to the window, we blow the fucker away."

With a grim smile, Frank whispered, "Tony, you never told me you had these hidden talents."

"Yeah, well, it's the best plan I got, but shit happens. Be careful."

They crept along the gutter until they were below the window.

Tony put his Glock on the gutter, knelt down and planted his palms on the gutter. "Go for it."

Holding the Glock in his right hand, his finger off the trigger, Frank braced himself against the side of the house with his left hand. Put one foot on Tony's back, steadied himself, then the other. Slowly but surely he straightened. Now his head was just below the windowsill.

Was Orazio in the room? The Kevlar vest would protect his torso, but Tony was right. His head would be an easy target.

When Tom Cruise did this in Mission Impossible, it looked easy. It wasn't.

He set his finger on the trigger. Gripping the sill with his left hand, he stood on his tiptoes and looked into the room. He saw no one.

"Clear," he whispered. Taking care to make as little noise as possible, he hauled himself over the windowsill into the room. Hot, sweaty and out of breath, he rose to his feet, stuck his head out the window, gave Tony a thumbs-up and waved him up to the window.

A burst of automatic gunfire erupted, deafeningly close.

Frank couldn't pinpoint the exact location, but some of the gunfire came from the second floor, part of it from downstairs. Fortunately, the shots masked the loud thud Tony made as he hauled himself inside and tumbled onto the floor.

Tony scrambled to his feet and whispered, "What's that?" Pointing to an open door on the other side of the room beyond a twin bed.

"Looks like a bathroom," Frank whispered.

"I'll check it." Moving silently for a such a large man, Tony slowly advanced toward the door, his Glock in firing position.

Frank spotted Natalie's leather handbag on the bed nearest the side window. He opened it, took the items he wanted and slipped them into his pockets. Quickly and quietly, he crept to the hall door, which was ajar.

Across the hall, another door was wide open. A woman stood near the window. Tomasso's wife, Frank assumed.

Catarina held an Uzi in one hand, but clearly wasn't ready to use it. The weapon was dangling from her left hand, and she was crying.

Tony came out of the bathroom and whispered, "Clear."

Frank beckoned him closer and whispered, "The mobster's wife is in the room across the hall with an Uzi. Let's rush her."

Tony took a look and nodded. "But quietly."

Weapons drawn, they crept across the hall and entered the room.

Catarina saw them. Her mouth sagged open and she dropped the Uzi on the floor.

"Don't shoot," she said, "I give up!"

Another round of gunfire exploded, downstairs and upstairs.

Frank picked up Catarina's Uzi.

CHAPTER 45

Orazio stood in the darkness, gripping his cellphone. "Where are your men, Silvano? We are trapped here, pinned down by a SWAT team."

"My men are in armor-clad cars at both ends of the block. But they just called and told me that sirens are approaching, a lot of them. I saw a bulletin on TV. Police action in Metairie it said."

"Silvano, we are outnumbered and low on ammo. We have to get out of this house! Two cars are in the garage, ready to go. Tell your men to pin down the men in the Hummer."

Silence on the other end.

A fulminating fury rose inside him. "Silvano, listen carefully. Do you want the cops to come in here and find three million dollars worth of diamonds in Tick-Tock's house? Tell your men to attack these FBI agents in the Hummer so we can escape!"

A heavy sigh on the other end. "Orazio, that would be foolhardy. Certain slaughter. I cannot order my men to do this."

Orazio ended the call, tossed the cellphone on his bed and clenched his fists.

La Cosa Nostra was about Family and loyalty. But sometimes even Family could betray you.

Trust no one. Father's words, spoken to him many years ago.

The sound of voices brought him to his senses.

Male voices in Tommy's room down the hall.

But Tommy and Rocco were downstairs.

Who was in the house?

He slammed a fresh magazine into his Uzi.

———

Frank gave Catarina his don't-fuck-with-me look. "Who else is up here?" Tony had checked the bathroom and found no one.

Catarina shrank away from him. "*Non loso,*" she said. I don't know.

Using what little Italian he'd learned from his grandparents, Frank said, "Dove Orazio?"

"*Non loso.*"

"*Parla inglese.* Where's your husband?"

Catarina pointed at the floor. "Orazio tells him go downstairs."

He released the safety on her Uzi and went to doorway. A flash of motion down the hall, Orazio poking his head out the door of his room. He spotted Frank and ducked back into the room.

"Orazio," he yelled. "Put your weapon on the floor and come out with your hands up."

Silence. He risked a quick peek and jumped back from the door.

A burst of gunfire from an automatic weapon sprayed the doorway. The frame shattered and slivers of wood scattered over the floor.

Tony shoved Catarina down on the bed to get her out of the line of fire. She looked like she was in shock, gasping for breath, her eyes brimming with tears.

Frank heard footsteps in the hall. He raised the Uzi, sprang to the doorway and saw Orazio run downstairs.

"Tony, the target just went downstairs. Catarina, who else is downstairs besides your husband?"

"A guard?" she whispered. "I not know his name."

"Tony," he said, "we need to immobilize her."

"No problem." Tony pulled zipties out of his pocket and cuffed Catarina's wrists, used more to cuff her to the spindles in the headboard and said, "Silencio or we'll be back."

She nodded vigorously, her eyes fearful.

To Frank, Tony said, "You believe her? We know Natalie's room is clear, but we better check the other rooms up here. Ya never know."

They cautiously advanced down the hall, weapons raised. No sign of life, no motion, no telltale sounds. Tony sprang across an open doorway beyond Natalie's room and motioned to Frank. He burst into Orazio's room.

No one was in there, but the odor of gunpowder was strong. Empty magazines and broken glass littered the floor beside the front window.

"They've got a fucking arsenal," Tony said, "Uzis and plenty of ammo. What else is up here?"

"I got no clue," Frank said. "Let's find out."

The door across the hall beside the stairs was open. They approached it warily and burst inside. Utility equipment for the house filled one side of the room, but along the left-hand wall, five CCTV monitors sat on metal shelves, displaying every side of the house.

"Jesus," Tony muttered. "They been watching the SWAT team!"

"Exactly," Frank said. "Conti and the FBI got more than they bargained for. The mobsters had someone watch the monitors and warn the shooters when the SWAT team attacked. But the shooters aren't up here. Orazio and Tomasso and the No-Name guard are downstairs."

"Great," Tony said sarcastically. "Three hoods packing Uzis."

———

Orazio burst into the dining room with his Uzi, poised to shoot. The smell of gunpowder was even stronger here. Holding their Uzis, Rocco and Tommy turned away from the front windows, gaping at him. He waved them closer.

"They are in the house. Cops. Upstairs."

"Jesus!" Tommy raked his fingers through his hair, agitated. "What about Catarina?"

"What about her?" he said. "If she'd shot them, we would not have this problem."

Rocco stared at him, his eyes wide with fear. "What do we do now? We're surrounded!"

"Grow some balls! We shoot our way out. I will guard the stairs. Take your Uzis and get in the rented SUV. Start the engine, Tommy, but wait for me. Don't open the garage door until I get there."

Tommy gave Rocco a look. Sending him a message, Orazio thought, a subversive message. Tommy wanted to play at being the leader. This he could not allow. He raised his Uzi. "Do it!"

Without a word, Tommy took an extra magazine off the table and stuffed it in his pocket. Rocco did the same, and the two of them ran down the hall toward the kitchen.

Orazio mopped sweat from his forehead and took stock of his situation. Catarina was upstairs, but he would get no help from her. He didn't know if she was alive or dead, and he didn't care.

Sweeping broken glass out of the way with his foot, he crept to the front window. Like a faceless monster, the big black Hummer stood at the curb beside the fence to his right. If Tommy drove the SUV over the lawn around the cop car and turned left at the end of the driveway, away from the Hummer, they might have a fighting chance.

But first, he had to take out the cops upstairs. There had to be at least two, maybe more, armed and dangerous, as these American cowboy-cops were so fond of saying. But not with Uzis.

He positioned himself at one side of the arched doorway, aimed the Uzi at the stairs and waited.

After a moment he heard stealthy footsteps creep down to the landing above him. Then, silence.

Sweat dripped down his forehead. He heard a grinding sound from down the hall. The garage door opening.

Merda! First Silvano had abandoned him. Now his brother was deserting him. A disappointment, but not a huge surprise. In Tomasso's world, he was the sun. Other planets revolved around him. To his brother, loyalty was an alien concept, easily abandoned. Tommy felt no loyalty to the Family, not even to his own brother. Or his wife. In a life and death situation like this, Tommy thought only about saving his own skin.

Orazio gripped the Uzi. He was on his own.

Soon the cops upstairs would attack. Rocco's car was in the garage. Were the keys in it?

Even if they were, he wouldn't stand a chance. More cops were probably out there, waiting. Drive with one hand and shoot cops with the other? Impossible. They would mow him down like a common criminal.

Fueled by the adrenaline racing through his veins, his heart was beating abnormally fast, his senses hyper-alert. The lingering smell of gunpowder. His sweat-soaked shirt damp against his skin. The creak of the stairs above him.

Was this how he would die? Alone in this house? Abandoned by Silvano. Betrayed by Tommy.

Perhaps not. He still had the diamonds.

And the Smith & Wesson inside his jacket.

He bent down and put the Uzi on the floor of the hall.

"Truce," he shouted. "My weapon is on the floor. Don't shoot."

"Raise your hands and keep them where I can see them." A deep voice from above.

A man in dark clothing sprang into view on the landing above him. Shocked, Orazio stared at his hands.

Merda! The cop had taken the Uzi he'd given to Catarina.

Orazio raised his hands, palms out, evaluating the cop as he slowly descended the stairs step by step. Mid-forties, just over six-feet, rangy and fit, black hair and a Roman nose. Italian, Orazio believed. But his eyes were the main draw, relentless and angry.

The eyes and the Uzi in his hands.

"Get on the floor," the cop said. "Keep your hands where I can see them."

Orazio raised his chin. "No. I am Orazio Antonetti and I have a proposal for you. What is your name, please?"

"Homicide Detective Frank Renzi, NOPD. Get on the floor."

"Please hear me out, Detective Renzi. You will not regret it."

The cop went still and a look of fury appeared on his face, a don't-fuck-with-me-expression. Orazio knew that look. He'd used it himself, many times. This did not bode well for his plan.

"I'll tell you one thing I regret," Renzi said. "You shot Natalie in the back."

"Natalie." Orazio grimaced. "She calls herself Laura. Another lie. But never mind. Upstairs in my room are diamonds worth three million dollars. I will give you half of them."

"How generous. In exchange for what?"

"You take me to the garage. We get in my SUV and you drive us past the police cars. I will hold a gun to your head to make it look like I will shoot you. It will not be loaded, of course."

A tight smile from Renzi. "Of course not. Then what?"

"You drive around the corner and I let you out. You take the diamonds, I keep going."

"Nice try," Renzi said, "no cigar."

Was this an American saying? If so, he was not familiar with it.

But the message in Renzi's eyes was crystal clear. No deal. And his finger was on the trigger of the Uzi.

Errant thoughts flitted through his mind. Would the whore in Venice miss him? He tried to remember her name. Ah yes, Rosalie, who never asked questions and did whatever he wanted. If he had sent Rosalie to the SUV and told her not to open the garage door until he got there, she would have waited for him until hell froze over.

But Rosalie was in Venice, and Tommy and Rocco were gone.

Faced with a cop holding an Uzi, he didn't have many choices. Should he try to convince Renzi to take the diamonds in exchange for giving him his freedom? No. He wasn't going to beg.

A profound sadness swept over him. As Father had told him many years ago, "We come into this world alone and that is how we leave it." As usual, Father was right.

What he needed right now was a cigar. Fortunately, there was one in his shirt pocket.

He reached for it with his right hand.

An explosion of sound hit him, then agonizing pain. Fighting it, he clutched his chest, felt the warmth of his own blood seep through his fingers. Now the NOPD cop was standing over him, his face blurry and indistinct. His mouth was moving but Orazio couldn't hear what he said. His ears were ringing and his vision was fading.

He tried to take a breath and couldn't.

Then the pain slipped away and everything faded to black.

———

Shaking with fury, Frank stood over Orazio. The mobster thought he could bribe his way to freedom, but he didn't know Frank Renzi. All the money in the world couldn't deter him from his mission. Catch the criminals and make them pay for their crimes.

And Orazio's crimes were worse than most.

He imagined Bianca, an innocent little girl, watching Orazio murder her mother. Pictured Natalie, his longtime adversary who had become … not a friend exactly, but no longer an enemy, lying on a blood-soaked blanket, struggling to breathe, her face ashen.

Shot in the back by Orazio.

Now Orazio was dead, or soon would be, his eyes closed, his mouth twisted in a grimace. Good riddance to a vicious killer.

When he realized Frank wasn't going to take the bribe, he had reached into his jacket. For a gun, no doubt.

"Frank, are you okay?" Tony thundered down the stairs, gripping his Glock in both hands, poised to shoot. Then he saw Orazio. "I can see you're okay, but he don't look so hot."

"He went for a weapon, so I shot him."

They squatted on either side of Orazio's body. With hands encased in latex gloves, they opened Orazio's jacket. His white shirt was drenched with blood. A cigar was in the shirt pocket. Inside the pocket of the jacket was a Smith & Wesson revolver.

"The miserable fuck," Tony said. "Puts down his Uzi, but he's got a fucking peashooter in his pocket. I heard him try to bribe you. If you hadn't shot him, you'd be dead. Four slugs in the chest, I'd say he's a goner. But where are the others?"

Frank had been so focused on Orazio, he'd forgotten about them. "I don't know."

"Nobody came running to help this guy, but we better check the rooms down here." Tony rose to his feet and crossed the hall, his Glock at the ready. He opened a door below the staircase, took a look and said, "Nobody in the powder room."

Frank picked up Catarina's Uzi, and they advanced down the hall to the kitchen. No one was in there, but doors on opposite sides of the room were open. "Garage," Tony whispered, jerking his head to the right.

Weapons drawn, they crept into the garage. One bay was vacant, a brown sedan sat in the other bay, empty.

"The garage doors are open," Tony said. "Maybe they split in another car."

"They won't get far. The neighborhood is surrounded by cops."

"And FBI agents could bust down the door any minute. We better get outta here."

"Let's check the other room first," Frank said.

They cautiously approached the door on the opposite side of the kitchen. The room was empty.

"Man," Tony said, gesturing at the big screen, "this place looks like a movie theater. Without the popcorn."

Frank went to an open door, looked into a walk-in closet and said, "No popcorn, but it's got an arsenal. Check this out."

Tony took a quick look and said, "Time to split. The feds will take charge of Catarina. Leave her Uzi here. Let the feds figure out who killed Orazio. They won't find your prints on it. You were wearing latex gloves."

"Thanks to you," Frank said. "Thinking ahead like a chess player."

"No problem." Tony grinned. "Us goombas gotta look out for each other."

CHAPTER 46

SATURDAY, December 25, 2010 – 11:00 AM – Swampscott, MA

Frank sat beside his father in a pew six rows back from the altar. The church smelled like Christmas, the odor of spruce trees permeating the air. Red and white poinsettia plants and green wreaths decorated the altar. "Red, white and green," Judge Salvatore Renzi had cheerfully pointed out moments ago, "the colors of the Italian flag."

Frank hadn't attended church in years, but his father was seventy-seven and as Art Blakey said, Tomorrow's not guaranteed. After the chaos in New Orleans, he hoped a peaceful environment and a dose of holiday cheer would ease his emotional turmoil.

On his way to the hospital after the shootout Tuesday night, Vobitch had called him and said, "Natalie's gone."

"Gone?" he said. "Gone where?"

"The doctors couldn't save her. The slug hit her lung, nicked her liver and spleen. After three hours on the table, her heart gave out."

Stunned, he said nothing.

"Frank," Vobitch said, "you still there?"

Unable to deal with it, he'd said, "Talk to you tomorrow."

For hours he had sat in his condo, drinking scotch on the rocks, overwhelmed by a deep sense of loss. Unable to imagine the pain Natalie had endured, he replayed their final conversation in his head. Pictured her in the hospital valiantly fighting for her life. Alone.

For years, Natalie had never been far from his thoughts. Now she was dead.

And four days later, he still wasn't over it.

The organist finished playing "Joy To the World," and a white-robed pastor rose from his chair to begin the service. Frank tuned him out and stared into space, reviewing what had happened since Tuesday.

A major battle had erupted over who would run the investigation. The mob house was in Jefferson Parish, but NOPD and an FBI SWAT team had been involved. The Jefferson Parish Sheriff, the NOPD Super and the FBI Special Agent In Charge were still fighting over it.

In their escape attempt, armed with Uzis, Tomasso and the mob guard had fired on officers in an NOPD cruiser. They escaped but ran into a roadblock four blocks later. Surrounded, they kept shooting. Two minutes later they were dead.

When FBI agents entered the house, they found Orazio, but they still couldn't figure out who killed him. The only prints on one Uzi were Orazio's. The prints on the other one matched those of Tomasso, now deceased, and Catarina Antonetti. And Catarina wasn't talking.

When Conti questioned her, she said the magic words, "I want a lawyer." Reluctantly, Conti dialed the number she gave him. Catarina spoke to her lawyer, in Italian, of course. Ten minutes later, Attorney Silvano Tucci arrived. Tucci wanted her freed on bail, but Conti played his trump card. Catarina faced accessory to murder charges in Venice.

On Wednesday, Conti and Catarina had boarded a plane bound for Venice. That night Frank got a phone call from Venice. Generale Cesare Valenti told him that Sophia's sister would fly to New Orleans and take Bianca home to live with her and her husband and their children. On Thursday, Frank drove Kelly and Bianca to the airport.

When Bianca's aunt came up the ramp to the arrivals area, Bianca seemed happy to see her. Before they left to board a flight to Venice, Bianca said, "Thank you for helping me, Mr. Frank." He didn't mention Natalie. Kelly didn't either. They kissed Bianca goodbye and handed her off to her aunt. Kelly boarded a flight to Chicago to spend Christmas with her extended family. Frank had called Tony Coppola.

He smiled, recalling Tony's reaction when he told him about the mystery regarding who killed Orazio. "Great news, Frank. Let the feds puzzle over it. You know me. Omerta to the max."

After the holidays he would face an IAD hearing for shooting King Rock, but not for killing Orazio. He figured Vobitch and Kelly suspected he was the shooter, but they didn't ask, and he didn't tell.

He hadn't mentioned these issues to his father. Why spoil the holiday?

Last night he'd taken his father to their favorite seafood restaurant. Before dinner they had a glass of wine at the bar overlooking the water, chatting as they often did about the Boston Celtics and the recent death of legendary coach Red Auerbach. Like everyone else in Boston, they also speculated on the whereabouts of Whitey Bulger and his girlfriend. The infamous Boston mobster was now on the FBI's most wanted list.

Organ music jolted him out of his reverie. The Mass was over. Now he and his father would visit his mother's grave and decorate it with red poinsettias, her favorite. After they had brunch at a local restaurant, his father would take a nap.

Frank would keep his promise to Natalie. Go to Chinatown and talk to Pak Lam. He wasn't looking forward to it.

———

2:00 PM   Chinatown

Following the directions Pak Lam had given him, Frank strolled through an open air food market past tubs of live eels, catfish and squid, and carcasses of rabbits and chickens dangling from hooks. It was unseasonally warm, and the market was busy, Asian families mostly. A little girl in a plaid skirt and a white sweater ran toward him, laughing. Her younger brother was chasing her, clearly enjoying the game.

Beyond the market he walked past four elderly Chinese men shooting craps on an inverted cardboard box. Crumpled dollar bills lay on the sidewalk. The men ignored him, cigarettes dangling from their lips, sipping tea from Styrofoam cups after they rolled the dice.

One block later he entered a narrow brick-paved alley. No sunlight here. Ahead of him, the alley dead-ended at a brick wall. He felt a sudden chill. Dark and shadowy, the alley gave off a sinister vibe. If he'd brought a gun, his hand would be on it. But he hadn't.

At the end of the alley, twin pagoda lanterns illuminated a flame-red door. On the door were three Chinese characters and, in yellow letters, ROYAL DRAGON. His destination.

A white-haired man with a wrinkled face opened the door and led him through a dim-lit room that smelled of incense. Faint music was playing, a haunting Chinese melody based on the pentatonic scale. Again, he felt a chill. The interior felt more sinister than the alley.

The white-haired man stopped at a door and tapped once. A slender man in black silk trousers and a white shirt opened the door. Pak Lam was taller than most Chinese men, five-foot-ten, and his dignified bearing made him seem taller. But this was not his most striking feature. An angry scar bisected his left cheek from his eyebrow to his jaw.

"Thank you for coming," Lam said, "It is a pleasure to meet you at last. Please, take a seat."

Frank settled into an easy chair beside a black-lacquered coffee table. Lam sat opposite him, shrouded in stillness, his expression unreadable, his black eyes distant. A confident man, bordering on arrogant.

"Natalie asked me to call you. She said you would be worried about her."

Lam put his palms together and bowed his head, a gesture Frank recognized as an Asian thank-you. "I am glad you did. When she lived in Venice, we spoke once a week on the phone. She was happy there, working at a shelter for domestic violence victims, teaching children to speak

English. She thought she had found the perfect sanctuary. But a man betrayed her."

"Agent Conti, but he wasn't the man who killed her. One of the mob thugs shot her in the back. The doctors tried to save her but they couldn't. I rode with her to the hospital. Her last thoughts were of you."

Still no reaction. Was the man incapable of feeling?

After a moment Lam said, "I am not her father, but I loved her like a daughter. What has become of this man who shot her?"

"He's dead. I shot him."

A flicker of emotion appeared in Lam's eyes and his posture relaxed slightly. "Natalie was right to trust you. She would be pleased that you have avenged her murder. As I am."

He felt like he'd passed some sort of test. Clearly, Natalie had told Pak Lam about him, which meant Lam knew he was the cop who'd been trying to arrest her.

Lam gestured at the lacquered table. A large tray held bottled water, cut-crystal glasses, a porcelain teapot, and two cups and saucers. "Would you care for some tea, or water perhaps?"

"Water would be good, thanks."

"Help yourself," Lam said and poured tea into a cup.

Frank opened a bottled water, poured some into the glass and waited.

"You may have heard about the Asian concept of saving face, Detective Renzi. But Westerners intellectualize the meaning of this. Asians live it every day. Natalie did not understand this until she was a teenager. After that, it ruled her life."

"She wanted to avenge her mother's murder."

"Precisely."

"It took her a long time to find the killer. Twenty years."

Lam sipped his tea. "She told you this?"

"Not exactly. I read her diary. It started when she was ten, after her mother died."

"Then you know that Natalie endured difficult times in her quest for vengeance. She told me about this when we met two years ago. Her tenacity and determination impressed me."

"Unfortunately, the police don't view this as a positive thing. There are warrants outstanding for her arrest in New Orleans. Well, there were. Not any more."

Lam remained silent, seemingly lost in thought. "When we met, Natalie had a problem. A man wanted her to steal some paintings. She wanted to get away from him."

"So you helped her escape."

Expressionless, Lam gazed at him. "She was afraid of you. She knew you were hunting for her."

Frank shrugged. "That's my job. I'm a homicide detective."

"Do you have a family, Detective Renzi? A wife? Children, perhaps?"

"A daughter. She's the light of my life." No need to get into the ugly divorce from his wife.

Lam gestured at a photograph on the wall. A boy and a girl—aged six or seven Frank guessed—stood hand in hand, laughing. They reminded him of the kids he'd seen in the market. A striking woman with beautiful almond-shaped eyes and flowing black hair stood behind them. "My wife and children," Lam said. "Two weeks after that picture was taken a rival tong murdered them."

Stunned, Frank remained silent for a moment, then managed to say, "That must have been devastating. I'm sorry for your loss."

Lam gazed at him, expressionless. "I grieved for my family, of course. But I could not allow their murders to go unpunished. It was a matter of honor. So I killed the men who took my family from me." Tracing the ugly scar on his cheek with a finger, Lam said, "They wounded me, but I cherish the scar. Each day when I see it in the mirror, I rejoice that justice was done."

Frank thought about it. Would he do the same if someone murdered his daughter? He studied the smiling children in the photograph.

And then it hit him. The boy and girl were twins. Pak Lam had given Natalie their passports, substituting photographs of her for theirs.

He reached inside his jacket and removed the items he had taken from Natalie's purse. He'd left the cash in her wallet but had taken her iPhone, her new passport and driver's license. He put the passport and the DL on the table. "Who is Bruce?"

Lam ignored the documents. "The friend of a friend of mine."

"A CIA agent, Clint Hammer, shot him."

"So Natalie said. But she killed him. This was as it should be." Pak Lam locked eyes with him. "Just as you killed the man who shot Natalie in the back."

"I'd rather you didn't tell anyone that I killed Orazio."

"Understood, Detective Renzi. Never give your enemies ammunition they might later use against you."

"Are we enemies?" Frank said.

For the first time, Lam smiled. "Not anymore."

———

Five minutes later he walked out of the dark alley into the sunshine, happy to leave the grim atmosphere inside the Royal Dragon behind.

He could understand Pak Lam's desire for revenge. But if every man whose wife and children were murdered took matters into his own hands, there would be no law and order, only chaos. Considering that Pak Lam knew he'd been hunting for Natalie, the meeting had gone well enough. They would never be friends, but at least they weren't enemies.

Basking in the warmth of the sun, he leaned against the side of a brick building. His father was taking a nap. He could do with a nap right about now, with Kelly O'Neil. He took out his cellphone and called her.

"Hey, Frank, great to hear from you. What's up?"

"Nothing special, just felt like talking to you. Where y'at?"

"My aunt's house and it's bedlam. My father, my three brothers and their wives and kids are enjoying the Zeppetella family pig-out. Every vegetable known to man, six kinds of pasta, and a roast turkey bigger than a Volkswagen Bug. Now we're gearing up for dessert: fourteen kinds of pie, topped with ice cream or whipped cream."

He loved her hyperbole, which was often an indicator of her mood. Maybe her guilt feelings about Angelica's murder and Jacques were diminishing. "What have you got on?"

"Frank," she said sternly. "This is no time for X-rated conversations. Little ears might overhear. I'm wearing my pretty red dress with the high neckline, very chaste."

"I can fix that. What time do you get home tomorrow night?"

"Flying into Louis Armstrong Airport at seven."

"Great. I'll be there to meet you."

She uttered a throaty laugh. "You better be. I miss you."

"Miss you too. Go eat some pie."

"Oooh noooo," she wailed. "Think of the calories!"

He smiled, enjoying her theatrics. "Don't worry. We'll work them off tomorrow night."

######

ABOUT THE AUTHOR

Prior to writing crime thrillers, Susan Fleet was a freelance trumpeter in Boston, a college music professor and music historian. The Premier Book Awards named her first book, *Absolution,* Best Mystery-Suspense-Thriller of 2009. Feathered Quill Book Awards named *Natalie's Revenge* Best Mystery-Thriller of 2014.

After living in New Orleans for nine years, the primary setting of her Frank Renzi thrillers, she returned to the Boston area, but she visits New Orleans at least once a year. See more about Susan on her website: http://www.susanfleet.com

Susan says . . . If you'd like an email alert when my next book comes out, sign up at http://eepurl.com/ExkX9 I promise never to share your email with anyone. If you enjoyed *Natalie's Dilemma* I would appreciate an honest review on the Amazon site where you purchased it. I know this takes time, but the review needn't be long, and whatever you do, please don't reveal the ending. Thank you!

Crime fiction by Susan Fleet

ABSOLUTION
DIVA
NATALIES REVENGE
JACKPOT
NATALIE'S ART
MISSING
NATALIE'S DILEMMA

Non-fiction by Susan Fleet

WOMEN WHO DARED: Maud Powell and Edna White
DARK DEEDS Vol 1: Serial killers, stalkers and domestic homicides
DARK DEEDS Vol 2: Serial killers, stalkers and domestic homicides

ACKNOWLEDGMENTS

Writing *Natalie's Dilemma* took longer than I expected. Like many of my readers, I love Natalie! So many adventures and narrow escapes. If you haven't read the other Natalie books, *Natalie's Revenge* and *Natalie's Art*, I urge you to do so. You're in for a treat!

In the interests of accuracy regarding the Mafia, I consulted two books. *Donnie Brasco: My Undercover Life in the Mafia*, by former FBI agent Joseph D. Pistone, and *Making Jack Falcone*, by former undercover FBI agent Joaquin "Jack" Garcia.

Writing a novel is a collaborative process and many people helped me along the way. My thanks to members of the crimescenewriters group for answering several questions. Thanks also to my beta readers, who read the final draft. Their suggestions greatly improved the book. Many thanks to John Amaral, who proofread the manuscript and made his usual helpful editorial suggestions. His astute comments on the use of firearms, weapons terminology, and ammunition were invaluable.

My heartfelt thanks to NOPD Detective Armando Asaro, who sat down with me in the District 8 station and patiently answered my many questions about police procedures and protocols. However, the events and actions in *Natalie's Dilemma* are fictional, and I have taken a certain amount of dramatic license. Any errors or inaccuracies are mine alone.

And finally, a huge thank-you to all my readers! Without you, all my hard work would be in vain. I would love to hear from you. You can send me an email at: susan@susanfleet.com

www.ingramcontent.com/pod-product-compliance
Lightning Source LLC
Chambersburg PA
CBHW070309260626
47160CB00003B/780